Beneath
the
Southern Cross

Published by Mackay Books.
350 Bothwell Park Road
R D 2   Waiuku
South Auckland 2682

Printed and bound in Shanghai, China.

Disclaimer: This novel is a work of fiction. References to real people, events,
establishments or organisations are intended only to give the fiction a sense
of reality and authenticity. Other names, characters, places and incidents por-
trayed herein, are used fictionally within the wider context of New Zealand's
history.

Heather Mackay
for *Mackay Books*

Cover by Jane Williams, Thames

National Library of New Zealand
ISBN 978-0-473-13216-3

Graeme Sturgeon

Beneath

the

Southern Cross

Author's acknowledgements

To my wife Julie, my thanks for her help. Without her patience and encouragement this book would never have seen the light of day.

To Jane Williams, my thanks for her art. The picture on the cover is her work, as well as the drawing of the maps. My gratitude also for being an important first reader.

To the first readers of the manuscript, thank you for letting me use you as a sounding board: Bill Axbey, Neil Allen, Denis Wing, Bruce McWilliams, Rob Law, Paul Burgess, Rob H. Bradshaw, Vicky Jones, Shirley Santos, Liz Sills, Marty Bowers and Kylie Sturgeon.

A special thanks and acknowledgement to my two editors for all the work they have done - Heather Mackay and Carol Dawber.

Previously by Graeme Sturgeon:
Dustoff for Willie Peters, River Press 1998, 1999

Foreword

The inspiration for this book sprang from the story of a young sealer named James Caddell who was captured by Maori on the southern coast of New Zealand. As near as he could recall, he was captured in 1806. He believed he was around the age of thirteen to sixteen when it happened.

His companions were all killed, but because Caddell touched the chief, he was considered tapu and his life was spared. He took the tattoo, then a wife, and went on to become a well known chief of this tribe.

Caddell's story can be found in the Australian newspaper, the Sydney Gazette, on or about the 3rd of April, 1823.

My wife Julie and I spent six years sailing in our yacht around the coast of New Zealand and we travelled the waterways and walked the ancient trails of Maori, visiting many of the places that are mentioned in this book. During a storm when we were visiting the area, large quantities of human bones were uncovered in Queen Charlotte Sound and it was believed that here one of the great feasts had taken place.

In the era in which this book is set, many great chiefs strode this land. The lives of some have been recorded in books such as The Musket Wars, by Ron Crosby, and The Life and Times of Te Rauparaha, by his son, Tamihana Te Rauparaha.

Beneath the Southern Cross is an historic novel set in time between 1800 and 1832. The known facts are scarce and in many cases only the bones of history remain.

Graeme Sturgeon
Coromandel, 2008

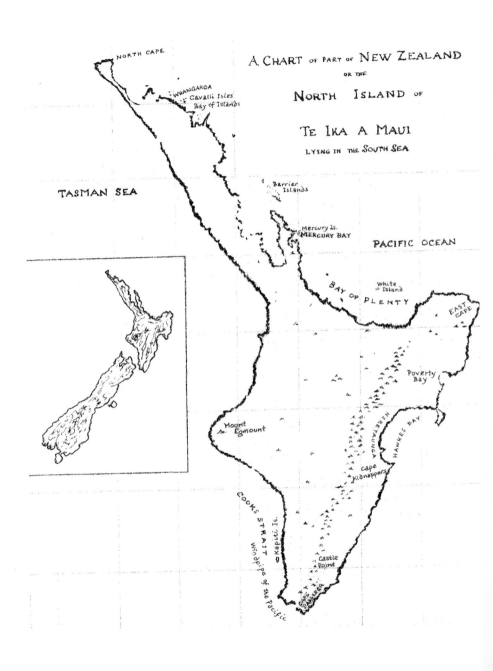

A CHART OF PART OF NEW ZEALAND

OR THE

NORTH ISLAND OF

TE IKA A MAUI

LYING IN THE SOUTH SEA

NORTH CAPE

WHANGAROA
Cavalli Isles
Bay of Islands

TASMAN SEA

Barrier
Islands

Mercury Is.
MERCURY BAY

PACIFIC OCEAN

BAY OF PLENTY

White
Island

EAST
CAPE

Poverty
Bay

Mount
Egmount

HEREETAUNGA

HAWKES BAY

Cape
Kidnappers

COOKS STRAIT

Kapiti Is.

Windpipe of the Pacific

Castle
Point

CAPE PALLISER

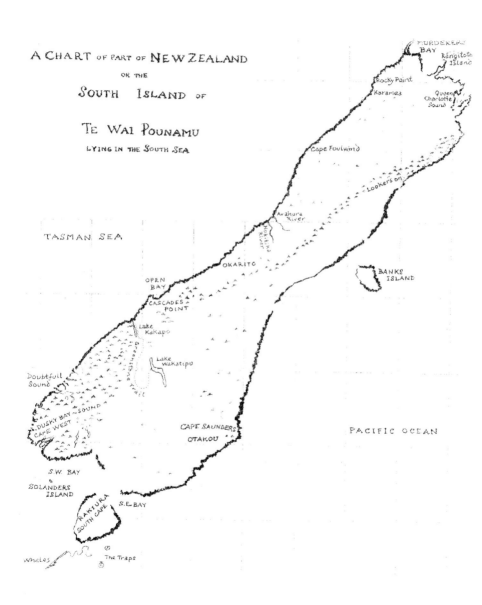

A CHART OF PART OF NEW ZEALAND

OR THE

SOUTH ISLAND OF

TE WAI POUNAMU

LYING IN THE SOUTH SEA

MURDERERS BAY
Rangitoto Island
Rocky Point
Karamea
Queen Charlotte Sound
Cape Foulwind
Lookers on
Arahura River
Hokitika River
TASMAN SEA
OKARITO
BANKS ISLAND
OPEN BAY
CASCADES POINT
Lake Kakapo
Lake Wakatipu
Doubtful Sound
DUSKY BAY SOUND
CAPE WEST
CAPE SAUNDERS
OTAKOU
PACIFIC OCEAN
S.W. BAY
SOLANDERS ISLAND
RAKIURA SOUTH CAPE
S.E. BAY
Whales
The Traps

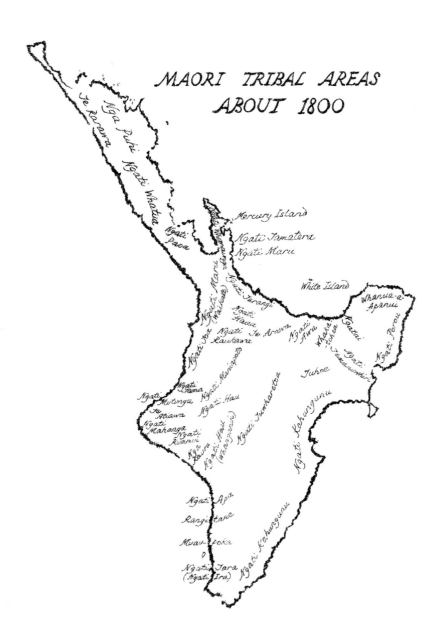

MAORI TRIBAL AREAS
ABOUT 1800

Nga Puhi
Te Rarawa
Ngati Whatua

Ngati Paoa

Mercury Island
Ngati Tamatera
Ngati Maru

White Island

Whanua-a-Apanui

Ngati Whatua (Kaipara)
Ngati Terangi
Ngati Haua
Ngati Te Arawa
Raukawa
Ngati Awra
Ngati Porou
Ngati Tawharetoa
Whakatohea
Ngati Kahungunu
Tuhoe
Ngati Tama
Ngati Matinga
Te Atiawa
Ngati Maru
Ngati Hau
Ngati Maniapoto
Ngati Tuwharetoa
Ngati Mahanga
Ngati Ruanui
Nga Rauru
Ngati Apa (Whanganui)
Ngati Kahungunu

Ngati Apa
Rangitane
Muau-poko
Ngati Tara
(Ngati Ira)
Ngati Kahungunu

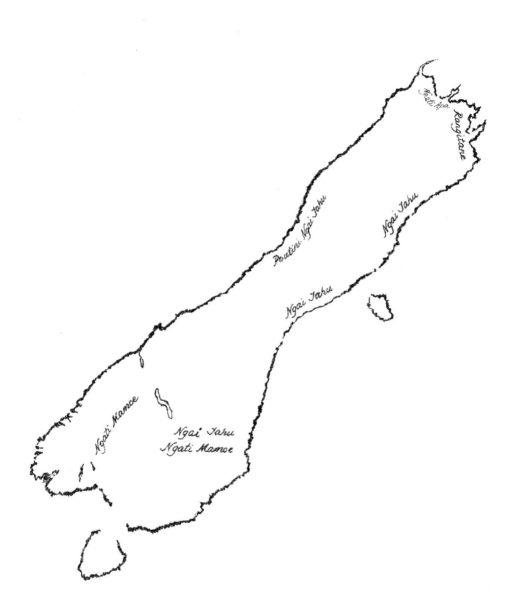

Ngati Apa

Rangitane

Poutini Ngai Tahu

Ngai Tahu

Ngai Tahu

Ngati Mamoe

Ngai Tahu
Ngati Mamoe

Chapter 1
3rd January 1800

Erickson, or The Swede as he was known in the shipping world, sat in his cuddy staring absently down river to where the Potomac River emptied its cargo of dirty spring water into Chesapeake Bay. He had been thinking hard and now it was time to act.

'Send for the boy,' he told the servant who stood by his shoulder. 'He will be back at the farm now, I expect. If not, wait for him and bring him straight here. Tell him the time has come and the ship is ready.'

Erickson picked up the ship's papers in front of him and read quickly through the parts that interested him most. He knew that by the time he had received them this new ship of his was already at sea.

All ships begin as an idea, little more than a dream, then for months they are no more than timber, rope and canvas. But at the first kiss of the sea and the first footfall of her crew on deck, she becomes a living thing. That is what his ancestors had always believed, and Erickson had yet to find to the contrary.

For a few minutes his thoughts were far away from the Potomac. In his mind he was on board his ship as she made her way down the Eastern Seaboard. He could almost feel the movement of the deck beneath his feet and he bathed in the rosy glow of ownership once more.

The *Northern Lights* was on her way at last, he thought. Hallelujah.

He had named her in memory of a country he had left long ago. His race was as old as any on earth, its legends and songs told of grand sailors, mighty warriors and explorers. Now generations of his people had made this vigorous young upstart of a country called America their home. If he was questioned Erickson would say, 'I am here living in this country, I think, because of the tale of the whale.'

Or more bluntly, depending on his audience, he would say, 'I followed the whales to this place and just never got around to going home again.'

He damned the bankers as he reread the papers before him. Erickson owned forty sixty-fourths of the ship *Northern Lights*, 450 tons registered, built in New Bedford, Massachusetts. The other twenty-four shares were held by his bankers as surety. This caused Erickson to gnash his teeth. To think that these bankers could take three eighths of each of his whales and at the end of the day not have a hair on their heads out of place was still a sore point.

When the papers were despatched this new ship of his, recently returned from sea trials, had been back in the yards loading her whale-chasers, lines, harpoons, and all the necessary tools that the chandlers of New Bedford supplied. She was purpose-built for the whaling trade and was being equipped for long voyages.

Once before, Erickson had owned a ship and was a very successful whaler in the Greenland fisheries. Then the war had come. British cruisers had blown his ship and most of what he owned in the world clean out of the water, less than a hundred nautical miles from his old home port of New Bedford, Massachusetts where men had for many years built whaling ships, re-supplied them after their long voyages and marketed their oil and bone when they returned home.

That was in 1783, Erickson remembered. Now, seventeen years later, it was three days into the new century. This vigorous young America he had chosen as his home, which had dared to challenge the might of the British Empire and win the war of independence, had finally made good its promise to repay him for the destruction of his ship.

For a long time he had pondered the wisdom of building another whaler, as the prime years of whaling looked like being over forever. The great whales were nearly gone from Greenland waters, and many of the other northern grounds were fished out. Even the best ships were taking as long as two years to fill their barrels, and many came home unable to pay even living wages.

But Erickson had his spies out. Few of the ships that plied the northern fisheries sailed without at least one Swede aboard. Some even carried members of the scattered and numerous Erickson clan itself amongst their crew, just as The Swede himself had worked his way up. Once he had been a young man chosen for his powerful frame as an oarsman. From there he had slowly but surely moved up through the ranks, always saving his money when the rest wasted theirs, until at last he became a ship owner.

It had taken twenty years, but what did that matter? When his boat fastened on to his first whale, when he took that glorious first great ride with the rope smoking as it tore from the coil, he thought he would faint from the thrill and excitement of it all. This was the famous Nantucket sleigh ride which could change a young man's life forever.

Now it was his son's turn to take some of the responsibility off his shoulders and add to the family fortune. Already the young man had worked a season in the fishery and, unless his father was a fool, Lafe Erickson would be one of the great whalers of the new century.

Erickson waited for two days for his son to return home, and while he waited he reviewed again the copious notes he had gleaned from his spies. "Fish," he said many times to himself. 'I must have fish.'

New grounds had been found in the vast Southern Ocean. New grounds with abundant whales, more than a man could even count. Information was hard to come by though. Most ships' officers were sworn to secrecy so few would speak, and few crewmen could read the charts. Some talked however, and little by little Erickson built his plans around the information he received. A whisper here, an overheard story there, and he had slowly built his whaling maps for the coming enterprise.

At last he heard the horses on the road outside and knew that his son had come. He put his maps away.

13

'I am back, Pa!' a young man's voice called as he took the stairs in great bounds, and Lafe entered his father's office and racked his musket alongside the many other firearms that lined the wall. Every type of firearm used in the last 50 years on sea or land seemed to be in the racks. Though hardly used now, the dull shine of their metal parts told of their care. These were more than just weapons; they were the tools of trade of this family and they were all there, from the bell-mouthed blunderbuss that fired a handful of lead balls that would clear the deck of a small boat to the heavy hunting musket that Lafe had just returned to the rack alongside numerous pistols of various calibres.

Erickson sat back in his chair and waited while his son stripped off his heavy deerskin jerkin and stood with his back to the fire. As he waited he studied the boy, aware that the time he had left to share with him was now short. He saw that Lafe had in this last year, his eighteenth, finished his growing and begun to put the muscle on his frame that gave him a man's stature. The boy had the size and colouring of all the Ericksons before him. They were a handsome race, his father thought. Lafe was just a shade over six foot tall in his moccasins. Where the sun touched his skin it was golden brown and where it touched his hair it was the colour of dark honey with bleached tips. His eyes were that intense shade of dark blue not uncommon in Scandinavia, but in other countries they would always draw a second look.

'How was the weather up where you were?' he asked the boy.

'Snowed two days. Fine two days.' Lafe's mouth broadened in a grin. 'We got a bear, Pa.'

Erickson knitted his brows and tried to look stern. He had already noted it was the heavy musket that the boy had returned to the rack, and as the young man's clothes warmed in front of the fire there was a distinctive odour of bear wafting into the room. He had told his son on more than one occasion not to hunt bear, especially in the dangerous fashion called smoking. This required the hunters to dig a hole into the bear's den then build a fire in the hole and shoot the angry animal when it charged out. But for one who had ridden a light boat attached to many tons of angry whale before his eighteenth birthday the old rules seemed not to be so appropriate any more.

14

Well, at least the larder has been well stocked these last months, Erickson thought. Deer, goose, duck and now bear. Deer and bear were no longer easy to find near the eastern seaboard so Lafe's hunting trips had taken him far inland to the foothills of the Allegheny Mountains of Virginia. He glanced again at the papers in front of him, enjoying the moment.

'Well son, our ship is ready. The *Northern Lights* has passed her sea trials with flying colours, according to Captain Olva.

'You are now the second mate of a new whaler. She's taking on supplies and her crew will be aboard now. She leaves for Virginia on the tide, if all goes well. What do you say to that?'

Lafe took the three strides from the fire to his father's desk in a single bound and shook his hand vigorously.

'I am more than ready, Pa. I have enjoyed the time here and the hunting has been good but I need to get back to sea. I will go down to the wharf and get the cutter ready.' The grin broadened even more and his eyes sparkled. 'With a bit of wind and the tide's help, we will sail for Norfolk in the morning.'

Erickson watched with pride and something like envy as the younger man strode from the room. Then he began to gather his papers and put his affairs in order, for he would be away for at least a month. He had a ship to send to the whaling grounds once more.

Before it was really light enough to see the other shadowy river craft beginning their day, the cutter had cleared the mouth of the Potomac and entered the wide reaches of Chesapeake Bay. The breeze was picking up as the light strengthened, and the volume of stars overhead promised a good day and fine sailing. Erickson had the tiller. From this position he could lean back and watch as Lafe fine-tuned the sails, finding the delicate balance that brought little ships like this cutter alive.

Her true description was gaff-rigged cutter. She carried a single gaff-rigged mainsail, with two triangular sails forward of the mast. With her transom-hung rudder and retractable keel, she owed much of her design to the oyster smacks that worked the Chesapeake. Being half decked forward of the mast gave her the ability to push her way through considerable seas without shipping a lot of water.

She was a sturdy, safe little boat, lap-straked/clinker-planked for strength, and at thirty feet she was a little longer than a standard whaleboat. Much of her design was based on the strong, light whale-chasers, and with her half deck removed, the mast and sails stowed and a full complement of oarsmen aboard she would serve as a spare whale chaser when needed.

Lafe had built the cutter himself, with the help of a skilled boat builder on the Potomac. She had been completed in the late summer of the previous year, and he named her *Aurora*. Her builders had used wooden pegs instead of nails, and they would be drilled out at Norfolk and the boat disassembled for storage in the hold of the *Northern Lights*. Like Lafe, she was going whaling.

As *Aurora* drew further from shore and the sun heaved itself over the horizon, the wind rose with it until the cutter fairly hissed along, shouldering aside the light swell that had come up with the wind. With the wind abeam, it was the little ship's best point of sail and Erickson smiled as he tested the tiller. If the breeze rose any more he would have to order his son to reduce sail, he thought. But Lafe had sailed her many times already, and would know that she was almost at the point of rounding up into the wind if she had an ounce more sail or even the slightest increase in wind speed. His father knew he was being challenged, and decided to say nothing.

The sky was the clear blue of fine winter weather that promised to hold, at least for the duration of the trip, but it was cold out there in the bay. Some of the upper bays and rivers of the Chesapeake were still carrying ice and would remain that way for a couple of months yet. But down near the mouth of this great bay, or drowned river valley as people were starting to realize it was, the water was saltier and held little ice. The men on the cutter were glad of their skin coats and fur mittens and the chance to lie below the deck, where a small charcoal stove satisfied their cooking and heating needs.

It was near midnight when they finally swung into the quiet of the James River and took in all sail except a small headsail for steering. It was much warmer now without the breeze of the boat's passage adding to the drop in temperature already caused by nightfall.

16

'You will recall this trip very well, Lafe, in the weeks to come,' Erickson said quietly, 'for when the *Northern Lights* leaves Norfolk it will be for the tropics and after that the doldrums. You will soon be dreaming of the sweet, cool breezes we had today.'

Lafe laughed. 'Pa, all I can think about now is islands in the sun. I have had enough of the cold this winter. But if I am right, we will leave here to sail to the southern winter?'

'Yes, but you will have had your fill of the tropics by then I hope. Then you start your real work – catching whales.'

By next evening the cutter had been taken down into its component parts and was ready for loading. Just as the light started to go, a ship swung around the point and prepared to enter the James River. The men stood eagerly watching, knowing the ship long before they picked out the name at her bow.

'Now that is a fine sight, Lafe,' Erickson sighed. 'At times I have thought I would never own another whaler.'

The younger man's eyes were bright with anticipation as he watched the *Northern Lights* turn into the wind, her sails losing their shape as the breeze now worked against the ship's passage through the water. As soon her upper sails were furled, the helmsman let her head fall away to pick up the wind again in her lower sails and she began her run into the river.

'For a new crew that wasn't badly done,' Lafe said quietly.

Erickson was aware of the relief he felt. The manoeuvre had been well carried out, but he had been holding his breath throughout most of it. If the furling had not been so fast and the ship had not been brought back so smartly onto the wind, she would have soon drifted onto the sand bar that guarded the river.

Many of the townspeople had turned out to see this new Erickson ship come in, for this was a sailors' town and a more highly-critical audience would be hard to find anywhere. Most captains, especially with such a new crew, would have reduced sail well out of sight of the watchers and the day belonged to Captain Olva for having the sheer nerve to carry it off. The confidence his manoeuvre would have imparted to the crew was beyond price, and Erickson knew that Olva had also been paying him tribute, as owner, by showing off the ship.

As soon as the anchor had buried itself in the mud a boat was swung out and four men rowed in to pick up the Ericksons, ship owner and second mate, from the town jetty. Lafe with his sea chest and box of delicate navigation instruments took most of the room in the whale chaser, but the four boatmen knew their job and they were soon alongside.

The great wooden sides of the *Northern Lights* smelled of new timber and paint and tar, and the masts and rigging looked dauntingly high from the level of the river. If it had not been for the formal joining of the ship that awaited his father and himself on deck Lafe would have been away up to the crow's nest, for it was her sails, mast and rigging that interested him most. Much of the work carried out aloft was hard, miserable and dangerous, especially in the blows, but Lafe liked being aloft. He enjoyed the hours spent looking for whales or just dreaming the days away, as the ship ploughed on through the sea so far below.

Erickson led the way up the ladder to the deck, as was his right as the ship's owner on such a formal occasion. Lafe followed closely behind, leaving his chest and boxed navigation equipment to be hauled aboard by the seamen, although not without a quiet word in the boatman's ear about what would happen if any of his property was lost in the river.

Captain Olva was waiting for them. He had changed into his best sea-going rig and he had the crew, also dressed smartly, drawn up into two lines to receive the new owner.

'You have chosen a good crew by the look of them, Captain Olva,' Erickson said as he moved between the two lines of men. He looked carefully into the faces of each of them and when he was done he turned back to Olva with a nod of approval. 'Send them ashore now, and I will speak to them tomorrow when we put out of the river.'

There was a race for the boats and soon all that was left on board was a small group of officers. Erickson had done the right thing in sending the crew ashore. It could be as long as two years before they set foot on American soil again, and some might not make it back at all. Whaleboats and even whole ships had vanished without trace before. It was part of the risk that went with hunting large fish in some of the farthest and least explored waters of the planet.

Not that a young whaling man would consider that he led a risky life. "It might happen on some other ship, but not ours," they would say. They were protected and guarded by the eternal optimism of youth. Today was today, and tomorrow would look after itself.

Now they would go ashore to drink, to sing and dance and tell stories, to talk of what they had done and would do, to boast of their ship, to calculate their lay, which was their percentage of the profits at the end of the voyage, and to speculate on the great numbers of whales they would kill.

And tomorrow, with hangovers fit to kill lesser men, they would wander the streets looking for women, talking to the bolder ones and looking over the town in a sort of desperate way as if to store as many memories as possible for the long lonely days and nights ahead. By nightfall, Erickson and Olva both knew, most of their men would be back on board with their heads down, catching up on sleep. Sleep was a luxury all too rare on a whaler.

'Good men all right, Captain Olva,' The Swede said formally as he watched the last of the crew into the boats. 'I guess many have been laid up over the last couple of years as the Greenland waters were fished out?'

'We had the pick of them,' Olva agreed. 'It was a sorry thing to see so many good men on the beach.'

He turned his attention back to matters in hand. 'Sir, would you and the second mate like to accompany me to my cabin?'

This is the first time the Captain has chosen to acknowledge I am even on board, Lafe thought. Olva was a stickler for regulations and protocol, which was only right and proper. While Lafe stood on the deck of this ship he was the second mate, not the owner's son, and he would only remain second mate as long as he was fit to hold the position. But Olva had been watching him, he knew that.

'We will get the chance for you to inspect your ship in the daylight, which may not be soon enough for the second mate by the look of him,' the captain chuckled as he waved them into his cabin. He did not need to tell Lafe that now in his own cabin, entered only by invitation, he was once again Olva. The families had known each other for a long time now. Olva was from the Old Country too, and that made them more than just shipmates. The two older men had shared berths together on many whalers over the years, and each regarded the other as the second best whaling captain sailing in any fleet on the ocean.

Lafe had served under Olva before, on his first and only trip to the fisheries, and considered him a good captain. Olva was tough and a firm disciplinarian, which Lafe thought was no bad thing as long as it was not directed at him too often.

Once, he remembered, he had left the hatchet out of a whaleboat he was in charge of, thereby endangering the whole boat. As Olva had told him in no uncertain terms, if the hatchet which wasn't there where it should have been had been needed to cut the boat free from a running whale, the boat and its crew could have been towed clear over the horizon and lost for good. Olva had demoted him immediately to oarsman and he pulled extra watches for a week until he had nearly learned to sleep standing up. But that was on another voyage, and Lafe had learned his lesson well. Now Cooky entered the cabin bringing each man a tankard of hot spiced rum, and at a nod from the captain he vanished hastily to catch the last boat to shore. The men sipped at their drinks in the small cabin, savouring the moment.

'Right. Let's have it,' Olva demanded.

The Swede smiled as he undid his case and pulled out his charts and a leather-bound and locked journal. Olva and Lafe were aware that this journal, along with the charts, carried all the distilled and re-ordered information that had been gathered on the various fisheries over the last ten years. While Erickson had waited and hoped that the new young nation would make good its promise to pay for his lost ship he had planned and schemed. Now he outlined his plans and the three of them pored over the charts, tracing the ship's most logical course across the oceans.

From Norfolk, Virginia, they would hunt their way across the Atlantic to the Azores. Any oil would be landed there and shipped back to Norfolk by the factors whose business it was to handle such precious cargo. From the Azores they would work the edge of the West African current to the southern tip of Africa then drop down to that band of constant westerly winds that circled the globe at latitude forty, hunting their way downwind until they reached the waters south of Van Diemen's land. These waters, Erickson had reason to believe, were rich fisheries holding good numbers of the valuable sperm whale. If enough fish were taken the ship would proceed to the penal colony at Sydney Cove in Port Jackson to unload. The British were paying a premium for whale oil, and there were empty convict ships at Port Jackson hungry for profitable cargo to carry on the return trip to Britain.

No food, and very little of anything else would be available in Sydney Cove. It was said the convicts were on half their penal rations, as the food grown in the Colony had fallen far short of their needs. This meant the *Northern Lights* would leave as soon as it had unloaded and cross the Tasman Sea to New Zealand. After rounding the northernmost cape the ship would enter the Bay of Islands, where food could be traded from native gardens established there. Once fresh food and water had been successfully obtained, the ship would fish the east coasts of both main islands, heading south.

'There's an anchorage on the southeast coast of the middle island at a place called Otako,' Erickson told Olva, who nodded slowly.

'I've heard of it.'

'According to my information it may be possible to pick up native guides there.'

The *Northern Lights*, they agreed, would need to be in a position to place a sealing party, with local guides, on the southwest coast of Middle Island on or about the month of November, when the seals hauled out for breeding and pupping. Once it had landed the sealers, the ship would go whaling to the south and west, where there was a newly-discovered whaling ground near the Solander Islands.

According to the reports Erickson had recently come by, this area was rich in right whales. When sufficient stocks of oil were stowed in the holds, the ship would travel back to Sydney Cove and load it on a merchant ship returning to England, then return to New Zealand to take on board the sealing party and their skins.

'Not later than April, before the winter begins to bite,' The Swede warned, 'Then, back home to Norfolk, Virginia.' He stabbed the chart with a stubby forefinger in triumph.

'A bold plan,' Olva told him. 'Though I must say most of my own sources back up what you say. I have heard of as many as 10,000 seal skins taken in a single season by a ship on that coast. A fortune was made in the skins alone.'

'And the merchants of England get hungrier for oil by the day,' The Swede reminded him.

'What of the natives, or Maori as I hear they are called?' Olva asked.

'There are places where contact has been established and there they are keen to trade, mainly for whale tooth and muskets. Cannibals still roam most of the country though, from all reports,' Erickson said with a grimace. 'You will take care, my friend.'

Many things were discussed around the table in that small smoky cabin and Lafe started to realize what planning went into such a voyage. Many of the charts that his father had brought with him were hand drawn, and must have come from the pen of one of the very few sailors to have visited that part of the world. Much of what the great navigator James Cook had charted on the coasts of New Zealand and New South Wales had been ammended and added to by careful hands, and the charts appeared both accurate and useful.

Lafe wondered how the crew would react to this news. A whaler went to sea, stayed as long as it took to fill her barrels and then returned to her home port. That was what her crews expected. Some whalers had stayed at sea for up to two years, but that was regarded as a long trip. This cruise might take even more than two years to complete.

Shipowners and sea captains very seldom discussed their plans with the sailors, Lafe knew that. Most officers reckoned on the fact that by the time the crew knew something different was happening they would be too far away to do anything about it. Whalers were usually single men, but some among the crew would leave wives and sweethearts behind them. This would cause a lot of sadness aboard the *Northern Lights*, but it was the nature of whaling, and whaling men, that such things were to be accepted.

If they met another ship out at sea, returning from the whaling grounds, and the sea was calm, they would join up for a 'gam' as the whaling men called it. Lying side by side in the ocean swells, the captains, officers and crews would swap news and socialize with their counterparts. Letters, catch records, dispatches and general news would be swapped and finally arrive at the home port where shipowners and crewmen's families would receive them with equal enthusiasm.

If they had success among the whales, everything would be all right and the crew would work hard because it meant money in their pockets when they returned home. But some ships went a year without boating a single whale. These were jinxed ships with unlucky captains, and their crews would desert the ship at the nearest port, ruining the shipowner if he could not attract another crew. This problem became compounded for the poor captain who was often afraid to come close to any land for fear he would end up the only one left on board.

A short cruise of around a year, with a ship returning home with all its barrels full, was considered a good cruise and every whaling man on board every whaling ship hoped for such a triumphant homecoming.

Scurvy, the age-old killer of whalers, was no longer such a curse. Since Cook's day ships' officers were more aware of the causes of scurvy and ensured the crew received better food. Various concoctions were also carried on board to dose the crew with. Such dosings were not voluntary for the sailors and some recipes, secrets known only to the captains, were good cause for fleeing the ship.

Northern Lights had a good captain and the men would be well looked after. But as second mate, Lafe would be in charge of the sealing party to be left behind on the southwest coast of New Zealand. There would be ten sealers and the two guides that they hoped to obtain at Otako. This would be quite a responsibility he realized.

When Lafe quit the cabin and sought his bunk, his father and Olva were still tackling the smaller details of the voyage. It was enough for him, for the time being at least, that he knew the major plan and the part he would play in it.

As he lay waiting for sleep to come he reviewed his own plans. As second mate he would be in charge of one of the two watches that ran the ship. When the crew arrived back on board the first of the watches would begin, and they would run four hours on and four hours off, with

23

shorter dog watches to rotate the hours, until the end of the voyage.

This meant that Lafe, as well as the crew, would need as much sleep as he could get from now on. Catching and boiling down whales would cut into any sleep time and there would be long periods where everyone would work to the point of near exhaustion. He would also, as the *Northern Lights'* navigator, take the noon shots with the sextant, wind the chronometer and plot the ship's daily course across the ocean. Boat crews would be chosen when they reached the open sea, and Lafe would have to train them and be responsible for his own whaleboat being ready to launch at a moment's notice.

He knew too that much of his time would be spent high in the rigging, furling and setting sails depending on the winds. Sails chafed and wore through, and had to be sent down for repairs. Rope frayed and needed to be spliced or replaced, and on a good ship this work never stopped. *Northern Lights* was new and so were her sails and rigging, but this was the source of the power that would carry them across mighty oceans, and it had to keep working.

Minor sail changes were his to decide, major changes were called by the captain, and then he would be just another hand high in the rigging. Lafe knew it would take a week or two to get himself and the crew seasoned to the work and knowing their jobs again. A sailor soon learned to hang on with his legs while trying to fist a large piece of madly-flapping canvas that threatened at any minute to hurl him from the top of the mast into the sea far below. If that happened, it was a lucky man that was ever picked up again. A small head was very hard to find again in any sort of sea, even if it was calm enough to turn the ship to search.   'One hand for yourself, friend, and one hand for the ship,' the old hands said.

This voyage his father had planned was ambitious indeed, but Olva was the man to pull off such an expedition, Lafe decided. The old man had salt water in his veins instead of blood, and in a few weeks when his crew got to know him better they would follow him to hell and back. Lafe reckoned that James Cook must have been such a man. He had taken his crew to the ends of the earth five times and brought them home again.

At cock-crow next morning, Erickson and Lafe made a full inspection of the ship. From the bottom of her large holds, where the oil would be stored, to the spar that supported the sky sail at the very top of the main mast, nothing was missed. When this inspection was completed to everyone's satisfaction, all three men rowed ashore for breakfast.

'I am satisfied,' Erickson told Olva. 'We have a good ship.'

'They build well at New Bedford,' the captain agreed. 'They used good heart oak, and I am damned glad you chose to copper her bottom,'

'I have heard the worm is bad in the tropics, and who knows what it is like where you are going?'

'How does she handle?' Lafe asked as he chewed his way through the large breakfast in front of him.

'She's a tough ship,' Olva replied, but it was to the shipowner that he spoke as he added, 'and all other things aside, a tough ship is what we need where we are going.'

Lafe finished his breakfast, excused himself and set off to find a couple of crewmen to help him get the dismantled cutter out to the *Northern Lights* and stored in her hold.

'Christ, that young man of yours can eat,' remarked Olva when Lafe had left them.

'He's a gannet if ever I saw one.'

'I am glad it is you, not me, who will have to pay for his food. At this rate we will be out of rations long before we sight New South Wales.'

Erickson laughed. 'But don't worry, my friend, I have provided extra for him so you won't miss out.'

His organisation had been meticulous and sound. The last of the supplies and the fresh food would be aboard by last light, and the water barrels filled. 'Your crew should be back on board by then too,' he told Olva. 'I doubt you'll have trouble there.'

He was right. By nightfall all of the last minute goods had been purchased and anything that needed attention had been repaired, and by the early hours of next morning not one of the crew had failed to return to the ship. This was a good omen according to Olva, who gave the quiet order to lift the anchor.

Daylight was not far away now and there was enough light to see when the anchor was straight up and down, while still holding the ship to the muddy bottom. When the tide just started to run out of the river the whaleboat towed the bow around until it faced the open Bay and the anchor was hauled aboard. One by one the sails caught the wind with a crack and were sheeted home, while the ship below felt the power of those sails and began to pick up speed in the muddy river. By the time the jibs were set and flying, the whale-chaser had been hooked on to the chains and its crew were back on board.

Erickson was still on his ship, enjoying the feel of the deck timbers beneath his boots. He had arranged to be picked up by the pilot boat outside the bay near Cape Henry. He wanted to see for himself how the ship performed under sail. With the amount of canvas she carried and the shape of her keel under the water, she should be as fast and handy as any whaler could be. He had chosen her design with care for just those reasons. All ships were a compromise though, he had to acknowledge. There was a balance to be sought between carrying capacity or cargo area, and speed. You could have one but not both.

Northern Lights was 110 feet, longer than most whalers. She had a narrower beam than most too, and she carried more canvas higher up on the mast where the breeze was stronger. Many whaling ships resembled bathtubs in shape and the sailors would joke and say they been made in one long length, with individual boats sawn off it as they were needed.

But American boat builders had learned a lot during their war with Britain. American frigates were widely respected by the navies of the world for being able to outfight and outrun their opponents. Erickson's old ship had been lost to a British attacker so it was fitting that much of the knowledge gained from that war had been incorporated into the building of this new whaler of his.

He took up a position in the stern and watched as more and more sail broke out aloft.

'Nearly half as many sails again as any whaler I have previously sailed on, Olva,' he said with quiet pride, and his captain nodded in approval as they stared into the forest of spars and rigging above them.

Soon each of the three masts carried its full complement of five sail, and three jibs were set flying from the sprit. That made eighteen sails in all and nine studding sails remained below. These were added only in light airs and were used to increase the width of the main sails.

Now *Northern Lights* was running fast for the entrance, where the huge Chesapeake Bay emptied into the Atlantic Ocean.

'She has the bone in her teeth now,' Erickson chuckled. 'She can already smell the open sea.' He grinned with pleasure, enjoying the feel of the ship under his feet once again. There was no sign of tenderness, no hint of an excessive heeling angle brought on by the press of canvas above. She sailed freely and well, and he was a proud man.

High in the rigging Lafe paused in his work and looked around as he felt the ship begin to lift to the first swells of the Atlantic Ocean, swells that may well have been born near the shores of Africa.

He watched the land fall away with a feeling akin to loneliness but not quite the same.

"Chesapeake, you are so beautiful!" he cried aloud. "I wonder how long it will be before I see you again." The wind carried Lafe's voice to the other sailors and one or two looked at him and smiled, sharing the moment. Some shouted their own farewells into the wind before sliding back down to the deck. Others, he noted, turned away so he could not read the expressions on their faces.

At Cape Henry the sails were slackened briefly while the pilot boat took Erickson aboard, then the ship pointed her bow toward the wide reaches of the Mid-Atlantic.

The voyage had begun.

Chapter 2

The *Northern Lights* was headed for the Azores, a small group of islands lying almost due east of Norfolk on the other side of the Atlantic. Near the same latitude as Chesapeake Bay, these little islands were much closer to Africa or Portugal than they were to any other place on earth. The Azores were under Portugese control and, having a prime position in an isolated part of the Atlantic they had become the crossroads of the ocean and a busy trading post for whalers.

It would have been relatively easy to put the bow of the ship onto a compass heading and sail down the latitude line to the Azores, but the *Northern Lights* was a whaler and she hunted the oceans like a solitary wolf. Her course curved south into warmer waters, where Olva's nose told him whales would be and where he had taken them before at this time of year.

The whales followed great migratory routes around the world from ocean to ocean but their routes scarcely ever crossed the Equator. That was what the whalers believed, and the fact that the stocks of whales were still abundant in the southern oceans after they had declined in the northern fishery seemed to prove it. Ships' logs would show that if you took fish on a certain day at a given position, the chances were high that on the same date a year later you would find a pod nearby.

Captains like Olva believed these things and kept catch records that were jealously guarded from prying eyes, while at the same time they kept their eyes and ears open and alert to any morsel of information that might slip from the lips of another whaler.

Once they had left their native coast and the light blue sea gave way to the deep blue of the true ocean, the boat crews were picked. Ropes, oars and other gear stood in piles around the four whale-chasers which were ranged on deck ready for lowering at the first sight of a whale. The masthead was manned now and would remain so till the end of the cruise, and the crew gathered on deck with more than a little excitement. Picking the boat crews was a major event on any whaler. From this moment until the last whale of the voyage was captured and processed, competition between boats and their crews would be fierce.

The sailors gathered around as the four boat captains stood forth and the picking began. Rank had its privileges in this time-honoured process. The first mate began the picking and chose his first man, then Lafe as second mate chose his, and on down it went until each boat captain had chosen his six men. One of the six on each boat was an experienced harpooner and they were regarded as a race apart from the common sailors, although they still pulled an oar during the chase.

The harpooners had their own weapons, the razor-sharp heads kept covered in soft leather pouches made from the gut of a young whale. These were the harpooners' tools of trade, often made to their own designs and scarcely ever let out of their owners' sights. Each harpooner carried at least three harpoons and two lances, minimum armament for the coming battles. The harpooners formed a little community of their own within the ship. They ate together and bunked in a no-mans-land, neither forward with the men nor aft with the officers. It was a masonic society, proudly protected, and God help the young sailor who wasn't aware that in the harpooners' hands alone rested the success or failure of any voyage.

During the picking of the boat crews Olva acted as the final arbiter, as it was in the interest of the ship to have the boat crews as evenly matched as possible. Each crew had a mixture of the strong, the brave and the cunning, according to Olva's rules, for if one oarsman got a scare from a whale, he warned his captains, it would never do if the whole crew followed.

Once the picking was done the whale-chasers were loaded under the careful eye of the harpooners. Some of the equipment, such as the harpoons, the lances and the whale line, would never be touched by the ordinary sailors. The whale line sat in a tub in the bow of the boat, eight hundred yards of it carefully coiled so that it ran free without a kink or twist. If the line threw a playful loop, a half-hitch or a hangman's noose as it rose from the tub it could take someone over the side and more than one luckless sailor had been whisked from the boat by a loop of errant whale line and taken down to the depths, his life crushed from his body, doomed to keep the whale company for many a day.

Those men not picked for a whale-chaser crew would manage the mother ship and wait to see if death or injury would suddenly elevate them to a more exciting berth. With her crew of forty the *Northern Lights* carried a slightly larger number of sailors than was usual with whalers of her tonnage so that when the shore party was left on the sealing grounds the ship would still not be short-handed.

The last part of the ritual was the nailing to the mast of a gold sovereign, so everyone could see it. This prize would go to the first lookout who cried from the masthead, 'She blows! She blows!'

It was the distinctive fountain of expired breath that gave the whale away, long before any physical shape could be seen from the ship. The sperm whale left its own signature hanging in the air above the pod, producing a spout not only upward but forward in the direction of travel. For a fish more valuable and more avidly hunted than any other on earth, it appeared unkind that the gods had made this so.

Often in that week before they met their first whale Captain Olva would stride the deck, checking wind and sea conditions. If they were suitable he would grab a light barrel, hurl it into the ocean and shout, 'A whale! A whale! Launch the boats!' The sleeping watch would boil up from below decks and the four boats would hit the water like ducks, racing each other to retrieve the barrel and return it on board.

'My regatta,' Olva called it and he would roundly curse the last boat crew back on board the ship. 'If that had been a whale it would have died of old age long before you lot got there,' he would tell them in blistering tones.

Just as every last sailor had become tired of looking to the masthead and wondering if they were all asleep up there, it finally came – the long-awaited, excited cry. 'She blows! She blows!'

Olva was up to the cross trees with his glass in an instant. One glance in the direction the lookout was pointing, and he had the pod clear on the horizon. Orders were shouted to the helmsman below and the ship began to swing, heeling savagely onto a new course. Olva slid down the ratlines surprisingly quickly for an old man, and was back on deck before the boat crews had finished gathering.

'A small pod, about ten sperm whales. All young bulls,' he told the boatmen. 'We stay on this course for fifteen minutes then launch the boats.'

He looked at Lafe and the other excited men sternly, choosing his words. 'Remember these are young whales, young and foolish like some of our crew still, and because of that they are dangerous. They will do what you do not expect them to do. Attack them head-on and remember – no noise!'

As soon as the chasers hit the water their little sails blossomed forth and they set off in a long curving course to get ahead of the pod. It took time and patience to sail to the ambush position, and once Lafe was sure that his boat was where it should be and the pod was sticking to its original course, he dropped his sail. Now the stalk began. They were bow on and right in the path of the whales. Although the young bull Lafe had picked out could not see them, its vision directly ahead blocked by its own enormous forehead, its hearing was extraordinarily sharp. Silence and position were the keys now. A careless foot knocked against the side of the boat, and the pod would hear it through the water as clearly as a flock of geese hears a shot from a fowling piece many miles away on a fine winter's morning. Olva had drummed this message into the men. 'And just as quick as bloody geese, a pod will scatter and vanish from the ocean,' he had warned them.

'Row easy and quietly now, they are close.' Lafe spoke softly to the crew, whose eyes were fixed on him as he stood at the steering oar. From this point on until the harpooner rose to throw his iron, only the boat captain would see the whale. Some of the faces before him showed

31

clearly that this was their first time, and they were feeling the strain so Lafe tried to look confident, and even arranged a devil-may-care smile on his face to give the new men courage. He could vividly remember what it was like to row into danger without being able to see what was coming, and knew it was at this point that new sailors had been known to jump clean over the side rather than meet the whale racing toward them. Poor devils, Lafe thought to himself as he watched the strained faces before him. This was how a foot soldier in Ancient Rome must have felt when an army of chariots bore down on him.

Out of the corner of his eye he could see the other boats in a rough line across the track of the advancing pod. They had all picked their whales and were just beginning to make their run in. Boats and whales were closing at speed and things began to happen very quickly.

'One hundred yards,' Lafe warned softly. Then, 'Cease rowing!' They were close now, almost bow-on to the enormous head. A touch on the steering oar and the whale they had chosen would pass down the port side of the boat, almost within touching distance.

'Face your front!' Lafe hissed at an oarsman who was trying to get a look over his shoulder.

The subdued roar of the whale's passage through the water could be heard clearly now, and the tension on the boat was almost tangible.

'Back oars!' Lafe rapped out and the men dug deep, wiping the remaining way off the boat and bringing her up sharp.

'Starboard pull!' Lafe ordered and, as the boat started to spin in its own length, 'Take him now!'

In one movement the harpooner rose from his bench near the bow. He turned, lifted his harpoon from the rack and braced himself for the throw.

It had been a good approach; the great arched back of the young whale was not more than ten yards from the tip of the raised harpoon. The first third of the sperm whale's length was taken up by head and bone that would repel even the sharpest blade but the harpooner focused on a spot forward of the dorsal hump. He drew back and, with a mighty throw, launched his harpoon.

He threw well. For a long minute the harpoon stood fixed deep in the muscle of the great broad back. Then the line started to peel from the tub.

'Ship oars!' Lafe ordered, and the long blades disappeared back on board with great speed. Now the oarsmen swivelled around to face the bow of the boat, grab the gunwales and hang on. The whale had felt the prick of the harpoon and had sounded, picking up speed as it headed for the safety of the deep. The harpooner whipped a single turn around the bollard and they were away on the Nantucket sleigh ride, the whale line tight enough to play a tune on. To feel the power of this great creature was an experience never to be forgotten.

This whale was a bull, still a few years from maturity but fit, powerful and full of fight. Down, down it swam into the depths, until nearly five hundred yards of line had been taken from the tub. Holding the line loosely in his hand, the harpooner tried to read the whale's movements as it swam deep below them.

'He has stopped going down,' the harpooner said after a minute or two of holding the line, 'but he still swims strongly.'

More long minutes went by as the little boat careered through the waves, bouncing off the tops of some, smashing down in the troughs of others.

'This will shake a liver or two loose,' Lafe joked, but he hung onto the gunwale as grimly as any other man in the boat. His steering oar was useless in their headlong rush across the sea. Where they went now was solely at the whim of the whale, and a couple of the oarsmen threw hasty glances over their shoulders to where they had last seen the mother ship. Lafe could tell from their shocked faces that the *Northern Lights* was already far behind, and he knew what they were thinking. Tales were told in whaling towns of boats that had been towed clean over the horizon, never to be seen again.

'He's coming up!' shouted the harpooner. His sensitive hands told him that deep down below the angle of the line had changed as the whale tired. Quickly he started to overhand the slack line back on board, while another man coiled it carefully back into the tub, but before they could close the distance to fix another harpoon into it the young bull was gone again, down, down again into the depths, taking all the hard-won line they had just regained. Lafe splashed water constantly over bollard and line, as by this time there was a distinct smell of burning from the bow, the wooden bollard beginning to smoke from the friction of the line.

This time the whale did not reach quite the same depth, nor stay as long. At each successive dive the great fish tired more and more and stayed down for shorter periods, until at last he lay spent on the surface. Tired, but still full of fight and at his most dangerous, Lafe warned as the boat closed in quickly. They stayed carefully wide of the huge tail that could stove the vessel in and kill the crew with one blow.

When he had the range the harpooner drove his lance into the bull's vitals, probing until he found the spot. The whale spouted a crimson fountain of blood from its blowhole then in its death flurry rolled over and shuddered its last breath, turning the sea to foam as a light mist of blood and water settled on the boat and its seven occupants. The mighty tail rose from the sea, lashing sideways, combing the air above the harpooner as the little boat scuttled for safety.

Once out of danger the men rested on their oars, and no one moved for a minute or two, all of them in awe of the mighty creature they had just slain. They looked at each other all speckled with blood. Some smiled, some were thoughtful, one or two still looked scared. The new men had ridden the Nantucket sleigh and their lives had changed forever in the two short hours since they had launched their chaser. They would never forget their first whale, nor the crew they had shared the experience with.

They could see the mother ship in the distance; she had put on a bit of sail and was bearing their way, and now those who had been more than a little frightened began to cheer and slap each other on the back. Lafe sympathized with their behaviour – how well he remembered his own first whale. He gave his men a few minutes to savour the moment and store the great chase and the killing away in their minds. It was a memory to be taken out again and again, to be savoured later in life when they were too old to go to the fisheries. A landsman could live his biblical three score and ten on earth, and not one minute of his life would come close to the excitement of this crew's last hour, Lafe reckoned. But there was work to be done yet.

'Right, let's get him back to the ship before he sinks or the sharks get him.' He gave his orders, the harpooner cut a hole in the large flukes of the whale, a rope was passed through it and tied, and they began to tow their fish in. In the distance the *Northern Lights* was now lying side on to the slight swell with the other three boats in attendance. One of the other chasers was also fast onto a whale and the mother ship looked as if she was in the process of hauling it alongside. Lafe calculated that the drift would bring the ship down on them in due course, but their own efforts would help speed the process.

'Put your back into it boys, if you want your dinner tonight,' he encouraged his men. 'Captain Olva won't let us sleep until the last whale is cut up and sent below. No shark will get a bite of his profits if he can help it'.

When all the whale boats had been hauled back on board and the two whales fastened on either side of the ship, they got a little sail on, just enough to give her steerage way and make a steady platform for the cutting in to follow. A quick meal was eaten and a glass of rum drunk to the first whales of the season, then the harpooners were over the side astride the whales and the cutting in began.

Already the sharks had started to gather, and there was no creature on earth that the whalers hated more than these thieves of the deep who could strip a whale before their very eyes. A man hovered in a bosun's chair over each of their catches, a razor sharp cutting knife ready to open the guts of each shark as it ran in to snatch a mouthul of blubber. As fast as the guts fell out of one shark it was swallowed by another but still around and around they went, until it was their own guts they were eating. The primitive brains inside the fish told them they were still hungry, that they must eat and keep on eating as if there was no tomorrow.

As indeed there wasn't, Lafe thought, for these fish. Not when they had swallowed their own guts. He took his turn in the bosun's chair, swaying above the whale, jabbing with his blubber spade as a shark dived in to grab a chunk of blubber and rip it away. There was a certain evil in a fish that would continue to eat and eat until torn apart by its own species in a swirling mass of gore. Lafe had heard the stories before, but here, not far north of the Equator, the inhabitants of the sea seemed to have a new and more ghastly set of rules.

Guided by the harpooner's knife, long strips of thick blubber were lifted from the whale's carcass using a block and tackle set up from the crosstrees on the main mast. These long heavy strips were dropped through the open hatch into the blubber storage room below. While the whales were being stripped the ship's carpenter was setting up the trypots to render down the oil. First, a large shallow tray was set on deck and filled with water from the sea to stop sparks from setting fire to the oil-soaked decks. Many a ship had been burnt to the waterline before this system came into general use among whalers. In the shallow trays, brick fireplaces were erected beneath the huge trypots.

All this activity was carried out under the stern gaze of Captain Olva, who once in a while gave a quiet command to one of the mates.

'Mister Erickson!' he bellowed suddenly. 'Will you leave those sharks alone and come up on deck to cut blubber? If you carry on like that they'll have you before you've even set eyes on Sydney Town!'

Lafe realized that he had pushed the boundaries too far and Olva was angry with him. He had been taking too many risks, he knew that, but he had found a deadly fascination in the battle going on in the sea below him. Olva, though he would never have shown it, was concerned for his safety.

Lafe knew that if he slipped into the water he would not live long enough to be snatched back on board. All he would add was a little blood and a little grease to the grisly scene. He signalled to the men above to haul him in, smiling a shame-faced apology to his father's friend as he took his place beside the trypots.

Many hours later when the body of the whale had been stripped of blubber it was cut free from the ship and slowly sank with its army of murderous attendants. The huge head was hoisted above the waterline and secured with its huge blunt snout pointing up to the stars.

The abrupt transition from light to dark was particularly noticeable on this evening, as they had raced to cut in the whales while they could still see the tools they were using. Lafe had noticed day by day the lessening of twilight hours, but that day when they most needed the light, it failed abruptly. One minute he was able to see to the horizon, the next he could not see his hand in front of his face.

With night upon them the fires under the trypots lit the scene while men staggered with exhaustion on the greasy decks. They could have been demons from hell. Their shadows danced across the mainsail as if down on the deck some primitive race performed a ghastly dance to an unknown god.

In the fires, whale consumed whale. The whale's own flesh, once the oil had been cooked out of it, was fed to the fires as fuel and as the flames leapt the whole reason for the ship's existence was drawn from the pots and poured into barrels. Some of the oil found its way into the new timbers and the ship began to take on that distinctive smell that all whalers carried with them. The *Northern Lights* would carry this smell to the end of her days. The New Bedford sailors always said you could smell a slaver before you saw her. Whalers smelled too, but the people were nicer.

For the boat crews it was the end of a long, long day. Some of the younger sailors, Lafe noted, were nearly asleep on their feet and he was not much better off himself. They would eat now, and hit the bunks after they had washed as much of the oil from themselves as it was possible to. Some had forgotten to change into their oldest rig before they took to the boats, and the clothes they wore would never be clean again. The older hands worked amongst the blubber and oil wearing nothing but old strips of canvas fashioned into loincloths around their hips. They washed themselves and their loincloths quickly and took to their bunks, knowing that now they were among the whales sleep was precious. New men, the ones who had caught and killed their first whale that day, were still too restless to sleep and gathered in little groups to talk over the chase and the killing.

Olva never seemed to need sleep. As long as there was a whale alongside he kept a small watch on deck to feed the pots and draw off the oil throughout the night. From his customary position next to the wheel, his eagle eyes missed nothing. If by chance a whale should appear at daybreak he would be ready to send the boats out again.

With the first of the tropical light beginning to paint the eastern sky, Lafe's watch was on deck for what he considered the most interesting part of the cutting in of a whale. In the forehead of a sperm whale is a reservoir of the finest and most expensive oil on earth. This was the treasure, the reason for the sperm fishery's existence, and the real profit of the voyage would come from this source. The harpooners, always aware of their position on board a whaler, acted as masters of ceremonies in this important event. Surveying the forehead of the whale carefully, the harpooner from Lafe's boat cut a small hole through the bone and into the skull. A dipper was passed into the hole and emerged brimming with the light, creamy oil and it was passed from sailor to sailor, each man dipping a finger into it to feel the delightful soft texture and to taste it on their fingers. The oil resembled the essence of man, and it was from this the sperm whale got its name. This precious oil would be used to lubricate the most delicate instruments man produced, like the chronometer which was the most valuable navigation instrument on the ship. Some would be used to light the houses of the extremely wealthy, as it burned cleanly without odour or smoke.

This cask in the whale's head they were tapping into would, on a good whale, produce up to 500 gallons of sweet oil. Whale men believed that the sperm whale's ability to dive so deep was in some way tied to this amazing product, which started to solidify into a wax-like substance in little more than a cool breeze. It certainly accounted for the huge, square-shaped head that was the most recognizable feature of this giant of its species.

When all the oil that could be reached with a dipper had been ladled carefully into the barrels, the hole in the whale's forehead was enlarged and the smallest crewman went inside to mop up. Not a drop of this oil was ever wasted.

Before the carcass was released the stomach had been searched for the mysterious substance called ambergris, a waxy secretion that was used as a fixer in the perfume industry. Weighing up to twenty pounds this ambergris was also a very valuable product, though no one could tell how or why the whale produced it. Owing to the scars that all sperm whales carried from their battles with the giant squid of the deep, some believed that ambergris was the indigestible beaks of these squid. It was usually found in a whale that was in poor condition and skinny, but no one knew why that was.

Once the ship cut free of the heads, the processing was over. The fireplaces were dismantled, the decks sluiced down and all sail was set as the Northern Lights once again bounded away before the breeze. She was still hunting, but her general course would bring her into the vicinity of the Azores within a week.

Lafe was in charge of the navigation as well as his numerous other duties. He was aware that Olva often ran checks on him, as he had seen the captain taking his own sun shots, but so far he had never corrected the log which meant he was satisfied Lafe was doing a good job. The navigator always knew where he was in this great big water-filled world, and this was important to most of the other officers too. Lafe was always surprised that a lot of the sailors did not care a damn.

His navigational duties meant that the second mate was mostly excused lookout duty in the crow's nest up at the top of the mainmast. Some days though, he climbed up to the masthead and sent the lookout down, for here high above the deck was the most peaceful place on the ship. Here he could have the place all to himself for an hour or two, and with his eyes half shut and his body in tune with the arc that the mast traced across the sky he would dream of the islands he was soon to visit. They were headed across the Pacific Ocean to one of the least-known places on earth, a place whose inhabitants, the Maori, called it Aotearoa or Land Of The Long White Cloud. Others called it New Zealand, the name given by the Dutch sailor Abel Tasman.

His father's journal contained many interesting facts about the place, mostly gleaned from the few whalers who had visited this lonely land at the bottom of the world. Lafe had read through the notes many times. If everything went to plan he would spend six months in the sealing areas of Middle Island and he wanted above all to be prepared. Meanwhile he dreamily searched the sea for the next pod of whales.

By the time the scattered islands of the Azores hauled themselves over the horizon, the ship had killed ten whales and the crews were well-practised and fit for the southern oceans where they were headed next.

The town of Horta, on the island of Fayal, held little appeal and the *Northern Lights* stayed only long enough to unload the oil for Erickson's factors to send on, to fill the water casks, and to take on board whatever fresh food the officers could find, then they were gone again. Horta's one or two small streets had not much to offer sailors by way of entertainments and most were relieved when they were under way again. They had not yet been at sea long enough to be desperate for land under their feet, nor to suffer unbearable desires for the company of women. Besides, Olva did not like these foreign ports. The risk of disease being brought on board his ship was too great.

Chapter 3

Lafe had mixed feelings as he watched the tiny islands of the Azores disappear over the horizon. This was their last port of call in the old world; the *Northern Lights* was now shaping her course for the Equator and the lower forties beyond. Many sailors believed that in the great southern ocean there were large sea creatures capable of dragging the ship down into the depths and destroying her. Moreover there were lands not yet trodden by civilized feet, inhabited by cannibals that bore only the most rudimentary human shapes. These were old stories, but at the Azores they had heard new rumours too, that the British and French were at war once again. Napoleon Bonaparte was in power and in Paris, and he was a strange and ambitious man with a military government behind him.

'The trouble with European wars,' Olva warned his officers, 'is that the combatants tended to regard any ships not involved as fair game, though the British are more likely to give us trouble than the French.

'A lot of British officers are still smarting at the loss of their American colonies, and some captains still regard anyone who sails under the American flag as a rebel. We cannot fight them so our only defence will be to run like rabbits. Keep your eyes open and don't let the lookouts doze off.'

The *Northern Lights* kept a man at the masthead night and day, and carried a lot of extra sail. Olva also had the cannons run out and fired, just for practice. The ship carried four rather small pieces, just enough to keep lightly-armed South Sea natives from taking the ship if they took it into their heads to try.

'Not many ships could catch us in a stern chase,' Lafe reckoned, and said so. 'Only one of those damned frigates.' They were the greyhounds of the sea, well armed and very, very dangerous. Both the British and the French were known to be prowling the seas and interfering with private traders. Olva knew how to run though, and with sufficient warning he knew he could keep ahead of a frigate till darkness fell and then lose it during the night with a judicious change of course or two. He made sure every one of his officers knew what to do if another sail was seen on their watch.

The *Northern Lights* was running now, racing to get clear of the slave routes out of Africa that crossed the Atlantic and attracted unsavoury attention. Still, it was a great big ocean. In all the weeks since they had left their home port only one other sail had been seen on the horizon and that, Olva suspected, was another whaler. Both ships had altered course away and were lost to each other in an hour.

'Which just goes to show, Lafe, how unfriendly the waters of the northern hemisphere have become in recent times,' Olva had told his second mate as they watched the strange sail recede over the horizon. 'It would have been nice to stop and have a gam, but who could take the risk? I can hardly remember a time when the English were not at war with someone. They say it's to protect trade, but the peaceful trader is often the victim and I won't have it happen to this ship.

'Time was I would have taken us around Cape Horn and into the Pacific after the whales, but those devious Spanish dogs have seized ten American whale ships around that coast in the last couple of years so we now have to enter the Pacific by the back door. Softly softly catchee monkey, you understand me?'

When Lafe was on the wheel, his body moving lazily to the motion of the ship, Olva often brought up this issue of the destruction or seizure of American ships. The whaling fleet had almost ceased to exist by the time the American war of independence was over, as most of the ships were either sunk or sailed to Britain as prizes of war. The thought that this fine new ship could be taken by the British was enough to make Olva's eyes nearly bulge out of his head with rage.

'God give me the day when America is powerful enough to field her own fleet of warships,' he would rail. 'Then we could protect our ships and wipe the sea clean of these pirates.'

They were still well north of the equator when they entered the doldrums, a mass of stationary air that varied its position and size from one year to the next. The sailors disliked the doldrums with a fierce intensity; the ship rolled her guts out when there was no breeze to fill her sails, and her rigging wore and chafed from one dawn till the next without producing so much as a knot of speed. Sails were set and then reset to try to catch a vagrant breeze until the sailors gave up and crept back to their patches of shade. The canvas wore thin in many places and had to be sent below for repairs, while the glare from the flat featureless sea gave no relief to the men's eyes.

Up at the masthead one day a lookout called, 'She blows! She blows!' But the whale was only his to see, and he was brought down a little mad and tied to the main mast for his own safety. He came round after repeated soakings in a seawater tub, but had to be lashed to his bunk for fear he would throw himself overboard during the night.

'Be patient,' Olva counselled. 'This too will pass, and one day soon the doldrums will lose their grip on the ship.'

As long as his own ship could not sail neither could the enemy, so he cancelled lookout duty and organized a party for the crossing of the equator. As the oldest of the few shellbacks on board who had crossed the line before, Captain Olva was both King Neptune and master of ceremonies so he and his two acolytes were decked out in seaweed wigs and fantastic costumes made by the sailmaker. Each young sailor was brought before 'King Neptune' to ask permission to enter his domain, and when they were answered in the affirmative they were seized by the acolytes, dunked in a mixture of rancid whale oil and suds and had their heads shaved, to the great amusement of the rest of the crew. The sailors took delight in the fact that the ship's officers received an extra dunking or two for good measure, and it took two full days for the whole crew to be

43

welcomed to the realm of King Neptune. It was a truly pagan ceremony, but it served as a welcome rest for everyone on board and was good for morale. It was the sailors' rite of passage, and now that the line was behind them they could properly call themselves blue water sailors.

Olva watched his crew closely during this time. He knew from experience that if there was trouble on board it would invariably break out in the hot airless days of the doldrums, but as time progressed he was pleased to see that he had chosen well from among the many young men who had asked to sail with him. They were all Americans but their ancestors had come from sea-faring races all over Europe and the names on the ship's muster list were English, Scots, Norwegian, Swedish, French and even German. The new country had served them well, they were strong and healthy young men, and with a gentle curbing of their high spirits and a touch of sensible discipline they would conquer the world.

Olva never gave a direct order to his crew but told his officers what he required and sensibly allowed them to take charge and see to it being carried out. From his position near the wheel the captain saw and heard everything. It was a very good way to study human behaviour, he thought. He was there yet he was almost invisible, the rock that life on board the ship swirled around like the currents of the sea.

He spent a good deal of his time watching Lafe in particular. His second mate was the owner's son and, more importantly, the son of a life-long friend, and sometimes Olva felt the responsibility weighing heavily on him. Lafe was young for the demands that would be thrust upon him during the voyage, but unless he proved incompetent, which was unlikely, it would be as Erickson wanted.

'That young man is a little too fond of taking risks for my liking, though,' Olva muttered sometimes to himself. His eyes often strayed to the rigging where Lafe moved with the casualness and the agility of a monkey, his poise and balance that of a natural athlete. No one else on board moved with such speed and grace.

In the last six months Lafe had filled out a lot. He had the muscular fitness and balance of a man used to the woods or the high rigging of a sailing ship, and none of the sailors would challenge him any more to a race to the top of the mainmast and back to the deck, for he had won all wagers and was now the undisputed champion.

Since Olva had eased the dress standards the young Swede had spent so much time in the sun in little more than a loincloth that his skin was now the colour of a ripe chestnut. His long, blond shoulder-length hair, carelessly tied at the nape of his neck with a piece of tarred string, ruffled in any breeze, and his dark blue eyes were intense for someone so young. He was handsome, but at only eighteen he was still unaware of the fact. There was an indefinable quality that attracted people to him, and they always came back for another look as if the picture they had seen was very complex and required further study.

Now and then Olva had seen Lafe receive one of those long lingering looks that asks a thousand questions. It seemed the young man had no trouble ignoring such looks from his fellow sailors; that sort of game held no appeal for him and Olva thanked God for it. Man love was not tolerated on Olva's ships.

'It makes trouble on any ship,' he had told his officers right from the start. 'I want any signs of it stamped out, and any offender will be dumped at the first port we come to. Let them know that.'

Olva placed more responsibility on Lafe as the voyage went on, but never more than he could handle. It would be a big responsibility, looking after the sealing crews on a strange and isolated coast for six months, and the captain wanted him ready for the job.

Not many men were born with the many moods of the sea in their blood, probably not more than a handful in every thousand sailors Olva thought. Like him, Lafe had come from a race of seamen and explorers who had conquered most of Northern Europe, the North Atlantic, England and, it was believed, America as well. These were the Scandinavians, Norsemen, or Danes, races that had burst from the north in their longboats and were called the Vikings. The lineage of Erickson, Son of Erick, could be traced right back to Erik the Red whose men had colonized many lands and spread their seed far and wide throughout the old world and the new. This young man Lafe, with a little bit of luck and if the fickle hand of fate allowed him a long life, would do the same. And I shall be watching, Olva told himself.

First it was a light breeze that tickled the sails, the first movement of the sultry air mass that had hung over the ship for days. It flickered for an hour as if it could not make up its mind whether to stay or go, then it grew into a real wind that heralded the end of the doldrums. With every sail up that could catch a breeze they sped south for the great fisheries in the latitudes of the lower forties. They sighted the odd pod of whales, slashed at them and killed three fish on the edge of the great current that surged up the coast of Africa, but they would not deviate from their course to search for more.

Olva had other worries about the shipping routes. If war was to break out or had already begun, would he be able to ship his oil back to London? Convict transports regularly sailed to Sydney Town with their human cargo but war could change all that, and this Sydney to London traffic was a very important part of his plans since London was where the profit lay. Industrial growth in England was now lubricated by whale oil and the demand was insatiable; if a product from the factories of England had moving parts, it needed oil. Olva needed the English ships so it was up to him to convince the ship owners and their captains, whom he regarded as little better than slavers, that they could do business together.

He had been pleased to learn from the talk among sailors in the Azores, a source he had found reliable in the past, that empty convict ships had gone to China to load tea rather than return to England empty. That sort of attitude gave him hope that in the end the desire for trade would overcome any prejudice the English might have in dealing with a Yankee. Shipping rates might be higher because of the risk of war, but the price of oil would go up as well.

'But first we have to catch the fish, our barrels are empty.' Olva chuckled as he spoke to the mate who was on the wheel. 'As a wise man once said, it would be foolish to sell a fur coat without first killing the bear.'

The first really good hunt since the doldrums was on another pod of young bulls. The ship was not yet far enough south to meet with the mature fish that sought their food in cooler waters.

It was like preparing for an ancient Roman contest, Lafe thought as he checked his whaleboat. The teams were ready and spoiling for action after so long a wait, and there was tension in the air as the young men stood to their boats waiting for the word to launch, their nostrils flaring as if they could smell the danger on the wind.

Lafe's boat was soon fast onto one of the bulls very early in the chase, and after a long gut-busting run their fish was finally brought to the surface. But as they went in close to make the kill the whale fish lashed out, catching the boat a heavy blow with its tail. With stunning suddenness an oar was driven into the ribs of one of the sailors and the boat was stove in near the bow. The little craft rolled and the men were tossed from their benches into the water, terrifyingly close to the dying whale still beating a tattoo on the water with its flukes. Each blow was enough to crush a skull so each whaler took the action he thought most likely to save his life. Most vanished under the surface and swam like otters to get clear, while the smashed boat floated upside down just outside the lethal range of the whale's tail.

Trapped air in the hull gave it a little buoyancy still, and when all the crew except for one man made for the overturned boat Lafe suddenly realized he had a crewman who could not swim a stroke to save himself. The hapless sailor was being pushed and pulled toward the hull by several other survivors, spitting water because his mouth had been open when he hit the sea. Lafe had been assured by all his crew they could swim tolerably well and was shocked that he had been lied to, even more shocked that anyone would go chasing whales in a small boat and not be able to swim half a dozen strokes to save his own life. What a strong desire the man must have to go whaling, Lafe thought inconsequentially, even as he gasped and fought to save his own skin.

Within seconds, it seemed, the unfortunate crewman was on the upturned hull clinging by his nails like a cat. Lafe quickly looked over the other five men as he trod water, and noted one of them was breathing harshly and blood was coming from his nostrils, but he knew there was no point in trying to persuade the man who could not swim to come off the hull so the injured man could be laid there. His fear might well make him fight and take someone with him. Two others helped the sailor who was hurt, and he soon had a grip on the hull. Between gasps he confessed that though he was still alive he thought he had been stove in worse than the boat.

Sharks! Everyone in the water knew they would come soon. The death throes of the whale and the vast amount of blood in the water would see to that. Each spasm of the dying whale's body, every flutter of its now nearly motionless tail sent a homing signal through the water for many miles around. Food, the signal said, tons and tons of lovely food just waiting to be eaten, and a few scraps of humanity around a half-sunken boat to scoff as well.

Lafe knew the other boat crews would be breaking their backs to get to them before the sharks did, but his boat had been towed quite a long way out from the rest of the chaser fleet. He watched his men trying to stay afloat with the minimum of movement so as not to attract any attention to themselves. He knew that if a shark attacked any one of them there would be a mad scramble to get onto the overturned boat and it would not hold them all but that would not matter, it was human nature to fight for life and the non-swimmer perched there would quickly find himself back in the water.

Lafe decided that if they were attacked he would go for the whale, dead now and floating well out of the water. He was not sure if he could climb out of the water onto its back but if the incentive was great enough he thought he would manage. Anything to get away from the horror of one of those brutes; he could almost feel the jaw clamping shut on his belly and tearing the life out of him.

Soon the injured sailor was having trouble breathing and keeping his head above water. He began to struggle and splash ineffectually and Lafe had to fight against his own survival instincts, forcing his limbs to move him closer to help support the man. Most of the others stayed as far away as they could, aware that the injured man sending wounded-fish signals through the water would be the first to go when the sharks came.

Lafe reflected that whaling must be one of the most risky jobs on earth, and tried to keep his thoughts away from what was happening in the water beneath him by thinking of happier times. For some reason he remembered his father telling him about a young immigrant relative who had made good money carrying gunpowder for a mining company. In the five years he was away working his hair turned grey and when he came home the family no longer knew him. Lafe would have gladly swapped occupations with the man right then.

One of the injured man's feet collided with his own bare toes and he rose nearly a yard out of the water, very nearly knocking the non-swimmer from his perch. Frightened nearly witless he slid back down into the freezing sea, thankful he hadn't overturned the boat. The long, lazy swell hid them from all but a small stretch of water in the troughs, but after what seemed like hours they heard the faint call of a boat captain encouraging his oarsmen across the water, urging them to dig deep.

'Pull! Pull! Come on boys, pull! We have friends in the water, lads! Pull! Pull!'

They were the sweetest words the men around the half-sunken boat had ever heard. They knew that the ordeal was nearly over, but the next few minutes were still the longest any of them had ever lived through.

Willing hands plucked them from the water before the rescue boat had even stopped its forward motion, but the man on the overturned hull was left there as there was no more room in the little chaser. He was safe enough where he was as they waited for the *Northern Lights* to sail down on them although he was an unhappy man, clinging to his risky perch while the sailors offered good-natured advice on the quickest way to learn to swim. He was finally prised from the water-logged hull by another boat's crew and he was the butt of many jokes after that day.

The four boats had taken three fish, which was a good tally from a single pod and evidence that the long hours of practice were beginning to pay off. On the debit side they had a very badly injured crewman and there was no medical attention but what the ship could supply, for by the time they made landfall the poor sailor would be long recovered or dead. However Olva's own medical skills were regarded as just as good as most doctors could provide. In his forty years on the sea, in both peace and war, he had acquired a great deal of experience and those patients

Perhaps it really was the captain's nose that put them amongst the whales from the beginning of this new course, or perhaps it was just good luck, but every few days a new pod was sighted and the boats were launched. The hunting had begun in earnest. These were big bull whales that filled many barrels with sweet oil as the ship slowly closed with the southern coast of *Terra Australis,* or New South Wales.

Lafe's crew caught their share even though there were two new men in the boat, one to replace the dead sailor and the other the non-swimmer whose courage had deserted him when it came time to launch the boat again. Although he promised to rejoin the crew as soon as he learned to swim there was little hope of that happening for many months, and he refused to go near the water for fear of sharks.

When the ship was not under way they were busy stripping blubber from freshly-caught whales. Their cruising days were over now, giving way to plain hard work and too little sleep as the *Northern Lights* ran like the factory ship she was. The whales were killed and towed in by day and the boiling crew's bizarre dance around the fire continued through the night. Off the southern coast of New South Wales the black or right whales were often sighted from the masthead. These were good whales that produced a lot of oil, but it was not as valuable as the oil of the sperm whale so they were left unmolested. If and when the ship was unable to find sufficient sperm whales they would turn to hunting this docile and easy-to-kill species that floated so handily for days after it was dead.

Storm after storm rolled in from the southwest, storms that had hatched down near the Antarctic throughout the months of June and July. These storms did not bring the snows that the men were used to in their own country but just endless sheets of grey rain that swept across the decks, and the sailors endured day after day when they were cold and wet as well as tired. Remarkably their health stayed good apart from the endless round of cuts and sprains and crushed fingers. They killed many whales and filled the ship until not a single empty barrel was left on board and even the lockers were full of the large sperm whale teeth that would be used to trade with the natives of New Zealand.

One morning the sailors found their ship nosing gently through the rock-strewn passage that separated Van Diemen's Land from the mainland, and when they had cleared the passage they turned north for Sydney Town. Already the water had become warmer again and the weather began to improve. It was September 1800, and the *Northern Lights* and her crew were eight months out from their home port.

As they headed north they closed with the coast for a first good look at this strange, grey-brown continent at the bottom of the world. Everybody called it New South Wales, although the many hundreds of prisoners from the rapidly-emptying jails of England already knew it by a different name, New Hell On Earth. From the moment their feet touched the red earth of the penal colony, men and women alike knew there was a fair chance they would never see their homes again.

The crew lined the rails, studying the first land that they had seen since the Azores. It was restful on the eyes after months of seeing nothing but waves that never ceased rolling across the horizon. A haze hung over the coastline and the offshore breeze brought the smell of dust from the warm land, laced with a spicy, alien scent of trees they had never smelt before.

It was a pity that the men could not go ashore in Sydney, Olva told Lafe, but it was not safe; in fact he would have armed guards on watch around the clock.

'From what I have heard the convicts here are desperate enough to try to seize the ship and sail her away,' he said soberly.

Botany Bay slid past as the ship moved with a gentle rolling motion. These calm waters, sheltered from the southwesterlies by the huge land mass, were a welcome change after the more vigorous seas of the south Pacific. Port Jackson and Sydney Cove were now only a day's sail away and then they would have completed the longest section of their outward voyage.

Olva gave the order they were waiting for, to prepare the ship for entering harbour, and with lots of noise and good humour the anchor was hoisted from down below where it had rested for the past eight months, and catted on to the hawser. Soon it would kiss the mud of Sydney Town.

The sailors had been told they were not going ashore but there would be things to see and not much work to do, that was something to look forward to anyway.

The ship passed through the rugged cliffs of the Port Jackson entrance and into one of the finest natural harbours on earth. According to Captain Phillip of the First Fleet, who had first reported its existence, it would hold a thousand ships of the line in safety. The calm sparkling waters of the harbour spread inland as far as the eye could see and laid a glittering trail for the *Northern Lights* as she ran all the way in to Sydney Cove in the distance.

There was not a sail in sight.

'Not much sign of people either, unless you included a few clouds of smoke curling up into the sky,' the sailors muttered to each other. They had grown tired of their own little world aboard the ship, at least for the time being, and needed to see other people even if they could only stare at them from a distance. But the strangeness of the dull grey-brown foliage failed to raise any great desires or recognition in their breasts. It did not look anything like the type of countryside they remembered from home. It had no real definition, only a sameness everywhere they looked. The ground rose only a little from the water's edge then stretched away into the distance in layers, all covered in dusty-looking trees of indeterminate blue.

Coasting along under a very slight breeze they came into a harbour edged by what looked like a small village. Olva brought his ship up into the wind while the men hurried to get the sails off her, and when she had lost her forward motion the anchor went down and buried itself into the mud of the harbour bottom. Then the sailors were free to line the rail again and stare at one of the meanest-looking villages on earth.

They could see little in the way of substantial buildings or development, just hundreds of the most rudimentary hovels stretching away into the distance. In places the bush had been cleared and gardens established, but those were the only signs of progress. Near at hand was a wharf, with a group of larger buildings that looked a lot more permanent. They were probably warehouses and food stores, the crew guessed, and beyond them appeared to be barracks and government buildings of the rudest type. A group of motley craft, from ships' boats to native canoes, had put off from shore and were now beginning to gather around the *Northern Lights* and the only thing stopping them from boarding was the armed men at the railings.

These poor creatures were hungry for news, Lafe could see that, but when they realized the ship was a Yankee whaler eight months out from her home port they started to drift away. A few stayed to offer their services but they had little to offer. Most were convicts that had served their sentences and were trying to make a living as best they could but few among them were sailors. Any sound-bodied and eligible men had already left on the first ships that would take them on board and sign them on.

There wasn't a surplus of food anywhere in the colony, no industry had been developed and so they offered their women, but the sailors on the *Northern Lights* eyed the poor skinny wenches and shook their heads. It was a poor indictment on any town that a sailor after eight months at sea would not give its women a second look, but Olva was relieved. A shipload of randy sailors was hard to control and he knew they would swim ashore if they saw women they desired. Even his armed guards might not stop them, and he wanted none of this port's diseases on his ship if he could help it.

He took six armed men and went ashore to see to the shipping of his cargo to his factors in London. It was easier than he thought it might be. A new fleet of convict ships was expected to arrive any day, and his oil could be stored in an empty warehouse until then. The town's officials were happy to sort out the details for the price of a large hogshead of rum, which was duly delivered.

'This is the only town I have ever visited with rum as its currency,' Olva told his officers in wonderment. 'If we had only arrived here with a cargo of the stuff a man would never have to chase the fish again, except that there is no money here and you would have to take rum in return for your cargo of rum. It is a strange and sad place, this Sydney Town.'

There were many Irish convicts among those on shore, always badly treated and on the point of rebellion. The militia were regularly called out to deal with them, and whenever there was a whiff of trouble the whipping posts worked day and night and the hangman never slept. Olva was horrified by what he saw and heard, and so were his men.

'We will double the number of armed guards from now on, offload the cargo and float it ashore at dawn tomorrow, and then get clear of this place as quickly as possible,' he ordered.

'Even the water is not fit to take. I have checked the stream and found offal in it and an outhouse perched above it upstream.'

He called the crew together on deck and informed them bluntly that if any man among them allowed their feet to touch the shores of Sydney Cove in the next twenty-four hours he would have their names removed from the ship's books and they would be cast back upon the shore among the convicts. To forestall any ill feeling he promised that within the next ten days they would be dropping anchor in a little paradise called the Bay of Islands, where they would remain for a week, and every sailor would get a rest and the chance to go ashore there.

Once the oil was on the beach and safely in the hands of the port officials, willing hands hauled up the anchor. No one wanted to linger, and soon the *Northern Lights* glided out through the entrance at Port Jackson and sought the clean smell of the open sea once more.

Chapter 4

Out on the Tasman Sea the stiff breezes soon blew away the memory of the poor town and its miserable convicts, and the men on the *Northern Lights* thanked God for the honest life of a sailor. Their new course was due east, into the eye of the rising sun. According to Cook's chart this would bring them to the northern point of the northernmost island of New Zealand, that odd-shaped group of islands in one of the far corners of the world. Several days' sailing to the north was yet another island and another convict settlement they called Norfolk, with an even worse reputation than Sydney Cove. It was reputed to be a place so harsh and cruel that convicts in despair committed crimes they knew carried the death sentence and then laughed as they ascended the scaffold to welcome the hangman's noose.

Further still beyond Norfolk were the Loyalty and Friendly islands. Many of these island groups had been well visited by whalers and every other boat that sailed the Pacific Ocean. Thanks to the reports written by ships' captains, books written by missionaries and explorers and the stories carried home by sailors, these Pacific islands were well known even among those who had never been there.

'Truly these islands are the Gardens of Eden,' quoted some of the more pompous writers as they searched their Bibles for specific mention of such places.

'Dens of sin and iniquity,' crowed the missionaries as they

packed their surplices and set off to do battle with the devil. Some islands already enjoyed the dubious honour of belonging to one major power or another as the British, French and Dutch governments expanded their trade monopolies into the Pacific.

'I wonder what the islanders said when they were told they now belonged to jolly old England,' Olva chuckled. 'I bet no one bothered to write that down.

'Thank God the islands we are heading for are still free of such trappings of civilization, particularly the disease called colonization. There are a few places where the British have planted their flag in the name of the King or Queen, damn it all I can never remember which, but otherwise the place belongs just as much to you and me as to the British. And as far as I can gather, the missionaries haven't got too much of a grip yet either. Nothing ruins a place quicker than missionaries.'

Their first glimpses of their destination was of a thin, low-lying strip of land running north and south, with a long, sandy beach that ran on into the distance in both directions. Strong winds out of the Tasman forced Olva to stay well clear of the lee shore and he turned north, coasting along in a light breeze until he found the large headland marked on Cook's chart that indicated the northwestern extremes of the country. Through the glass they could see that it was here the powerful tides of the Pacific and the Tasman seas met. This was Cape Maria Van Dieman, named by the Dutch navigator Abel Tasman on his brief visit to the coast in search of the great southern continent. Away to the northwest was a group of islands Tasman had named the Three Kings, and this confirmed the correct landfall Olva and his navigator had made.

The tides round this cape created a vicious rip that for a time took control of the ship, pushing her eastwards towards the true northern cape which was a very formidable series of rock cliffs. Olva paced the deck, his mouth tight with worry until a good westerly breeze working in their favour enabled the ship to claw her way off shore and so escape the fang-like rocks reaching for her hull.

'Well, I hope there are not too many headlands like that along the coast,' he muttered at last. 'I have never seen such ferocious tides.'

58

As they looked back at the surging white overflows of water that they had just escaped, some of the men laughed and grinned and Lafe realized just how much the tension had mounted. They had not crossed the wide oceans to be wrecked now, and it was a timely reminder that the sea was a cruel mistress. Olva continued his easterly course until they were well clear of land in case of a sudden wind change, and as night closed in the sails were dropped and the ship settled to drifting in the light westerly breeze. They dared not travel further along this unknown coast once darkness had fallen.

A Pacific sunrise greeted their first morning off New Zealand and the *Northern Lights* was framed in red and gold as they closed again with the shore and turned south to run down the east coast. It was like entering a different world with a completely different set of rules; in a distance of less than fifty miles the ship had left the boisterous Tasman Sea for a much kinder and gentler ocean. With a gentle breeze setting from the land and a clear blue sky overhead the sailors happily set the lighter cruising sails and the ship began to make way in a sea that settled to a lake-like flatness with a sparkle in it. They knew now why this great ocean was named the Pacific.

First impressions were of a dark green land of a colour not quite anything like they had seen before. In the distance, white sand beaches rose to meet forests that clothed the slopes of the hills in soft greens, running to merge with hazy blue hills. At its lower levels the forest appeared to contain an abundance of ferns that assumed the size and status of trees, giving the landscape a pleasing balance. In places these tree ferns were thick enough to form ancient-looking forests in their own right. No one on board had ever clapped eyes on such a forest. It was both primitive and vastly attractive, and set off the white sand beaches in a most fitting manner.

A cry from the masthead alerted them to the fact that they were not alone on this attractive coast. Thin columns of smoke rose from the terraces above several beaches, and the lookout reported canoes drawn up in one of the coves. Olva had a party of sailors haul up the four cannon from below and range them on the poop deck with powder and shot at the ready, and they had just finished the task when a deep and sheltered harbour began to appear from behind a headland. Like the rest of the crew Lafe began to hope the ship would put in and anchor. The land offered a gentle and subtle invitation to a sailor who had not set foot on land for over eight months. Come, walk on my sand, wade in my streams and explore my wonderful forests, the country seemed to say to them, for the sailors and officers who lined the rail were heartily sick of the sea. It was only a temporary sickness and it would pass, but right now they wanted to plant their feet firmly upon the land and feel the sand beneath their soles and let it run through their fingers.

But the decision was Olva's to make and his only, and the *Northern Lights* slipped steadfastly past on a course that would take her inside a small group called the Cavalli Islands. Cook had made extensive charts of this coast and had named many of its islands and bays after prominent figures or friends at the Admiralty. Doubtless Bay showed itself, with many a hopeful glance from the crew to their captain, but slowly faded to starboard. Olva could not risk his ship along this rocky coast in the dark so he had two choices; to shape his course for the open sea and spend the night offshore, or to choose an anchorage in one of the many bays or inlets.

'A sail! A sail! Three points off the starboard bow!' came the cry from the masthead. Without waiting for orders Lafe grabbed the telescope and swung up into the ratlines. Within seconds he was on his way up to the masthead high above the deck.

'A whaleboat with half a dozen crew, put off from shore and on a course to intercept us!' he shouted down as he swung into the ratlines. Down he came like a monkey and dropped lightly back onto the deck.

'A whaleboat? Aye then, it seems then we are not the only ship in these waters,' Olva mused. 'I wonder where he is holed up? But I guess we will find out soon enough.'

All eyes were on the stranger's boat as it ran down the wind, cut across the bows with exquisite timing, ran down the big whaler's side in the wind shadow and tacked again to come alongside. It was a beautiful piece of seamanship and some of the crew cheered in the general excitement of the occasion.

'Permission to come aboard, sir?' called the tall skipper as he scaled the ladder that had been lowered for him.

'Jeremy Haste, out from Salem a year.' He held out his hand to Olva, greeted the officers one by one then quickly convinced Olva to join his ship at anchor. 'It's the finest little bolthole in the whole Pacific, with the friendliest natives you ever did see,' he assured them all. Within minutes his whaleboat was tied off to the stern, the *Northern Lights* had a new pilot and they were skirting a small island and heading for the shore, sailing directly towards a set of high cliffs that from seaward showed very little sign of any entrance, let alone a harbour.

Olva's long fingers tapped against his thigh as he tried not to let his anxiety show, and the deck fell silent, but as they grew closer they began to discern a gap in the cliff and then a slightly angled entrance into a steep-sided valley. With Captain Haste's confident directions, the tide in their favour and the offer of a tow from the whaleboat if they needed it, Olva relaxed as the *Northern Lights* glided through the narrow entrance and into a magnificent drowned mountain valley.

Just inside the entrance was an island, terraced and fortified with fighting positions right up to the flat crown of its top. On the lower slopes a series of small grass huts were set out in seemingly haphazard fashion and natives stood staring at the strange ship that had appeared in front of their village. One ship was a rare sight in a place such as this; two was something that would be talked about for years. As the ship slid past, the natives gathered on the beach and broke into a spirited war dance, its strange, fierce rhythm and tight coordination of movement remarkable to see.

Opposite the island the ship turned north again under topsails alone to ghost silently down to the head of one arm, where the other whaling ship lay quietly at anchor in beautiful surroundings. Olva backed his sails and brought up hard against his cable as the anchor dug deep into the sandy bottom. A cheer went up from both the crews and echoed from the rock faces and there they sat, two ships from the other side of the world come together as strangers in an idyllic place.

Their chance meeting had come about because Jeremy Haste, captain of the *Salem,* enjoyed fishing. He had slipped out through the entrance and was busy filling his boat with tamure, as the natives called them, when the sails of the *Northern Lights* hove into sight. He had recognized her at once as another New England whaler.

'Now here we are floating together on the other side of the world, and our home ports are less than a day's sail from each other,' he chuckled.

'This is truly a very strange meeting,' Olva said, and he raised his voice to hail the *Salem*'s officers. 'You Massachusetts whalers certainly get around, don't you?'

'Wait until you see how the natives welcome you, Captain!' one of the mates called back, and Olva raised an enquiring eyebrow to Jeremy, who grinned widely.

'You have got about an hour before the Maori arrive in their canoes. They will want to put on a display to welcome the new ship in,' he said. 'Don't be alarmed by the dance, the haka they call it. It looks very warlike, but in this case it will be a welcome dance.'

'And how should we respond to it?' Olva asked.

'I suggest you dress up your crew and arm them, load your cannon and look very warlike yourselves, and you will gain no end of respect from them.'

Lafe could already hear the rhythmic beat of paddles across the bay as the native canoes closed in on the ship. He inspected the crew who had been quietly preparing for an encounter with unknown forces ever since they closed the coastline. They had managed to look quite regimental for a change. They all wore their best coats, each man had a powder horn and bullet pouch on his belt and they carried their primed and charged muskets as if they meant business. Many carried razor-sharp tomahawks in their belts at the small of their backs. These were very effective weapons when it came to close fighting on board a ship.

Suddenly ten great canoes swept past the *Northern Lights,* the largest carrying up to fifty warriors, and circled the ships. A haunting chant from the canoe singers kept the timing while every single paddle flashed and dipped into the sea in uniform perfection. Lafe had never seen anything like it. What he took for a medicine man, with feathers in his hair and wrapped in a great feathered cloak, stood in the stern of each canoe looking straight ahead and calling the beat. Lafe calculated the speed of the canoes at around twelve to fifteen knots, and was impressed by the seamanship as well as the visual effect. A formidable enemy, he thought, and filed the information in the back of his mind, resolving never to underestimate these natives.

'These truly are a race of boat people,' he said to Captain Haste, who nodded soberly.

'You've seen nothing yet. Wait till they really get moving.'

Manoeuvering as a single unit, the fleet of canoes changed direction several times at high speed before arranging themselves in a semicircle on the starboard side of the *Northern Lights*. At a signal from the chief medicine man the rowers rose as one, lifted their knees high and brought their feet down with a crash that sent the shags madly flapping into the air from the trees around the bay.

Lafe was delighted with the way the Maori handled their canoes, each of which appeared to be a work of art in its own right. He ran his eyes along their lines, from the highly-carved and decorated prows to the equally-elaborate sterns. They looked to have been carved from single tree trunks, and if that was truly the case this country must have some mighty big trees, he thought.

The warriors themselves were well made, no darker than the Indians from his own country, and but for their hideously-tattooed faces and buttocks they were a pleasant-enough looking race. Again the haka began, and Lafe watched with interest as the witch doctor led the chanting while the warriors beat time with their feet, at the same time rolling their eyes and hanging out their tongues in the most ferocious manner.

After the dance was finished and the thunderous echoes had stopped rolling around the bay Olva invited twenty of the dancers, including the several chiefs and minor chiefs, on board to receive gifts he had prepared for them. Jeremy Haste helped him to communicate through one of the natives who, surprisingly, could speak a little English. He had been in the Bay of Islands and had spent a season on a whaler.

Led by Chief Kaitoke, the native group shook hands and pressed noses with all the officers in turn in a serious and dignified way. Lafe was sure a lot of humour lay behind all that dignity, for he had seen a sparkle in the old man's eye. Chief Kaitoke was older than the rest and had the most regal and dignified bearing. He touched Lafe's hair and gazed into his eyes for a long moment, then he made a little speech that was translated by the English-speaking native beside him.

'My chief says that your head is far too pretty to remain on any man's shoulders. It would be safer amongst the extensive collection of shrunken heads he has at his home.'

There was a great deal of laughter, from the crew of the *Northern Lights* as well as from the natives, and this caused several of the latter to fall to the deck helpless with mirth while the old chief grinned and nodded at the whalers.

Olva had mustered their small band of musicians, fifeplayers, drummers and a trumpeter of no mean ability, and at his signal they began to play as loudly and tunefully as they could manage. The natives listened politely but seemed to think this was a challenge to their own musical abilities and more were summoned up from the canoes until a full fifty ranged across the deck. When the fife and drums had played out their last notes the Maori launched into the most vigorous haka yet, until Olva feared for his decks under their stamping feet. It was only the coming darkness and the empty bellies of the natives, for Olva made it clear there were no refreshments on offer, that cleared the ship in the end and allowed the sailors to go below for their own dinners.

All the *Northern Lights'* officers except the man in charge of the watch set off for the *Salem* where they had been invited to dine. As they entered the wardroom the first thing that caught Lafe's eye was a whole family of dogs that seemed to have the run of the place. The ship's bitch had given birth to her litter of pups several months into the voyage and they were now nearly fully grown, all six of them. They were of a breed that was new to all the visitors, none of whom had ever seen dogs like that before, and there was much discussion about them. Jet black and smooth-coated with a very powerful frame, their temperament and good nature were obviously the best points of the breed. Their owner explained that the dogs, bred for hunting and known for their powerful swimming ability, came from the Labrador coast.

Olva soon urged them to forget the dogs; he had more important matters to discuss. First he needed to know about whales and seals and where they were to be found. The *Salem* had been in the fishery for a year and was nearly full of oil. She had come into Whangaroa, as the natives called this place, after a hard but successful season to the south.

Jeremy Haste told Olva he had found out about Whangaroa when he met the chief at the Bay of Islands. 'He urged me to visit, which we did in the early part of the voyage. As a reward to my men for their hard work, I promised I would return.

'When my crew have rested we will head for Massachusetts via Cape Horn, staying well to the south and away from the Spanish Coast.

'Though *Salem* is only a whaling ship, yes, I have seen many seals,' he said. 'Rest here for a few days then go to the sealing grounds.' Olva had brought his charts on board and soon he and the master of the *Salem* were both bent over them, which left the other officers to talk between themselves. There was much to talk about. This meeting of whale ships was like a gam that took place in the open sea where, if it was calm, they could tie their ships together for a couple of days. This meeting was all the more enjoyable because of their surroundings, and the *Salem* men were just as eager to show their visitors around as the officers from the *Northern Lights* were to explore.

They sauntered up on deck as evening approached, so they could take in their surroundings and listen to the new sounds of the land. The arms of the sea stretched into the mountains and had turned light blue as the sun slid behind one of the many mountains, and the water was as smooth as glass. Close by, the silence of the evening was broken by the discordant cries of the gulls, but from the forest in the distance came the song of birds. The sound drifted across the water like small waves that crept up the sand and men from both ships listened in silence, trying to envisage the number of birds involved in such a chorus.

The next morning the dawn chorus of the birds was even more memorable, and half an hour after first light the songsters outdid each other to lift the sun into the heavens. Lafe sought Olva's permission to have the cutter brought up from below and reassembled, and when it was ready he and Olva set off to the village, with a small armed guard, to see the old chief.

Kaitoke appeared genuinely pleased to see them, Lafe in particular, and made a great fuss greeting him and pointing to his hair. It was obvious that the old man's remarks about Lafe's head had been repeated far and wide, and the young Swede made quite a stir around the village. Wherever he looked he was greeted with broad smiles and much merriment, and the girls peeped at him from the background and hid away when he looked back at them. As much as he tried to see these tantalising young women he was always disappointed because they ducked into their houses where they could watch him but he could not follow.

Lafe studied the village closely. This was a winter settlement and there were no gardens or animals other than a scruffy dog or two that looked to him more like a fox than a dog. Olva made an agreement with the chief to purchase twenty pigs and a small quantity of potatoes. It wasn't a lot, but the village didn't have a lot to share as it was the hungry season near the end of the winter, and the *Salem*'s captain had already purchased most of the surplus. Mostly the tribe lived on the fish that moved into the shallow waters at this time of the year, and the chief had already sent his warriors with their biggest net to catch fish for the two visiting ships for fear they would eat him out of house and home.

It was no accident that the *Salem* had put into this port. Captain Cook had brought hogs to the north, and later whaling ships had brought potatoes, but while many other tribes had eaten their gifts before the sails of their benefactors disappeared over the horizon, Kaitoke's people had bred from the pigs and planted the potatoes.

Lafe was invited to go with the men to fetch the pigs Olva had bargained for, and away they paddled in several canoes to the forest at the head of the bay where the animals lived in a semi-wild state on the sunny fern faces. It was hot, dangerous work. When the angry boars were bailed by the dogs they charged anything and everyone that came within range, and used their wicked tusks to lethal effect. A good many spear thrusts were needed to end the rampage in the thick fern where the hogs invariably stopped to fight their last battles. Except for a couple of bites and a few small rips Lafe thought the young warriors got off lightly, as their courage bordered on the foolhardy at times.

The pressure was on to display bravery and prowess, and comical things happened. When one warrior came bounding down through the fern with a large angry pig on his heels and tried to take cover in a hollow tree, his exposed and naked buttocks earned a painful swipe from the boar's tusks. Lafe laughed as loudly as the rest of the warriors, but their subsequent behaviour surprised him. They did not rush to help. On the contrary, they seemed to believe that the gods would be offended if mere mortals interfered with the master plan, and they rolled around the ground holding their ribs and dashing tears of laughter from their eyes while they shouted foolish suggestions to the victim.

Even he laughed ruefully as he limped away after extracting himself unaided from the tree, and he performed a short but defiant haka to show the now-dead boar he hadn't really been frightened after all. Lafe wondered what would have happened if the dogs had not arrived to divert the boar's attention before more serious injuries were inflicted. Would the man's friends have helped him? He suspected not, and was puzzled.

As a people, they had the most well-developed sense of mimicry Lafe had ever seen. A dozen times before the hogs were loaded into the canoes the scene between the hog and the warrior with his head stuck in the tree and the rip on his buttocks had been acted and re-enacted, each time with no less enjoyment and humour than the original event.

Once the hogs were delivered on board the *Northern Lights* and accepted as being in good condition, Chief Kaitoke came on board to bargain for his price. The Maori was an able man when it came to commerce, Olva soon found out, and he set a good rate which became the baseline for all future trade between them.

Much of the time the crews of the two ships mingled, either on one ship or the other, and as long as there were enough people on each to form a good armed guard night and day their captains were content. Olva spent much of his time updating his charts from the new information Jeremy Haste could give him. Lafe meanwhile was free to explore or fish as he chose. Two of Kaitoke's sons, along with the English-speaking Maori, were delegated to accompany him, but whether as guides or guards he was not sure.

These two young men who were the chief's sons were not much older than himself, Lafe guessed, and they were very interested in the sailing ability of Lafe's cutter. Their names were Rua and Matai. Rua's name meant double or two of something, Lafe learned, and Matai was named after one of the giant trees of the forest. Rapidly he and the young man who had been on a whaler found a common language and communication became easier.

Lafe was impressed that the tribe could recount legends of the sailing canoes that had brought them from their island homes in Hawaiki to this country they called the Long White Cloud, but the great double-hulled canoes came from a time when their people made such long sea voyages and they were things of the past. The natives travelled only from harbour to harbour around the coastlines now, relying on the power of their paddles and the strong backs of their warriors.

The windward sailing ability of the cutter intrigued the young men until Lafe drew a picture in the sand of how the keel prevented it from sliding sideways in the water away from the press of the sail. In this way he picked up his first word of the Maori language, the name waka which meant a ship, boat, or canoe. He filed this and other knowledge away for later use.

One bright morning they loaded the cutter with fishing gear and headed out through the gap in the cliffs to the fishing grounds off the harbour entrance.

'It is the season for tamure and kahawai, they are fat and easily caught this time of the year,' the interpreter explained. The tamure, or snapper as the English called their similar species, was a bottom-feeding fish of gluttonous habits that would take a bait of almost any edible product of the sea. Once the hooks were taken they were hauled on board in their dozens, their beautiful copper-gold skins coloured with a patina of blue spots flashing in the sun. In a morning's fishing Lafe and his three crewmen half-filled the cutter with tamure and delivered them to the cook on board the *Northern Lights* who chuckled with delight and set some of the crew to preparing them for cooking.

'A corpse would rise again from the deep for such a meal as we will have today,' he said happily.

It was the first of many such expeditions. Once the sea breezes had risen around early afternoon the four young men would leave off fishing for tamure, cram on as much sa.l as the cutter could carry and head out looking for schools of kahawai. The cutter would slice through large schools of fish that m.de the sea boil as they chased the smaller prey they fed on. Lures that the Maori had made were towed behind the boat, cleverly mimicking the escaping flutter of smaller fish, but the difference now was that each lure contained a hook of good American steel. These kahawai closely resembled the trout and salmon of the Northern Hemisphere and could be caught in great abundance when they were on the bite.

Most of the fish, which ranged in size from four to eight pounds, were dried, smoked and stored in barrels on the ship for later in the voyage. Racks were set up on the beach near the ship and soon they were full of drying fish and had to be guarded from the predations of the crew who became fond of them.

Not many sailors would normally eat fresh food from choice, and in most circumstances they preferred what they were used to at sea, salt beef and salt pork out of the casks. Olva alternately cajoled and threatened them, warning them of scurvy and other unmentionable diseases, but still they muttered and tried the cook's patience until the food stores were locked and they had to exist on what was caught and gathered daily or go hungry. It was a strategy that worked, and the men quickly adapted to their new diet.

Chief Kaitoke was the paramount chief of Whangaroa harbour, much of the surrounding area and also the little island at the entrance with its powerful stockade and defensive positions. One day he decided that the honour of having two ships in his harbour deserved a great feast, and he set his people to the task of preparing food on shore for all the officers and crews except the watch that remained to guard the ships.

Leaning back a little to study Lafe's face, he gave a slight smile of satisfaction at his plans while Lafe carefully arranged his expression so as not to show the surprise he felt. He thought about the proposal, which he understood was more of an order than a request, remembered Olva's warning and struggled to find an answer equal to the occasion.

Could he live in such a place for the rest of his life? It was an attractive thought, and the harbour would make a fine base for a whaling ship. The chief's granddaughters were very pretty girls, one of them especially, and a year was a long time. By then he would be nearly twenty years of age. And the tattoo? Well, he would face that problem if and when the time came, if he ever came back here at all. Aware of the honour that was being bestowed on him, and more importantly of the possible consequences of any negative reaction, he made a silent apology to Olva and his father and smiled calmly at the old man.

'I agree.'

Over the next couple of hours Lafe was made aware that this was no mere whim of Chief Kaitoke's. The old man was making long term plans in the best interests of his people. He had gained insight into the fact that the White Faces were a very large tribe and he judged that with their weapons and their ships they would gain more and more power and influence over his country.

When the chief had finished all he had to say, and that was rather a lot, there was a long silence and it was clear the floor now belonged to Lafe. He searched his overwhelmed and reeling brain frantically for something fitting to say, and gave up. He knew that in any race there was a certain latitude allowed to youth, and blurted out what he really wanted to say. 'Can I see your shrunken heads?'

The chief laughed, this was a very fine joke that he would relay to his friends at the first opportunity and many times in the future.

As Lafe sailed his cutter back out to the ship he reviewed some of the main points of the long conversation he had had with the chief. One piece of information he remembered was that the bay where the ship lay at anchor was called Pekapeka. The chief had explained that pekapeka was the Maori name for the bat, so it was Bat Bay.

Almost every island had its village or pa, each with the stockade that the Maori were so fond of building. These dominated the routes among the islands and were built either on very steep hilltops or, in some cases, on the tops of nearly unscaleable cliffs. Access was in most cases by a single well-guarded path, and Matai demonstrated by gesture and grimace how the fighters above would drop boulders onto any unwelcome guests who might try to use the tracks.

Olva had his crew armed and the cannon run out. People who built such elaborate defences were either at war or preparing for war very soon, according to his view.

The French had made a mistake here and paid the price for it, perhaps lulled by the lapping of the waves on these oh-so-perfect little islands. They had let their guard down. Marion du Fresne, captain of the *Mascarin*, had allowed himself and twenty-five crew members to be lured away from their ship to inspect some timber they needed, but once away from the security of their ship they were surrounded, overwhelmed, killed and then eaten by the cannibal Maori.

Olva considered this was worse than bad luck; it showed a fatal flaw in French strategy, an underestimation of the cunning and ability of their adversaries. For these natives were adversaries, no matter how friendly they seemed. He, Olva himself, had been accused of being poor eating, perhaps by one of the very people who had devoured the unfortunate French sailors. That reference to a morsel of human flesh sitting a little uncomfortably in the belly of some Maori was in itself very poor taste, Olva thought, though horrified as he was he could see the funny side. It was as if the French had let the side down by being lean and scrawny.

The massacre of du Fresne and his men happened in 1772, nearly thirty years before, but many of the older Maori they were about to meet at Bay of Islands would have been part of it. Members of this tribe had been killed in retaliation and, as the people of Whangaroa had cheerfully informed the sailors on *Northern Lights*, eating people was still an honourable activity. There were many who remembered the Wi Wi, the name they had given to the French sailors as they listened to them talking.

Skirting around the edge of the islands, the *Northern Lights* made her way slowly up a mighty tidal river and came to anchor outside a village Matai called Waitangi. Here was an established and well-ordered tribe, judging by the neatness of the cultivated kumara and potato fields that ran from the bay up to the lower hills. Well-fenced and hog-proofed, these gardens were obviously the real wealth of the villages and were highly organized to provide a trade surplus to sell to the infrequent ships that called.

Sometimes the Maori must curse the pig that Cook had given them thirty years before, Lafe mused. A great deal of time and effort was spent by these poor villagers trying to keep Captain Cook's razorbacks away from their crops, but they were a valuable food source and an extremely valuable trading commodity. He had seen no evidence of other edible animals and suspected that the cannibalism so entrenched in Maori culture was in some way related to this lack of meat.

The hogs were of a very primitive species with long snouts and a formidable set of tusks, their hairy bodies tapering back from heavy shoulders to lean and cat-like hams, and they ranged in color from black, often with ginger patches, to a great variety of spotted hides.

It was early spring, and the Maori were only now planting new crops so there was little chance to buy any other foods here but pork. Still, Olva had put into this bay in the hope he could fill many more of his casks with meat for they had not laid up enough at Whangaroa for the sealing gangs he planned to land further south in four to six weeks time.

Soon after the anchor had hit the mud the ship was surrounded by a swarm of canoes and this time the formal ritual of the haka was replaced by smiling faces and shouts of welcome, the more relaxed manner of the natives indicating that contact with European ships was not unusual in these waters.

'Don't take anything at face value,' Olva warned his officers. 'They might seem friendly, but perhaps it is just that they are sharp traders.'

By the next day a brisk trade was organized. Pigs of all shapes and sizes were dragged down to the water's edge trussed in flax ropes, the officers weighed them, the price for each animal was then agreed on and the next hog hauled down by the sweating, excited natives. It was a day of great delight and excitement for sailors and natives alike. The bartering was conducted with great vigour by both sides amidst the squealing of the hogs, the barking of dogs and the laughter of natives and boat crews as the savage and frightened animals were carried through the light surf and loaded into the whaleboats. Men of both races were bitten, and one pig escaped into the forest after swimming for half a mile, pursued by a boat crew and half the village.

A good natured dispute arose over who owned the pig now in the forest. The Maori claimed that as the hog had been weighed and the price agreed, it was properly the property of the white man. But Olva laid out his defence cleverly, claiming the hog would be recaptured and sold to the next ship and that possibly it had been trained to escape, therefore turning over a great profit for its owners. The villagers enjoyed his reasoning and talked it over among themselves, each of the orators of the tribe taking his turn at haranguing the crowd. This was a weighty matter that required serious consideration. It was finally settled that Olva was to pay only half the value of the pig, and if it was recaptured then one of its offspring would belong to the ship and be given to Olva next time he visited.

'These people are better traders than the Jews,' Olva roared in mock rage, which pleased the Maori no end as his dramatic tone, words and gestures confirmed that they had got the better of him. Once honour was satisfied, half a dozen warriors trotted off to the village and returned with a nice pig as a gift to Olva so that he would not feel bad after being so outsmarted.

Chief Te Pehi arrived from his home on one of the fortified islands. He was a man of immense dignity, with a deep and obvious liking for these visitors from far across the sea, and he settled happily on board for a couple of days eating the ship's food with obvious enjoyment. He was very happy when those on board indicated an interest in his extensive tattoos. These were his pride. They covered his face, thighs, and buttocks in large scroll-like patterns, and appeared to those unused to the tattooed form rather ugly at first. While he was on the ship Te Pehi would eat with obvious enjoyment anything set in front of him, but he would not touch the rum that he was offered. His name for this beverage was Stink Water. Lafe thought Te Pehi was one of the most dignified men he had ever met. He was a blood relative of Chief Kaitoke of Whangaroa, and of the *Northern Lights'* new crewman Matai who greeted his elder kinsman with great respect. Like Matai, the chief was learning to speak English.

He gave his permission for Lafe and Matai to visit the vast forest at the head of the river in search of suitable timber for ship repairs. The ship's carpenter might be glad of such timbers after a hard season down in the rough seas of the sealing grounds, but Olva was wary and mindful of the French experience. He insisted that his second mate take four armed men with him on board the cutter when they set off up the rather lazy tidal river to a place on the upper reaches Matai called Kawakawa.

On the river terraces the great trees hung over the water. The little cutter had truly entered a forest of giants, and Lafe and the other sailors stared in wonderment. They could see the trees climb layer upon layer, right up the hillsides to the peaks in the distance in an unbroken sea of green. Here stood the mighty forest they had come to find, but unlike the forest back in their own country this was a dark and shady domain, perhaps even a bit sinister.

Three or four different tree species seemed to dominate and they were the largest trees that Lafe had ever seen or believed that the earth could support. Tree after tree soared a hundred or more feet above their heads without a single branch for two thirds of its height and the wealth of clean, unknotted timber was staggering.

A fleet of whale ships could be built from this river flat alone, Lafe realized. Many of these giant trees could not be spanned by all six men with their arms outstretched, and there were others of smaller diameter with very little taper that would make fine masts and spars. With Matai's help they located a fine specimen of the tree he called the totara, used for canoe building, and a length of trunk was cut to size. It was fine looking timber, straight-grained and easy to work.

Another one of the great trees was the matai, the young Maori told them proudly, touching the tree and his own chest to let them know this was his own namesake.

80

Olva wasted no time at the Bay of Islands. Once the timber had been towed back down the river and safely stowed on board the *Aurora* was hauled back on deck too and the *Northern Lights* headed out through the islands into the open sea. The crew was rested, fit and healthy, the water casks were full and the ship had fresh victuals on board. Now Olva was going hunting.

They soon cleared Cape Brett and set course for a pair of islands away on the horizon. Cook named this group the Barrier Islands for the protection they offered to the great gulf of water inside them. The waters were rich with fish and great clouds of gulls wheeled in the air, diving on the schools below while the porpoises chivvied from the edges like wolves, slashing into the solid mass of fish and taking easy prey. Deep below them other predators attacked until the sea rose in a great bubble from the heave of the harassed fish pressing up from below.

A dozen or more of the crew had purchased lures from the Maori and these were towed behind the ship for most of the daylight hours. Sea trout or kahawai abounded, with several types of tuna. These were school fish and sometimes up to ten lures were struck at once. Many fish were lost on the way up the high sides of the ship, but the catch was still heavy and between them the keen fishermen caught enough to provide meals for the rest of the whalers who seemed finally to have lost their prejudice against seafood. Such a supplement was a boon to any captain, because as long as the crew had access to fresh food the risk of scurvy would be much reduced. Olva had stocked orange and lime juice in the Azores but wondered at its continuing effectiveness as it had been stored so long it was very sour and the crew would only accept it mixed with rum.

'Thank God for rum,' he would say as he ordered the juice served with the tot at the evening meal.

Off the Barrier Islands they came across whales again. These were the less-desirable right whales, but Olva gave the word to launch the boats and three whales were killed and towed in. That evening, he justified the catch.

'I want all of the men on board to know their prey,' he told the mates. 'Once we land Lafe and the sealing party we will be short of a

81

chaser and her crew, so from now on we will target this docile and easier-to-kill right whale. That way we will fill the ship quickly, get the oil back to Sydney Town and return in time to pick up the shore party.'

Once the oil had been rendered down the ship moved across the arms of the Bay Of Plenty where White Island, an active volcano, trailed its permanent marker of smoke downwind. It was a fine landmark that could be seen for many miles out to sea.

When it came to naming features James Cook was a very descriptive man, Lafe mused as he studied the charts. The great British navigator's charts reflected his moods and the receptions he had received from the tribes he encountered. Bay of Plenty and Poverty Bay were good examples, not much more than a day's sail apart yet each name told a vastly different story to the men on the *Northern Lights*.

'To have the power to name a new country, and to wield it in a fashion that will colour the thinking of generations not yet born, that is a fine thing,' Olva agreed rather wistfully. 'Take the Dutchman and his one and only attempt to land on New Zealand soil. After some of his men were killed by Maori that place is known to us all as Murderer's Bay, but he might well have named the whole country Murderer's Islands. Is that fair?

'On a ship the captain sits on a lofty perch, but to hold the naming rights to a new land, now that is real power.'

Lafe wondered if he himself would ever hold such powers, perhaps even put his father's name on a chart like the one they were poring over. To be able to write Cape Erickson or Erickson Island and have other men know the name for all time – that would be a truly great thing. For a moment his vision of the future was clouded by the memory of his promise to Kaitoke but he put that from his mind again. Something would happen, and right now he was second mate on an Erickson whaler.

Adult right whales were now in the midst of their southern migration to colder waters again after their breeding season further north around the Friendly Islands. The *Northern Lights* was on a roughly similar course to that of the whale pods, and the cries of, 'She blows! She blows!' came more regularly from the masthead. Once more the fires on the deck flamed and smoked through the night.

Cook's landmarks came up over the bows one at a time and went down by the stern as they followed the *Endeavour*'s path. East Cape, Young Nick's Head, Cape Kidnappers, Cape Turnagain. Then one morning a snow-covered range of very high mountains loomed ahead at first light. This was their first sight of Middle Island, and how different it looked from the North. The noon shot put the ship east of Cape Palliser, Cook Strait was off their beam and already there was a noticeable drop in the temperature of the water. The bay ahead, dominated by those same high craggy peaks, took a day and a night to close with.

Cook had called this place the Lookers On, an odd but rather beautiful name recalling the group of natives that had paddled out to his ship and just sat and watched, perhaps stunned at the sight, as the *Endeavour* sailed by. It was an interesting place, and in the clear air the mountains appeared close enough to reach a hand out and touch them, but the *Northern Lights* had bloody and profitable work to do further south and so she hurried on.

Though they hunted whales and launched their boats often, their progress was steady as she made her way down the coast. One morning Banks' Island, which was really a peninsula and joined firmly to the mainland, was in sight but by evening it was far behind again, still on the horizon but now over the stern. They left off hunting whales at Cape Saunders to enter the harbour at the place Erickson had told them about, the settlement called Otaakou. It was here that they hoped to obtain a Maori guide with knowledge of the sealing grounds and the islands and harbours off the South Cape.

On the way up the harbour Matai managed to convey the fact that these people were enemies of his own tribe, and in a fit of something close to terror he indicated that either they would eat him or he would eat them. No one paid him much attention, for he had said the same about every tribe on the voyage down the coast. Lafe was sympathetic to his friend's fears, but sceptical about any possible contact by tribes so far apart and thought it more likely that any tribe that was not Matai's own kin was perceived as his enemy.

Their approach had been seen and a line of warriors above the high water line broke into a spirited haka when the ship drew near.

'A sign of friendship or an indication of their intention to fight with us?' Olva wondered aloud. 'It is so hard to tell the difference.'

Lafe watched Matai, who seemed to catch the beat and rhythm of the haka like a strange disease. His eyes rolled in his head, his head jerked involuntarily up and down to the beat and his feet drummed a tattoo on the deck in time with the dancers on the beach. Olva hoped Matai would not cause a war as he answered each of the challenges with one of his own, but it all seemed friendly enough when they were invited to land, and at the village they found warriors who had been to the sealing grounds and could speak reasonable English.

Before long Olva, Lafe and another couple of officers were seated with Matai on flax mats, and after the lengthy courtesies they now recognized as common in that part of the world had passed, the negotiations began. A guide would go aboard the ship only if a musket and a considerable amount of powder and shot were delivered to the chief prior to him leaving the village, the whalers were told, and when Olva tried to offer a different price they turned their faces from him. This was the only deal that could be struck with this tribe, a musket was what they wanted and a musket they must have.

Like most whalers Olva did not believe that arming the tribes with muskets was in the best interests of visiting ship such as the *Northern Lights*, but he met his match when he tried to bargain further. Jimmy, as the native guide called himself, came on board only after his chief had tested the musket and was satisfied that it was a good one. Olva secretly hoped he would overcharge it one day and blow his bloody head off, preferably when the *Northern Lights* was well on its way home.

Jimmy was a small, wiry man who appeared to be in his late twenties or early thirties. He was familiar with shipboard life and fitted in well, unlike Matai who when the country he knew had first disappeared over the horizon was so overcome by homesickness that he lay around the deck and wept for a week.

Lafe had been forced to lead him to his meals at first, and at night to his bunk, for fear he would lie where he was and pine to death, but now he was daily becoming more cheerful and would attempt to race

Lafe to the top of the mainmast when his mood suited. He reaffirmed his promise to his father Chief Kaitoke by speaking only Maori in Lafe's presence, though his own grip of the English language was improving daily. Jimmy had a reasonable grasp of English and, in spite of Matai's fears, seemed to establish a reasonably cordial if somewhat distant relationship with the other Maori on board. Both understood and respected the captain's role as chief of the ship, but looked to Lafe as their mentor and leader.

Another crew member that had adjusted well to life on the *Northern Lights* was the Labrador pup given as a gift to the ship by the departing *Salem*'s captain. It had spent a few nights crying for its litter mates but, like Matai in whose bed the pup found comfort, it had got over its homesickness eventually. It was just as well, as Olva had threatened to maroon them both on an island somewhere for the rest of the season if they did not cease the nightly caterwauling that kept all their shipmates awake.

In the last few weeks at sea the dog, which they named *Salem*, had lost its puppy shape and begun to grow into its own over-large feet. It was already a powerful animal, with shoulders that showed promise of great swimming ability and a short, thick coat of dense black hair that kept it warm in almost any conditions. As the days passed the dog became a favourite on board and they all wondered how they had managed so long without one. Olva begrudgingly admitted that when it came to keeping the ship's morale up, the dog was the best mascot he had ever seen.

Once clear of Otaakou Olva set his course well to the east so he would clear the southern cape by a good margin of safety. Though Jimmy insisted that the southern cape was an island, Olva's chart did not show it as such and he was suspicious of Jimmy's motives. They were still close enough to Otaakou for Jimmy to have them on the rocks for his friends to plunder. Cook had thought the cape part of the mainland and drew it as such, warning of many dangerous rocks to be found in the area. One set of rocks in particular had almost caught his ship, and he had named it The Traps.

The cape that the *Northern Lights* was heading south to round, and that Jimmy insisted was an island, was called Rakiura or blushing skies. According to Jimmy the island of Rakiura blushed on certain nights of the year like a young man at his own wedding. He described the lights that danced across the sky when his tribe came there to collect titi or mutton birds from their burrows.

'That would be the aurora,' Olva exclaimed when he heard about it. 'A phenomenon I would dearly like to witness in this far-flung spot. I did not even know there was such a thing here.'

It was the northern aurora, or northern lights, that the ship and the little cutter were both named for, and it made a lot of sense that there was a southern counterpart. The atmosphere was so clear in these new latitudes that the stars hung close in the sky above the ship with a clarity and a sense of nearness that the whalers had never seen before.

As the ship passed by the great southern cape that Lafe and Olva were now willing to admit might have been an island, she began her run north again. Many of the little islands and rocks the ship passed were awash with foam, and most could be seen to hold seals in good numbers, but Olva would not launch his boats against them. The crew were not yet sufficiently skilled at skinning seals nor, more importantly, at recovering skins and men from the rocks in such conditions, he warned, and his officers realized the truth of his words. The southerly blow was piling the white surf against rocks that were surrounded by forests of bull kelp and the long arms of the weed waved in the current, thick and tough. In the clear water it could be seen growing from a great depth.

'These seals will keep until the weather is more moderate,' Olva assured the men. 'And have you ever seen such a forest of bull kelp? It will hinder the rowers no end. If a boat turns over in the kelp, we will have drowned sailors, nothing surer, and a drowned sailor is no use to us or the ship, nor to his sweetheart back home.'

Already the mainland was starting to show again away in the north, where the tops of many tall, snow covered mountains stood out clearly in the chilled air. Directly ahead of the ship now were the Solander Islands, two great humps of rock many hundreds of feet high, sticking straight up out of an ocean that gave the impression of being very deep. Windblown, bleak, and inhospitable though they were, these were the islands Erickson the Swede had sent his ship to find because they marked one of the greatest whale fisheries and sealing grounds yet discovered in the world. From the day Olva sailed the *Northern Lights* away from the New Bedford docks, this area of ocean surrounding these great rocks had been her destination. It was here the mature right whale returned from the Pacific after breeding, bringing its calves with it to fatten in the cold, plankton-rich waters.

They passed the desolate western cape, still carrying little sail but making a fast passage owing to the strong cold southerly winds that drove the ship. Closing quickly with the land she nosed her way carefully between the rocky islands that guarded the entrance to Dusky Sound. This was a very large fiord carved out of the mountains by an ancient glacier, a fiord so deep that the lead line could find no bottom except very close to the shore. This fiord had been explored and carefully mapped by Cook and his men on their second voyage around New Zealand. It was a place of great enjoyment and wonder for them, and had become a place of refuge and renewal.

'Thank God for our safe arrival,' Olva exclaimed as his ship picked its way around the many islands and rocks that dotted the entrance. 'If the wind had turned fluky on us we would not have been able to hold her off the rocks with her anchor, the water is too deep for that.'

The sea had been too rough outside the entrance to launch the whaleboat to assist with a tow, and there had been tension on deck as Olva took the ship in. It was a grand harbour though, and now the ship was out of the wind in the lee of the high ridges it was warm and the waters were as placid as a lake. Snow-capped mountains were reflected on the still water, and the silence as the ship ghosted along, after the scream of the wind in the rigging outside, was balm to the senses.

The many arms of Dusky Sound stretched away in front of them for miles into the mountains both distant and close, mountains so high that the peaks were just weathered rock covered in deep snow. Some of the mountaintops forced the sailors to crane their necks and look straight up through the cross trees of the mainmast to see the tops of them. In many ways the forest covering the shoreline was the same as in the north except that it lacked the larger tree ferns and the trees here did not appear to have the height and girth of their northern relatives. Though the forest was a dense mixture of light and dark greens and looked very thick and almost impenetrable down near the water's edge, the trees grew smaller and more stunted as they ran up onto tussock benches into the sub-alpine terrain higher up. Those upper benches gave way to steeper grades that climbed on in turn to where the tussock faded away as it joined the snowline.

As the ship glided toward the anchorage at Pickersgill and the shore on either side of the ship drew closer, it was the birdsong that stilled the talk on board. It was still springtime here in the south and the birds were taking full advantage of the sunshine to sing their courtship songs. The sheer volume of the noise was so great it seemed it must have issued forth from a million throats, and though the birdsongs were far from unpleasant it required a conscious effort to speak above the noise. Best of all, the seals were here. A good number had been seen on the islands at the entrance to the sound, and all the rocky points around the bay seemed to hold colonies of the creatures basking like fat slugs in the sunshine.

Once the anchor streaked down through the clear water at the little anchorage of Pickersgill, trailing a string of bubbles behind it, a whaleboat towed the ship back into a small cove where her stern was tied to two trees, perhaps the same two trees that Cook himself had used.

After an hour or two staring at their new surroundings the crew began preparing for the seal hunt that would take place next day. Barrels of salt were hoisted from below, muskets, powder and shot were readied and the many harpoons and knives that would be needed for the hunt were sharpened. While this was going on Lafe, Matai and two other crew members known for their fishing abilities were sent out in the whaleboat to find out if the harbour would still produce fish as it had for the *Endeavour*'s crew. The fish were certainly still there. No sooner had the lines been lowered into the water than Matai had his up and a large blue cod lay kicking in the bilges nearly scaring the wits out of the dog. They all bent to their lines in intense concentration. Down went Matai's line and up it came again with another cod, while Lafe's line was empty.

'You must think like a fish to catch a fish,' Matai patiently explained, and he went on to catch five fish to every one the others caught.

Soon they had enough cod on board to feed the ship so Lafe aimed the cutter towards a rock where Matai's sharp eyes had picked a seal basking in the sun. Rowing as stealthily as Indians they closed in on the sleeping seal's blind side but, just as Lafe prepared his musket to fire, the dog barked to let the hunters know he had spotted a strange creature on the rock up ahead. A cuff across the ears taught him his first hunting lesson, silence at all times.

Though the seal sat up and looked sleepily at the boat, neither he nor any of the many generations before him had ever been hunted. Fear, or even the urge to escape, was not part of his conditioning. In fact, the seal could not possibly know that danger was coming as it came in a form it had never seen before. Gliding quietly across the water towards him was a creature of great interest, his poor eyesight told him. It was alive and had many limbs, like an octopus, and so he sat and stared at it trying to make up his mind just what it was he was seeing. Lafe's musket ball took him behind the eye and smashed his brain to a pulp so it ran down the side of his head, and without even an inkling of alarm he died and rolled off his rock into the shallow water.

For many seconds the sound of the shot echoed from mountain to mountain, sending flocks of painted ducks flapping down the fiord, their calls coming clearly back to the hunters in the sudden quiet that followed. The forests where the birds had sung seconds before fell silent and now all the inhabitants of the valley seemed to hold their breath for what might happen next. This, the dog decided, was where he should take action. He leapt over the side of the whaleboat, nearly knocking one of the sailors into the water, sank his teeth in one of the seal's flippers, hunched his back and hung on tight.

'Ka pai te kuri!' Matai's musical voice rang out, laughing at the sheer fun of it all.

'Good dog,' Lafe quickly echoed, and once the dog had been forced to release his hold on the flipper the seal was rolled into the boat with the rest of the fish and the whaleboat set off back to the anchorage. Now a powerful hunting instinct had been awakened in the young dog, who kept his eye closely on what he regarded as his contribution to the day's bag just in case it tried to escape.

The seal would be useful for food but it was also useful for a skinning demonstration. One of the sailors on board had done a season or two as a sealer and the whalers all gathered round as he stripped the seal of its hide efficiently, showing them the best way to skin it and explaining how to handle and preserve the skin. For these men accustomed to handling whale blubber the seal meat looked easy to extract and they looked forward to their first meal of it.

Away to the west above the entrance to the fiord, the setting sun painted the sky a stunning red and crimson that gave the promise of another fine day to follow, and that night Lafe lay awake in his bunk long after the rest of the crew slept. Somehow he missed the sound of the ship at sea. There was no sound at all here at the anchorage in the cove, no sound of the sea passing the hull, no creak of ropes, not even the comfort of a watchman's tread on deck. Lafe could not remember such a total lack of sound ever before in his life. He rose and made his way quietly up to the deck, followed by the soft pad of Salem's feet. The moon had risen and he could see far across the fiord and up to the tops of the mountains at the head of the bay in almost as much detail as during the daylight hours. It was, he decided the stillness of the night, the awareness of being so far from home and his awe of their surroundings that disturbed his soul and caused his loss of sleep.

As he watched the rings spread across the surface of the water from a rising fish, he wondered about the future. More and more he was aware of the strong pull this vigorous, beautiful, young country was exerting upon him. It was, he imagined, like the soft urgent arms of a woman enfolding him, and he could not help but believe that his destiny lay somehow entwined with this land. His own mother had died when he was a very young boy and from then on he had travelled with his father, who made his living from ships and trade. Now he sometimes felt he had many homes and sometimes that he had none at all. He realized this had effectively loosened the bonds of country, home and hearth, because now he could feel the ties of his past life slipping away like the current of an outgoing tide.

Suddenly his reverie was broken by the call of a night owl from Astronomer's Point. It was the morepork and its call said exactly that. Matai had told him the owl's name was Ruru and he was the messenger of death who called from the graveyard. It seemed to Lafe from what little he understood so far that the Maori world was full of gods, ghosts and bad spirits.

He was still on deck when the first pale light started to colour the sky above the peaks and the birds started their dawn chorus, first just one or two testing their voices, then more joining in until the very air pulsed with their songs. One bird's call had a bell-like clarity that made it hard to believe it was made by a small, green bird whose voice was far bigger than itself.

Shortly after sun-up the crews had put away a substantial breakfast that would last them the day and the boats set off for their respective hunting areas. The whaleboats were to work the closer rocks and coastline, while the cutter headed out through the northern entrance to search the rocky ledges washed by the Tasman Sea. Although Cook had seen a small family of Maori in Dusky Sound, it was believed that the country was relatively unpopulated, at least as far as tribes of any size went, but Olva insisted nonetheless that every boat carried two muskets and that the sailors should keep their eyes open. He warned them not to fire their muskets unless they were under attack, and at that signal the other boats would race to their aid. There had been no sign of smoke hanging in the still air of the evening or morning to show that the bay was inhabited, and it was accepted that no one could live without fire in this part of the country, even in summer.

It was near evening when the last boat pulled into the anchorage

91

and began to unload the skins they had taken. The carpenter had spent the day building drying racks on the beach from timber cut from the hillside above. All the boats had skins on board when they returned, and the crews were covered in blood and gore, their voices pitched high as they described their own parts in every chase. Competition among the boats remained very fierce, and although there had been the usual crop of accidents there was nothing serious. One man had been bitten and thought he would perhaps die of distemper, but Olva dosed him with a foul concoction that he made up to his own secret recipe and he never came back for another dose.

The *Northern Lights* would stay only a week in Dusky Sound, as Olva was anxious to get among the whales again while they remained in the southern waters, and Lafe was responsible for gathering as much fresh food as possible for the whalers who would be at sea for the next six months. Birds, fish and the odd seal were eaten fresh as they were taken and the remainder was salted or smoked and stored in casks.

Although there were no animals to hunt in Dusky there were many birds, ducks and pigeons and they made up a goodly part of the ship's diet. The little woodhen, or weka to use its Maori name, was a fine eating bird whose curiosity certainly helped his own downfall. A weka would stride from the bush right up to a sailor's feet, with his head held at an inquiring angle as if to ask, 'Haven't I met you somewhere before?' This appeared to be because the poor bird had no natural enemies and had a natural desire to see that affairs were conducted in a polite way in his own little piece of the world. The dog Salem caught many of them on the various beaches and coves by running them down and holding them with his big feet until the sailors took them from him and wrung their necks. Lafe thought that by comparison to the wary turkeys he had hunted back home they were easy prey and it almost seemed a shame to kill such a bird, but sailors had to eat.

Jimmy the Otaakou Maori insisted that the weka had no sense of direction at all and was always lost. If you listened in the evening he told them, you would hear the weka call his friends to find out where he was.

Olva gave permission for a party to climb one of the near peaks in the hope that they may be able to get a view into a large fiord to the south and learn a little of the country that surrounded them, so Jimmy and Lafe left the ship early one morning with a couple of companions and headed for the tussock tops they had viewed from the cutter. It was splendid weather, and after five hours of solid bush bashing through what turned out to be a mixture of vines, moss and close-growing small trees the four finally broke out onto a small plateau covered in tussock and small herbs and grasses.

Exhausted, they threw themselves on the turf in the warm sun to rest and to gaze at the view that now stretched out before them, from the bays almost below their feet to the mountains that filled the horizon inland. The view alone made the climb worth the effort, and they ignored the many small cuts and scratches that they had received from some very unpleasant thorned vines that wrapped around their limbs on the way up the steep face.

They lay there and studied the country dreamily. The grand sight of the coast to the north disappearing behind the mountains was a disappointment to their plans and they discovered they would have to climb even further up to see into the fiord to the south. But they could go no higher that day. The climb up to the tussock benches had taken too long, and trying to return through the country they had come through in the dark would be to have a death wish. They sat entranced, looking out over the sound and pointing out the known features of Cook's chart, the deep passage that linked their own sound to Breaksea Sound and the northern entrance. They discovered there were more than twenty islands, both large and small, clustered around Five Finger Point, the landmark they had used to find their way into Dusky Sound.

Lafe wondered at the bravery of Cook and his crew and others like them who pushed their way into such places, unknown and uncharted, and later he and Olva shook their heads in awe at the risks the great navigator had taken.

'Bad enough just to risk shipwreck,' Olva commented, 'but in many places in this country you might well be eaten even after you made it safely to shore.'

The deep blue of the water at the entrance contrasted markedly with the white foam forming a ring around each of the rocks and small islands where the waves of the Tasman washed over them. Near the entrance of the fiord the water was light blue where the retreating glacier had dropped its spoil, but that quickly changed to the dark blue of the deeper water. The country was a blend of blues, deep blue water, light blue water, the forest a smoky blue in the distance and the sky a lighter blue again. Inland, the picture changed again and had still another dimension. There the snow on the higher peaks broke up the blue of the forest and sky with a set of jagged white teeth, fascinating to stare at.

Up on the plateau, Lafe's daydreams were broken by Jimmy rousing himself and demanding, 'We go now, it get cold soon.'

Lafe knew he was right, though he was loath to leave the spot where he was, but he hoisted himself to his feet and they started back down the way they had come.

'You just want your dinner, don't you Jimmy?' Lafe teased him.

He was answered with a wide grin.

'Jimmy is the eatingest man I have ever seen in my wide travels on this earth,' Olva once declared after watching him put away a meal. 'And I thought you were pretty keen on your food.'

Lafe could put away a lot of food in a single sitting , but he had to admit he was an apprentice compared to the two Maori they had on board. As long as there was food in sight they would both continue to eat. A whale or a seal did not mean oil or skins to them, it was simply food, and when they left the ship for any reason their eyes never stopped searching for more sources of food. Nothing was too large or too small to be brought back for the cooking pot, though the cook was not always pleased when they sought to throw their unmentionable delicacies into his pots. Honour was satisfied only when they were given their own pot.

After a week or two, the crew realized the dog was starting to look a bit ribby; there were just never enough leftovers for him since Jimmy had come on board. But Jimmy had his talents. He insisted that a whaleboat take him to the entrance where he happily dived around the rocks and came back with a supply of black shellfish with an iridescent shell. Jimmy called them paua and Olva identified them as a type of abalone, and everyone agreed they were fine to eat.

Most of the seals had now been killed in Dusky Sound so Olva prepared to dispatch his boats up the coast while he went south to hunt the whales. Supplies were unloaded from the ship and shelters built well above high water mark. This camp would be used as a base camp and a skin shelter. Ten men would make up the sealing party, the two Maori guides and eight Americans; enough to crew both the whaleboat and the cutter. They would live together and hunt seals until the *Northern Lights* returned at the end of summer. Lafe would be the only officer in the party, though he had with him a harpooner who been elevated by Olva to the rank of mate.

The fine weather had gone now and the wind came in bringing heavy-bellied clouds. When the *Northern Lights* lifted her anchor and put to sea in a strong northerly, the men left behind experienced some of the heaviest rain they had ever seen. Soon the quiet little stream they drew their water from was a raging torrent and the sheets of rain that came down the fiord kept them inside their shelters for the first three long days of their new venture.

Chapter 6

'**God, it can rain** in this country!' the mate moaned as he wrung dirty water out of his woollen boot liners. Like everything else that had been on the floor of the shelter when the flood came through it, they were tangled with debris. Once the wind swung to the north it had been only a matter of time before the rain driving down from the mountains had washed them out of their little huts.

'First things first,' Lafe told his men. 'Today we will move the shelter to higher ground and build a moat around it. We've certainly learned something from this; in future we never put up a camp until we've had a good look at the terrain. Down by the mouth of the stream there's driftwood in the lower forks of the trees that makes this rainstorm look like a sunshower.'

The sailors had yarned away the hours as sailors do, their two guides and Salem the dog had slept, and Lafe had kept his journal up to date and planned for the fine days until the flood had galvanised them all into action and they had hastily grabbed up their belongings and rushed for the trees where Jimmy and Matai kindled a small fire for them to huddle over. The shelter they built on higher ground was a makeshift one, but at least they were no longer in danger of having their gear swept away.

When the wind swung south again it turned cold, but then the cloud broke and the sun arrived to dry out their tents and bedding. Very quickly the streams returned to normal and the birds burst into song with the utmost vigour as if to make up for time lost during the storm.

With the end of the rains came the sandfly, a small black midge with a bite that a creature ten times as large would be proud of, and very soon the men were driven mad by them. Jimmy told them a story that his tribe often told.

'In the beginning when the gods had finished making this land here in the west, they saw that it was very beautiful and they became concerned that the people would become idle and lie around looking at it all day. So, being wise gods, they set Te Namu the sandfly loose on the land to keep the people moving'.

Jimmy roared with laughter as he told the story, waving his arms to imitate the way the sailors swatted and scratched at the little midges, and he and Matai chuckled together as they repeated, 'Te Namu. Ko Te Namu ia.'

Lafe would have liked to know more of these local gods, but for that to happen he would have to improve his Maori or Jimmy would have to improve his English. Jimmy was better at telling stories than answering questions, he quickly learned.

Meanwhile the sandflies persisted and the men had only two choices, to crouch over a smoky fire till they were nearly suffocated or to push off in the boats and go hunting. They begged to go hunting, anything to get away from the little demons even though the rough seas would keep them hunting inside the sounds for a day or two yet. Besides the sandflies, the birdsong which had at first entranced them was also getting on everyone's nerves so Lafe decided it was time to leave. They baled the water from the boats, prepared food and loaded everything on board.

'These are probably the spring rains,' he had assured his men. 'They'll be over soon.' But after carefully questioning Jimmy, and finding more driftwood high in the forks of trees along the banks of the streams, he was not so sure. Jimmy stated that Murihiku, or 'the tail of the fish' as the place where they had camped was called, was notorious for heavy rain at any time of the year.

Rough seas, caused by the big southerly swells sweeping up the coast from their birthplace down among the icebergs, were still too much for the small boats to handle outside the fiord but that same bad weather had chased the seals in to rest in the sheltered rookeries and the hunting was good again. For safety's sake the two boats now worked together, the cutter sitting off the rocks while the whaleboat worked its way in to drop off the hunters. The men quickly spread along the water's edge to cut off the seals' escape back to the sea, then killed them with hard blows to the base of the snout. It was hard, dirty and at times exciting work and the whaleboat turned over more than once, spilling its crew into the foam to swim for their lives. The half-drowned sailors struggled amid the forests of kelp and the seals plunging from the rocks among them in their bids to escape back to the open sea, and Lafe had to stop the whaleboat from landing hunters on one or two well-populated headlands because getting ashore was too dangerous. If a sailor was badly hurt he would die in this lonely bay.

While the killing and skinning went on Lafe and Matai often gathered mussels from the rocks or dived for rock lobster and paua. Lafe had been around ships and the sea all his life and thought he was a good swimmer, but Matai swam like a seal and could dive to depths that astounded his friend. Sometimes he would emerge from the water with a big lobster in each hand and a grin on his face.

'Ka pai te kai! Good food!' he would cry out, his laugh ringing across the quiet bay. It was very good grub indeed, and it was a challenge for Lafe to do as well. Though sometimes given to strange moods and fears of gods and ghosts, Matai was a fine companion and was never happier than when he was gathering food. He would always choose the fishing spot, moving the cutter carefully into position as he peered into the depths looking for some sign that Lafe could never fathom. When the Maori was satisfied he would cheerfully announce what type of fish he was about to catch, making sure Lafe could pronounce it correctly, then send his line into the depths. It seemed to Lafe that if the gods had so much say about what a fish was going to do the whole process could be simplified by simply dropping a hook anywhere and letting the gods send the fish to it.

'Why is it not so?' he asked Jimmy one day. It was a serious matter that the Maori gave some thought to before replying.

'The gods are not always as attentive to their duties as they should be,' he finally explained. 'Some days they are distracted by other important things.'

'Such as?'

Jimmy's grin broadened. 'They might be away making love, as even gods do.'

Lafe was made to understand that men should play their part to help the gods by placing the bait in the right place, so as not to make the business of catching fish harder for the gods to organize. There were also many rules to be followed. No women were allowed near the tribe's fishing gear, Jimmy explained. Women were profane and would bring bad luck to the canoe.

'And you must not cook fish within sight of their living brothers. To cook a fish by the sea would cause great offence.'

'There is a lot more to this fishing than I thought,' Lafe replied.

One day Matai selected his biggest hook and strongest line, then took several dead cod and sliced them with care before clambering on board the cutter. He indicated that Lafe should take her out through the heads where she buried her bows into the rollers of the Tasman Sea until she reached the quieter waters beyond. Lafe suspected this was not a cod fishing expedition and watched with interest as Matai carefully studied the water, the breeze and other things known only to himself. He chose a spot a mile off the headland then took a whole cod, its flesh opened up to simulate the action of a butterfly's wing in the water, threaded it to the hook and lowered it over the side. As the cutter drifted over his chosen spot he watched, muscles tensed, poised for the strike. This was repeated several times, Lafe manoeuvering the *Aurora* while Matai peered carefully down into the deep water. Then suddenly his whole body went rigid.

'Don't move!' he whispered urgently. 'He comes, Te Hapuku!' He grinned and held his arms satisfyingly wide to show the size of the fish. Then for a minute or more he balanced the line across one finger, hissing with excitement as he picked up faint vibrations from the fish.

It seemed to Lafe that he was in direct communication, through the slender line, with the unseen fish far below. This was a masterful performance even for Matai. To him fishing was an out-of-world experience, something shared between him and his gods, and Lafe could feel the tension as the Maori gently let a little line trickle out over his finger.

'He eats now,' Matai whispered as he struck at the fish, sinking the hook into its jaw.

'Ah! I have you now, great fish,' he crooned. His line sang with the tension as he struggled to stop the hapuku returning to its rocky cave among the debris left on the ocean floor by the glacier. This was where he could lose the battle very quickly, he told Lafe as he worked the line. If the fish got back inside its cave no fisherman would ever get him out again. But these were the hands of an expert and, slowly but surely, the fish lost the battle. When it lay sulking and exhausted Matai pinged the line like a banjo string to keep it moving. Every run the fish made in the direction of its cave was carefully headed off, with just enough line given out to ease the strain but not enough to let it make the sanctuary.

Though it was a very strong fish and its cave was not far away, Matai slowly gained back his line until suddenly the fight was over. The hapuku was a deep-water fish and its bladder had ruptured in the shallower water. Now there was no fight left and it was a dead weight on the line as Matai brought it up hand over hand, laying the cord neatly at his feet as he did so.

Lafe was not prepared for the size of the fish that finally broke the surface. It was a bug-eyed, huge-jawed solid lump of a fish and he guessed it weighed around a hundred pounds. It took both men to roll it up the cutter's side and over the gunwales to lie in the bottom of the boat where it still twitched, giving the odd powerful thump with its tail on the boards. It was very thick at the girth, a deep-bodied fish with grey and blue shading together at the top of its body fading to white on the belly. Its mouth was so large Lafe could put both fists inside and its long bottom jaw protruded beyond the top to give it a belligerent look even in death. Lafe thought it resembled a type of bass or wreck fish he had seen in books.

Just for the fun of it he went through the ritual of asking if it was good to eat, and watched Matai's delight give way to a look of hurt and indignation.

'Have I ever dug up, caught, shot, or speared anything that was not the best eating?'

This was part of the ritual too, though in truth the sailors would testify that there were many things Matai ate that they did not find such good eating, like the foot-long worms he found in the forest and the sea egg or kina he had talked them into trying.

Matai cleaned the fish while Lafe got some sail up. Lafe knew from experience that his friend's haste was so he could investigate whether there were any other tasty titbits inside the fish that might be overlooked, and sure enough, as Lafe raced the cutter back through the entrance, there were happy chuckles and approving clucks of the tongue. By the time they got in Matai had two large fish roes, each as large as a man's head, laid out next to his hapuku.

The next morning when the boats left for the rookeries Matai stayed behind to prepare a feast for the hunters, and Lafe carefully laid out the supplies before they left for fear that Matai would cook all of their six months' food in one grand feast.

When the men pulled back into the bay at the end of the day, their boats loaded with skins, Matai met them at the water's edge dancing with excitement and worry that the food might have cooked too long. He urged them to hurry and take their places.

Early in the day he had begun his preparation by digging a square hole in the earth four times the measure of his foot by four times the depth. It was behind a sand hillock so that no fish in the fiord could possibly see him at work on their dead cousin. He had filled the hole with dry wood and river stones and fired it, letting it burn for most of the morning, then once the wood had burned away the ash was thrown out and the white hot rocks were retained on the bottom of the hole. Using layers of wet fern he had covered the rocks, laid the hapuku on top then added more layers of fern, placing a different food between each according to the cooking time it needed. Duck, pigeon and lobster were near to the fish, and the bush vegetables he had collected while the rocks heated went on last. There was bush cabbage taken from the tops of palms, fern fronds, cress, seaweed and kelp, all arranged at different levels closer or further from the hot rocks. Flax mats had been carefully placed over the food, a measured amount of water sprinkled into the hole, and the oven covered with a mound of earth and left to steam for the afternoon.

Now as the hungry sealers watched he carefully removed the soil on top of the hangi then lifted the flax mats one by one to expose the layers of perfectly cooked food underneath. Right at the bottom was the fish, a fragrant masterpiece steaming on its bed of fern. Even the fish looked pleased as Matai leapt into the air with a great cry and performed an impromptu haka around it. He raised his knees high in the air and thumped his feet down on the dirt, while the sealers cheered him on.

'Except for the ship's salt, every single piece of food that Matai has laid before us has come from the bush or the sea within sight of where he is sitting. There is a lesson here for all of us,' Lafe told his men. 'We look to the ship's stores for our survival but these two Maori who travel with us see their whole world as one big storehouse full of food. According to their culture this is food provided by the gods and it is there for all of us to use and enjoy.'

Lafe did wonder sometimes if civilization was not rushing along a little too fast and losing sight of these simple ways that allowed men to harvest what they needed from the world around them. The food was good, the fish the best that Lafe had ever eaten. It lay on the mat in front of them in mounds of succulent white flesh, and Matai showed them how to spread fish roe on it like a type of relish. Even the seaweed steamed inside the hapuku was good, and he wondered why as a sailor he had never eaten it before. Surely sailors and seaweed went together, and he wondered just how many sailors had died of scurvy within sight of this food that might well have saved their lives.

'I have seen whalers put into port with dead and dying sailors on board,' he commented to the men around him, 'but there are no signs of scurvy among the Maori. Indeed, they appear to be the healthiest people I have yet seen. If we eat as they eat we should come to no harm.'

Long after the sailors had eaten their fill and rolled away from the fire to lie contentedly puffing on their pipes, Matai and Jimmy continued to feast. They were watched by the dog with an expression that Lafe fancied was one of admiration. Even Salem had given up eating, glutted by all the leftovers thrown his way.

Jimmy and Matai loved the dog and were in awe of him as he filled out more each day and grew to his full weight. He was endlessly compared to the small, fox-like creatures back in their own villages.

'Eh, the pigs we would catch with such a dog,' Jimmy would say. But Lafe now understood enough of their language to fit together words and sentences he overheard in the course of the day, and he knew that they had also talked about how nice the dog would look emerging from an earth oven surrounded with vegetables. It wasn't that they didn't love Salem dearly, it was just that if the dog fell in the oven one day when they were really hungry they wouldn't be in a hurry to throw him out again.

Once the southerly eased the camp was dismantled, except for the skin shelter where their haul of sealskins was cached for the *Northern Lights* to collect, and the two boats cleared Dusky Sound and headed south around West Cape into the next fiord. This was another huge inland waterway which in fact had two separate arms but lacked the internal link that Dusky Sound enjoyed, and its entrance was guarded by reefs and rocks that would exclude larger ships from using it. The rough entrance had in fact turned Cook back, and he went on north to enter Dusky Sound instead.

Inside, the fiord was calm and deep and promised good shelter. A camp was soon set up on a sheltered sunny beach and the hunters were on the water again to attack the seals around the entrance. The hunting was good and Lafe made three trips back to Dusky Sound in the cutter, each time heavily laden with skins, before the weather broke and the rain came, binding them to their camp once again while the rivers swelled and waterfalls gushed from every cliff face.

It was during these spells of confinement that Lafe felt a deep loneliness. As an officer he was expected to keep his distance from the sailors, and the sailors respected that, but the sailors had each other to talk to and to laugh with. The two Maori were from different tribes and may have been sworn enemies but they chattered, laughed, sang and slept while the rain drummed on the canvas roof and walls. Lafe belonged with neither group and had only his journal and a few books for company. He spent his days listening to Jimmy and Matai talking in their own language, picking up words here and there and fitting them into sentences where he could, puzzling his brain with words that had obscure or double meanings.

The season passed from spring to early summer and the temperatures became mild and pleasant. Except for the downpours of rain that they received on a weekly basis and the sandflies that plagued them each day it was the grandest place in the world for a young and healthy man to be.

It was the season for the seals to come in to the land to rear their pups, and the hunters found that the rocks were inhabited by more seals each morning. Killing and skinning had lost all its excitement by now and had become just hard, remorseless toil, but their tally of skins mounted steadily. It was a dangerous, dirty job, with the constant risk of overturned boats and the ever-present smell of the skins, and it was little wonder the men's thoughts roamed far across the sea to their homeland and their loved ones.

Lafe knew that the sailors dreamed of home and their share of the voyage profits, and constantly reminded them to keep their minds on their work. Lack of concentration could mean he would one day bury them on a lonely beach in this far-away country, he warned, and their families would never see them again. For some, the money they earned on this trip would give them a valuable start in life, but for others it wouldn't last long; it would soon be gone on women and grog, and within a few months they would be looking for another ship heading for another lonely part of the world to start all over again.

Lafe found he had his own dreams, but they were of dusky-skinned women rather than the demure young girls of his own country and more than once he woke to realize that he had been transported back to his first landfall in New Zealand.

Which of Kaitoke's two granddaughters would be his wife? Would he choose, would she be chosen for him by the old chief of Whangaroa, or was he destined to sail away on the *Northern Lights* back to where he had come from and never see either of them again? He decided such dreams were not healthy and he tried to put them far from his mind.

After nearly a month it was time to head back to Dusky Sound. It was like returning to an old and much loved home; the islands and the waterways were familiar to them now and Pickersgill, where the *Northern Lights* had anchored, was the centre of their universe.

There were only a few seals left in Dusky and it was scarcely worth the effort to hunt there. As soon as the weather was right they would head north up the coast to new hunting grounds. Meanwhile the fish were biting so Lafe and Matai went off to explore Wet Jacket Arm, a long, deep and narrow reach between two mountain ranges that soared so high either side of the cutter the two men had to lean well back to view the tops. It was a pleasant place to spend a summer's day, with deep, still waters reflecting the mountains in such exacting detail that Lafe turned the *Aurora* aside rather than run the boat through such a masterpiece and shatter it.

No doubt it would be a cold and gloomy place in the winter, Lafe decided. Very little sun would ever reach the dark foliage at the water's edges. Even the name that Cook had bestowed upon the place had no obvious explanation but carried a hint of things uncomfortable or better left unsaid. And there was no trace of the natives that he had described as living in Dusky Sound in 1773, only twenty-seven years before the sealing crew from New Bedford set up their camp. They seemed to have gone forever.

Perhaps one morning the elderly and only warrior of the group had woken to find that his spear no longer flew straight, Lafe mused. Did they then linger for weeks, growing weaker from starvation, and die wrapped together in a little cave on the hillside? Were they truly the lost tribe? And if so, why had the old warrior that Cook had met, with his two wives, a young girl, two children and a baby, left their own people to travel to and live in this wilderness? So many questions, Lafe thought. The lost tribe might well remain one of this country's mysteries.

105

The sealers found signs of human presence in other parts of Dusky Sound. In some bays there were tree stumps, in one place an old fallen dwelling, but this was the work of steel, not stone. Sealers had been there before. Maori had been there, Cook and his crew had been there. Who else? Lafe could not tell, but he still searched the secluded bays with his eyes every morning looking for the spiral of smoke that would tell of the survival or return of the lost tribe.

The plan he and Olva had put together before the *Northern Lights* left was for the two little sealing boats to work north from Dusky Sound, moving in turn through each of the many sounds still to be explored. Caches of dried skins would be stored at suitable places to be picked up when the ship returned from Sydney. They would hunt as far north as The Cascades, a place Cook had described as a series of torrents falling from the cliffs into the sea, and this was where they expected to rendezvous with Olva in the first week of May.

Once they had moved from Dusky Sound Lafe and his men led a nomadic existence. Camps were set up in each sheltered bay in turn until the seal numbers dropped and the tally of skins had risen, then the hunters moved on. Sometimes they were weather-bound for three or four days at a time in tents that thrashed in the winds and soaking rains, in weather so bad the boats could not even put off from the beach and were carried bodily up into the tree line and tied down for fear they would be wrecked. At other times the sky would remain clear for a week, not a breeze ruffled the water and they sailed or rowed through reflections so exquisite it was almost a crime to shatter them. On those days they fell among the seals and killed them in their hundreds before moving on. Boots, skin, and clothing became so matted with blood and fat that their sense of smell became dulled and everything smelled, felt and tasted the same.

As the sealers moved steadily north they moved into summer and the fine, hot days reduced them all to working in only their boots and strips of cloth around their loins. The work was hard and the days were long, but they were healthy and ate well and there was little or no animosity among the gang. Perhaps they were lucky with the choice of leaders and crew, or perhaps the credit should go to Olva for picking those who were to stay for the sealing. He was a successful captain, Lafe reflected. His crews always came back with money in their pockets so he always attracted the best men to his ship, and now it was paying off. The young Swede hoped one day to be able to boast such a reputation himself and he bore his responsibilities as he knew Olva would have done, feeding his men as well as was possible and respecting their wants and needs. His sealing crew had been picked from the best whale men on the ship, and for this he was grateful.

Only for the worst crimes on board would Olva allow a man to be flogged. Marooning was still the most common way to deal with crew trouble on a ship. A persistent troublemaker would be dumped ashore in an isolated spot with a little food and left to shift for himself. If the ship came back for him at the end of the season he was lucky, and most captains did not bother to return. Lafe was glad he would not have to make a decision like that, because nearly always if the victim was still alive he was reduced to gibbering madness by the time his ship returned for him. Marooning was the cruellest of all punishments, especially here in New Zealand, but the crew knew and had to respect the fact it was an option for any officer in charge.

One morning they landed on a beach that showed signs of human use; at some time in the past year a large party of Maori had camped at this same spot. Jimmy had told them it was not uncommon for tribes to travel along this coast to gather stone. This pounamu, as Jimmy called the stone, was the colour of the leaves of the greenest tree in the forest and had a value greater than any other thing on earth.

Lafe felt a slight lifting of the hairs on the back of his neck when he looked at the old camp fires and the area that had been cleared for sleeping.

'The only way to have got this number of warriors here was by canoe, and big, sea-going ones at that,' he told his men. This camp had obviously been used many times over many years judging by the size and number of the cooking fire places.

'Would this lot have come from Murderers' Bay?' Lafe asked Jimmy. Their guide had warned them that the northern tribe was well known for its bad ways and the sealers would no doubt be eaten when

107

they were caught. Lafe did not pay too much attention to Jimmy's stories; he used the same words as Matai had used to describe every tribe in the North Island except his own. But a shadow had been cast over them all and they were a lot less carefree and happy than they had been. Muskets were carried everywhere now and were carefully stacked near to where they were working. Lafe sat with his musket across his knees in the cutter when the men were on the rocks killing seals.

No war party came to disturb the hunters and Lafe began to think it might not be the season for stone gathering, but he and the men built a small stone hut on a bluff so they could retreat there and defend themselves if need be. The site he chose was at Open Bay, a day's sail north of The Cascades at the very northern end of their summer wanderings.

The country past there showed more evidence of periodic Maori visits. Most beaches they landed on showed signs of occupation for at least part of the year and Lafe knew the danger was greater there than anywhere else they had been. As they travelled north from those first Maori campfires Jimmy and Matai became sullen and very seldom spoke. They wanted to return to Dusky Sound and they considered Lafe to be dangerously mad when he continued north in the direction of their enemies. Nor would they work any more. Matai showed more signs of homesickness than ever before, and there were days now when he would not leave his bed. He began to lose weight in an alarming fashion, and it was only when the boats were loaded and ready to leave the shore that he would climb aboard, his face showing tired resignation, rather than be left alone on the hostile shore.

Already the seals were starting to leave their summer ground. The breeding season was over, and as the sealers started back over old ground the number of skins they took was much lower. Lafe knew that discipline could soon become a problem and he decided to keep a close eye on the men until the *Northern Lights* hove into sight. Still, the ship should arrive in the next couple of weeks and the season had been good. He calculated that they had around eight thousand skins cached in a number of bays stretching right back to Dusky Sound.

Then one evening a man went missing. He had told his friends he intended to walk a little way up a nearby river to get away from the sea for a few hours by himself, but when he was not back by dark the sealers became alarmed. Lafe had warned his men not to leave camp except in numbers and to be armed at all times, but the constant companionship of the same small group was wearing thin after months of living and working together and they were all starting to feel the need to escape, at least for a couple of hours here and there.

The missing man had taken a musket, powder and ball with him, but they would have heard any shot quite clearly in such a quiet valley and there had been none fired that day. It was hoped that the sailor was not foolhardy enough to have left the riverbed and become lost.

'If he has, he is a dead man. No one would ever find his way out of that forest by himself,' Lafe told the rest of the party. 'We'll look for him in daylight.'

No one slept that night. They sat around the fire with their muskets across their knees, waiting for something to happen. Some dozed a little where they sat but most were watchful, believing their friend had already been taken by Maori and an attack was likely at any moment. That night the moreporks called, first from one place and then another, as if they were gathering to spread the word. 'A man has died here today,' they seemed to say. Lafe would have liked to ask the two Maori what they thought but it seemed wiser to keep his own counsel because Jimmy looked grim and withdrew into himself, saying nothing, while Matai sobbed quietly throughout the night.

At first light Lafe took half the men up the river to search for the missing sealer. They found the first tracks in the silt of the riverbank, and they were not hard to follow as the man seemed not to have moved with any great purpose in mind but to have simply wandered. More tracks in the soft sand showed where he had stopped to gaze into a deep clear pool where a pair of blue ducks cavorted, as tame as a couple of yard chickens.

'Just a man happy to be away from the sea and the killing for a few hours,' Lafe said softly. The man's tracks showed his mood as clearly as if they had been witness to his movements.

Lafe led his war party, for that was what he believed it was, moving in a tight group up the riverbed like a porcupine, muskets primed

109

and cocked and pointing outwards to cover each likely point of attack. Before leaving camp Lafe had his men load with buckshot. Any battle, he told them, would take place at very close range, probably no greater than a spear could be thrown, and buckshot was murderous at that range.

The silence was broken only by the river chuckling its way through the boulders. Even the birdsong was subdued, as if the birds too held their breath for fear of provoking the violence they could feel in the air. The sealers found a place where a tree had fallen into the stream, leaving a hole in the forest canopy that let in a little sun, and here the sailor had laid himself down on the sand with his musket propped next to him against a log.

In the soft white sand was a pool of thick, coagulated blood teeming with glossy blue-backed flies, and there was another lumpy substance that Lafe strongly suspected was brain matter. He did not look closely. His belly began to heave in a terrible manner so he quickly turned away.

The tracks showed clearly how a party of Maori, perhaps fifteen or twenty, had crept up on the sealer as he rested. The river chuckling over the rocks would have covered any noise, or maybe he had fallen asleep, and one of them had struck him on the head before he could rise. More patches of blood on the sand across the river showed where he had been carried off and his friends soon found the small trail through the forest that snaked its way to the north, showing tracks of unshod feet both coming and going from the area. But though they followed the trail for many hours they could not find the sailor's body, his musket or his murderers.

By the time the war party arrived back at the camp with the bad news it was late afternoon and Lafe ordered guards to be posted in the forest at least a hundred yards out from the camp while the rest of the men packed all the gear and prepared the boats for immediate departure. If they were attacked they would have to defend the boats to the death, because if they lost those they were doomed.

A hurried council of war was convened and it was decided that though they may lose a few skins if the Maori attacked the stone hut, they would rather leave it undefended and protect the boats. They could not take to the water in the dark but at first light they would begin their retreat back to Dusky Sound.

Though Lafe thought they would be able to defend themselves against the fifteen or so Maori who had killed his man the previous day, he believed them to be part of a much larger group. He and his sailors would fight for the boats if they had to, but they would rather run. A battle in this thick forest would be a murderous thing.

'Even now they might have reached their village and be making ready to return and wipe us out,' he told the men. He could almost feel this in his bones, and knew they had no time to lose.

They settled among the tree roots with their muskets held firmly, and only the gamest among them dared to close their eyes. They knew it would be another long night, and they also knew it was a long way back to Dusky Sound.

Chapter 7

To fight or flee, that was the question that burned in Lafe's brain. In the end it would be the weather that would dictate what happened in the next twelve hours, but he had to have a plan in place. The cutter with its fore and aft sailing rig was the more versatile and seaworthy of their two boats as the whaleboat, like the Viking ships of old, carried a simple, square sail that was useful only when sailing before the wind. It was helpful when they were towing in a whale or making a silent approach on a pod, but any whaleboat relied on the muscles of its crew at the oars. It was one hundred and fifty miles back to Dusky Sound, as near as Lafe could figure it, and with one oarsman dead the remaining crew would need all the help they could get. An unfavourable wind could keep them from leaving, at least until the next change in the weather.

When he watched the sky at dusk, long streaks of cirrus cloud blurred the setting sun. It was a hopeful sign that the fine, windless days they had been enjoying were coming to an end, and if the weather followed the pattern he had observed recently the wind would come away from the north during the night to build in velocity the next day.

What he feared most of all was an attack from the sea as well as from the land, and he dreaded meeting the huge war canoes on the open sea. He could defend the stone house but that would leave the boats exposed to an attack, and if the boats were lost he and his men would be effectively marooned. That was a situation he could not risk, in spite of their muskets, because a determined enemy could lay siege to the hut and starve them out.

That murderous band from yesterday would have canoes somewhere not far up the coast, he decided. He had to try to put himself in their shoes and second-guess them. His men relied on him. The natives would know the sealers had boats, so the only way for them to prevent their prey from escaping was to block their retreat and that meant an attack from the sea.

The more he chewed it over the more he knew he was right. After the demonstrations in Whangaroa Harbour, when Kaitoke's people had showed their awesome seamanship and the manoeuvrability of their canoes, he had a great respect for the Maori navy. But how long did he have before an attack was launched? That was the burning question.

Every hour during the night he changed the sentry whose job was the loneliest of all, sitting by himself in the forest frightened by owls and every creak and rustle from the ancient trees. It was vital that the men got what sleep they could under the circumstances. Jimmy claimed that his tribe would never fight at night, but Lafe wasn't so sure about this mob; night attacks were not unknown.

By five o'clock in the morning he had made his decision and he gave the order to move quietly to the boats. For an hour or more he had watched the sky and felt the breeze slowly building. Though it was still light and fluky, it was holding steady from the northwest, and in the next hour it would fill and strengthen as the dawn broke. The slight wind signalled bad weather to come, although perhaps still a day away.

'This is both good and bad,' he murmured to the men, keeping his voice low so it would not be heard over the lapping of the waves. 'It will be unpleasant out there but it might let us get fifty miles down the coast before we have to hole up again, and it might keep the canoes at home. Their canoes are a lot less seaworthy than the cutter or the whaleboat.'

There were only nine of them now, and seven were needed to row the whaleboat. He sent Jimmy with the mate to take an oar, telling him his life depended on his pulling with the crew. Matai crept on board the cutter and curled up on the bench seat, wrapping a piece of canvas around his shoulders, while Salem the dog took up his position in the bow. Lafe decided Matai looked more like a whipped dog this morning than ever and could not decide whether he was suffering from sheer funk or if he really was a sick man. Lafe would have liked to whip him to see if that would cure him of his cowardice. When he really needed another oarsman to handle the cutter but all he had was this useless creature who could not even help himself, let alone hold a musket.

Lafe had put the crew to work the night before muffling the oars with bits of canvas, and as quiet as death they put out from shore, the whaleboat towing the cutter until the two boats could clear the headland and pick up the breeze. But even as the two sails were being hauled up the masts and set to catch the wind one of the oarsmen gave a cry and pointed to a huge triangular sail that could be clearly seen crossing the path of the waning moon. It was an ocean-going canoe.

Lafe had not expected this, and for a moment he was too stunned to think. He was quite prepared to meet canoes with warriors paddling them and knew they were fast and deadly, but this was a ship, a sea-going craft of a type he had been told was now rare in this country, and it was swooping down on them like a bird of prey. For a moment he considered running back into the bay and making a stand at the stone hut, but a quick calculation told him he and his men would be overtaken if they tried. The mate in the whaleboat had already dropped his sail and the boat streaked away into the darkness, heading south as fast as his oarsmen could propel her. The choice had been made for everyone, and there was no going back to the stone house now.

As the breeze began to fill the *Aurora*'s sails she picked up speed and started to move along through the water. Lafe set off in pursuit of the whaleboat but the cutter only loafed along as it ran before the light breeze and when he looked back the triangular sail had grown a lot larger. He knew he was in danger of being overtaken within the next half hour and he leapt at Matai, picked him up bodily and flung him behind the tiller, shouting at him to hold the cutter steady. His only hope now was to head west, out into the open sea where there was at least a chance of finding some wind, so he let the boom swing across and re trimmed the sail faster than he had ever done before. Even then he lost several hundred yards of the precious lead he still had. The speed of the big canoe bearing down on them was mind-numbing and in the strengthening light of dawn it was now close enough for Lafe to see what he was up against. He realised he was looking at a relic from the past, a double-hulled sailing canoe with room for at least twenty paddlers in each hull. Forty warriors – a much more formidable enemy than he'd ever thought to meet in this part of the world.

'The big bitch is running downwind on sail and paddles!' he shouted to Matai. No wonder she was eating up the sea miles. He calculated that the canoe would overtake the whaleboat within a couple of hours at most as his oarsmen would not be able to keep up the killing pace that they had begun. Hour after hour, slowly but surely, the big canoe would overhaul them as they rowed for their lives.

Lafe glanced back to the bluff where the stone house stood and was just in time to see a flaming torch arch out of the gloom under the trees and land on its canvas roof. Within seconds the oil-soaked canvas was in flames. So I was right, he thought, it was a two-pronged attack and we were lucky to escape at all. If this was escape, with such a ship closing in on him. But the big sailing canoe did not alter course when he did, although the cutter could easily have been overtaken as it headed out to sea, and Lafe knew the attackers had singled out the whaleboat full of men as their quarry. He looked at Matai in disgust and resisted the urge to throw him in the sea to swim ashore and meet his enemies.

'You and I should be dead by now, and it is no thanks to you that we are still alive,' Lafe told him gruffly. 'When the day comes to fight, you fight, my friend. And today is the day!'

Slowly the sun climbed into the heavens and slowly, as often happens near the coast, the breeze rose with it. Now the cutter started to heel to the wind as it picked up speed and the small wavelets broke over the bow as Lafe turned south again, running parallel with the big canoe but well out to sea. Now that he had the wind his confidence was starting to return. It had been touch and go for a while, and he knew he had come close to continuing out to sea and abandoning the whaleboat to its fate but now he knew what he must do and he prayed the wind would hold so that he could work himself within musket range.

'Then we will see if we can whittle down their numbers a bit,' he told Matai, more to put steel in his own backbone than with any hope of stiffening up his crewman. He fired both muskets in the general direction of the canoe to get rid of the old charges that might have got damp overnight, then set about carefully reloading them while Salem looked on from the bow with approval.

'I wouldn't grin too much, they eat dogs on that waka,' Lafe told him. 'Get ready to bite first, boy.'

The whaleboat was clearly visible again, the men still rowing strongly but Lafe knew they would be tiring and as soon as the canoe closed in their sheer terror would make them lose their rhythm. Once that happened the canoe would probably ram them, and once their muskets were empty the fight would be over. A crowded whaleboat was not a good platform to fight from.

Further out to sea than the other boat, Lafe was still running parallel with the big canoe and now slowly he was gaining and creeping ahead. He held his course until he was well forward of the enemy bow then took a deep breath and tacked until the bow of the cutter pointed at the dead centre of the nearest hull. With the wind on the beam the cutter fairly flew through the water while Lafe hung grimly onto the tiller, the two loaded muskets near at hand. He'd done it now, he was committed and he felt his own warrior spirit rise.

He could see that his bold approach was already affecting the speed of the big canoe, the paddlers losing the rhythm as they watched the cutter and tried to fathom its next move. He studied the huge triangular sail and decided it would be limited in any tacking dual with his own boat. Downwind with forty paddles and a sail this Maori ship was fast, and if they dropped the sail and just used paddles alone they would still be faster upwind than most boats. But on all other points of sail he thought the *Aurora* would have them beaten. He would use the wind to get in quick, do some damage to the canoe or its paddlers and hopefully get out again fast.

He trimmed his sails until they were drum-skin tight and closed in, holding the cutter on a collision course aimed dead at the guts of the nearest hull. He noted with grim pleasure that some of the warriors had

116

laid down their paddles and seized their weapons, realising at last that the white devil was intent on ramming them. He held his course until a collision seemed almost unavoidable then slammed the tiller hard over, cutting across the stern of both hulls. As he drew level with each hull he emptied a musket into the mass of bodies, the shot sweeping the canoe from stern to bow plucking feathers from cloaks and pieces of flax from the kilts of the warriors. Salem barked furiously, adding to the pandemonium, and Matai screamed in fear.

Both muskets had been double-loaded with birdshot, and from the reaction on board Lafe guessed that this was a tribe that had never heard a musket fired before. Those nearest the cutter went over backwards, whether from the charge of shot or from sheer fright he couldn't tell. He let the *Aurora* run well clear of the big canoe but when he looked back he could see no sign of pursuit; in fact there was very little sign of anything above the gunwales of either hull. A satisfactory number of yips, yelps, and squeals had greeted his charges of birdshot as it tore into the flesh of the canoe's occupants, and he guessed he had not only shocked the warriors but injured many of them.

He brought the cutter around in a half circle, re-loaded his muskets and began his run back toward the canoe. This time he had loaded with buckshot. He might have slowed the enemy down but now they were as dangerous as wounded bear and he had to immobilize their canoe. A glance into the distance told him the whaleboat had started to increase its lead and pull away, but that would last only as long as the oarsmen's strength held out. They would be very tired by now and their desperation-fueled burst of speed could not last much longer. It was only because they had spent much of the summer sitting on those same benches behind those same oars, working hard and staying fit, that they had the stamina to keep ahead of their enemies so far.

Back to the task in hand he judged the wind carefully and edged the cutter in from slightly behind the big double canoe, staying just out of spear-throwing range until he drew level with the big-bellied sail. He wedged the tiller between his knees and emptied both muskets one after the other into the sail where he judged the wind pressure was greatest. Small pieces of the weft flicked away from the sail and spun off downwind as the dozen or so small balls chewed their way through its soft belly.

The dog, his feet wide spread for balance, gave a few loud barks to show that he was ready to join the fight if Lafe would just take him in close enough for him to do his bit. A head and an arm appeared above the gunwale of the canoe and several spears splashed into the water just short of the cutter's side as Lafe widened the distance between the two vessels again. This time he reloaded both muskets with good solid ball, confident he had the enemy's measure. He had seen that the sailing canoe with its big rig was limited to sailing downwind, as it risked turning over in anything less than a light breeze at any other angle, so he brought the little cutter in as close as he dared. Then as fast as he could load and fire his muskets he poured shot after shot into the protruding belly of the sail until it looked like a tattered basket. The finely-woven flax fibres, cut by the musket balls, began to unravel and the wind did the rest. The speed of the big canoe slowed to a crawl.

Lafe eased his own sails and waited for the next move, which wasn't long coming. Someone on the other vessel slashed the rigging holding the two masts up and the whole lot, sail, masts and all, disappeared over the side into the sea. Lafe watched in awe as forty paddlers jumped into view from where they had hidden from the gunfire and reversed their positions until they faced the way they had come. Then they churned the water into a foam as they dug deeply, heading back in the direction they had come from. Their ship was like a wounded beast, Lafe thought, more dangerous than ever and ready to fall on anything that crossed its path. Once more he set a course out to the open sea and noted the still freshening wind with hope.

'As long as we hold the wind, we can run down on them at any time and let them have another charge from the muskets,' he shouted to Matai, hoping to stir some spark of hope in him. 'We will shadow them until I am sure they will not change their minds and take up the chase again.'

He fervently hoped that these warriors he was up against would know they were still being watched, and that now they knew the quality of his weapons the tribe might decide to stay at home in future. One thing he would not do, he resolved, was to let them burn all the hard work of the summer months. To lose the cache of skins at the stone hut was bad enough; to lose any more would mean all their efforts had been for nothing.

Now the immediate crisis was over he had time to draw breath and he sat down heavily, his body shaking with the reaction to the fight, and re-loaded the muskets while he thought about his other problem, Matai, who was huddled in the corner of the transom wrapped in a dirty piece of canvas. As Lafe watched, the young Maori's head lolled back and forth with the motion of the boat and his eyes appeared to focus on nothing, in this world at least. Lafe was shocked at the sudden deterioration in his condition and for a moment thought his friend was already dead.

In the last few days so much had happened that he had not been too aware of problems close to home, and Matai had simply been a burden and a nuisance. Now he thought that perhaps the man had picked up some disease from the whalers, some minor complaint for Europeans that affected Maori badly. Certainly there had been no sickness to mention on the voyage out or in the summer sealing camps, but Lafe had heard that Maori were very prone to catching new diseases and often fell to common colds, measles and such like. There was no doubt now that Matai was a very sick man, he realized. He might even die in the next couple of days without good care, and a good wetting from the dark rain clouds moving in from the sea could be the end of him.

Reluctantly he tacked again, letting the boom sweep across the boat with a flourish that shook the teeth in his head, and headed back toward the shore which was now some distance away. Urgently he began to search for a secluded creek or lagoon that would hide the boat and themselves and where he could set up camp before the storm arrived. The darkening sky promised that the storm would be a good one. Already the sea was starting to get up and unless Lafe found shelter in a creek or river soon, landing would be a problem as the rollers showed a lot of white where they broke along the open beaches.

Wind was piling the breakers up on the sandy beach of Big Bay as he searched for a river he remembered close by. He found what he was looking for just south of the beach and for a moment he wished that he hadn't. The large tidal stream was running out, the river a mass of white water pouring over a treacherous-looking bar. It was going to be an evil entrance to run, but he had little choice now. He chose a big wave and shot the cutter towards what he hoped was a gap in the bar, riding the wave all the way in with as much sail as the little boat could bear. If he lost this wave the next one would either fill the boat or lift the stern and she would broach and roll, tipping her passengers into the water where they would have little hope of surviving the breakers.

It was a wild ride. With the sea roaring in their ears they slipped past a bunch of scattered rocks and tree trunks whose shattered limbs protruded from a mass of foam that hid them from view until the cutter was safely past. It would have done me no good to have seen them earlier, Lafe thought with a shudder as he glanced sideways. The wave had control now and they were in its power, but it expended its energy quickly against the more docile outgoing current of the river, and soon the boat was released into quieter waters.

When he had a chance to catch his breath and look around he saw a number of large snags that would be a problem at low tide, but right now there was sufficient depth over them not to worry the little *Aurora*. He shortened sail and the cutter nosed her way into a tidal river maybe a hundred yards wide or maybe more. It wound inland along the bottom of a U-shaped valley with low scrub on both sides rising to solid forest and the high peaks of some distant range at its head. A spit of very white sand lay on one side of the river above the reach of the waves, as if the wind had carried it inland from the beach and left it shaped like a sculptured wave of sea.

This was a river unlike any Lafe had seen on this southwestern coast. The other rivers whose lives began high in these mountains mostly crashed and roared their way right to the ocean waves as if they did not have a second to spare in their rush to mix their snow melt with salt.

'A different breed of river,' Lafe told his non-comprehending shipmates. It was good to hear his own voice after the wind and the wild ride through the surf, and he earned an encouraging tail wag from Salem at the bow. 'This one ambles its way down to the sea in a leisurely fashion and makes the most of just being a river. It's in no hurry to lose its identity and change its ways.'

There was the music of ducks in the air. The muddy flats uncovered by the tide held uncountable flocks that took to their wings as the cutter bore down on them, only to land again around the next bend. Rows of shags dried their wings on dead branches, and several white herons stood in the still backwaters and watched the little boat pass. The surface of the water was ruffled now by the gusts of wind coming in from the sea, and Lafe scanned both banks for a suitable place to build a hut. He sailed on around sweeping curves and was well inland, away from any prying eyes that might be looking for them, before he was satisfied he had found the right place. He set up their camp next to a small stream overhung with thick forest that trailed its moss nearly to the water's edge, and dragged the cutter up into the stream easing her mast as it passed through the trees. He was soon satisfied he had hidden her well, and Salem showed no sign of anxiety as he ranged around the area. The scrub on the riverbanks had given way to pure forest now, away from the salt air that only a few scrubby plants could tolerate.

Lafe soon had Matai laid out on a fern bed next to a small fire built among the rocks, but his friend lay unseeing, uncaring. Driftwood and the sails from the cutter were enough to build a hasty but comfortable little hut that would shelter them from the storm and allow a fire to be built inside for the cold nights ahead. After trying unsuccessfully to speak with Matai and warn him that he was leaving for a while, Lafe took the musket, called Salem to his side and went upstream to stalk a flock of ducks he could hear chortling and quacking upstream. By lying flat on the bank and firing when the ducks swam into a line he got four with one charge of powder and with the next he got a couple of woodhens that came out on the river bank to see what all the noise was about.

With Salem's help he retrieved his game, and with the provisions he had on the cutter he figured they had enough food to last a fortnight. He did not want to risk firing the musket again for fear of attracting unwelcome attention but had thought the risk worth it to secure a little fresh food for his shipmate. The wind had got up quite strongly now and would have masked the sound of the two shots, and hopefully the coming storm would have sent anyone else in the area looking for cover.

A great duck soup was set bubbling in a pot slung over the fire and then he finally had time to attend to his patient. He stripped Matai of his foul clothing, washed him thoroughly from head to toe and wrapped him in a couple of warm blankets, but to his disappointment the Maori took only a few sips of the duck broth and refused any more, turning his head to the wall and appearing to drift off to sleep again.

Lafe sat looking at him and wondered again what ailed the man, who had suddenly gone off his food about three weeks earlier. He had spoken a little when pressed but did not give any clues as to what was wrong with him. It was about the time the first Maori fireplaces had been found, Lafe remembered, and it was a noticeable event because up until that time his nickname was The Gannet and the whole crew knew that nobody enjoyed food more. All the sailors were of the same opinion as Lafe at the time, that the young Maori was just frightened. It would soon pass, they believed, and he would be back laughing and eating as much as before.

Lafe could sense the danger in trying to hide away here in this mountain valley, and already he found creeping up on him a feeling of being alone. The last he had seen of the whaleboat and its crew was away on the horizon to the south, where they were still rowing strongly and showing no signs of looking to land.

Salem crept close and nuzzled at his hand and Lafe stroked him absently, his thoughts turning back to his patient. The careful examination he had made while he was washing Matai left him even more baffled. Except for the whites of his eyes being a muddy yellow colour, his breath smelling of death and his ribs showing, there was nothing obviously wrong with him. No pox, no fever, no congestion of the lungs, nothing in Lafe's experience of the normal complaints found on board a whaling ship. However he had heard stories from the slave ships out of Africa, stories of slaves who just decided they were going to die. Nothing would change their minds and they simply lay down and died.

There were other stories from the native world, of voodoos and curses that killed at a distance as surely as musket balls. Primitive races, Lafe knew, were prone to more elementary fears than his own people, and over the last few months he had learned a lot about tapu and about the host of gods in both the upper and lower order that plagued the world of the Maori. Spirits inhabited most of the known things on earth, it seemed, and they all needed to be placated in different ways to avoid the most horrible punishments that were sure to follow the slightest mistake or the breaking of these laws. Lafe decided he would question Matai when he woke in the morning. Perhaps there was a ceremony or ritual that could be performed to placate the spirits and make things right again.

He lay on his back on the soft fern mattress he had plucked from the forest, covered himself with a blanket and listened to the building storm outside, thankful it had given him grace to build such a snug cabin. He thought through the long day that had passed. It had been one of those days when but for the luck of the devil none of them would have lived to tell the tale. Why had he turned back to attack the canoe when all his instincts told him to run for his life? He still did not really know where that courage had come from but thought the answer lay in the fact that he was a ship's officer on the *Northern Lights*. He was Olva's officer and his father's son, the whalers were his men and their lives were his responsibility.

He admitted to himself that under his skin he didn't feel very brave. If the wind had not come to his aid the canoe would easily have run down the little cutter, finished off her crew, and still caught the whaleboat. He, Matai and the dog would have been dead.

He chuckled as he thought about Salem. Even the dog had put up a good show that day. All the Maori they had met on their travels had been frightened of him at first sight and his barking at the warriors in the canoe had certainly added to the impact of the little cutter's bold attack. Lafe had heard Matai call Salem 'War Dog,'

'And even now, war dog, you guard him while he sleeps,' Lafe whispered sadly across the tiny hut, and the big black dog thumped his tail and snuffled closer to the still, sick figure.

Lafe saw again in his mind the rows of tattooed figures that had risen in the canoe to meet him when he closed in on them the first time, unaware that he brought a new type of warfare to this land where battles had always been fought hand to hand and eyeball to eyeball.

123

I am pleased I did not have to kill them, Lafe thought, even though they would have killed us. For a space of time he had debated whether to pick off the crew one at a time or fire at their sail instead, and he was pleased with his judgement. A few warriors would be picking birdshot out of their hides for days to come but they would soon recover. He chuckled quietly and stretched to ease his tired muscles. All in all he was glad the day was over, and could only hope the whaleboat was by now safe in some hidden cove.

Now it was totally dark and he listened to the whistle of the ducks' wings as they lost height, the hiss as they slid into the river ahead of the coming storm, and the sighing of the wind in the tops of the trees that sheltered his camp hidden away in a little hollow in the riverbank. Finally the rain came, first softly and then in torrents drumming on the sail that sheltered them.

'Tomorrow will be a day when even the birds will be walking,' he whispered to the dog before sleep claimed him.

Before daylight he woke again. The rain was still heavy and with nothing else to do he began to review his plans. The whaleboat should be safe from any raids during the storm but the sealing crew would not be back for them, he knew that. He had told them whatever happened they were to head for the safety of Dusky Sound and prepare for any attack that might come that way. If Olva found there was no one to meet him at The Cascades, the plan was that he would make his way to Dusky Sound and hopefully at least someone would be there waiting for the ship. Then the *Northern Lights* would come up the coast looking for Lafe and Matai, and all would be well again.

But the *Northern Lights* would not close in on the coast in a storm like this. Olva would stay well out to sea away from the lee shore until the next weather change came through.

'You and I, dog,' Lafe told Salem. 'It's up to us to keep a watch for the ship as soon as the storm has blown itself out.' The big dog had sensed that he was awake, and at the sound of Lafe's voice he crept across from Matai's bed to offer a little company. Lafe was glad of the warmth and dozed again.

That morning Matai seemed to have a need to talk but Lafe missed some of the meaning because he was not quite good enough with the Maori language yet. Sometimes his patient was lucid, sometimes not, but he had the desire to speak of many things; his childhood, his tribe and his ancestors. He spoke of Tane, god of all green and growing things, of Tangaroa, god of the sea and fishes, and of the great Tu, god of man and of war. These were gods that Lafe knew about from the talk of the two Maori on the ship, and he had already asked many questions of Jimmy from Otaakou.

Matai had stuck very rigidly to his promise to his father, the chief Kaitoke, that he would teach Lafe to speak the proper tongue, and so the young whaler had learned much, but now he wished he had been more attentive in those eight months since Matai joined the ship for now he had no interpreter and no other help to understand what was being told to him.

Matai spoke sometimes with the voice of a poet, at other times in the voice of the chief that he might well be if he ever returned to his tribe. There were things he thought important for Lafe to know, things he made him repeat until he was sure what he had said was understood and would be remembered. Thus Matai in his own way added his story to the oral traditions of his own tribe. Generations yet unborn would tell of this chief's son who went whaling and sealing on a ship far to the south and died in a strange place that nobody even knew the name of, except that it was near Murihiku, The Tail Of The Fish. Lafe realised that Matai was writing his own book, and he was the bearer of the story.

'You are my brother now,' Matai said. 'You will return to Whangaroa and take my place in the tribe.' He rested for a long while, and Lafe thought he slept, but then his eyes opened again and he turned to Lafe with a weak smile.

'I have been thinking hard to find the good words and now I have them,' he said. 'These are the words you will say to me when it is the right time.

'They are not sad words. They are words used when two people are parting for a time only,' he said earnestly, willing Lafe to understand.

125

'It will be good to hear them said in the Maori tongue, and you have time to learn them.'

He gripped Lafe's hand and whispered, 'Haere ra, e tama e. Mou te tai ata, Moku te tai po.'

'They are good words, Matai, and I will learn them,' Lafe promised. 'Farewell, my friend. The morning tide is for you, the evening tide will be for me.'

Matai smiled again, and his expression was sad and gentle. 'What more could I want than my friend the dog and my brother from across the sea to attend to me in a warm hut?' he whispered. 'There is much to eat, though I don't have such an appetite as I used to.'

'Ka pai te kuri. Good dog.' He trailed his fingers through Salem's thick coat and closed his eyes again.

Lafe watched him drift off to sleep, hoping that he had not just heard his friend's final farewell, but Matai woke several times during the night and summoned Lafe to his side each time. He seemed to have an urgent need to talk again.

'You have much to learn of our language and customs yet,' he told Lafe. 'I don't think my father understood what a slow person you are. I hope you carry on and learn much more before you meet him again, I don't want him to think I did not try hard enough.'

The next time he woke his mind was on something else. 'Do you know what I would like to eat? Kumara. That is my favourite food. Never mind the white man's potato, the kumara is better for Maori.

'If I cannot have kumara, I would like eel instead, I am very fond of eel. Tomorrow I will instruct you on the best way to catch one,' he said in a languid way.

All that day and night the wind thrashed through the tall trees that towered above the camp. The massive trees groaned and cracked under the strain, sometimes losing branches, and large, dead falls crashed into the soft ground near where the two men and the dog lay protected only by their canvas roof. Lafe cursed the fact that he had built his camp in such a dangerous spot. It was the need to hide from the big canoe that had caused him to risk having their heads stove in by falling pieces of timber, but it would be an even wilder night at sea, and for all the risks

126

they now ran he was thankful for the river and its many other blessings. While the storm raged they were safe from their enemies, at least.

On the third day he finally emerged from the hut to find the rain had eased, but the sky was patchy and the wind still in the northwest and he knew the storm wasn't finished yet. Soon it would swing to the south, growing colder and bringing near-tropical downpours before it finished.

He was going after an eel, but until Matai explained the ritual that he had to go through, he had no idea they were such finicky creatures. He wasn't allowed to wash his hands in the river, nor could his lips touch the water in which the eel was to be caught. When he wanted a drink he must use two cups, one to dip the water out of the river and the other to drink from. Otherwise, Matai told him, the eel would know that someone in the vicinity meant him no good and he would slither away to the deepest part of the river and hide.

Lafe made up a line as instructed, took the leftover leg of a duck for bait and set off, his musket carried at the trail with a strip of canvas wrapped carefully around the lock to keep the moisture out of the priming. Calling the dog in close he headed upstream, intent on exploring toward the head of the valley as well as fishing for Matai's eel.

There was something about the river and the valley beyond that did not fit right. Ever since he had crossed the river bar, he had felt that way about the place. He battled his way upstream, leaving the bank to wade around dead falls and at times crossing patches of swamp up to his knees. He had covered perhaps a mile when he realized that the valley was opening up in front of him. Through the larger trees ahead he caught a glimpse of a large body of water, far too large to be a river, and beyond that some very tall mountains. When he stepped through a screen of bushes he realized what had made the valley feel so different from all the rest on the coast.

A beautiful mountain lake lay hidden in the forest. Its clear waters were surrounded by high mountains on all sides except for its river, where the camp was hidden, and the outlet to the sea, and as Lafe stepped from a gloomy swamp into the huge vista of still water and beaches of sand the contrast stunned his senses. The surface waters were touched by the wind in places, but elsewhere it was sheltered and calm.

127

The mountains girdling the lake, whose tops now carried early winter snow, appeared to plunge so steeply downwards that they disappeared into the still water itself. From the shingle beach at his feet the lake ran, Lafe guessed, ten miles or more up toward the head of the valley. It was quite narrow for its length, maybe a mile and a half at its widest point, and a quick check of the sun confirmed that it ran roughly north and south. It was a great jewel of a lake, hiding away from the eyes of man. He stayed for many minutes drinking in the scenery, his eyes moving from the lake to the snow covered tops and back again. Perhaps a glacier had carved the lake out of bedrock, he thought.

This valley had the shape of the fiords further south, but it was different in its own special way. It could be that this glacier's journey to the sea had been interrupted by some great event in the past and it hadn't made it all the way. He tasted the water and found it fresh and quite drinkable with just a hint of brackishness from the sea.

While he was exploring he came across an old trail that snaked its way just above the lake's edge then up and over the ridges. It appeared to come up from downriver past his camp and lead up toward the head of the valley, and from it Lafe deduced that the lake and the hinterland beyond it was of some importance to Maori. There was no sign of recent use but just being on the man-made track made the hairs on the back of Lafe's neck stand up like the ruff on a dog's back. He knew he was no longer in a wilderness but in known territory, where men had come and gone and would come again.

The lake had suddenly lost its beauty for him and he headed back towards Matai, stopping to cast his duck-baited hook into a deep hole near the riverbank. In a few minutes Matai's eel lay flapping on the bank beside him and he wrapped the still-wriggling fish in fern leaves and carried on, following the Maori track until he was above his own camp. There he cached the eel and followed the trail further in the direction of the sea. It snaked its way through the tall trees and dropped down to a sunny, dry clearing in the lower scrub of the riverbank not far from the open beach, and from where he crouched on the edge of the forest he could just make out four or five small grass huts dotted around the edges of the scrub, their openings facing into a clearing.

128

He signalled Salem with a warning hand to be quiet and still. His first instinct was to run back to his camp, push his cutter out into the river immediately and take his chances with the sea. He wanted above all to flee for the safety of Dusky Sound, but he didn't need to see the river bar, the roar of the surf told him he would not get the cutter out of the river until the sea dropped. And that could still be a week away.

After watching the huts with his musket cocked and ready for a few minutes, Lafe sidled down through the scrub like an Indian for a closer look. He had not seen either the huts or the clearing the previous afternoon because of the screen of bullrushes on the rivers edge. He listened carefully with his ear against the rear wall of one hut before he crawled through the low entrance at the front. Each of the little huts would sleep about six people, he estimated, and they had been used within the last month. A formidable number to meet, according to the piles of refuse scattered around the clearing. Shellfish, ducks and fish bones. At least there was no sign of human bones among them, he saw with relief, remembering the shipmate who had been dragged away a few days before.

Heading back to camp he racked his brain for an escape plan, but knew that until the sea dropped he was effectively bottled up inside the valley.

Matai was no better. Lafe cooked the eel according to instructions but his patient only nibbled a little before sinking back into his bed and declaring, 'Ka pai, it is good. A fine fish.' Lafe tried to entertain him by describing the cunningness of the eel and the tricks he had been forced to perform before it allowed itself to be captured, and Matai smiled and nodded, pleased with the story. But Lafe did not tell him of the huts downstream for fear the shock might kill him outright.

He kept the worry from his face with an effort and told Matai of the plans he had to sail to Dusky Sound when the weather turned fine and of the wonderful lake he had discovered just a little way beyond their camp. He hid his misgivings well, but knew that even having a fire going in their little hut was risky now although it was a risk that had to be accepted. The camp would soon become cold and clammy without it and his patient already felt cold most of the time.

During the night a viciously cold wind blew up from the south, bringing with it the first real bite of the winter to come. All through the next day and the night that followed, rain hissed through the tree canopy onto the canvas roof of the cabin and Lafe kept the fire going night and day. Now he was forced to accept the fact that Matai was dying and had only hours left to him in this world. He hung on to life with barely a fingernail grip through the night, and when dawn broke on a new and silent day he barely breathed.

Some time during the night the wind had dropped and the rain had ceased, and Lafe had dropped into a dreamless sleep that lasted several hours. He woke with a start, guiltily checked the fire and realized it was out and his patient appeared cold in the early dawn light in spite of the extra blanket Lafe had wrapped around him from his own meagre supply. Before he lit a new fire he thought it wise to scout the area in case anyone was on the move, and to catch some food before they both starved to death.

He grabbed his musket and eel line, whistled the dog and headed for the lake, his breath like steam in the cold morning air. He did not like leaving Matai in the state he was in but he needed to find a quick supply of food then get a fire going and dry the camp out before they both died of pneumonia.

'You poor dog, your ribs are showing,' he told Salem, and the Labrador wagged his tail and managed to look solemn. Since they had stopped killing seals his food supply had been very meagre but Lafe did not dare let him stray from the camp to hunt for himself.

They broke out onto the lake edge and into a new world. Heavy snow had fallen during the preceding night and it now covered the mountains down nearly to the water's edge. The lake was smooth and mirrored the deep blue of the sky in the bright sunshine that as yet had no warmth in it. Again Lafe was astounded at the way these lakes and fiords captured the perfect reflections of their own mountains, laying them out like an artist's canvas at his feet. But if a good artist painted such a scene he would go mad trying to decide which way up the canvas should hang on his wall. Individual rocks jutting out from the white peaks thousands of feet above the lake, stark, black, and too steep to hold snow, were picked out in absolute perfection on the lake's still surface.

Then a movement far down the lake caught his eye and a moment later the reflections were shivered by three large canoes which had just pulled out of a little bay and were shaping their course for the river mouth near where he stood. Lafe stepped hurriedly back behind a screen of bushes, his hand on Salem's head in warning, his heart threatening to leap from his chest in sheer terror. For a moment he considered running for the cutter, launching it and heading for the sea, but he quickly realized there wasn't even enough breeze to carry him out of the river, even if he had the time to seize the sail from on top of the hut and fix it to the mast.

Frantically he reviewed and just as quickly discarded all the courses of action he could take. He could abandon Matai and set off across the mountains for Dusky, but with the winter snows now down to low levels he knew that was an impossible task to set himself. A great number of fiords penetrated far inland between where he stood and Dusky Sound and he had no way of crossing them, even if he could find his way across the ranges and through the forests that divided them.

To the north there was nothing but danger; unfriendly tribes all the way up to Murderers' Bay. Inland. The high mountain passes that might have led him to the country of the friendly tribes of Otaakou were now closed by snow and he would die of exposure if he climbed.

The canoes came on at great speed, eating up the distance to the river mouth where he stood. They were faster than he could bear to calculate and he strained his eyes to see if they had women and children on board. If they did, he still had a chance. If they don't, it is a war party and I will run and take my chances in the forest, he promised himself. He remembered Jimmy's warning about war parties, or ope as they were called.

'He maroro kokoti ihu waka,' the guide had told him. 'The flying fish that cuts across the bow of the canoe.' Apparently it was an inflexible rule that anyone caught by an ope was killed and eaten. Lafe was shocked to learn that no one was spared whether they were friend or foe, and sometimes even brothers and sisters of the warriors in the ope were killed. But Jimmy had quite cheerfully told Lafe that such actions were necessary and therefore acceptable.

'That is the way it has always been' he said. 'You can't change the rules while the game is in progress.'

But if it was not a war party, there were other choices. In the condition he was in, Matai would die if he was moved now and Lafe couldn't bring himself to abandon a good shipmate to die alone on this strange coast, near a lake with no name. He was in many ways responsible for Matai being there so far from his home. Kaitoke himself had placed his son on board the *Northern Lights* to ensure that Lafe would return to Whangaroa a well educated young man, suitable to marry one of his granddaughters.

When Lafe was sure he could pick out several women amongst the paddlers on the canoes he trotted back down the trail to his camp, his mind churning. Matai appeared even weaker than an hour before, he was on his last legs and sadly Lafe realized that his friend would die that day. A faint death rattle had already begun deep in his chest and his breath fluttered in his throat like the wings of a moth. Even Salem seemed aware that Matai was dying and crept under his blankets to stretch out next to him and offer what comfort he could.

A feeling of immense sadness settled its load on Lafe's shoulders as he realized that he alone would have to face the dangers that were rapidly bearing down on the camp. He strained his ears to hear the canoes when they passed down the river and struggled to think of a good way to bring about a peaceful meeting between them. An unexpected face-to-face meeting in the forest could only lead to violence where otherwise cooler heads might still prevail. Both his muskets were loaded with buckshot and he knew that he would kill many Maori if it came to a fight, but that was exactly what he hoped to avoid. In the end he would be killed too and that would accomplish nothing.

He watched the dog closely, knowing he would hear the canoes first, and when he saw Salem's ears prick and his hackles started to rise he gave him a good rap on the head with his knuckles to warn him to keep silent. Lafe dearly wished that the canoes would just keep going but he knew they would not head out to sea that day, no one would, not for two or three days yet. In his mind's eye he saw them heading for the little grass huts he had discovered not far down the river, their intentions clearly to camp there for a few days.

Lafe had made up his mind now and knew what he must do. He struck a match to the pile of brush and wood he had kept dry in the hut during the storm, and once the flames had a good hold he dumped an armful of green rimu branches on top of them. Soon a greasy column of smoke filtered through the trees and rose into the still air in a signal that could be seen for miles around. It said here was somebody who wanted to be found.

Lafe knew what would happen next. The warriors would creep in close and surround the hut, and they would quickly gain confidence once they saw that no great numbers of enemy were lying in ambush for them. Then it would be up to him to make the next move before they rushed the cabin. A certain amount of bluff, he decided, might just win the day.

With shaking hands he selected and donned his best clothes, his coat with brass buttons and a scarlet neck cloth, and around his waist he strapped his knife belt, tomahawk and powder horn.

'A quick face wash and a comb through my hair and I am ready for my own funeral, if need be,' Lafe told Salem lightly. He waited quietly inside watching the dog. An hour passed and then Salem's hackles started to rise. He had heard or smelled the enemy as they crept up on the camp. Lafe picked up his musket and stepped quickly out of the hut before the fear that threatened to take control of his muscles rendered him powerless to do so. He stood with his weapon across the crook of his arm, searching the shadows with his eyes until he located them.

Thirty paces away, just off the trail near a large beech tree, stood six tattooed warriors, poised in limbo between fight and flight. They had been watching the entrance to the makeshift shelter and he had startled them with his sudden appearance. The dog advanced stiff-legged toward them with his bristles erect, growling deep in his throat, and then barked twice, the noise shockingly loud in the quiet air as it echoed two or three times from the valley walls. Lafe spoke abruptly and Salem turned and stalked back to him, his ruff erect like a wolf's, and took up a position at his leg. In the silence following the echoes of Salem's defiant bark the two sides stared at each other. Lafe felt the tension and could see his visitors were on the knife-edge of shock, unnerved by the dog as other Maori had been.

'Haere mai, haere mai, haere mai,' he intoned in the best modulated voice he could manage. 'He Pakepakeha ahau.'

The silence weighed heavily in the morning stillness. A bellbird dropped its three opening notes into the silence where they echoed and spread like ripples on water. Still no one moved, and there was no answer.

Ever since he had read of Cook's successful meeting with a tribe in Dusky Sound twenty-three years before, Lafe had contemplated such a scene, and much thought had gone into choosing the words he had just spoken.

'Greetings, greetings, greetings,' he told them. 'I am Pakepakeha, an imaginary being with white skin.'

Except for those few Maori who had contact with white men it was generally believed that such a race existed, a belief that may have started when the Dutchman Abel Tasman made his first attempt to land at Murderers' Bay. When Cook sailed around the coast some years later the word of his coming travelled faster than his ship. 'The Pakepakeha have come,' runners told the people. The Lookers-On off the Kaikoura coast had noted that when the sailors rowed their boats it was with their backs to the direction of travel and it was accepted then that they were in fact Pakepakeha, white goblins with eyes in the backs of their heads.

Now Lafe declared himself a white goblin and stood for what seemed an eternity staring impassively at the warriors, who stood without movement as if carved in stone and stared back at him. Their tattooed faces and shoulders above their flax cloaks blended well with the shadows cast by the branches overhead. Careful not to make any sudden movements, Lafe stood the musket against the side of the hut then sent the dog inside to slump down next to Matai. Then, holding his hands wide from his body to show he was unarmed, he advanced a few hesitant steps and stopped to wait for a response.

One of the men stepped forward, with a high-stepping gait that reminded Lafe of the movements of a heron. He advanced to meet the young sailor until they stood no more than three feet apart in the middle of the clearing.

Lafe found himself looking into the face of a man he guessed to be around thirty-five years of age. Beyond the black tattoos that scarred the man's face from forehead to chin he thought he could sense a degree of kindness and humour, but overlaying all that was apprehension and fear. This was the chief, Lafe decided, who had to show his courage before the others. It was his duty, just as it was the duty of a ship's officer to show bravery in front of a whale, but it had cost him dearly to walk that few yards to stand face to face with the white stranger.

Lafe was in a fine pickle of fear himself but he reached forward, laid his hands on the chief's shoulders and bent his head, touching his nose to the Maori's nose in the formal ritual of greeting. Then he turned and strode back to the hut, leaving them to follow if they wished.
He called Salem and ruffled his coat reassuringly, and soon the dog was in a friendlier mood and ready to greet the visitors.

The chief came closer, screwing up his courage as he advanced toward the dog, his eyes wide open with wonder. Salem indicated that he was actually very good friends with the whole human race and he was sorry for the fuss he had made earlier, and he sat quietly and warily near his master to watch proceedings. When he was beckoned to enter the hut the chief obeyed smartly enough until he saw Matai, whom he mistook for a dead body, and backed rapidly outside again. Lafe tried to find the right words to ask for help for his dying friend, but the chief had found the axe and was examining it with all the delight of having discovered the crown jewels. A knife that Lafe produced created as much interest again as the chief tested its keen edge and discussed its usefulness with the others. But when he was offered the knife as a gift he waved it away, indicating it should stay with its owner.

Politely but firmly the chief indicated that there was no need for such a gift, as he of course owned the Pakepakeha now and everything that went with him. Or so Lafe understood his meaning, and so he expected it to be. He returned to his patient who had been sadly neglected for most of the morning, and found that Matai was alive still but deeply unconscious.

He cleaned his friend's face with a cloth and did what little he could for him in his last hours on earth. He heard his visitors depart, and when he stepped outside again he was in time to see his cutter being floated out of the creek and taken down stream to join the canoes.

'Well,' he muttered quietly to Salem, 'I am truly a prisoner now.' But with the optimism of youth he did not yet despair. He was alive and did not appear to be in any great danger of losing his life in the near future, and there was always the chance of escape as long as he remained alive.

An hour after noon, according to the sun, a party arrived to move Lafe, Matai and all their belongings down to the lower camp. Matai was lowered carefully into a canoe by four women who, it seemed, were to take care of him now, and the remains of the old hut were burned. Lafe was escorted down to the clearing with Salem at his heels and found himself the object of everyone's attention.

This was not a true tribal family group, he noticed. There were no old people and no young children and he suspected that he had made contact with a group of hunter-gatherers. Somewhere, possibly to the north, the rest of the tribe must have their village. The canoes lay upturned on the solid ground near the river, ready to be launched and he noted that they were big solid single-hulled coastal canoes that showed good workmanship.

The four women who had been detailed to tend the patient stayed near Matai and quickly threw up a little grass hut to cover him, but the other women retired to their own huts and Lafe could feel their eyes watching him from the darkened interiors. Only the chief walked next to him and the dog as they circled the clearing, the rest of the warriors bringing up the rear guard. It was a sort of victory parade, Lafe understood. It was obviously a great feat to capture a Pakepakeha, and although there was no violence nor threats offered to his person there was no doubt that he was the chief's prisoner. He noted that there was a second new grass hut being built at the edge of the clearing away from the rest. One was for Matai and the other, it was indicated, was for him. Meanwhile all his worldly goods had been carried down from the cabin and were laid out on a flax mat before the warriors who sat gravely and contemplated the different treasures.

The chief pointed to each object in turn and Lafe was required to demonstrate its use, a performance accompanied by loud grunts of wonder or approval from his audience. Anything of steel or metal was exclaimed over and passed from one set of hands to the other and it was obvious that they valued metals above all else.

His muskets were something else. So far no one had ventured near the two of them leaning against the hut wall and Lafe wondered who had been ordered to carry them to the clearing. It was a good thing that they were kept aside, and he tried to convey the message that they were to be touched only by his own hands. He was acutely aware that they were both still charged and primed and if one was accidentally discharged someone could be killed. Then his own life expectancy would be brief.

He suspected that although these tribesmen had never seen a musket before they might have been made aware of them by others who had seen them in action. He went over and picked one up as carefully as he could, signalling to the chief his intention of firing it. The chief looked decidedly nervous about the whole business but he did not refuse, and Lafe guessed he did not want to lose face with the tribe by appearing to be frightened by anything the Pakepakeha did.

Lafe picked a gourd twice as big as a man's head, filled it with water and set it on a rock on the bank above the river. Waiting until the drama had built up a little, he looked around and saw that all the women had vanished inside their huts again and the warriors stood well away near the edge of the clearing. He grinned at the chief who stood bravely by his side, though Lafe could tell by his expression that he would rather be elsewhere.

He took his time sighting the musket, drawing the moment out until he knew everyone in the audience was holding their breath, and then he stroked the trigger. Through the smoke he saw the gourd explode and send a sheet of water flying up into the air, while out of the corner of his eye he saw the chief's feet leave the ground. Thousands of ducks, shags and other birds rose from the waters of the river and lake and fled out over the sea on whistling wings while the echoes of the shot were flung

137

back again and again from the bluffs at the end of the lake.

For a second or two after the explosion the chief blew through his nose like an angry bull as he stood rooted to the spot, slowly recovering from the shock.

'You are a wicked Goblin!' he told Lafe. His voice was pitched high with surprise and shock. But when he looked around he was more pleased with himself than ever as he saw his shamefaced warriors creeping out from where they had taken cover in the scrub.

'Such fine, brave warriors!' he chided them. Stalking over to the riverbank he picked up the smashed gourd and puzzled over just how it had been killed. He had not seen what hit it and in his experience such a noise, though terrifying, could not kill alone.

Lafe was given some food and realized he was badly in need of it, as he had not eaten much over the last two stormy days when the food in the camp had run short. But while he was eating he saw the four women leave the hut where Matai had been taken, their voices raised in a soft keening, and he knew then without needing to be told that the end had come for Matai. When all was quiet and everyone had gathered in the clearing he spoke the words his friend had taught him.

'Haere ra e tama e!
Mou te tai ata,
Moku te tai po.
Farewell, friend!
The morning tide is for you,
The evening tide is for me. Aueee!'
And his voice broke as the people wept with him for Matai.

Chapter 8

Matai was buried that day, with all the honours due to his rank, in the dunes above the sea. In the clearing by the river the high-pitched keening of the women blended with the distant throb of the sea in a final farewell as the sand was tramped firmly on his grave.

'It is a good place, with the quiet river on one side and the wild sea on the other,' the chief told Lafe and he agreed, knowing that according to Matai's own beliefs his spirit had long since fled his body and flown to the north to begin its departure into the underworld.

It was a sad day for Lafe, and when the time came to sweep the white sand over the face of his young friend it was a hard thing to do. They had shared many adventures in the eight months they had travelled together, first on the ship and then on land and in the cutter, exploring new places. But more than that, Matai had tried to share his language and his way of life and had done his best to teach Lafe the stories and beliefs of his tribe. Now with his death and the burning of their hut the past was over, and Lafe had to face the future with what little knowledge of the Maori people he had been given.

With Matai dead and buried it occurred to him to wonder what the future now had in store. A lot had changed since he had awoken in his driftwood hut that morning. I am a prisoner yet not quite a prisoner, he decided. Although his movements were not restricted he noticed that if he left the camp several warriors would get to their feet and find an errand that took them in the same direction. The cutter had been hauled from the water and rested next to the chief's hut, where the men spent a lot of time fingering the metal fittings and wondering at the workmanship of the overlapped planking on the hull, and Lafe was afraid that the chief might have it stripped, in his greed for iron fittings before he had a chance to demonstrate how useful the little boat was.

He knew he would feel the loss of the *Aurora* deeply if that happened; not only had he helped to build her but she was also a link to his home and family. Her wonderful clean lines still reminded him of the oyster boats that worked Chesapeake Bay, but those memories were rapidly fading away into the dim past. More importantly, this little boat still represented his only hope of escape back to his own people if the opportunity ever presented itself. At all costs he must try to preserve her, Lafe decided.

The man who held Lafe's life in his hands was Tama, the paramount chief of the tribe. Lafe soon established that the rest of his people lived to the north and this party had been far up the valley at another lake gathering eels. There were many flax kits of eels, dried and smoked, stored in a small shelter and more were drying on wooden racks in the sunshine. Lafe found out a great deal that first day by listening and asking careful questions, but he did not understand many of the answers he was given. He would have to be particularly careful not to make them think they had captured a particularly stupid goblin, he decided.

He suspected that when the sea calmed again his captors would travel north to their main village and join the rest of the tribe, taking him with them. A certain restlessness about the group told him they would move again soon. He did not want to go north but he was aware he had little choice in the matter.

The *Northern Lights* was due any day now and he hoped more than anything in the world that she would hove into view and rescue him, but he had to accept that the ferocity of the storm just passed might have pushed her a hundred or more miles to the south of where he now stood. She would have had little choice but to run before the storm with bare poles wherever the northwesters took her; no ship could have carried sail in the near-hurricane conditions that had existed throughout the better part of the last week. Lafe and Matai had experienced the storm onshore and it had all but carried their little hut away. All he could hope for now was that the ship was late and had missed the storm.

He no longer feared for his own life, at least not in the short term. Tama and his people had shown him considerable kindness since Matai's burial, he noticed, and he didn't have to worry about Salem who had made friends with everyone in the camp and was eating well.

He sat and repaired some of his clothing while he studied his captors. This was a picked group, able to travel fast over quite long distances, and they looked hardy and strong. Among them were young men and women, some no more than thirteen to fifteen years of age, he guessed, and possibly on their first expedition. The oldest of the group was Tama who was the undisputed leader and whose word was obeyed instantly. They were a robust and healthy looking people, though shorter than the men of his country, and they were thickset and well muscled. Mostly their skins varied from light brown to a darker hue and were nowhere near as black as the Negroes he had seen but more like halfway between them and the colour of the Orientals, perhaps like the native Indians of New England. But these Maori warriors had most of their faces, thighs, and shoulders covered in deep scarring that had been rubbed with black. It gave their faces a dark, scowling look.

Some of the women had small motifs tattooed on their chins below their lower lips, which were also blackened, and from what he had seen of them they were generally attractive and well formed. The young men were quick to accept the stranger in their midst, but not so the young women who kept to themselves and vanished into their huts like rabbits into their holes if Lafe moved in their direction.

Most of his days were spent with Tama, who seemed to have a great thirst for knowledge and never seemed to tire. When Lafe stumbled over an explanation in his new language the chief waited patiently until he had finished then ordered him to begin again. Nothing was so small or insignificant that it did not capture his interest.

On the beach in the smooth sand Tama drew a remarkably accurate map of the three islands that made up his country, and asked where Lafe's tribe of Goblins came from. Lafe indicated where Matai

141

had come from, far to the north, then he drew Australia and America, keeping them and the ocean to scale in a drawing that took him far along the beach. Tama was very thoughtful for a long time after that.

Many of his questions concerned the muskets so Lafe decided to kill a seal for meat for the group. He still had a musket that was loaded and wanted to discharge it for safety's sake, but when he stepped from the hut with the weapon in his hand the rest of the people vanished into the scrub and into their huts. He and Tama headed for the rookery at the point where Lafe crept in quite close to an enormous bull seal and, taking careful aim, gave it a charge of buckshot into the head. At such close range the bull's skull was quite stove in and its blood and brains splattered the rocks and stained the sea below. Tama was thoughtful and said nothing until the seal had been cleaned and the carcass carried back to camp by men who had come to retrieve it when they heard the shot.

'This is a terrible thing you have brought among us,' Tama said finally. 'With this weapon even the lowest born, or mokai, could kill a chief. No matter how skilled he was with his arms, even if he was the most skilful man in the tribe with his weapons, it would not matter, he would be dead.

'That is a very wrong thing, Goblin,' Tama warned. 'Do you understand me?' His scowl was threatening and Lafe nodded soberly.

That afternoon a school of about thirty porpoises crossed the river bar and passed the camp heading up the river to the lake. Everyone dropped their weaving, tool-making and other pursuits and trotted up the track towards the lake too. The porpoises gave every sign of having come to play and they rolled, leapt and cavorted the length of the waterway, carving their way through the reflections on its surface with great abandon. Finally they came close to the shore where their human audience stood, as if they had sought them out on purpose.

'For a porpoise, it is better to have your tricks admired by people,' Tama explained. 'They know they are a long time dead, and perhaps there will not be anyone to admire their skills in the underworld.'

Lafe sent the dog out into the lake and the porpoises cut playful rings around him as he tried desperately to close the distance between them and sink his teeth into one. It was a great game for the playful mammals and they effortlessly avoided the dog with flicks of their tails. They sped in from the side and behind, each one diving under the dog to reappear on his other side so that he was always changing course to chase a new fish. The people on shore thought it was the funniest thing they had ever seen and it was obvious that Salem was rapidly finding his way into their affections. They owned no dogs in their tribe, they told Lafe. Other tribes kept dogs, but none like this one.

Soon the sun dropped behind the mountains to the west and a chill settled over the lake. Reluctantly the people left the porpoises to their games and set off back to the camp, the women to prepare food and the men to resume whatever they had been doing before. Lafe saw that the canoes were being loaded, which probably meant an early morning crossing of the bar; the sea had been dropping all day and it looked good for passage making.

It was a well-run expedition; everyone had their duties and went quietly about them without any apparent dissent. Like a well-run ship. Lafe mused as he got busy fitting his sail to the mast of the cutter and stowing his gear on board. He presumed that he was going with them, no one tried to stop him and he guessed that if he had not begun his preparations he would have been told to do so.

Before they left the camp he took his knife and carved his name and the date in the smooth bark of a prominent tree. Lastly he added an arrow pointing north.

'This is Goblin talk,' he explained to the puzzled Tama. 'When another Goblin comes to this spot he will understand that I have been here before him.'

The way Tama's eyebrows disappeared into his hairline confirmed that this concept of a written message was quite different to anything he had previously encountered. Taking up his knife again, Lafe cut a copy of the chief's facial tattoo into the tree trunk next to his own message. He had already noted, and Matai had confirmed, that no two tattoos were ever the same and therefore he surmised that the recipients had chosen them after much careful thought and that each was in its own way a signature. And I was right, he thought as he saw Tama recognize this image of himself on the tree.

'Now people will know that Chief Tama and the Goblin stood at this place,' he explained, and saw with relief that the message got through. It had been difficult to get the chief to understand what he had done, and with all the inbuilt tribal fears of witchcraft and magic hanging in the air it was something he perhaps should not have attempted. It would pay him to be more careful in future, he cautioned himself. To be accused of using witchcraft against the tribe would have serious consequences.

Long before sun-up Lafe could hear the camp stirring around him. Tama had been to the river mouth to consult with the weather gods and when he returned to camp he commanded, 'We go now!'

Food for the journey had been prepared the day before and now the boats were launched into the river, sleeping mats were rolled and stored on board and the canoes led the way out through the reeds into the open river. The air was crisp and the sky was clear, the stars hanging so close in the heavens that Lafe felt he could reach out and pick them from the deck of the boat. There was a crackling frost on the ground and the light mist rising from the river promised a fine day.

'Only the morepork is still awake to witness my departure and to know of Matai's grave in the dunes,' Lafe said sadly to Salem as he looked back for the last time.

Soon they rounded the last bend of the river before the open sea and the little fleet rode the ebbing tide to the bar. There wasn't even a hint of a breeze so one of the canoes had to tow the cutter over the bar and into the smooth water beyond, where the westerly picked up a little from around the point. There was no escape for Lafe. Tama rode with him in the cutter and had brought on board another solid-looking warrior who watched every move the sailor made. On a thong fastened to his wrist hung a patu, a lethal-looking club of black stone shaped like a question mark, finely ground and polished with edges on it like a meat cleaver. Though it was only eighteen inches long, it had weight and balance and was obviously designed for the speedy cracking of skulls. It was a fine weapon for close fighting and Lafe knew it would be quick and deadly.

Tama had a patu hung from his own wrist, though his was made of the finely polished greenstone that was valued above all else. His was the weapon of a chief.

When the sun finally hauled itself up over the mountains it was into a cloudless sky with the sea as calm as Lafe had ever seen it on that coast, and he was sure Tama's weather sense had predicted such a day for his northern migration. To undertake such trips in canoes with so little freeboard would take very accurate judgment of the weather, he acknowledged, and his respect for the Maori grew.

The first forty miles of coast offered nothing but high cliffs and sunken rocks which had to be passed before a suitable place could be found to beach the canoes. For the first hour of their journey the breeze was light, but it held from the southwest and soon started to build. By then, however, the canoes had built up a long lead on the cutter. Tama wore a face like thunder and Lafe could see that being left so far behind was a considerable blow to his dignity. The chief indicted several times that perhaps the canoe was a better form of transport, and it was only his endless desire for knowledge that had led him to the decision to travel in the cutter.

The crews of the canoes were very well balanced and they handled their craft well, Lafe decided with a whaler's critical eye. Once the paddlers got the rhythm they looked as if they could keep it up for many hours, their muscles developed from childhood for such journeys. He saw that the warriors and the women ate and rested where they sat on the benches, a fresh set of muscles taking up the paddles whenever someone began to tire. There was a grim purposefulness in the way they wielded their paddles, and he decided he would not like them on his trail.

The very air on that part of the coast had been scrubbed clean by the storm of the previous days, bringing the magnificent views up close. The layers of the forest where it ran up the mountains were displayed in great detail from the sea and a small range of red mountains, noticeably different among the dun and black rocks of the other ranges, reflected the morning light. Perhaps there was some new mineral waiting to be discovered, Lafe thought, and wondered at the sight. The red range stayed visible from the cutter for a long time as they sailed along on the quiet sea, and he remembered the red cliffs from which the Cascade River tumbled further along the coast and the dreams of gold and silver he had had when he saw them. These red mountains that drew his eyes now had gone unnoticed on his previous trip up the coast; then the cutter had been in close to the shore hunting seals, and on the voyage south he had been engaged in his running battle with the big sailing canoe. It looked possible to climb the red range from the little camp he had made for Matai by the lake, and he would have liked to do that. He wondered if he would ever pass that way again.

He knew there was a chance he was being taken north to be eaten at some great tribal feast, and shuddered at the thought.

Though it appears Tama has other plans for me, he mused. The chief obviously expected to gain great mana by owning his own personal Goblin.

Once in a while, without making it too obvious, Lafe took back the spyglass from Tama and searched the open sea for the *Northern Lights*, hoping against hope that she would haul herself over the horizon all sails set and come flying to his rescue. But the sea remained empty of all but the three canoes and the little cutter making their way slowly north. Not even a solitary whale broke the smooth surface of the sea as far as he could see, and sadly he accepted that his last chance was falling away behind him.

As the sun warmed the air over the forest and caused it to rise up the steep mountain faces, the cooler sea air moved in to take its place and a fine sea breeze started to blow. Lafe hauled the sails taut and sent the cutter hissing through the wavelets at a fine speed.

'This is more like it!' he yelled at the wind as they rapidly began overhauling the canoes. Tama had a smile on his face again for the first time in the voyage. He stood with his arms folded in what was obviously his normal stance in the leading canoe, but it was not appropriate for a sailing boat and Lafe knew that if he made a mistake or the wind shifted suddenly and the boom swung across, Tama would be smashed into the sea and probably badly hurt. His chiefly dignity would take a blow it might not recover from and not only that, his bodyguard would think he had been attacked and probably rap Lafe across the head with his club. How could he persuade Tama to sit down?

In this type of vessel an officer sits at the tiller where he does a little steering and gives orders without compromising his rank and status, Lafe reasoned to himself. But chiefs in this country were not in the habit of even chasing the flies off themselves from what he had observed. He decided to take a chance on Tama's curiosity and thirst for new experiences.

It wasn't so hard in the end. Once the Maori chief got the feel of the tiller alive and kicking in his hands, the wonder of steering a boat by such methods was enough and he was soon entranced by his new occupation. Very quickly he learned to call, 'Tack!' and put the tiller over while Lafe eased the boom across with the boom sheet so the little ship would pick up the wind on her other side and quickly settle on a new course. As she heeled nicely to the wind on her beam Salem, in his normal position at the bow, spread his legs a little and crouched lower to maintain his balance, his mouth open and his tongue lolling as if he was laughing at a good joke.

'The dog is eating the wind!' Tama shouted, his eyes shining with excitement as he urged every last bit of speed out of the boat. Slowly but surely the canoes were overhauled and dropped one at a time behind the cutter. They drew level with the streams that flowed down the cliff faces Captain Cook had called The Cascades and here they shaped their new course for the point at Open Bay. The breeze held up for the rest of the day and they rounded the bay in the late afternoon.

Lafe looked hard for the little hut that had covered their last cache of skins, but there were only a few fire-scarred trees to mark the spot. There was nothing else left to see and he decided it would not be wise to bring to Tama's notice the fact that there had been a sealing party, an attack and a sea battle there.

An hour before dark the cutter crossed the bar and entered a tolerably wide river mouth that gave way to a navigable river leading inland. Tama called the river Okahu. As they neared the bank Salem leapt out and went splashing ashore and Lafe got ready to jump in too so he could drag the cutter to the bank, but the chief took it upon himself to teach his captive some manners. He raised his hand. 'Stay where you are!' he ordered. With an imperious flick of his eyes he sent his bodyguard over the side into the muddy water to drag the cutter ashore and moor it to the trunk of a tree that jutted from the bank. Then patiently sloshing his way back through the mud the man offered his back to his chief, deposited him gently on the bank and returned to the cutter to offer the same service to Lafe.

'It is time you showed you have mana,' Tama told Lafe curtly. 'To own so many precious things you must be the son of a chief. It is time to act like one.'

This was a new development that Lafe did not quite understand. Was he to have rank and status? He thought that was what the Maori was saying to him, and decided it was in his best interests to accept the role. He learned that the warrior who had carried him ashore was a mokai, or slave. He had been taken as a young man in a war with another tribe and was the personal property of the chief.

He didn't appear to be oppressed by his status, Lafe thought as he watched the slave collect driftwood and bustle about lighting a large fire. Most of the conversation that flew backwards and forwards between Tama, who sat on a mat near the fire, and the 'emoki', as the chief called him and who appeared to do all the work, seemed more like that of friends than slave and master. Lafe understood enough of the words that passed between them to know the emoki was full of praise for the Goblin's sailboat that had carried them to their destination without a paddle being plied throughout the whole journey.

On the bank of the stream were six grass huts similar in design and construction to those at their last resting place and Lafe was sure that the same people had built them. These were obviously regular stopping points used by the tribe for voyages up and down the coast according to the seasons.

'At this camp we gather eels and titi which are the young of sea birds,' Tama explained. 'This camp is our own and we are masters of all the land to the north until the land runs into the sea.' He drew a map of his territory in the sand and Lafe knew then that these people were probably the inhabitants of Murderers' Bay. There were many questions he wanted to ask, but they would have to wait until his command of the language was better. He missed so many details by understanding only half the answers he was given and by not being able to put his questions into the right words.

Not being able to understand had its advantages though, he thought, as he was able to avoid some issues by pleading ignorance. When Tama questioned him as to the whereabouts of the rest of his tribe, Lafe continued to draw his maps of America in the sand. Not being familiar with the behaviour of Goblins, Tama seemed prepared to believe he had travelled alone in his small boat from a land very far away.

Lafe understood that he was at all times to remain at the chief's side. Though he was not quite a prisoner he was not his own master although his status was considerably higher than the emoki's, and the slave served his food and saw to his comfort as he did for Tama.

The *Northern Lights* was due back along the coast at any time and Lafe watched for an opportunity to escape. While the sea remained calm he could steal the cutter and travel well out to sea to meet his ship, or even head back to the rendezvous at Dusky Sound, but as the tribe moved further north his chances of escape would diminish. Stealing the cutter would not be easy – already Tama had ordered the emoki to remove the sails and oars and store them in his own hut.

The three curled up in their blankets and robes around the fire and it was long after dark when they were woken by a hail from the first of the canoes as it put into the river. The emoki kicked the fire together and piled on dry wood, and in the light of the flames the rest of the party staggered ashore. They were exhausted from fifteen hours at their paddles, too tired even to eat properly and they simply chewed a little dried eel, washed it down with water from the river then crept into their huts to sleep. Men and women went into separate dwellings, Lafe noted.

He had been given a hut to himself where he could store his possessions. He had mats to sleep on and with his warm blankets and Salem beside him he felt like a chief. The hut was small with an entrance that had to be entered on hands and knees. There was a space for a small fire but no chimney, and the smoke exited via a small hole under the eaves or filtered through the smoke-blackened thatch of the roof. When Lafe thought of the six or maybe seven people sharing each of the other huts, which were the same size as his, he realized that was probably the preferred way of keeping warm. Without good woollen blankets in this climate it would be better to roll in together like piglets, and Salem was better than any extra blanket on a colder night.

The clearing was well warmed by the sun before the camp bestirred itself next day and the people crawled from their dark huts to check the weather and the direction of the breeze. Once they had decided what the day would bring they sauntered down to the river and Lafe sat and watched as both men and women, after discreet trips to the bushes, set about washing and grooming their hair. The warriors were a vain bunch, he decided, taking a lot more time with their hair than most European women did, and he chuckled at the comparison. First they washed and combed their long black hair then they wound it into elaborate buns, fastened with combs and one or two feathers piercing the topknot as a finishing touch.

A vain lot all right, he decided, but he viewed his own tattered clothing with distaste and sniffed his own body. His personal standards of cleanliness had slipped considerably since the *Northern Lights* had departed near six months before.

Perhaps that is why I am given a hut to myself, he conceded. Perhaps the unwashed savage is repelled by this unwashed savage. Sniffing his armpits and his clothing again he realized that both gave off a rank smell, the fat of long-dead seals and the smoke of numerous camp fires mingling with other less identifiable things in the general fug. He hunted up a long-forgotten piece of soap, a pair of clean trousers and a shirt and headed for a quiet bend in the river bank to take a bath. Soon he stood shivering in the cold mountain water up to his knees, as naked as the day he was born as he soaped away the months of accumulated grime from his hair and body, cursing the cold water that made his knees knock together and the soap that burned his eyes. Suddenly he realized that he wasn't alone and looked up to see the women of the tribe all gathered on the bank to watch.

He lowered himself quickly into the stingingly cold water until his nakedness was hidden and waited, hoping they would soon get tired and go away, but to his dismay they stayed and continued what he gathered from their laughter was an animated discussion on the parts of his anatomy they had managed to get a good look at before he dived. He remembered the mana Tama had conferred on him, summoned all his dignity and his limited vocabulary and ordered the women from the riverbank before he froze to death. They obeyed with clear reluctance, and he quickly finished his bath, leapt for the bank where his clothes lay and then wandered nonchalantly back to the fire.

'Ho, Goblin!' Tama greeted him. 'The women tell me you took to the water like a shag when they looked at you!'

His jest caused a great deal of merriment around the fire.

'Could it be that the cold had shrunk your piri piri so that you were ashamed to stand in front of them?' The chief roared with laughter, pleased with his own witticism at Lafe's expense. 'Now their curiosity is satisfied, they are happy that you Goblins are the same as real people. There has been much debate as to how Goblins beget their children.'

Lafe's embarrassment deepened when he realized that Tama had not finished yet.

'Take off your cloak so I can see the two colours of your skin,' he ordered. 'I do not have to hide on the riverbank to satisfy my own curiosity.'

Lafe removed his shirt to show where his shoulders and arms were tanned a deep brown from the summer's sun, while his belly and back which were usually covered by his vest were much whiter. Tama grinned as one of the younger women stepped forward, urged on by the rest of her sex, and walked boldly up to him. Lafe had noticed her already. Taller and slimmer than others of her group, her skin was the colour of light brown honey and she had the grace of a young queen.

She looked boldly into his Lafe's eyes, her expression unreadable, and reached out to touch his skin. For the space of a second her fingers fluttered like a butterfly across the hard ridges of muscle on his stomach and in spite of himself he jumped as if stung by a bee. It was the first time a woman had ever touched him intimately and the quiver that ran through his body was obvious to all those watching. The blood rose quickly to his face when he heard the laughter from the other women.

Still boldly holding his glance, the young woman reached up and lightly touched the pulse in his throat with her fingertips. She allowed her fingers to linger there for a minute. Momentarily her cloak slid aside and an exquisite brown-tipped breast was exposed to his view. As she dropped her hand Lafe looked into her brown eyes and felt himself drawn into their depths like a drowning man, reading love, sorrow and passion in those fleeting seconds. For a heart-stopping moment it was as if they were together and alone, and they had eyes only for each other.

Time seemed to last forever as their gazes remained locked together, and Lafe struggled to control senses that threatened to run wild. It was only a greater outburst of laughter and ribald comments that made him swing away from the girl in confusion, put his shirt back on and seat himself before the food.

Many in the party had seen the spark that was struck between man and woman and recognized it for what it was. Speculative glances were cast in Tama's direction but he stared blandly back at them as if he had seen nothing at all amiss.

The mood of this camp was happy and carefree. There was plenty of food, talk and laughter and it seemed there was no hurry to resume the voyage now that the worst part of it was behind them. The warriors attended to their weapons while the women wove new mats or clothes in intricate designs from the grasses and flax that grew in abundance near the river. Two heavy flax kits were carried out of the chief's hut and when he sauntered over to investigate he saw they held pieces of pounamu, the wonderful green-tinged stone that Jimmy had said was found only in this part of the country.

'It is more valuable than any other thing the earth produces.' Matai had agreed. Now the warriors and their women each chose a piece of greenstone from the kit and began to work on it. From the bushes around the camp they unearthed pieces of sandstone that showed signs of much use over the years. Wet sand was dashed from a gourd onto these blocks and the greenstone was slowly ground away by hard rubbing. Each of the pieces that Lafe examined had been broken from the mother lode somewhere in the mountains, and each was now roughly shaped out to its desired shape and polished towards its final form. This stone was a greyish green colour shot through with highlights of different shades, not the dark green stone Lafe had seen worn on the neck and in the ears of some Maori, and it seemed that it was being worked mostly into adzes and chisel heads.

The stone appeared to be very hard and could be brought to a high polish that had a certain warm glow to it. The woman who had been brazen enough to touch Lafe wore an exquisite piece of carved stone around her neck that looked like a little laughing gnome.

'We gathered this stone at a lake high in the mountains, above the lake where Matai died,' Tama told him when he saw Lafe's interest, and he sent the emoki to his hut to get the chief's own weapon, a greenstone club shaped like a question mark. It was made of the richer, dark green stone and when Lafe felt the weight and heft of it he had to admit it was a fine weapon.

'This stone came from a river further up the coast,' Tama told him, and Lafe gathered that there were different values attached to the different shades and hardness of the stone, but all was rare and precious. The greenstone they carried represented a fair amount of the tribe's wealth.

As the day wore on, Lafe noticed that one or another of the warriors would casually get to his feet and look towards the group of women. Obeying an unseen signal one of them would leave her task and join him on the other side of the clearing and they would saunter hand in hand towards the sand hills or upstream into the forest, not reappearing until the warmth of the sun had gone. Soon there were few men and women left in the clearing. Lafe dared a glance at the girl with the mischievous fingers and was met with a look full of both promise and challenge.

Tama had Lafe lay out all his possessions and went over them once again, exclaiming over the sharpness of the razor when he was shown how it was used. There was nothing that escaped his notice and the kit that held all the small tools, screwdrivers and flints that Lafe used to repair and service the expedition's muskets were of particular interest to him, as were the muskets themselves.

'I have the desire to learn to shoot the musket myself,' he announced. 'Today would be as good a day as any to begin, don't you think, Goblin?' It was a command, not a question. Lafe figured that to Tama's warlike soul, one musket would be a powerful weapon to devastate his enemies with but two would be much better. At Tama's insistence, he gave him instruction on the loading of the musket, demonstrating it over and over until the chief was satisfied he had mastered the art. Then Tama seemed to tire of his lessons, or perhaps he was not yet ready to take the next step. He turned on the girl with the bold eyes, who was working on a flax kit.

'Make up this Goblin's hair like a warrior's. It looks like a toi toi bush on a windy day,' he ordered. Lafe found it was an exquisite form of torture to sit still in front of this young woman while Tama looked on, because out of sight of the chief the girl's fingers played a subtle game on the back of his neck. Deftly she combed the knots out of his blond tresses and wound them into a topknot into which she placed a single black and white feather. Then at Tama's nod she moved reluctantly away from his side and back to where her work lay on the ground.

Lafe wanted to call her back. His senses were swimming still from the very nearness of her body and her touch. He had never felt like this before with any woman, nor did he have any real experience to call on. He was aware that Tama watched him closely, his face impassive. Perhaps he was not unaware after all of the subtle byplays that had passed between the two young people in the last few hours? Even though the blood pounded in his temple, Lafe maintained an even stare in return. He knew that he was alive only at the whim of the chief who, if he grew tired of him, could snuff out his life like the swatting of a fly. He knew also that if he broke any taboos concerning the women of the tribe he would be done for. Only that morning he had heard Tama remind his tardy slave that the oven was gaping for him if he did not hurry himself.

That night Lafe waited a long time for sleep to come, his mind full of the strange feelings that had overtaken him during the day, and his dreams when they came were of a honey-skinned girl whose name he did not even know.

Towards the end of the afternoon the women had set up food drying racks and early the next morning Tama divided his people into groups of equal strength and they were sent to different places to catch eels, fish and birds. Lafe was pleased to see the girl was in the same party as Tama and himself. Canoes carried them a short way up the river to where a set of rapids barred any further progress, then they beached the boats and travelled overland at a smart pace to a small lake set deep in the forest. Four eel traps, cleverly woven out of vines, were brought from their hiding places and baited with an unlucky woodhen that Salem had caught on the track.

An old canoe was dragged from among the ferns and the traps were lowered into the lake and left to do their work. Lafe passed out lines he had brought from the cutter. He knew Tama was interested to see if the Goblin's iron hook was as successful as the Maori method of wrapping a piece of bait in a ball of scrapped flax that looked like cotton and would entangle the eel's teeth while it was hauled swiftly into the boat and killed. Both methods produced many eels and soon the flax kits held as many as the slaves and the women could carry.

All day Lafe waited his chance to speak to the girl alone, and when the moment came he searched desperately for the right words in this still-strange language.

'What is your name?' he asked her.

'I am Marama,' she said with a smile. 'And I am the daughter of Tama.'

Lafe stared at her. He had not expected that, and in his confusion he forgot what he had planned to say next. She was a very beautiful woman though very young, perhaps not more than fourteen years old. Then she heard someone moving towards them through the fern on the edge of the lake and quietly edged away.

'I will sing for you,' she whispered, and she went off quickly to load up her flax kit with eels.

They fell into formation for the return journey, fighting men to the front and rear, slaves and women carrying their heavy loads in the middle. The tall trees formed a canopy overhead of cathedral-like

155

grandeur, forcing the party to travel in single file on a track that snaked its way around the trunks of the larger trees. High above in the canopy the bellbirds dropped their clear notes into the silence. Then Marama began to sing, so delightfully that to Lafe it seemed that even the birds stilled their own voices the better to listen to hers. Though he did not catch the meaning of the song it was enough to know it was sung for him alone.

Next morning before the sun had showed itself over the mountains Tama had the different groups on the track again, some to the lake to empty the eel traps, some to fish and his own party to the cliffs to gather seabirds. They spread out along the cliff tops to search for the burrows where the birds nested and once a nest was found a hand was thrust down the entrance and a large, fat fledgling of a seabird was dragged out by its neck. With Salem's help Lafe soon had more birds than he could carry.

'Good, good! Soon the hungry times will be on us,' Tama encouraged. 'We must work hard to gather what we can before the winter comes.'

That evening Lafe watched as the women plucked and cooked the birds then sealed them in kelp bags preserved in their own fat. They would keep all winter if needed, a woman assured him. But if the hungry times were coming, the present was good, and even with Matai he had never eaten so well. The ovens overflowed with food, fish, shellfish, lobsters, eel and birds, and always the women urged him to eat more.

'Here, Goblin, try a little more of this, or this,' they would say. 'You are too skinny, the winter will kill you.'

'Look at Tama. He is fat like a seal, that is the best way. Do Goblins eat only the wind?' they asked.

Now there was a noticeable restlessness among the group of gatherers and Lafe knew they would move again soon. All the kits, including many new ones that had been woven out of the nearby flax, were full of smoked and dried food now and the drying racks were empty. All day Lafe watched Tama as he studied the sky and the breezes and that evening, when he was sure the signs were good, the chief gave the word.

'In the morning we will go.'

The wind off the land had reduced the waves to mere ripples at that early hour before the dawn when the heavily-laden canoes cleared the bar, and there was breeze enough from the south for the cutter to make its own way out to sea. As they headed north the country along the shore began to change, with extensive flat plains running back to the ranges beyond. They were all covered in tall forest with rimu trees towering high above the canopy, and the rocks and cliffs that had shielded the land from the sea on the previous leg of the voyage began to give way to long sandy beaches.

Late morning saw the boats safely past two lonely islands that stood off a great river mouth. The flow of the river could be felt well out to sea and Lafe speculated that this river could penetrate well into the mountains, perhaps providing a pass that would allow a man to escape to the other coast. But he was careful in his observations, aware of the chief's eyes always watching him.

'Look! There are many seals still on the rocks,' Tama indicated, calling his attention back to the nearer view. 'Maybe some are wintering over and that will be good when the hungry days come around. We might need to come back soon.'

They spent that night rolled in their mats on the sand in a little cove. No fires were lit, food was passed from hand to hand and they chewed it where they lay. By dawn the next morning they were gone again, the muscles of the paddlers scarcely rested and the women quiet with weariness.

The cutter forged ahead with a good wind, and as they moved steadily up the coast Lafe had his best view yet of the extensive range of mountains that made up the spine of this southern island. High mountain peaks with permanent snow towered above them, their great ice fields and glaciers laid out to view as they carved their way through the forest to the lower levels of the land.

'These are our mountains,' Tama indicated. His hand swept across the sky taking in everything they could see in the vast distance. 'This is our land.'

Late that afternoon the canoes, escorted by the cutter jogging along with eased sails, approached their destination.

'This is the home of my people.' Tama pointed, and Lafe could see a narrow entrance leading into a huge lagoon separated from the sea by a long sandspit. In the distance columns of smoke rose from a number of fires. 'This is our home, Goblin,' Tama said again, and his pride was apparent.

Lafe was on edge. He had worried during his journey north that this could also be the home of the warriors who had killed and carried off one of his men and whose great double canoe he had fought the running battle with.

It was obvious that their arrival had been watched for and soon more than a hundred men and women were gathered at the entrance of the lagoon to greet them. To Lafe's nervous eyes it did not look like a welcoming party; the men were heavily armed and drawn up in fighting formation, while the women stayed well back on the dunes. A fierce haka was underway as a canoe darted out of the lagoon, skirted wide of the cutter and joined the other canoes. A long, animated discussion took place while Lafe, Tama and the emoki sat with slackened sails and waited for the canoe to come up to their chief. Tama stood with his arms crossed, looking pleased with himself. He knew that capturing the Goblin would enhance his reputation immensely, and that was good for any chief.

But when he studied his people ashore with a practiced eye, a frown creased his forehead. He had expected the sight of the cutter to create a minor outbreak of hysteria but this was something different and Lafe's heart sank as tried to read the chief's expression.

'There is more to this than meets the eye,' Tama muttered to the emoki. 'My people are ready to attack. Something is wrong, I can feel it from here.'

He summoned the canoe over to the cutter with an imperious wave of his hand. 'Where are their manners? They should have come to their chief first anyway. Someone will be sent to the ovens for this.' His warning was deliberately pitched loud enough for Lafe and the emoki to hear, as if he already suspected what was amiss.

Finally the canoe came to them with a couple of flicks of the paddles that quickly brought it alongside. The six warriors on board were very heavily armed and their eyes shifted nervously from the dog to Lafe and back again so Lafe stared back as bravely as he could. Tama spoke angrily to the skinny middle-aged warrior who seemed to be the spokesman for the welcoming committee and Lafe struggled to pick up some of the key phrases of their conversation.

'This is no way to greet your chief after a long voyage across the sea,' Tama snapped angrily. 'I have single-handedly captured a fierce Goblin.' When he had finally finished a long speech he listened to what the skinny one had to say, his eyebrows disappearing into his hair line as he showed the whites of his eyes, and the more he heard the angrier he became. Lafe could not follow much of what the skinny one said in his high-pitched lisping voice, but the word utu was mentioned several times with dark glances in Lafe's direction.

Tama had worked himself up into a fine state of rage. He snorted through his nose like a wild bull for a second or two before snatching the emoki's patu from his hands and fanning himself vigorously with it. Then he spat out a string of orders that even Lafe could see were not to be questioned, and the canoe pulled hastily to the shore. Orders were shouted, the warriors on the beach began to break ranks and the women burst forth with a song of welcome.

One by one the heavily-laden canoes with their weary crews headed for the shallow outfall of the lagoon. As each canoe touched the sand it was grabbed by willing hands and warriors up to their knees in water dragged it over the bar and into the lagoon beyond.

Tama fixed Lafe with a steely glare. 'So, Goblin! It seems that you have already meet the tohunga, and you took utu against him for killing one of your men. This is the first I have heard of other Goblins?'

His voice was very soft but there was a menace in his tone that made Lafe shiver with fear.

'This is a very strange story, Goblin! I cannot wait to hear more.'

The chief waited until the last canoe crossed the bar and had launched into the lagoon before he gave the signal for the cutter to begin her own run to the shore. The breeze was holding well and the little *Aurora* made a fine show coming through the surf under full sail. Lafe could see a hundred or more watchers standing up in the sand hills staring at the new craft that they had heard so much about. Already the story had flown from mouth to mouth about how Tama had captured this strange waka and its fierce occupants, the white Goblin and his big black dog. Now Tama was putting on a show, as befitted a chief, and Lafe decided to help him to make the most of it.

He lifted the keel as the water shallowed quickly at the bar and dropped the sail at the last minute, letting the cutter sledge its way up on to the sand. Tama hailed his warriors and rapped out a series of orders that sent half a hundred helpers into the shallows to grasp the gunwales and race the little boat over the sand and into the lagoon, occupants and all. Once inside Lafe whipped the sail up again and as it filled they set off in style across the sheltered waterway towards the village they had seen from out at sea.

Tama stood with his arms crossed and his great greenstone patu dangling from his wrist, every inch a victorious chief returning home in triumph. And here I am, his captive, Lafe thought wryly. But he could not complain, at least not yet. The chief had treated him fairly in every way, and he was still alive and unharmed.

All that long day he had watched the horizon for a sail, knowing that every mile he travelled north the further he was from where the *Northern Lights* might be already searching for him. Now that he had crossed the bar and was about to enter the village he realized he truly was a prisoner and hope started to fade.

Chapter 9

It was a very still, quiet piece of water, this lagoon, and it had a primitive feel to it. Huge trees appeared in places to grow out of the water itself. From the cutter Lafe could see long ropes of moss hanging down from trees whose lower limbs drooped to touch the water, while vines as thick as a man's thigh wound their way around the trunks of other large trees intent on strangling the life out of their hosts. Dark, silent waterways that could be travelled by canoe appeared to lead far into a forest, and the lagoon itself was alive with ducks and other water birds. He wondered if the Everglades in Florida, an area he had only read about, was not a little like this place.

The village held a strategic position on the edge of a headland that butted out above the lagoon. Thirty or forty large huts sat on a sunny bench inside a strong looking palisade of sharpened tree trunks. These sturdy posts were sunk deep into the earth and lashed together with vines and resembled to Lafe's eye some of the forts out in the American northwest. The main gate of the fort, towards which the cutter's bow was now pointing, had a fighting platform above it that tapered inwards like an eel trap and would be easily defended by a small group of men. This was a tribe that had many enemies and expected to have to defend itself at any time.

He counted ten canoes pulled up on the beach by the main gate of the fort. And there she is, he thought to himself, and his spirits sank.

The great double canoe that he had attacked so desperately down the coast was here, pulled up against the palisades on rollers so that she could be launched again in seconds. He had known in his heart since their first meeting on the water that he would see her again, but it was still a shock and an unwelcome one. He wondered exactly what sort of trouble was waiting on shore for him.

He became aware that Tama was studying him closely, and as they approached the fort the chief spoke softly.

'You need only to know one thing before you go ashore. In my village you are the son of a chief and I expect you to act like one. If you remember this, there will always be a place for you among my people.'

The words were not said unkindly and Lafe took heart from them, hope building again as he ran the cutter onto the shore where many hands caught her and dragged her high up onto the sand. He curtly ordered Salem to stay where he was, fearing the dog would cause panic among those who had not seen him before.

Tama stepped from the cutter with dignity, adjusted his cloak and weapon and signalled for both Lafe and the dog to join him, then glancing neither to left nor right he strode regally through the two lines of people that stretched from the little boat to the gates of the village. Lafe followed closely at his heels, feeling the hostility of the crowd. Only Salem seemed unaffected by the tension and walked easily at his master's side, senses alert.

They entered through the great gate and found themselves in a sort of well-trodden courtyard with dwellings opening onto it. Most of the village's domestic chores appeared to be carried out here but mats had been laid out around a fire in front of the most imposing building, a house whose intricately-carved face boards displayed likenesses of ugly little bowlegged men with protruding tongues and seashell eyes.

Tama took his seat and indicated a mat on his right hand for Lafe. Most of the other mats were occupied by men who were obviously the elders of the tribe, although there were one or two younger warriors, and all were tattooed. Lafe recognized the skinny tohunga from the double canoe who responded to his glance with a belligerent scowl. Beyond the firelight other villagers, both men and women, had laid out their mats

162

and sat quietly near so they could hear the talk. It was shaping up to be an important meeting.

And I bet my own fate will be on the agenda, Lafe decided. He could feel the tension in the air. Matai had told him that in some tribes the tohunga was priest, sorcerer and witchdoctor all rolled into one, and often they held the real power. Their magic scared the people and could reduce the tribal chiefs to little more than figureheads.

A woman brought him food, and he was so intent on watching Tama as he consulted quietly with the elders that it took a few seconds to realize it was Marama herself who served his meal. There were generous portions of food in a plaited flax bowl, some type of fish, eel and duck with bush vegetables. It was most welcome as it had been a long day and he was hungry. He also needed to keep his strength up and his wits about him for whatever ordeal was next.

Marama stayed for a minute to talk, whispering that he should show courage and honour. These were the most important things to remember, as his behaviour and bearing would help to strengthen Tama's arm against the tohunga. Lafe was aware that her actions in serving his food herself were deliberate and calculated, and would be interpreted by the people as a mark of favour for the Goblin.

When they had all eaten an expectant hush fell over the people and they waited in silence for what would happen next. Tama sent a messenger off to get a musket, which the chief placed in Lafe's hands. He checked the priming just in case, but as he had expected it was unloaded and would be of little more use to him than a club if he was attacked. Then he looked at the musket more carefully and realized it was not one of his own but was a ship's musket from the *Northern Lights,* a weapon that could only have belonged to the sealer who had been killed and carried off from the stream by the rock hut. Now the link to that murder was clear; there was no doubt that these were the warriors who had killed his crewman.

He was still assimilating the implications when Tama signalled for the tohunga to begin the meeting. Leaping to his feet with a short wooden stabbing spear in his hands, the skinny man began to harangue the crowd in a bitter voice. Lafe had never seen such an impressive performance and almost believed himself that he was guilty of the crimes he was being accused of. Even with his limited grasp of the language he could follow enough of the speech to know that he would be killed and consigned to the oven within the hour if the tohunga had his way.

The man was a master orator. He shouted, wept, rolled his eyes, screamed and made little dashes in Lafe's direction with his upraised spear, all the time working the tribe up to a feverish excitement. Lafe feared the speech could only end with his ritual demise and wished he had picked off the tohunga with his musket in the canoe when he had the chance. Making this powerful man run away from the fight was probably the most insulting thing he could have done to him, and the tohunga was in a poisonous mood because of it. He had obviously had time to brood over it, and that had deepened his rage. Lafe was awed but not surprised by the strength of his anger, as he knew the Maori were a very touchy race where their pride was concerned. A man's mana was at the core of his being, Matai had explained.

Night fell, but the chill that Lafe felt in his bones had nothing to do with the sun going down. The face of the mad tohunga darting in and out of the flickering firelight held him spellbound. Then finally, after holding the enthralled crowd in the palms of his hands for over an hour, the exhausted orator threw himself dramatically down on his mat as if to say, 'There, now I have done for you, Goblin! Who will kill him for me?'

Tama looked at nobody but sat for a long period with his head bowed as if in serious thought, and only when he sensed the crowd was ready did he stand and begin to speak. In stark contrast to the tohunga's impassioned performance he spoke slowly, with long pauses between his words as if to weigh them carefully before they were uttered.

'Cast your minds back, my people, to our first and only home at Taitapu away to the north from here, a place that some of our young people have never seen. Remember the day when Ngai Tahu came at us in the early morning, when the birds had only begun to sing their songs to the sun?'

'Auee!' he cried in anguish, as if even now the memory was too much to bear. 'That morning we fought hard. All day we fought Ngai Tahu but we were defeated still. We lost the battle.

'Why were we defeated?' Tama asked. 'I tell you why, my people. We were defeated because the enemy carried weapons of iron. They had somehow got their hands on the Goblins' axes, axes that cut us like no other weapons we have ever fought against before.

'Our wood and stone weapons were not enough! Our fighting skills were not enough!

'Not until we have our own weapons of iron will we be able to return to our homeland and take back what is ours.' Tama paused, long enough for his people to absorb what he had said.

'Long it has been our intention to find a Goblin who will make these things for us. But when we found him, this first Goblin who might have helped us to make these weapons, what did we do?' He glared around the group, his eyes seeking the mat where the tohunga sat.

'We have killed and eaten him already!'

He let the silence stretch again, repeating his words for emphasis. 'Ae, we have killed and eaten him already!'

Lafe saw one or two of the elders glance from him to the tohunga and back again, and knew Tama's point was getting through to them.

'But not this one!' Tama roared fiercely, on the attack now as he gestured in Lafe's direction. 'This is a fighting Goblin, and a good thing he is too, or he would have already been eaten and be of no use to this tribe anymore.' This raised a slight murmur of appreciation, and Tama pressed home his advantage.

'Is it not better to keep the bird alive and pluck a few feathers each day for your cloaks, than to kill the bird? I ask you this. We have a Goblin here, my Goblin. I, your chief, have captured this Goblin for our tribe. Shall we not use him?'

Tama stood silent for a long minute watching his people, meeting their eyes one by one in the firelight. Then he nodded abruptly, as if satisfied. 'I have spoken,' he said simply, and returned to his mat where he sat down in the silence.

He glanced at Lafe then, and signalled for him to move closer. 'There is one small matter to finish,' he told Lafe. 'I will call forward a warrior and you will present him with that musket. By doing this you will make him your friend and he will not seek utu against you. You will see when he comes forward that one of the bullets that you fired a few days ago knocked out his eye, and he has reason to hate you for that.'

At his signal a young man, no more than sixteen, stepped forward into the firelight and Lafe could see the empty red socket where his eye had been. Lafe was sorry that one of his random bullets had disfigured the youth and cost him so dearly, and he willingly leapt to his feet to present him with the musket. There were many nods and grunts of approval from the elders near the fire and the youth indicated that he was honoured by the gift.

It seemed to be over then. Marama came forward to lead Lafe to a hut which she indicated was his, and he found that all his possessions had been unloaded from the cutter and safely stored inside. She squeezed his hand quickly before disappearing into the darkness to the other side of the compound. Lafe dared not emerge again so he rolled himself in his blankets on the clean mats that had been provided, and counted himself lucky to still be alive. It had been a long day but now, with Tama's support, it seemed he had won a place for himself in the tribe. The rescue he had hoped for was not going to happen, so this new situation was the best he could hope for, and he was very thankful indeed for it.

Tama was with his wives all that next day, which left Lafe free to go where he wished. He used the time to explore the village and all the surrounding area with Salem at his side and the emoki as his shadow. Most of the villagers were friendly, though a little frightened of him, and the children followed him at what they hoped was a safe distance. Lafe played games with the dog on the beach and hurled sticks far out into the lagoon for him to retrieve so that the people would quickly realize how friendly the strange dog really was.

Many of the men who had not been south with the expedition were out fishing or hunting still, or putting up new food stores to hold the extra provisions for winter. These storehouses were small buildings erected on top of a single slippery pole that could foil the best efforts of the rats to climb them and would, when they were finished, hold the tribe's winter supply of food. To Lafe's surprise there were no crops or areas of cultivation, and when he asked about this he was told that in their previous home they had grown gardens but since they had been

166

forced to flee after being defeated in the great battle they had only hunted and fished.

Everything seemed to be dated by the tribe from this war, which had happened about five years previously as far as Lafe could find out. Everything was spoken of as 'before the war' or 'after the war'. The first two years after the war the tribe had led a totally nomadic existence, one of the elders told him. They were then little more than a few scattered groups of people heading further south every day, many of them hurt in the fighting. Frightened of everybody and always ready to run, they had finally reformed themselves, amalgamated with other lost groups and mopped up any refugees on their route south into the largely unclaimed and unpopulated area where they now lived.

It had been a difficult time when every hand in the land was against them, and they had crept out of the swamps only when they felt strong enough to survive. Here on this spot they had built their village only three years earlier, and they were still not sure it was defendable as it had never been tested. Some believed the best thing if they were attacked was to flee to the bush and swamps and hide, hoping that when the enemy went away there would be survivors to rebuild the tribe.

Their most important possession was the great double canoe that some of them had managed to launch during the heavy fighting. They had used it to escape, sailing it south to this place and hiding it in the swamps, and some of the elders had travelled this way while many others had struggled overland down the coast. One of their first priorities had been to build the smaller canoes their fishing and hunting parties used, and now the food stores that had taken all summer to lay up and the extensive number of greenstone pieces that the tribe now owned meant once again they had possessions to be defended.

'We do not fear attack from the sea for we are the Boat People,' they told Lafe proudly. 'We are masters of sea warfare and our big canoe is feared around the coast.'

The emoki told him that there was a well-fortified village about five days' journey further north, with a tribe of nearly equal strength to their own. 'Though we do not fear them so much, they are vassals and a sub tribe of a more powerful tribe on the east coast.'

167

These, he guessed, were the Ngai Tahu that Tama had told him about. Because they had already been defeated in war and driven from their village, many of Tama's people believed that they were already living on borrowed time and an attack could be expected daily.

'If they come this year it will be soon, before all the mountain passes are blocked with winter snows,' they told Lafe. 'Nearly always attacks are made by other tribes when the food stores are full.'

'There is an age-old saying among us,' the emoki said. 'When the harvesting of kumara is done, the harvesting of man will begin.'

That time was not far away, Lafe realized, vowing to keep his muskets ready at all times in case they were needed, and he spent the next day in his hut working on his armoury. When the cutter was built a cleverly-designed compartment had been set into the underside of the deck in the forepeak, and in it were stored two small tarred and canvas-wrapped barrels holding between them nearly forty pounds of gunpowder. That and the two full horns he carried gave him a goodly supply that would last a long time if he was careful with it. He also had a good supply of lead in rolled sheets and enough bullet moulds and flints to start a war of his own, and now he had a third musket on his side he felt a little more confident. He began to make his plans.

First he would talk to Tama. He would need to train One Eye and another warrior as soon as possible to handle the spare muskets. That would go a long way towards breaking up any attack on the village by natives, especially if they had no experience of musket fire.

The next day Tama came to watch him making bullets and Lafe had to spend a lot of time answering his endless questions and walking around him. First, the chief pounced on a piece of sheet lead that Lafe was cutting up ready to melt and cast in the bullet moulds.

'It is too soft, this iron. Is it young iron?' the chief asked again. He had already seen and felt the lead's softness some days before when he was going through Lafe's belongings, and its inability to produce a cutting edge had disappointed him as he had hoped to make dozens of axe heads out of the flat sheets. Now he returned to the problem.

'Surely if we heat it in the fire, like we do wood and some of the stone we use for weapons, it will grow harder?'

Many of the tribe's tools and weapons were indeed fire hardened, as Lafe knew, but why this would not work with lead was proving difficult to explain. He cut a piece of lead in the shape of an axe head and passed it to Tama, who laid it on the red hot coals of a nearby fire. A couple of minutes later he gave a loud snort of astonishment as his axe head of young iron turned into a blob of molten liquid before his eyes, ran down through the hot coals and disappeared into the ash below.

This stunned Tama like a blow to the head. In all his time on earth he had never seen such a thing and it defied all logic. In his world stone remained stone, it did not become liquid, and fire made such things harder, it did not devour and destroy them. He spat into the fire to show he wasn't pleased, then watched in wonder as Lafe poured water on the fire, retrieved the shiny disk of lead from the ashes and presented it to him. After that he watched in silence as Lafe melted the lead in a little pot, poured it into the moulds and knocked out the perfectly-formed round bullets as they cooled.

Tama was happy to agree that the one-eyed warrior should learn to shoot the muskets as soon as possible, but he claimed the other one of Lafe's muskets for himself. The warlike old devil had already thought it all out, Lafe realized. Three muskets, three owners – but the chief already owned the one-eyed warrior and the Goblin so the mana of the muskets was his alone.

Tama and Lafe inspected the defences around the village. The palisades and the fighting platforms were in good condition and Lafe estimated that there were around seventy warriors available to defend the place, an adequate number for the size of the fort although some were a little too old, he thought, and others too young.

'What we really need is this many muskets,' he told Tama, holding up the fingers of both hands twice to denote twenty. 'I hope your enemies don't have muskets?' Tama admitted he did not know.

A group of young men was undergoing weapons training and Lafe was pleased to see this, though their weapons were more suited for hand-to-hand fighting than defending a fort.

'How many warriors can Ngai Tahu put in the field?' he asked.

'As many as there are stars in the sky,' Tama told him cheerfully, but by using a stick in the sand and drawing the comparative sizes of their villages, Lafe came to a figure of around five hundred men. He was sure then that their only hope of turning back such a hoard was to rely on the shock power of the muskets so the next morning he began his own weapons training class on the beach.

Teaching Tama and One Eye to load and fire was easy enough, but it took time to overcome their tendency to shut their eyes when they pulled the trigger. Tama also had a bad habit of pouring an extra measure of powder down the barrel for greater effect, reasoning that if a musket could kill then surely it would kill better when it made more noise, but Lafe drilled them day after day until they were proud of their ability to load and fire at a rapid rate, and he was satisfied with their competence. Tama still used too much powder and could not be swayed from his belief that the bigger the enemy the more powder was required. If he ever got a Ngai Tahu chief in his sights he would probably blow them all up. Still, Lafe slept easier at night knowing the three muskets were loaded and ready for action and that others were capable of using them.

When the first heavy snowfalls of the year filled the passes the risk of invasion faded for another year and the people relaxed. Lafe was pleased at how readily the tribe came to accept him into their midst. He was made welcome at every fire and was offered good food and talk. Tama told him one day that he had earned much of the respect he was afforded; the warriors were impressed by the way he had taken utu on the men of the double canoe for killing his fellow Goblin.

'To the Maori, utu is a very right and proper way for regaining a man's mana,' Tama explained. 'Mana is important, a man cannot expect to be a warrior without it.   The shooting out of the sail was a stroke of great cunning and it will be talked about by my tribe for many generations. That is why it was necessary to present a valuable musket to the man whose eye you knocked out. After such a victory you could afford to be generous, and any bad feelings the man or his family might have towards you would be a case of bad manners now that you have restored his mana with such a gift.

'My people all think it was a good solution and the right thing to do. The tohunga would have it otherwise,' he confided with a chuckle, 'as he was the canoe singer that day when you attacked our waka. He lost a lot of his own mana that day, but he is only a spell singer and has an inflated idea of his own value to the tribe anyway.'

Every few days a tired and hungry-looking scout would come in from the forest to report to the chief, and Lafe was invited to sit in and listen to their news. The scouts kept constant watch on the tribe to the north and the mountain passes that might still be open. It was a dangerous time for any tribe. In this country, it seemed, there were always wars, though he gathered from the old ones that it had not always been so.

Day by day Lafe was introduced into more and more of the tribal customs and he found one of them particularly interesting. Now that the tribe had become settled and the food supplies more secure Tama had brought in the custom of whakatupu tangata, the making of warriors to fill the ranks. Lafe was puzzled and asked what it meant.

'This is a very important thing for our people,' Tama told him with a stern look. 'Every able-bodied man and woman is expected to apply themselves to the task.'

Lafe was not sure that he had caught the proper meaning of this conversation and sought clarification on the matter from other sources. The warriors were quick to confirm that it was a tribal duty and they were all busy night and day complying with Tama's wishes.

'Making babies!' Lafe exclaimed at last. 'So that's what he was talking about. That's what I thought.' For days he had been aware of the lovemaking going on around him and he thought about little else but Tama's daughter Marama. He summoned up his nerve.

'Chief Tama, can I help in this great enterprise?' he asked. But Tama was already several steps ahead of him.

'No, Goblin, it is the duty of warriors and their wives only.'

'Am I not a warrior? And could I not find a wife?'

'No, Goblin,' the chief said firmly. 'As you can see, all warriors carry the moko, the tattoo, on their faces and bodies. No woman would even consider coupling with a man who had not undergone the tattoo. That would be like marrying a child.'

Even in his wildest dreams Lafe could not imagine undergoing a full tattoo, though he had to admit he had got used to them and no longer

171

regarded the blue-black whorls and ridges that scarred the faces around him as ugly. He was told that each young warrior chose the basic design for his first tattoo and, year by year, his own personal triumphs were added as new lines until by old age a brave warrior's face was nearly as black as coal. Apparently the flesh was heavily ridged and gouged with a small chisel, the lines and circles radiating outwards from nose, mouth, and eyes. Then ink made from the soot of a certain tree was rubbed into these wounds so the flesh was permanently stained.

Not for me, Lafe told himself. He wondered whether it was ever done to a person by force, and was told with some astonishment that such a thing was unheard of. No one would consider doing that to another person. The moko required willingness and bravery on the part of its wearer and considerable skill in its execution, and sometimes warriors went without a tattoo for many years until a famous tattooist was captured by the tribe or they could afford to pay for his services.

Village life, Lafe found, was very agreeable. In the mornings after a meal he would join in with the young men as they trained with the patu, a small fighting club, and the taiaha, a short wooden stabbing spear. These were their main fighting weapons and the young warriors practised in pairs the various forms of attack and defence, concentrating on the best moves with each weapon. They advanced and retreated like gladiators, accompanied by the crack of fire-hardened spear against spear ringing around the compound. They also trained in wrestling and running. Lafe enjoyed these exercises and with his long legs and slender, well-muscled frame he was soon able to beat the best of the young trainees in a race, which improved his standing with the tribe even more.

Lafe enjoyed the long, fine but cooler days of what his people back home would have called an Indian summer. Most afternoons he went with off into the bush with one of the gathering parties to find more food to swell the food houses. In this way he became familiar with the country round about – the wide rivers that were so prone to sudden rises and falls with the mountains in such close proximity, the two lakes and the lagoon that provided so much of their food. It had been a good year for man and beast and every living creature they harvested was fat. Long bags made from the bladders of the kelp, split and dried, were filled with

172

a dozen varieties of birds cooked and preserved in their own fat. In spite of the hunting the birds still came to their favourite trees, the miro and the kahikatea which were heavy with fruit, and beautiful fat pigeons fell in their hundreds to the spearmen who lurked in the upper branches. With their twenty-foot long spears these men stalked the birds silently along narrow paths formed by the larger branches.

The hunters had their own captive birds, reared and trained from the nest to act the perfect Judases and lure their unsuspecting wild cousins within range of the spears. Lafe spent time in the upper branches with a spear one of the old men had made for him and his enjoyment was so obvious that one of the women warned him to take more care.

'If you are good in the trees you will soon be food for the roots. This is a favourite saying of us women, you know, so take heed.'

Of all the foods the villagers had access to, Lafe enjoyed the pigeon best. If it had been eating miro berries then the crop of the pigeon was not removed before cooking because it was the berries that gave it such a rich flavour, the women explained.

Much of the time he watched for Marama as she went about her many duties. The women seemed to have much more to do than their menfolk and were seldom idle, but one day Marama invited him to visit a stream to see the kotuku, the white heron. In the spring, she told him, the herons would gather only at this spot to nest and even now there would be some living there. The emoki would accompany them, of course, because it could be dangerous for a woman to travel so far from the village. She smiled as she told him this, and his heart thumped as he realized the hidden meaning of her words.

Lafe had seen the kotuku only at a distance but this time they crept in close to where a bird fished in the shallow waters of a small stream. They watched as it stood motionless, gazing into the water near its feet for so long that Lafe began to doubt if it would ever move.

'We have a saying,' Marama whispered in his ear. 'He kotuku kai whakata – the white heron feeds on its own reflection.'

'That is nice and it fits the bird perfectly,' Lafe replied. He tried the taste of the words on his own tongue and filed them away in his memory.

'The most valuable gift from one tribe to another is the gift of a plume from the kotuku, but unfortunately those feathers can only be owned and worn by a chief. My father keeps his in a specially-carved chest and they are brought out and shown only at feasts.

'It is such a waste of good feathers,' Marama lamented. 'If they were mine I would wear them when I sing and they would look so fine in my hair. But Tama has placed a tapu on the plumes to keep his daughter from touching them.' She said this matter-of-factly but Lafe had learned something of the concept of tapu and knew that if such a spell or curse was placed on a location or an object there would be dire consequences for the unlucky person who broke it. Thanks to the emoki he had already learned to avoid burial sites and holy places, and the knowledge that the skinny tohunga was watching him made him particularly careful not to infringe any other unwritten rules of the tribe.

Even now Tama lurked in the background, sending the emoki to see that he did not break any tapu involving this daughter of a chief. It did not seem fair. Mostly he enjoyed the company of the big slave, but today he would have much preferred to be alone with the beautiful young woman beside him.

From where they were crouched in the undergrowth watching the heron he could see the emoki on the bank of the lagoon cleaning mud from between his large toes with a stick. Marama, being high born, never saw the big man at all. He had been with her family since before she was born and she took it for granted that he would always be around somewhere watching her.

Now that she had the Goblin to herself she wanted to talk of love and poetry and hopefully to learn how such beings were different from her own people and how they were the same. It was strange, she thought, that a man who had travelled so far and visited so many strange places should be so lacking in social etiquette. The way he stared at her breasts when she let her robe slide down her shoulders a little way was like a starving dog looking at a bone, she thought to herself, and chuckled. How would he behave if he saw her secret place? The women in her tribe displayed their breasts freely when they were feeding their babies, swimming or just sitting around in the summer sun.

Perhaps, she thought, if this Goblin saw her breasts more often he would become more used to them and not stare at them so. She shrugged the cloak from her shoulders and smiled at him, but his indrawn breath hissed through his teeth as his eyes feasted hungrily on the upthrust breasts with their brown aureoles. His hand stretched out and the tips of his fingers brushed lightly across both her nipples. Marama was startled: he had moved so quickly. She drew the robe tightly around her shoulders once again but she had felt again the current that flowed between the two of them, and knew that the game was over. Her own body had betrayed her, she had felt her nipples tingling to his touch and the warmth that flowed into her loins was a new and disturbing sensation.

The sheer depth of feeling in the Goblin's deep blue eyes had nearly been her undoing, she knew. He had such sad and yet such bold eyes, they had stolen into her heart and now a seed was lodged there forever. It would flourish, she had no doubt of that, and would not be uprooted without tearing the whole fabric of her being apart.

Without being fully aware of her own actions Marama found herself drawing Lafe to her body until, eye to eye, their noses touched and they breathed deeply of each other's essence. The smell of his maleness made her senses swim and when he touched his lips to hers she had to break away before the sensation totally overwhelmed her. She scrambled to her feet, giddy with desire. Under her cloak the Goblin's hands had made free with her breasts and now her nipples strained against the rough fabric of her robe as if they still longed for his touch. She moved to the edge of the lagoon, close to the protection of the emoki, and tried to think calmly.

Marama had reached the age of fourteen summers and was more than ready to choose a mate and raise a family as many of her friends in the tribe had already done, but she was the daughter of a chief and so could marry only into another royal blood line. That was her fate, and there was no such husband to be found in her own tribe. Tama had sons but the taint of incest was the one great tapu that could never be broken, and because the old tribal connections had been broken by the war there was no husband to be found who was even remotely suitable. She was too valuable a prize to be cast among the warriors in Tama's own tribe, she knew that. In better times she would be married to a chief of another tribe, and her blood would be used to cement an alliance that would strengthen her father's mana. Her body and spirit were not her own, she belonged to the people and her duty lay in such an alliance. No man in her own tribe had ever sought her as a wife for that reason.

Until now she had not minded that no one sought her out as a wife or asked her to walk with them into the forest for whakatapu tangata. All this she had known and accepted as right and proper until this Goblin came along, but now everything seemed to have changed so quickly. *I feel like a butterfly that has just hatched and dried her wings and now sees how short the summer really is*, she admitted to herself.

But Tama alone held the key to her future. Would he let the Goblin take her for his wife? It was for men to make the decisions and for women to carry them out; that was the way it had always been. Even young sons were expected to give advice to their mothers, and it was for the chief to make the decisions for his people. She knew she had a special relationship with her father though it was within the strict bounds of what was right and proper between a chief and his daughter.

I will ask him, she decided. She regained her feet and moved away. Lafe leapt from the ground to go after her but in his passion he had quite forgotten the large emoki who now rose to his feet and gave him a ferocious scowl, making little chopping motions into his cupped hand with his patu. The message was clear. Lafe was glad he was not armed as in that wild lustful moment he would cheerfully have blown the slave's head clean off his shoulders. Frustrated and disappointed, he turned on his heels and made his way back to the village.

Over the next few weeks he found no chance to get Marama on her own again. It seemed that the whole world conspired against them ever being alone. If Marama went for water and Lafe followed then every woman in the village found they had run out of water at the same time, and now in the evenings he never lacked company around his own fire. People came to him for advice, to teach him something or just to talk away the hours until it was time to sleep again. Now that the food stores were full there was much time for visiting and storytelling and the cooler weather of early winter kept the men close to home.

It was the time to make new weapons, and although there was much talking done the hands were never still while the tongues were busy. Everyone had a piece of greenstone that they were shaping. The more ambitious worked on great clubs called mere and even the children worked the smaller pieces into ear pendants and the ugly little gods that were worn around the neck.

Lafe started noticing a subtle change in the people's behaviour toward him, as if he was being tested. It was nothing really obvious, but now even Tama spent more time asking him questions and probing his background. Lafe could answer freely now, because he knew that the *Northern Lights* would have left the coast and be well on her way back to America. For days after he knew she must be gone he was cast down, but sometimes when he thought of Marama he surprised himself by being a little glad that he was here instead of on the ship.

One day he was challenged to a wrestling match. It was a popular pastime but although he had often watched such matches he had never been invited to join in, let alone been formally challenged, and this challenger was one of the best fighters in the village. Lafe was allowed to choose an adviser who would act as his second and he chose the emoki, who went to see the challenger to arrange the day and the place of the fight. He also instructed Lafe on the rules, which were few. He seemed more interested in teaching the Goblin how to lose gracefully and obviously thought there was little chance of any other outcome.

In fact, no one seemed to hold out much hope of him winning the fight, Lafe decided ruefully, but he would have to put up a good battle. This was a serious challenge that he faced, and it dawned on him that he could take a really bad beating. When he saw looks of pity on the faces of his friends he became even more worried, and asked the emoki if it was possible to issue a counter challenge. There seemed to be no reason why not and so it was done. There was a lot of talk about this second challenge. This had never happened before, at least in the memory of the elders, and wisely they considered the matter before delivering their verdict. On the day agreed on by each party, it was decided, the two would fight in the Maori style and following that another fight would be fought in the style that was practised among Goblins.

It wasn't considered bad form to watch the enemy training so Lafe strolled down to see what he could learn. He watched his opponent oil his body carefully, warm up with a series of exercises then demolish his sparring partner with what looked like incredible ease. The rules seemed not to be that different from the rough and tumble matches that took place on whaling ships to entertain the crews in port. The object was to pin your opponent helpless on the ground to score the point, using whatever holds and throws a very desperate man could think of.

By the day of the match excitement had reached fever pitch around the village. People stopped to talk at Lafe's fire, to clap him on the back and sometimes just to stare at him as if, he thought, they knew they wouldn't see him around afterwards. When the time came his adviser escorted him to the ring, a flat area normally given over to games and kite flying and where the entire village was already seated and waiting. He sought out Tama with his eyes and nodded to him respectfully, receiving the same acknowledgment in return. Tama's manner seemed just as open and direct as ever. Why then had he given permission for his Goblin's bones to be broken, Lafe wondered? He was sure that no warrior would have dared to issue such a challenge if the chief had not given his permission beforehand.

Now that he lived with a race of people whose rules and laws had of necessity become his own he could not and would not refuse the challenge, even if he had to take a whipping. He looked down at Marama and received such a sad smile in return that he felt he was already sentenced and on his way to the gallows.

He eyed his opponent who stood buck-naked a few yards from him, the whites of his eyes startling among the black whorls of his tattooed face. The warrior's skin was oiled and glossy and his muscles rippled as he strutted backwards and forwards in front of the crowd, raising the dust in little puffs around his feet as he stamped them down from the height of his thighs. This was his day, and he was the tribe's champion.

Lafe thought he saw a few sorrowful glances cast his way, mainly from the women of the tribe whose hearts were a lot softer than the rest. His opponent, he guessed, was about four inches shorter than he was but with a trunk as round and stocky as a wine barrel, and probably weighing thirty pounds heavier. He cast a last glance at Marama, lifted his chin and flexed his muscles to face the challenge.

At a signal from the chief the two wrestlers crouched and readied themselves, eyeball to eyeball, and when the war horn brayed they rushed in and grappled, each trying to keep his own balance and at the same time toss his opponent into the dust. Lafe realized in the first few minutes that his opponent's strength was much greater than his own. The man had his feet planted solidly and his great thighs were like the trunks of trees, and slowly Lafe was forced to give ground under the pressure. But he wasn't going to go down easily. He crouched suddenly, catching the big man off balance, and tried an ambitious hip throw he had been taught by a Chinaman on his first ship. The abrupt change of tactics caught the other man off guard and Lafe managed to roll him onto his back for the first point of the match.

He saw a new respect in the warrior's eyes as they closed in and grappled, but try as he might he could never manage to get the other man off his feet again and he felt his strength slowly drain away. His face was regularly rubbed in the sand and his legs and arms ached from the pounding and twisting they got until his breath came in strangled gasps. Finally the match was over. His lip was badly split, his bones felt like they had all been pulled from their sockets and his legs were like jelly as he was lifted from the sand for the last time and declared the loser, and the whole tribe leaped to their feet and launched into a impromptu haka led by his opponent.

Winner and loser together washed the dirt and blood from their bruised bodies in the lagoon and went back to the fire where the women had prepared a feast. The match had put everybody in a happy frame of mind and ribald comments flew to and fro among all ages, as everyone agreed it had been a great fight. Lafe was the butt of much of the laughter that flew backwards and forwards across the fire, although he felt it was not unkind. The early point he had scored was much discussed and he had, it seemed, gained much mana from the surprise move. It was so unorthodox that no one could remember it being used before.

'Eh, how we all enjoy a good fight,' they told him. Then, fed and rested, they moved back to the fighting ring anxious for the second half of the day's entertainment to begin. This was a Goblin fight and everyone knew that many of the things Goblins could do were different, but the general feeling was that their man would give this Goblin another good walloping he wouldn't forget in a hurry.

Lafe produced some long strips of canvas and had his own and his opponent's knuckles bound as he explained the rules of combat in a loud voice so that all the spectators could hear him.

'The way we fight is not so different from the way your young men train against each other with their fighting sticks. For every move there is a counter move,' he explained. He hoped that the contest would be one of skill, but after the war horn brayed he quickly realized he was dealing with a slugger who stalked him around the ring lashing out with blows that threatened to knock the head from his shoulders. Soon Lafe was using every inch of the area just to stay out of his reach and stay alive. Once in a while he managed to slip a punch through a gap in his opponent's defence, but for all the notice the big man took of the blows he might not have bothered and he knew he would have to think of something better pretty soon.

By the third rest break he realized he was lucky to still be in the fight. A wicked roundhouse blow had caught him on the ear and sent him to his knees and right out of the ring, and in the eyes of the audience he was down a point and still had made no impression on his opponent. He danced and swayed his way through to the next session content just to stay out of range of the other man's fists, but then he began to notice that holes were appearing in the warrior's defence. His opponent was becoming over confident. He moved in quickly and hit him hard on the breastbone, hoping he would lower his hands to cover the spot but the ruse was recognized for what it was and the man's guard stayed up.

Lafe leaned against the side of a tree during the break, breathing hard and wondered why he hadn't just been content to accept the beating he received in the first fight. Both fighters were now covered in blood and great welts stood out on Lafe's ribs where he had taken some bad blows. He could feel one of his eyes slowly closing and he bled from a badly-cut lip as the emoki fanned him with a flax blanket. His only pleasure was that his opponent was starting to look the worse for wear too.

180

He glanced at Marama and received a shocked look in return. Her face was full of horror at what she had seen, and as Lafe watched she leaned across to her father.

'Won't you order them to stop the fight?' she begged.

'No, I cannot. It must go on to the end now or these two will always be at each other's throats like dogs,' he replied, 'though if I had have known that the Goblin's way of fighting was so gruesome I would never have allowed it to begin.' There was regret in his voice as he signalled for the men to fight again.

Now is the time to finish it, Lafe told himself, or I will never be able to do it. He moved in quickly to land blow after blow, reducing his opponent's face to pulp. The big warrior's brain was beginning to slow down now, but instinct still told him to keep his breastbone covered even though Lafe had changed his target. The crowd was silent now, realizing that the two men were each determined to finish the other off. More and more often their champion's hands failed to rise to cover his face, but his return blows were still as vicious as ever.

Finally the chance came and Lafe took it. He mustered all his remaining reserves and swung his right fist, with all the power he could put behind it, at the warrior's uncovered jaw. With a shock that felt as if it had broken his wrist he connected and the big man went down like one of the giant trees of the forest that had been cut through, pitching slowly face forward onto the sand. Lafe's legs threatened to buckle beneath him as he waited for his opponent to rise, but the fight was over and the fallen warrior did not move.

Marama came to lead him to the lagoon to wash his wounds, and then took him back to the fire while his opponent was being attended to. She said nothing, and Tama's face was grave. The chief waited until Lafe was seated before he spoke.

'You have brought many new things to this tribe, Goblin. Some are good and some are not so good. This fighting with the closed fist is not a good thing, and we will have no more of it.

'Now it would be a good idea to present one of your axes to your victim, just to avoid any bad feelings that might arise from the damage you have done to his feelings. The small one will be sufficient.'

181

At this rate he would very quickly be left without any property at all, Lafe thought to himself. It occurred to him that no one had presented him with a gift to solace his hurt pride when he had been the loser, but he shrugged the thought off. The tribe's rules must be his rules now, and he could see that the big man armed with a sharp axe would be a great asset in any form of warfare with hostile forces.

Winter set in properly and sheets of icy rain spread down from the mountains. The village took on a nearly-deserted look in bad weather as its occupants simply wrapped themselves in their flax mats and slept. Only when the sun was out and the air balmy was there any sign of life outside those fuggy, fusty little houses. Lafe had never seen people who could sleep so long; some days right around the clock, men, women and children all mixed together in their nests of soft dry grass under layers of mats. It was like hibernation through the cold days and nights.

There had been many births during the autumn and the women all seemed to have babies at the breast. Long winters would not be so bad if there was someone to share his bed with, Lafe reckoned. He had Salem for warmth but there were other needs too.

The tribe was sustained during the winter by love and music. When the sun brought people from their houses to sit on mats out of the breeze and polish their greenstone pieces, someone would invariably shout the opening refrain of a song and they would begin. In this village all the women sang, and what voices they all had. Marama seemed to love singing best of all, and it was her voice that called the others to song more often than any other voice in the village. Lafe could hear and recognize her voice from any part of the lagoon and it reminded him of the bird of the forest called tui, whose clear, liquid notes dropped into the still air like honey. When Marama sang a hush descended over the valley as the inhabitants, small and large, paused and held their breath to listen.

The men loved music too, but theirs was a more vigorous, martial song and dance that was wonderfully coordinated. If Lafe happened to be talking to a warrior when the opening refrain of a haka was called, he would see the man's eyes empty of all conscious thought and his head start to jerk up and down on his neck like a disjointed puppet, just as Matai's head had done, and already his feet would have begun to stamp an almost involuntary dance in time with the beat. Lafe had never met a race of people with rhythm and song so interwoven into their very souls.

For much of this early part of winter he suffered from homesickness, brought about by his aloneness and the knowledge that the *Northern Lights* had now almost certainly left for America without him. For good or bad, these Maori people were now his people too. He spent much of his time in Marama's company but he was never again alone with her outside the confines of the village.

It was no longer enough for him just to be with her. Like a starving man he needed more than a trifling smile or the quick touch of her fingers and in desperation he finally persuaded her to climb a hill with him to where they could get a fine view of the mountains. The faithful emoki trailed them all the way to the top and Lafe would gladly have given him the slip but he guessed Tama had laid down the firm rule that the two of them could not be allowed to be alone together. Even as they climbed, Lafe sensed that Marama was afraid of the consequences of her actions. Slipping away to the forest with him had been a rash choice for her.

When they reached the top of the hill they sat and looked for a moment at the stunning view, then their eyes searched each other's faces.

'Marama, I want you for my wife,' Lafe said. His urgent need made the words much harsher and blunter than he intended and she looked at him seriously for a moment before she replied.

'I have asked my father if he would let me become your wife but he says he would never let me marry a man who is not a warrior. And he will never allow it. I know him well.'

'Does he think I am not a warrior?' Lafe asked, his voice tight with fury. He was stung by the insult, even more by Marama's quiet reply.

'Without the tattoo, Tama will never accept that you are a warrior. Without the tattoo you cannot be my husband.'

Chapter 10

Winter spread its grip over the land, staying warm and dry was the priority and almost all activity ceased. Occasionally an unusually warm and sunny day brought people from their homes but just as quickly a cold southerly would send them all into hibernation again. Lafe found the long days and nights with no other company but his own unpleasant until he too learned to doze and daydream away twenty out of each twenty four hours. It was the worst time he could remember. He was young, restless and homesick and had too much time on his hands, and the long periods of inactivity did nothing to ease his desire for Tama's daughter. He spent long hours brooding on his fate, little realizing that he was being subtly drawn into the tribe by minds far more cunning than his own. He was a very useful catch and Tama was not going to risk him running off the moment another sail came over the horizon, or worse, running off to join another tribe. Very cleverly, Tama had set out to bind his Goblin with silken strands in such a way that he did not even know he had been caught.

Am I a warrior or am I not a warrior? Over and over again the same thoughts spun in his head. The tribal council had agreed that he could be accepted into the ranks as a warrior on every other criteria but this, that he did not bear the warrior's mark. That damned tattoo! He had been over this same argument hundreds of times and there was no other answer that he could come up with, nothing that would satisfy both his own needs and the tribe's requirements.

There was no doubt that this matter of his manhood was the main subject of discussion right around the village. From the youngest child to the nearly toothless grandmothers, the whole damned village seemed to take it for granted that he would soon become a full member of their tribe with all the status and honour associated with marrying Tama's daughter. They refused to believe that he would allow the little matter of a tattoo to stand in the way. Didn't all men dream from childhood of the day they would receive their own tattoos?

Such remarks were often made in his hearing. It was cleverly done, this pressure that was brought to bear on him day and night, and Marama played her part too. Some days she would smile hopefully at him and his heart would nearly jump out of his chest, and the next day she would look sad and distant as if her life was ended. Tama himself spent hours asking questions, drawing Lafe out as a prospective father-in-law might back in America, except that the chief was a lot more open and direct with his questions than one of Lafe's own countrymen would have been.

'How many ships does your father own?' Tama would ask. 'How big was the ship that brought you here? How many men did it hold? How many muskets does your tribe own?' Lafe always smiled to himself when his answers pleased the chief, who was impressed that his white captive was the son of such a rich and powerful man.

'A great chief! Truly a great chief!' he would exclaim. 'And so wealthy too!' Tama was well satisfied, believing there would come a day when much of that wealth would find its way into his Goblin's hands and therefore his own.

Most of the people who came to Lafe's fire now to talk away the winter days seemed to be the heavily-tattooed warriors whose faces and bodies were living works of art. Against his will the young sailor found himself becoming interested in their tattoos and the names and reputations of the tattoo artists known to be the best. Some warriors even came to him with sheets of bark on which they had neatly drawn tattoos for his inspection and consideration, and as they left his fireside they would toss encouraging remarks over their shoulders in a very off-hand manner.

'The pain is nothing,' they would say. 'Not that you would be afraid of a little pain anyway.'

Lafe knew that this statement was untrue and that the pain would be excruciating. It was not unknown for a man to die under the needle, which was in fact more like a small chisel made out of the bone of an albatross wing and which was tapped into the skin with a light wooden mallet. Though it really wasn't the pain that stopped him, he admitted to himself. It was all a matter of perception. The tribe recognized him as a useful member of their warrior race and they wanted to keep him so they were offering all the privileges of a warrior to bind him tight, but he still saw himself as a prisoner hoping to escape and return home to his own country. These two contrary views should cancel each other out and remove the need for any action over the tattoo, but for Marama. In his heart Lafe had to admit he might not be ready to take an opportunity to escape even if it was offered.

For weeks he had wanted to go back down the coast to the two islands they had passed on their way up two months earlier. The islands had been crowded with seals and he craved a change of diet. He could do with some fresh seal meat and, more importantly, the chance to get away from the tribe and do some serious thinking. To his surprise, Tama agreed that he could go, and the chief himself would go with him. As usual, the emoki would accompany them to look after their needs while they were camped on the islands. It was just a matter of catching the right winds and a long enough break between the endless storms that blew across the Tasman Sea at that time of the year.

The night before they left, long after the last of the village lovers had fallen asleep, Marama crept into Lafe's dwelling. He was stunned that she would take such a risk and he quickly and nervously checked the darkness for the emoki before joining her on the sleeping mat.

'I know that you are struggling to make a decision and you are going away to the island for just that reason,' she whispered. 'I want to give you this gift before you go, to help you make up your mind.'

His senses reeling, he held her close and tried to kiss her but she held her finger to his lips. 'Give me your word that you will not penetrate me, and I will give you love tonight. There are many ways to make love, as you will find out. But you must promise. I must go to my husband as pure as my tribe expects me to be.

'If you do not control yourself I will scream and Tama will no doubt have you killed.'

Lafe would have promised anything to have her near him. He did not need her warning to understand the terrible risk she was taking for both of them, but he was powerless to do anything except nod his agreement and hold her close.

'The women have taught me the many ways to please a man,' she whispered in his ear. 'Let me show you how unmarried women practice lovemaking in our tribe. And then the next time we are together perhaps we will be man and wife, and then, of course, you will be in charge.'

She stood and cast off her robe, then slid under the blankets. His hands roamed her supple body, encountering nothing more than a strip of fine leather she wore over her loins held up by a thin leather belt. This loincloth was made from the pelt of the ground-living parrot, a bird whose pelt was so fine and soft it was like another skin. It was a prize much sought-after by hunters as gifts for their special women. What lay beneath it was a prize that Lafe knew he could not yet claim.

Three times before the dawn Marama raised him to the point of exquisite agony before bringing him to a blessed release with clever fingers, lips and tongue. Then, just before the first colour of dawn stained the sky, she slipped away into the darkness, as quiet as the hunting owl, to return to her own hut. Lafe was totally disarmed as he lay alone, wide awake, thinking of the even greater pleasures of his wedding night and all the nights to follow. When the emoki came to fetch him at first light he pretended to be in a deep sleep, though even to his own nostrils there was a strong smell of lovemaking hanging in the air inside the hut and he could only hope the slave had not noticed it.

The cutter had been packed and made ready the night before and now Tama, Lafe and Salem the dog scrambled aboard. The coldness of the air burned their throats if they breathed too deeply. The water in the lagoon stung their feet and ankles and must have numbed the emoki's legs as he pushed them off before clambering on board himself. For weeks

187

past the storms that raged the coast had flung angry waves ashore, waves that had pounded the beach with such fury that the earth had trembled underfoot, but now the open sea beyond the lagoon was so calm it could scarcely be heard.

All the way down the coast Lafe could hardly dare to meet Tama's eye, fearing that the chief would read on his face the secret smile of a man who had spent the night in paradise. When he let his guard down and thought of Marama he could feel the silly smile start to show, and hastily hid any sign of the delight he felt at sharing her bed. Several times during the voyage he caught Tama looking long and hard at him, frowning as if he had seen something distasteful, but his enjoyment in handling the tiller seemed to keep his mind from straying too deeply from the job at hand.

They made it to the island after spending a night up one of the many rivers that entered the sea on that section of the coast. Tama was anxious to put his skills with the musket into practice, and shot two large male seals that had tarried too long after the rest of the herd had headed south for the colder waters to fatten up. The seals were dragged out of the sea so the emoki could clean them, while Lafe made camp in a little thatched hut that Tama's men had built years before for seal hunting and the gathering of seaweed.

In this Maori world, taking food was a very special thing and was strictly controlled by laws of tapu. Every food had its season, there were places allotted for its gathering and to take certain foods out of season was to break a tapu. Such rules were strictly enforced, and a man who talked of eating pigeon in spring would be thought dangerously unbalanced. The complex system had evolved over centuries so that food sources could be managed and preserved and the hunter gatherer could not afford to take fish or game that was out of condition or skinny because it would not reward him for the energy he expended.

'There is a time and a season for everything,' Tama told Lafe.

'A time to sow, a time to reap,' the American replied, vaguely remembering his Bible. Although this tribe did not sow, they cared in their own way for nature. They would take a bird's eggs but would not take a sitting bird, allowing her instead to raise the next clutch. Shellfish were taken only when they were fat, otherwise they were left to spawn and replace themselves. Tama could point across the water from the island to any stream on the mainland and say, 'On the first big tide in spring, when the moon is little and thin in the shape of a fingernail, we will go there and fill a canoe with flatfish.' Or it might be shark or some other delicacy, each with its time and place of harvest. Without a written calendar these facts of moon and tide, fish and bird behaviour were stored in the tribal memory and if Lafe was to point to a stream and ask its name he might also be told that it produced very fat eels at the first full moon after the highest spring tide. This knowledge was gained the hard way, by trial and error and death through starvation, and if it was ever lost the tribe would probably perish with it.

The more Lafe learned, the more he realized how little he really knew of such a way of life. He was aware that the chief made the decisions about where to go and what to hunt and that the advice of the elders was sought and listened to, and he had already noticed on his first trip up the coast that the people never moved from a camp or began a trip until the food supplies had been carefully rebuilt to sustain them. Now he understood how important such decisions really were, that every time an order was given for the tribe to move out to hunt a certain food there was a very real risk of starvation if they were unsuccessful. If the chief got it wrong, the tribe would cease to exist.

Already on the little island where they were camped the seals were being prepared for transport back to the village, the emoki had dived repeatedly into the cold water for the black shellfish called paua, and many pounds of seaweed were already on drying racks in the sun. Tama often rested from his labours to sit in the sun and think, which was after all what a chief must do best, but the emoki was kept busy as long as there was a single edible thing left to gather and there was still light to see it with. There were several hundred hungry mouths to feed back at the village and that took some doing, but he did not seem at all unhappy with his lot. He had even been allowed to take a wife, which gave him a sort of superior slave status as long as he gave good service. If he did not, Lafe had heard Tama say many times, 'Eh, how the ovens are gaping for you!'

189

To Lafe's surprise, he found that for the first time since he had been captured he also felt a strong obligation toward those hungry mouths at home. When another large male seal swam in to the island and was killed and prepared he was delighted with its fine condition and felt grateful to the rich waters for providing such fine food.

Like Tama he also had time to think, and it was on this sealing expedition that he conceived the idea of fitting the big double canoe with a modern fore-and-aft sailing rig of a similar design to the one on the cutter. A new sail would have to be made for her anyway since he had destroyed the old one and he decided to seek Tama's permission to rebuild the boat's cross-deck platform and fit her with a single mast. With such a rig it would be the fastest and most powerful sailing vessel on the coast and, armed with a couple of muskets, would be a very useful addition to the tribe's defences.

Once again the cutter crossed the bar in triumph, this time with Tama at the helm and Salem barking a greeting from the bow. To return in the hungry months with a load of fresh meat was indeed a victory against the winter and the village came to life again. The ovens were heated and filled with fresh seal meat and the tribe sat down to a feast that lasted two days. It was pure gluttony; man, woman and child ate until they could hold no more, staggered away from the table to rest then creep back to the feast as soon as their stomachs allowed them. Now he understood the fine line between feast and famine Lafe could accept this culture of gluttony more readily and he reflected on the way Matai and Jimmy had eaten every scrap of food available to them.

The tribe had no way of catching whales, but he was told that in the rare event of a whale stranding on the beach they would camp next to it and stagger away only when the last morsel had been eaten. He remembered his days on board the whaler when the first whale of the season was hauled on board and men worked in the flickering firelight to extract every ounce of useful meat, oil and blubber.

Lafe had used his holiday away from the pressures of the village to think about the decision he had to make. He had no illusions about what was at stake; if he had the tattoo he would sever the last link with his own country and family, the hope that he could one day return to

190

New England. With a tattooed face he would become a native. He knew that the prospect of returning home was not high, but he could never forget his own first reaction, and those of others on the ship, to the faces of these tattooed warriors. Such a deliberate mutilation was alien to his own race, and he had drawn back with a feeling of revulsion. It would not matter that his own face was white and his hair was golden, if he wore the tattoo it would evoke that same response from his countrymen, a feeling of revulsion and perhaps disgust. And such an act would be deliberate on his part. There was no force involved, it would be his choice to submit to the chisel, his hand that slashed the umbilical cord that still bound him to America.

He knew that if he wished to survive and have any life at all it would be with this tribe, and that although they were far too polite to put it into words they had given him a clear choice. He could remain their prisoner or he could become one of them. Perhaps it could be called fate, but from the moment he had first seen New Zealand he had felt that his life was in some way bound up with this land and its people. Now he had returned to the village in triumph with the cutter loaded with food he found he had made his decision. He was part of the tribe, one of their warriors, with all the duties and responsibilities that entailed, and he let it be known that he would seek the tattoo.

Memories of that erotic night with Marama still made him blush and he hoped that the news of his decision would forestall any action Tama might take. The chief was quite capable of having Lafe seized, forcibly-tattooed and delivered to his future wife with an armed escort if he thought that this would provide an answer to his problems, and Lafe guessed that Marama would agree with her father's solution. For the good of the tribe, that was the way Tama would always act and it would be wrong to think otherwise.

To his surprise, once he had told a few people he would have the tattoo it was as good as done, and in the eyes of the village he had joined their ranks. He made no promise and swore no oaths, but he was now a warrior, with all the privileges and responsibilities that entailed. He would be expected to give his own life, if necessary, to protect the members of the tribe.

He could take his time over choosing his own personal design, because this was one of the major decisions in a man's life and should not be hurried. Even more surprisingly, it dawned on him that the tribe had no tattooist of its own and he would have to wait until they captured or otherwise acquired the services of one. It seemed that an artist with the required skill and experience was not that easy to find, and Tama's tribe had no affiliation with any other group that had such a man in their ranks. According to the chief it was not unusual for an important warrior, or one with royal blood, to wait many years for a favoured artist to become available. If another tribe had a good tattooist famous for his skills, that was good reason to launch an attack on them.

'Such a thing is not unknown,' Tama explained. 'Many have become slaves or gone to the ovens because a young chief's face ached from the lack of a tattoo.'

'Surely then the tattoo artist whose people had been treated so badly wouldn't apply his skills for his new tribe?' Lafe asked, but Tama looked surprised at his unworldliness.

'Of course he would. You must not think we are backward in this part of the world, Goblin. We would keep his family alive and only eat them one at a time, to reward him for his good work. If his chisel was clumsy we would eat him and his people all at once and his family would cast no further shadow on the land.

'Now you will have to be patient, and maybe this year or maybe next year we will find an artist and you will have your moko.'

Lafe had come to like and respect his future father-in-law. Tama was in most ways a good man, though necessarily an authoritarian figure. He was, after all, the chief. He had taken over the role from his father before him, and he would continue to rule as long as he was successful and the people liked him. The moment he failed to satisfy either condition he would be replaced.

Lafe accepted all these things, but what he found difficult to stomach was that the man was a self-professed cannibal with a genuine love of human flesh. Lafe had skirted the issue in all the many conversations that they had together, careful to hide any signs of disgust when the subject arose. Tama thought no more of eating a human than eating a seal, though he professed to enjoy the former more.

'How do you think a war party travels so far and so fast, Goblin?' he said one day. 'We haven't got time to grow food or to stop for the many days it takes to gather fish and birds. Of course we eat our enemies. Doesn't everyone?'

He stared at Lafe, wide-eyed as a new thought struck him. 'Is this not so in your own country?'

'It is not done in my country,' Lafe told him, but his answer only confirmed in Tama's mind how wealthy and wasteful a race the Goblins were that they could ignore such a food source. Lafe decided he could never ask Marama if she had partaken of human flesh. He would rather not know the answer.

The Maori New Year began in mid-winter with the appearance of the stars Lafe knew as the Seven Sisters in the night sky. This was around the shortest day of the year, when these stars that Marama called Mata Ariki or the Eyes of God appeared low in the northeast, not far from the bright planet Venus. That loveliest of pale green heavenly bodies was always the first to show in the evening and the last to leave the sky.

An hour before sunrise the tribe gathered on the sand hills to welcome the Mata Ariki.

'Ah, the Seven Sisters in all their glory. They are perhaps the most beautiful group of stars in the heavens,' Lafe told Marama as they stood close together in the chill morning air, but though the idea of sisters intrigued her she preferred to see them as the eyes of her gods and ancestors. The stars reminded Lafe of night watches on the *Northern Lights* and he wondered where his ship was that day. She would have crossed the Pacific and rounded Cape Horn and would be well on her way home he guessed, and he hoped that Olva and the men had found his note scratched on the tree. At least then they could tell his father there was evidence he still lived.

Thoughts of home and family could come upon him suddenly, taking him unawares and saddening him, although mostly he managed to shut such longings from his mind or keep them in a secret compartment so they did not intrude on his new life. Marama always sensed this mood and she did her best to bring his thoughts back to the present.

When Lafe finally managed to borrow his spyglass back from Tama he sat and looked for the stars he knew best of all. They appeared very different in this new hemisphere and he recited the English names for the ones he knew, keeping them alive in his mind. The tribe had its own names for all the main stars and planets and he was learning them too, and learning about their annual paths across the sky. The stars helped to tell of planting times and other specific events in the food calendar.

No one left the sand hills that morning until the sun had hoisted itself above the ocean and the stars faded back into obscurity. It was a day for talk and planning, a day to look at the year ahead, and all the elders settled near the fire with their cloaks wrapped tight around them. Tama had decided that he would have more men under military training this year than ever before.

'This will mean a lot more work for the rest of the people, but no matter, this is what we must do,' he told them with a gleam in his eye.

'When the weather has improved we will raid the stone fields and we will take slaves this time, now that we have the thunderstick. It will be a good raid. Our enemies will be terrified when they hear the noise and we will take them easily. We need more women for the tribe, and more boys to replace those training to be warriors.'

Lafe listened carefully, and understood that the tribe would go to war in the coming year, probably in the autumn, although Tama was keeping the timing very much to himself.

'Tama never stops dreaming of taking utu against the tribe that drove us from Murderers' Bay. It might not come this year, but it will come one day,' Marama whispered to Lafe, confirming his guess.

Once prayers had been offered up to the stars for victory against potential enemies and prosperity in the year to come, it was time to fly the kites. For days the village had hummed with activity as new kites were built and old ones lovingly refurbished. They were mostly built in the shape of birds, cleverly fashioned out of light plaited grasses over a sturdy framework of hollow and light reeds. Some even had feathers cunningly attached to them and talons poised to strike, like the great eagle that once inhabited the land. Tribal memories of this bird so powerful it carried off woman and children were very fresh.

The kites were objects of great beauty as they swooped and soared, and to Lafe's surprise they caused great excitement not just among the children but among the warriors themselves. These were not mere toys and he realized that to fly a kite on this day of Mata Ariki was to worship the gods and ask for the tribe to be remembered in the coming year. Marama had made a beautiful kite that showed off her artistic talents and Lafe was soon tearing up and down the beaches among the most fearsome warriors of the tribe who were all doing the same thing, shrieking and laughing and trying to get their individual kites into the air. The object of the game was to out-fly all the other kites and at the same time launch aerial attacks on those still trying to struggle into the air. This mid-winter making and flying of the kites was an activity that lifted spirits and brought the tribe to life again before they settled back to semi-hibernation with the coming of the spring rains.

The barriers that once existed between Lafe and Marama seemed to have been miraculously swept aside by those few simple words, 'I will accept the tattoo.' Now they were permitted to work and play together, with the approval of the tribe, and they often shared a fire and a meal with other couples their own age. There were babies everywhere and Lafe was cheered to see the affection lavished on children, not just by their parents but by everyone in the tribe.

Only the sexual tapu remained and the emoki was there to see that Lafe did not stray beyond the right and proper boundaries for a high-born and well-brought-up young woman. When the weather was fine and warm the courting couple explored the many special places that Marama wished to show Lafe, and he felt sorry for the emoki who plodded stoically after them when he would obviously much rather have been sitting in front of his own fire.

Just south of their village at Okarito and high on the side of the great inland range was an ice field with its attendant glaciers that Marama called Roimata o Hinehukatere, the Tears of the Avalanche Girl. It was a poetic and very lovely description, Lafe thought. The furthest advances of the ice did look like tears, and Marama likened the great curving tracks of the glaciers to the moko or tattoo on a man's face.

This island that Cook had named South Island was known to Maori as Te Wai Pounamu or the waters of jade. Marama told him that Ngahue, an ancestor or god who came from Hawaiki to this new country, had a pet fish which turned to greenstone wherever he put it down to rest, which explained why greenstone was found in some parts of the country and not in others. Lafe always thought the boundaries very blurred when it came to distinguish between gods and ancestors, and he guessed that Hawaiki, which he had also heard Matai speak of, was a great land somewhere in the central or southern Pacific Ocean. The tribe had stories to explain most of the wonders of the world that surrounded them and most of these stories had gods or spirits involved in them somewhere. Many attributed to the gods a wicked sense of mischief at man's expense.

Everything to do with greenstone was of tremendous interest to the tribe, and it seemed to Lafe that when they were not looking for food they were engaged in a great treasure hunt. Once or twice he heard whispers that many caches of finished greenstone tools and weapons as well as boulders still in their raw state were hidden along the coast.

On their way down from seeing the glaciers Lafe and Marama went to the stream to see if the white heron was at home and while they watched it flew lazily across the lagoon towards them and over their heads to vanish among the trees. Marama was entranced and stood poised in silent wonder as the bird passed with its slow, stately wing beat, a pure white shape silhouetted against the deep blue sky.

'Do you see the same beauty as I do?' she asked in a voice filled with awe. 'I swear that bird is a god, and we have seen it.

'Now you will understand why we say to a most honoured visitor, he kotuku rerenga tahi, which means that the visit is like the flight of the white heron, a wonderful experience.'

So sensitive a woman, Lafe thought fondly, with so much poetry in her being. He knew that Marama's mother, Tama's first wife, had been killed in the fighting at Murderers' Bay. Marama had been their only child and Lafe knew just what she must have gone through because he too had lost his mother when he was a young child. Tama had two new wives and three very young children now, but Marama occupied a special place as his firstborn and the daughter of his first love.

Marama, Tama and the tohunga, who seemed to have got over his bitter hatred of the white Goblin although they were still far from friends, decided on a date in early spring when the stars would be favourable to the gods and suitable for the wedding. All Lafe could do now was wait, but at least he did not have to undergo the ceremony of moko first as he had expected.

It would be a relief in more ways than one to have a wife, because his clothing had started to disintegrate and was slowly turning to rags as the days went by. Already his boots had been discarded as no longer repairable and he now wore plaited flax sandals on his feet. None of the men had the skills to make their own clothing; that was women's work and until a man was old enough to acquire a wife his garments were made by his mother. The women prided themselves on their weaving and cloth-making skills and the people were always well dressed, but without a woman to do such work Lafe was well on the way to being the poorest dressed person in the tribe.

Marama promised him a new cloak for his wedding day. These were the finest of garments, woven out of fine grasses and flax then dyed to give the best effect. Finally, bird feathers were cleverly fastened into the weave, and the finished cloak was a work of art rather than a mere garment. To make and give such a beautiful thing was to be lifted to a higher spiritual plane and the people held that this talent, like the ability to sing and dance, was a gift from the gods.

Storytelling was another such gift, and with no books to fill in the long hours Lafe found himself an avid listener at first and then a storyteller in his own right. The people loved stories, preferably ones they had heard many times before, and he was often asked to repeat one particular story that had captured the imagination of everybody in the village.

'Tell us again, Goblin, about how your people ride to war on the backs of large dogs,' someone would cry out, and Lafe would begin his story. It called for him to draw a life-sized figure of a horse in the sand.

'But surely the beast's legs were longer than that last time, Goblin?' they would challenge, and only when they were satisfied that it was the same horse as last time would he be allowed to proceed. If his story varied even a shade from the original version they would be on to him like a flash. Every part of it was taken apart and carefully scrutinized, debated at length and reassembled again. War stories fascinated the tribe, and to ride to war on the backs of dogs was an idea that was so novel to them they never tired of hearing it. Lafe would finish the telling and wait for the same questions.

'Does this animal have teeth? Does it bite? Does it have hair?'

'Yes, this is true,' Lafe would patiently answer each question, knowing what was coming.

'Then it is a dog!' they would yell in great mirth wiping the tears from their eyes and pointing at Salem the Labrador, now so big a small child could have ridden on his back if he had allowed it. The only land mammals in the country, excluding the seal, were the rat, the dog and a small bat, and even the rat and the dog had been brought across the Pacific by Maori in their canoes. Salem was far bigger and stronger than any dog these people had ever seen before. It stretched their credibility to think that Goblins could ride to battle even on a larger dog, but to conceive of an animal the size of a horse was far too difficult.

The birdsong of the forest grew louder each morning as its inhabitants began courting, reminding their spouses that the summer was almost on them and there were nests to be made, and a new house was built inside the stockade for the chief's daughter and her husband. The frame was of saplings, the walls were panelled with tightly-tied bundles of swamp reeds and sweet-smelling grass was used to thatch the roof. As soon as it was finished Marama moved most of her personal belongings into it and made it a home, although she would not sleep there until the night of her wedding.

Finally the day came. Early that morning the ovens were opened, stones that had been heated on fires overnight were lowered into the pits and the food was put down to cook. Many new cloaks were on display besides his own wedding gift from Marama, proof that not all the tribe's energies had been wasted or spent making babies through the winter. There had also been lots of singing and haka practice, toning up the respective groups who promised a spectacular performance.

The hungry months of June, July and most of August were behind them now and the food supplies put aside in autumn were holding well.

'Many times in the past the food stocks have already been gone at this time of year and we foraged on fern root and whatever else we could find until the fish arrived,' an old woman told Lafe. Much of the food allotted to the wedding feast was drawn from the reserves saved for emergencies and the storehouses were left nearly bare, but the tohunga banished any feelings of guilt by assuring the tribe that the omens were good for an early and orderly spring. There was enough food in the ovens for three or four days of supreme gluttony to celebrate not just a wedding but another victory over those hungry winters that they had beaten one more time.

It had not always been so. When the tribe had been so abruptly forced to return to a hunter-gatherer existence after the war with Ngai Tahu, leaving behind the settled agricultural life they had enjoyed for generations, they had suffered harsh winters with many deaths among the young and the very old and pinched bellies for the rest.

The wedding ceremony began with the lifting of the food from the ovens followed by a gigantic feast. Then came the speech making and that went on for many hours. Tama took up most of the time reminding them of the homeland they had been driven from and the need to retake their land again in the future.

'These young people who are ready to share the flax mat will live their lives in that land that is ours,' Tama promised them.

'We have interesting times ahead of us, Marama,' Lafe whispered into his bride's silky hair. 'Tama has just promised to go to war.'

A beautifully-woven flax mat was draped symbolically across the shoulders of the bride and groom as they sat together on a low rise outside the meeting house. This told the world that they now shared a sleeping mat, and every man, woman and child in the village, except for a handful of scouts who watched for the enemy on the trails that led through the forest, was present to witness the ceremony. From their elevated position Lafe could see the face of every villager watching him and Marama as they listened politely to the long-winded speeches. Every one was dressed in their finery, everyone had been working and planning for weeks for this feast and the dancing and singing that would follow.

Soon an expectant hush fell on the crowd. The speeches were finished. A song rose from the forest, a challenge to sing and dance away the night, and in an instant the whole village was on its feet and men and women formed into their opposing groups. Each took part of the songs for themselves. The men's voices and gestures brought exciting thoughts of war and adventure, while the softer and richer notes of their women reminded the listeners of love and beauty.

Long after Lafe and Marama crept into their own dwelling the music swelled on, and as they spent the remaining hours until dawn loving each other and talking quietly of the future the revelry continued. The two lovers had only to look out of their entranceway to see the dancers silhouetted against the redness of the built-up fires and feel the ground shake as the warriors advanced and retreated across the clearing. As emphasis to their haka the men would crash their feet down hard on the soil in perfect coordination, sending the frightened water birds flapping into the darkness while the strong, clear song of the women floated across the lagoon and out to sea.

Lafe enjoyed married life. At times during the last few months he had felt very alien and different from the others in the village and had suffered attacks of dreadful loneliness but now that he had a wife and companion it was different. His fears and worries were gone and he looked forward to the nights that he had once found too long.

Marama was happy too, working harder and singing more often than she ever had before. Named for the moon that shone over their lovemaking, she was a woman of the Pacific and had ripened early in the warm sun as her ancestors had before her. She was now a sensual woman of fourteen summers and had been more than ready to take a husband and have children. She was as delighted as Lafe with their nights on the flax mat and, although she would not know it for many weeks, was with child within a few days of their wedding night.

Chapter 11

One morning the scouts who had been sent to watch the rivers came trotting into camp in a lather of excitement to say that shoals of inanga were gathering at the river mouths. They had been visiting the streams down the coast for weeks, watching for the schools of succulent, almost transparent little fish to come in from the sea and run up the rivers to mature. Inanga were the young hatchlings of fresh water fish, little more than an inch long and seen as great delicacies. Now, according to the scouts, they were ready to run upstream on the next series of high tides. This was what the tribe had been waiting for weeks for. It was the first fresh food of the season.

Scarcely anything compared to the excitement of food for the tribe, and Lafe always enjoyed the good-natured, organized chaos that broke out when a new source of food arrived. Soon canoes loaded with nets darted through the entrance and out to sea, heading south to the most productive of the tribe's rivers, while the women and older children slung their flax baskets on their backs and set off to trek the long miles down the beach to join the fishermen.

Tama wanted the big double canoe turned into a proper fighting ship and was keen to take up Lafe's suggestions for a new rig so he ordered him to stay behind with his wife and start rebuilding the vessel. As they worked the remaining villagers watched and waited for the arrival of the first shoals of the little white fish to appear at the entrance of their own lagoon. When they did come, they came in an endless stream of silver across the bar and along the edges of the stream banks, heading upstream where they would mature into adults in the mountain rivers and lakes. So clear and translucent were these little inanga that their whole inner structures could be seen through the skin. The villagers dipped their nets into the stream until every container they could find was filled to overflowing, then began the most important part – the serious eating.

Lafe had been at several native feasts by now, but he thought he had never seen or taken part in such wanton gluttony. Several duck eggs would be added to half a pound of the little silver fish and whisked with a stick, then the mixture was poured onto a hot flat rock that cooked it in seconds. The resulting omelettes were the most delicious that Lafe had ever eaten. Everyone agreed it was the most satisfactory way for the new season to begin, another celebration of the tribe's victory over hunger. Over the next few days the canoes arrived back at the lagoon from the rivers, every inch of space on board filled with inanga that had already been dried in the sun ready for the storehouses.

Once the weather warmed and the food supplies were built up again, Tama began to plan a trip into the hinterland for more greenstone. Most of the pieces that had been worked on through the winter were now finished and the chief much preferred to keep idle hands busy. These beautifully-finished weapons, tools and ornaments were the tribe's wealth; even the functional chisels and adzes were exquisite examples of the craftsmen's skill in working stone and those pieces which had been roughly gouged and smashed from the original boulders had now been rubbed and polished with sandstone until they were as smooth as ice. Many hei tiki had also been given their final polish. That bow-legged little god worn around the neck on a string of twisted human hair was a favourite, the eyes, tongue and even fingers picked out in bold relief, and they became more beautiful as the oils of the wearer's skin gave the stone warmth and lustre.

Such precious ornaments were handed down in families, and in the greenstone-starved northern island such hei tiki were so valuable that tribes fought over them. Many a beautiful daughter's marriage was confirmed with a piece of greenstone, Lafe was told. Some patu and hei tiki had acquired names because they had been with the tribe many hundreds of years and handed down from one generation to the next. To lose any of these treasures in warfare was to lose one of the main pillars of the tribe's existence and was regarded as a disaster. Tama had plans to use this wealth in some way to make his tribe powerful again, but he kept his plans to himself.

Lafe was told he could go on the next expedition but Marama would stay behind at the village. It was a sign that the honeymoon was over and, now it was openly acknowledged that Marama was with child, Lafe had mixed feelings about the proposed trip. An expedition through the mountains into the land of high lakes had strong appeal but he was not really ready to leave Marama or her bed so soon and already he felt a little lonely again.

Tama began to spend time on the sandhills studying the weather, while the canoes were being provisioned and made ready. Then one evening the chief returned at sunset and gave the brief order, 'We go tomorrow'.

'This trip has the feel of a war party about it,' Lafe said to Marama that night. 'Only the best young fighters in the tribe, and no women on the trip? I think we are going to battle, what do you think?'

'Only Tama knows what Tama knows,' was her reply, and that was the only answer he got.

The whole village was up long before dawn to run the boats over the bar on the last surge of the outgoing tide. Out on the ocean the powerful young men soon picked up the stroke and, responding to the calls of the canoe singer, drove their vessels south at a great speed. The cutter had to work her way out from land until the breeze filled her sails and then she too shaped her course south. Once again they travelled in easy stages down the coast, living off the land and rebuilding their food supplies as they went. The sea was kind and it was now the season of plenty so the journey was good. Soon the little fleet entered the river that led into the lake Lafe now knew was called Kakapo, and in the bow of the cutter Salem's ears pricked up and his tail wagged as he barked in recognition. This was a place where they had been before.

Lafe stood on the sad and lonely dunes where his new friends had helped him to bury Matai only a short few months back. All that remained of the little hut he had built for himself and Matai during the storm was a wet pile of ashes on a flat spot by the riverbank. He sat for a while and listened to the great trees that had sheltered them both, but now there was only a light breeze and the sounds were more subdued. He thought of the changes in his life since that day, and wondered what other sad events had played out among the roots of these giants of the forest in the thousand or so years they had claimed this spot.

Once they had caught and dried enough inanga the party would be ready to push on to the mountains, and while they waited for Tama to give the word everybody attended to their clothing and footwear. It was still early in the year so the chances of a snowfall were high and every man carried several pairs of double-layered sandals, plaited from the fronds of the cabbage tree, to wear on the sharp stony mountain tracks. Their womenfolk had made them leggings by the same method and these would be stuffed with dry moss to wear if and when they met snow on the passes. Inner cloaks of finely-woven grass kept the warmth of their bodies in, while outer cloaks of heavy flax with the leaves layered like thatch kept rain and snow out. They also wore undergarments of bird skin to trap the layers of warm air close to the bodies, but their real protection lay in the fact that the party was made up entirely of fit men, able to keep moving fast even in extreme conditions. This was no hunter-gatherer party meandering from lake to lake and food source to food source and limited to the pace of the slowest woman, this was a lean, efficient and dangerous force.

Once he was satisfied with the amount of food on hand Tama ordered the cutter to be beached above flood level and they boarded the canoes for the run up the lake to the river mouth at the inland end. They would follow this river until they reached its headwaters high up near the pass. Lafe craned his neck to see the tops of the mountains and the stark scarring of the riverbed that crawled its way down towards him while he plied his paddle with deep, strong strokes, keeping time with the others and half-mesmerised by the canoe singer's chant. The canoes sped like a flight of arrows down the placid lake to scatter the reflections of the mountains into a million tiny pieces that ran together again behind them, and the noise of their passing sent several pairs of Captain Cook's paradise ducks winging their way down the lake. The birds' sad and lonely calls penetrated every nook and cranny of the valley, telling anyone who was there to listen out for the sounds of a war party on the move.

Tama had outlined his plans the night before as they sat warming themselves by the fires, drying the last of the eels on racks in the smoke.

'This is our last trip south, for in the future our interests will be concentrated to the north once more,' he told his men. 'This is why this ope is on the water, to raid the best greenstone sites in the south and in the east behind the mountains.'

An ope was a small, fast-moving raiding or war party, Lafe knew, and he listened carefully as Tama laid out his plans. He noticed that the fun and laughter he normally associated with these people had been left behind with the wives and children and a strict discipline seemed to have taken its place, running from Tama through his two senior men down to the lowest ranked warrior in the ope. Everyone except Tama himself showed signs of nervousness, flaring their nostrils and showing the whites of their eyes, and Lafe prepared himself for whatever might come his way by checking that the flints of his musket struck a good spark and that his powder was dry. The tomahawk in his belt and large knife sheathed on the other side were already honed to razor sharpness.

As the canoes glided one at a time onto the sand at the river mouth they were hauled ashore and hidden in the forest. The scouts set off upstream at a steady lope, ranging far ahead of the main party as they climbed forever upwards from the lake shore. The mountains closed in on them from both sides as they followed a rough track that wandered from one side of the river to the other, always finding the easiest grades. Lafe enjoyed the climb; he was fit and the mountain air was sweet as he pulled it deep into his lungs. The muscles of his legs felt good.

My winter back on the land and the long walks through the hills with Marama have done me well, he thought, and he smiled to himself as he remembered Marama telling him, 'If you keep asking how far it is, the journey will be long.'

The scouts were waiting on a clearing near the snow line. They had already cut armloads of grass and were busy gathering more as fast as they could. Lafe noticed the chill in the air the moment he stopped climbing, and saw that the sun had already left this part of the mountain for the day.

'The sun grows dim and hastens away like a woman from the scene of a battle,' Tama quoted with a wicked grin as the men looked to their comfort before the night air froze them. Before they left the lake each warrior had chosen a stout stave, about six foot in length, to use as a walking stick and now these staves were gathered and lashed together to form the frame of a long, low hut. Grass thatch was quickly lashed to the roof and sides of the hut, a thick layer was spread across the floor and a fire was lit in a circle of rocks in the centre. Outside in the middle of the clearing others had built a large cooking fire which cast a circle of warmth and everyone huddled around it. Already the white frost was starting to creep across the ground toward the fire.

Lafe was glad of his blanket that night. Tama had the other and Salem slept between them, sharing his warmth, while the other warriors had to be content with burrowing into the grass like piglets and relying on the warmth of their cloaks. Without the collective heat of so many bodies crammed into the near airless little hut, Lafe realised, they could not have dared try to cross the mountains at that time of year.

Everyone was glad to be on the trail and moving again the next morning even before the birds had stirred in the trees. They walked the stiffness from their bodies in the first hour but did not stop to eat until they had climbed up into the sunlight again. The next night they camped at the top of the pass at the head of the valley, high among the tussock and the native grasses where the last of the snow lay in small drifts. Soon they would begin to descend, following a small stream that would become a river and lead them down to a great mountain lake they called Wakatipu.

Again the weather gods promised Tama that the days would stay fine and clear. He sent his scouts on ahead before word could get out that a war party had crossed the range and was loose in the vicinity.

'Do you see this?' He showed Lafe a tiny drop of dew trembling in the early morning sun from the leaf of an alpine plant. The droplet had been solid ice only an hour or two earlier and now it shone like a pearl.

'We say that a drop of dew is the beginning of a great river,' Tama told him. 'What do you say, Goblin?'

Lafe watched the drop and waited for it to fall.

'Up here on the great divide, I ask you this question. Does this drop of dew make the river that drains to a lake where we are going, or is this the beginning of the river we have climbed beside these last days?'

Tama was pleased with the answer and thought it over as he lay in the tussock like a contented seal. They were high above the world in the morning sun and they were moving cautiously, waiting for the scouts to return before they could move from the hills into the river valley. Once they knew the path was clear the chief led the advance down into the greenstone river where various tribes over hundreds of years had exploited the stone. Small mounds of chips dotted the banks where the stone had been roughly worked before being carried out of the valley. Again the ope moved fast. It was imperative that they travelled faster than the news of their coming, or the fish might slip out from their net.

The country changed quickly once the divide was behind them, and the warmer, wetter coastal weather patterns gave way to a drier and cooler inland climate. They were leaving the dense forest behind now for long, sweeping tussock and snow grass basins with wide mountain views. Their pace was rapid now, almost a trot as the scouts swept ahead to sniff out the enemy. Vast piles of greenstone chips showed where another tribe had smashed large pieces of stone out of a seam that ran up into a cliff face, and several other work sites were inspected but no one had visited them since last summer.

The country on either bank of the stream became forest once more as the ope moved lower down the mountain away from the alpine tussock and grasslands, and early the next day the scouts returned to report that they had found the enemy. Tama took the lead with his musket at the ready, and they sped at a dog trot over the shingle and sand river terraces to close in on their prey. Long before their first sighting of the enemy they could hear the regular crack of rock smashing against rock downstream,

207

and as they got closer they moved more cautiously. Lafe was aware of the faint tremble of excitement in his limbs and the flaring of his own nostrils, sensations he recognised from the run-in on a whale.

At a signal from Tama the ope split into two groups and swept down upon the enemy who were still unaware of the danger approaching, so intent were they on the task of smashing a large greenstone boulder they had unearthed from the banks of the stream. There was a short, brief scream from one of the women around the boulder as the fast-moving warriors closed on them. The men who had until then been intent on their work leapt for their weapons and quickly formed a defensive circle around their women. They had little choice. Tama's ope had arrived so swiftly that their only other course was to abandon their women and flee into the scrub on the side of the riverbed, but they were brave men and chose to fight. They were outnumbered two to one as they lowered their heads and prepared to fight like cornered rats, still shocked at the suddenness of the attack.

Panting from their charge along the riverbed the war party stopped only yards away, leaning toward their opponents and waiting for the word to spring. Lafe had a quick count; there were about ten women and the same number of men in the ranks they were about to attack. He was surprised at his own aggressive desire to fight.

'Shoot the chief!' Tama ordered. Lafe threw his musket to his shoulder and fired at the man Tama indicated, hitting him in the chest and killing him instantly. The shock of the musket's discharge was so great that several of the enemy warriors jumped aside and stared at their fallen chief in terror. Before they could recover their attackers were onto them and the blows flew thick and fast until the last enemy warrior crumpled onto the sand. Lafe could see that two of the younger ones were only rendered unconscious, felled by blows from the flat of the patu, and their hands were quickly tied behind their backs with flax cord. The rest were either dead already or were quickly finished off with blows to the head.

The women had scattered at the first attack but they were quickly run down. Hands tied behind their backs they were pushed together into a group where they sat in a dazed state, barely able to understand the enormity of the tragedy that had overtaken them so swiftly.

Lafe's blood was up. He went among the captives, looking them over carefully until he saw a young girl that he liked the look of. She was about the same age as Marama and he realised that he had already totally freed his mind of the sexual repressions of the old world. He would ask for this girl when the time came, as was his right.

He went over to have a look at the boulder the little party of stone workers had been trying to split. It was of considerable size and would take a lot more work still before it was smashed. A smaller greenstone boulder was lashed to the trunk of a tree and the workers had been lifting it with ropes around a branch overhead and repeatedly dropping it onto the bigger boulder below. Both boulders hid their beauty and wealth within a rime of rusty white nondescript coating, and only a man with a practised eye would have known what treasure lay inside.

Tama ordered his men to prepare the bodies by cutting them into joints so they would be easier to carry, and the women were made to load the dismembered bodies into their baskets to be carried down to the lake where their canoes would be hidden. There was a fearsome wailing when the woman were ordered to carry the remains of their husbands, fathers and brothers, but they were quickly cuffed into silence and the threat of sending them to the ovens was enough to get them to their feet and staggering under their heavy loads. In a surprisingly short time the chief had established a semblance of order and the ope moved off again.

At the lake edge were a canoe and several flax boats that Lafe learned were called mokihi, made from the light seed stalk of the flax plant tied into tight bundles and built into watercraft shaped like ducks which could be sat on and paddled. Such a vessel lacked the sides to stop waves from sweeping across its upper surface but it was an ideal lake or river boat because it could be built in a couple of hours from the abundant flax that grew on the banks nearby.

Several warriors stayed to watch the prisoners while the rest of the ope boarded the canoe and the rafts and paddled across the lake to take the islands. Only a few old men and women and about twenty children were left on the island while all the fit adults had gone to work the stone. When they saw their own boats paddled by strange warriors the people on the island knew the worst had happened and the women began the keening that meant death had occurred. There was nowhere to run or hide – the little island wasn't big enough for that. There were no other boats, the water was too cold to swim to the mainland and even if they were to try the canoe would quickly catch them.

They were soon rounded up and the children clung together like monkeys in fear while the old men and women were made to clean out the ovens and get the big fires started. Soon, to Tama's obvious satisfaction, the rocks that would be needed for cooking were added to the burning piles of wood and when all the dismembered bodies and the prisoners had been transported to the island Tama put some of the women to work preparing the food. The others were ordered to build more shelters for the war party.

Tama demanded that every bit of greenstone on the island be brought from its hiding place and laid before him. He looked long and hard, carefully inspecting every piece that the island dwellers produced. He would hold it to the light, clucking his tongue when he was pleased with a piece and frowning as if to say, you can do better than this, when he wasn't. He held the attention of his captives, who stared at him knowing their fate was entirely in his hands. He is like a fox in the hen house, Lafe thought as he watched.

Then Tama looked up casually from the stone he was stroking with his finger tips and, just as casually, clicked his fingers and pointed at the oldest person present, an old man of sixty or more Lafe guessed. One of Tama's warriors pulled his patu from his waistband and dashed the old man's brains out on the spot, starting his eyes completely from their sockets. Nothing was said in the silence that followed, but the pile of greenstone at Tama's feet doubled and then doubled again. The message was clear. He would let them keep their old people, but only at the cost of their stone.

Such are the spoils of war, Lafe told himself as he watched the warrior, who still brandished his patu, strutting among the prisoners like a barnyard rooster. There was a good deal of boasting among the warriors about the days events, but the honours of the day went to Lafe who had struck the first blow by killing the enemy chief with his musket.

210

He heard his fellow raiders describe their victims as 'the fish who have swum into our net' and the chief that Lafe had killed was called 'the first fish'. He remembered Matai talking of 'the flying fish that cuts across the bows of the canoe', the flying fish being any poor creature that the ope might come across in its travels. He remembered how horrified he had been at such a description, little realising that he himself would be part of such an ope.

Every bit of food on the island was rounded up for the hungry victors who wolfed it down as they waited for the joints to finish steaming in the ovens. There was an undercurrent of excitement among the warriors and among the woman captives as well, and Lafe realised that Tama was about to begin the most important event of the day, the dividing up of the women. The captives were once again pushed into a rough group where they waited apprehensively for what they knew was to happen next.

It was the lore of the land and Lafe found himself watching the captives as avidly as anyone else, aware that he had never before felt such a tension in the air or such a build up of rank sexuality and lust. The evening atmosphere was charged with excitement and he felt his own weapon stiffen and push out the front of his robe. He had what he had once heard a sailor describe as 'a bone that not even a dog could chew'.

He stared at the young girl he would choose when the time came, only to have her return his look with equal intensity. He was aware that he was the object of great attention and wonder – this tribe had obviously never seen a blond, blue-eyed Goblin before and he was impressed by her bravery in meeting his eyes. Like all the other woman in the group she wore the expression of a mouse that has been played with too long by a cat and finally seems to lose all fear and to advance almost joyfully to its jaws. Or was she responding unknowingly to the rank desire that filled the evening air and the primitive urges that would not be denied? Perhaps he would never really know the answer.

Tama strode forward first, as was his right, and the front of his robe bulged obscenely as he signalled to a prisoner and strode to one of the huts without a backward glance. The chief had chosen a comfortable, plump and attractive woman of around sixteen summers whose appearance under better circumstances would have been happy and good natured. Taking his cue from his father-in-law Lafe rose next and walked to the woman he had chosen, touched one of her shoulders and strode away to a vacant hut. He noticed the momentary flash of relief in the girl's eyes as she rose to follow him. The rest of the women would be shared by the warriors who outnumbered them two to one, and they had a hard night ahead of them.

Shyly the girl followed him into the grass hut and stood like a deer ready to flee at any moment. She no doubt would have run, but the thought of falling into the hands of the warriors outside was more frightening than what was inside the hut. She would have to take her chances with this Goblin.

'What is your name?' Lafe asked, taking her by the shoulders and touching his nose to hers in the Maori kiss.

'Tui,' she said softly. Lafe felt her tremble under his hands.

'Are you afraid of me?'

'A little,' she answered. 'I have never seen a person such as yourself before. You are a Goblin.'

'Goblins make love the same as ordinary people,' Lafe replied as he gently pushed aside the hands that fluttered helplessly like a butterfly against his own. He undid the fastenings of her robe and slid it from her shoulders before she could resist him, catching his breath as his eyes travelled the length of her body from the still-developing breasts to the triangle of dark hair between her legs.

She was younger than he first thought, and he caught the look of dismay on her face as he cast his own robe aside. He swept her from her feet and laid her gently on the mat where the evening light allowed him to admire the golden tones of her body. On his knees he hungrily explored her with fingers, lips and tongue until she began to move under his hands, then mounting her he took her for a gentle ride until she began to rise to meet his thrusts. Soon they both caught the urgent rhythm and they moved together more and more violently until Lafe exploded in a shuddering climax, planting his seed deep in her belly.

Tui snuggled up close to Lafe and wept a little. She was not sure what she had done but she sensed she had pleased the man and at the same time she had felt a deep awakening of her own body. Perhaps he would want to do it again soon, she thought, wondering just how often men did that to their women. She decided that the Goblin had been very gentle and she thought she would not mind if he did it again.

This was her first and probably her last trip to the Greenstone Lake. She was the niece of one of the women that the warriors were now bedding furiously in the other huts, and it was this aunt who had sought permission from Tui's family to bring her on the expedition that had gone so horribly wrong. Her people were the Ngati Mamoe who had come up to this lake each summer for as many years as they could remember to collect stone, and they had always camped on the island. The tribe had been numerous on the east coast and to the south of where she now stood, near The Tail Of The Fish, in times past, but now they were being pushed further into the less accessible parts of the country by more powerful tribes from the north.

Once a tribe began to lose in battle it was nearly impossible to reverse the trend, it seemed to Tui, and it was not an uncommon thing for the women of the losing party to be stolen in this way. In the last few years many of her people had been taken by other tribes and it had made their enemies stronger as her own tribe had grown weaker. Most of the stone gathered every year had gone to buying protection from their most powerful neighbours, but in the end it came down to the number of fertile wombs, like her own, rather than the number of warriors that a tribe could put in the field.

In the end the women would be the key to her tribe's ascendancy or extinction, she knew that, and she lamented that she had become one of those who were lost to her people. But she was alive. Her aunt had whispered to her to try to catch the Goblin's eye and to please him and she had managed to do so. Her cousin, two years older and recently married, had been chosen by the enemy chief so at least Tui would have a friend in her captivity. She wept again as she thought of the mother, brothers and sisters she knew she had seen for the last time.

But for me all that is now in the past, she thought. My future now belongs to this stranger from across the sea, and I will resign myself to trying to find a way to live with as much enjoyment as I can find under the circumstances.

As the first noises of a waking village reached his ears Lafe was happily making love once again to his woman. He had woken from a good night's sleep after thoroughly staking his claim to every inch of her body the night before. When he finished Tui crept down to the lake to bathe her tender organs and clean herself in the freezing water while Lafe tended to the cleaning and reloading of his musket.

From the moment of waking he had been aware of the rich smells of cooking meat, a smell that made his mouth water against his will. The smells that filled the air were like roasting pork but he knew it wasn't pork. He still had a little fish left, saved from the supplies he had carried with him over the mountain, and he shared it with Tui to spare her from having to eat the flesh of her tribesmen and relatives. But soon, he realised, they would both have to eat the flesh that his friends were enjoying with so much relish, or starve. There was no other food on the island and already the vanquished children were fighting for the bones and scraps that were thrown to them, not caring at all who they might have once belonged to.

The victors spent the day eating vast amounts of roasted human flesh, dancing victory haka and boasting of their achievements in the battle and on the flax mats of the island, while their captives tried to stay as inconspicuous as possible. The two very young warriors whose lives had been spared existed under particularly delicate conditions. They were walking food, and they would live only if they pleased their new owners and if hunger did not strike to spoil their chances. If they grew to be great warriors or had other special talents or gifts they could aspire in some distant future to being familiar and favourite mokai, like the slave who had been befriended by Tama's family, or even to becoming full members of the tribe. The captive women, however, would have to form bonds or relationships with one or other of the warriors as best they could and hope for fertility or they would go to the ovens.

Tama now had one eye on the sky, and the women were set to plaiting many pairs of flax sandals for the mountain crossing ahead of them. Much of the meat left over from the feast was cut into long strips and smoked over a fire for the journey ahead. Hau hau tangata, or preserved human, was the name for this food. Lafe ate reluctantly and sparingly of it for a start, his stomach threatening to reject every mouthful, but soon he was hungry enough and managed to eat and keep it down.

When Tama gave the word the lightly-laden scouts led off, followed by the main party then the slaves. Both women and men bore heavy packs of stone and meat on their backs. Some of the women had children to tend as well but the old ones were left behind on the island to fend for themselves, thankful to be still alive at the end of the day.

Tui was young and strong and stood up well to the journey over the mountains. Lafe could show her kindness only when she shared his blanket each night, and it was then that he gave her the extra food he kept for her during the day. For many of the prisoners crossing the mountains was an ordeal, but the weather was kind and they made it back down to the coast without any losses. They settled for a while where the river met the sea, living on fish and seal meat from the few seals that returned that year to the rocks at the river mouth. Soon the air was full of the sound of happy children and the chatter of the woman as they brought the nets in full of fish and ate as if there was no tomorrow.

Lafe mentioned to Tui one day that he thought the women had recovered very quickly from the sadness of their kidnapping and the loss of their menfolk.

'But who can check life's stream, or turn its waters back? 'Tis past,' Tui quoted. 'A woman has little choice, and a woman with children has none at all. We have to make the most of what the gods send our way. As sad as our spirits may be, a woman will always choose life in the end.'

As soon as sufficient food had been gathered the women with children were sent north along the overland trail with a strong guard of warriors to make their slow way back to Okarito, each carrying a parcel of valuable stone in their packs and food for their journey. Tama kept the two women belonging to him and Lafe, however, ordering them to

215

take up paddles beside the two young slaves and lend their strength as the canoes headed still further south on a whim of the chief. He wished to visit a place he had once seen as a young man and they travelled the whole day before resting on a small beach overnight.

The next morning they entered a very deep sound called Piopiotahi. They had come to hunt for more stone on the beaches below snow-covered mountaintops that took a man's breath away. Tama showed them a waterfall that tumbled down from the dizzying heights of a mountain above direct into the waters of the ocean. He was proud that he alone knew of this place.

'I have been here three times now, and two times it was as if the gods were pissing out of the clouds,' he told his men. 'This is the first time I have seen where the water comes from.'

That day they looked long and hard for a seal to augment their supplies, while others in the party hunted for stone on the beaches to the south of the big sound. Until they had secured their seal Tama and the other men were worried, and Lafe began to realize that the actions of his sealing party the previous summer had a telling effect on the wellbeing of this tribe and any others that passed this way. When an otherwise reliable source of food failed there was disbelief among the people and an uneasiness that bordered on fear. Suddenly a link was missing from the food chain, and the further south they went the greater was the worry that the paddlers would not have the strength to return to the last known food source. Then there was the added possibility that they would be delayed, the food they returned to find would be finished for the season and the problem would worsen.

The two young men, not much older than boys, who had been captured as walking food would be lucky to see another sunrise, Lafe reckoned, and although he felt sorry for them he found himself running an eye over their frames to see how much meat was on them.

Many were the groups of rocks visited that day by the hungry paddlers, but they were empty of seals. Yet Lafe could easily remember the large numbers of seals he and his men had killed in these very spots less than a year before. He was relieved when the ope finally managed to ambush and kill two large male seals and the canoes towed them to a sheltered beach. Willing hands dragged the carcasses into the shelter of the sand hills, fires were lit and every one fell to devouring vast hunks of seal meat half-roasted on sticks over a driftwood fire. Rich and still bloody, most of the first seal was gulped down in that half-cooked state until not another morsel would stay down in the overloaded stomachs of the hunters and yet again Lafe was astounded at how much they could eat. The mere hint of starvation was enough to see them loading up like bears before winter.

'Your people are the gluttons of the world. I have never seen anyone eat like them,' Lafe told Tama who laughed, pleased with such a compliment.

The remains of the seals were dried and smoked above the fire and then a serious hunt began for greenstone. Old reefs that Tama had taken stone from in the past were reopened and pieces of the stone broken out of the seams with hammer stones. This was the much loved tangiwai stone, a clear, pale stone ranging from soft green to shades of blue with clear lights shot through it resembling tears. The name of this stone meant crying water and Lafe could see why it was so.

'A piece of this stone from here to here,' Tama said, indicating the space from his finger tips to his wrist, 'is worth as much as any other stone from here to here.' He measured from his fingertips to his elbow. The stone that they had taken from the people at the lake was pure green with a black streak running through it. Another stone, taken around the Cascades, was pearly white or grey green and Tama called it inanga because it had the colouring of the little fish they caught in the rivers.

'The inanga is an attractive stone, but tangiwai is a jewel,' Tama said, and Lafe agreed with him.

These were happy days for Lafe as he searched for traces of the great rift that had broken the valley walls in early times and exposed the beautiful stone. The weather was fine and warm and the countryside was in the thrall of spring. He was enjoying his new woman too, as Tama was enjoying his, and the chief encouraged him.

'Be like a warrior and drive all other thoughts from the woman's head but love,' he urged. Lafe did this and more and still he found himself desiring her, until hours of the day would slide by as they dallied away

217

the afternoon in some warm and sheltered place. Tui responded like a flower unfolding into the sunlight, no longer just allowing Lafe to use her body but giving it willingly and taking her own rewards in return. Lafe decided he would not discard her when he reached his village but would keep her as his second wife. Among the people he now lived with that was a perfectly acceptable arrangement.

All too soon it was time to head north to Kakapo River for more food, and then to await the right weather to return to Okarito. That return was an even greater triumph than when Lafe had arrived as a captive, because the women and children prisoners and their warrior escort had arrived the day before the ope returned in their boats and the place was buzzing with excitement.

Marama greeted Lafe like a returning king and led the songs of welcome, but he could see the hurt in her eyes. That he had returned with another woman was not a surprise to her. The news had reached her ears with the first party of returning warriors and the demons of jealousy and self-doubt had worked their mischief. Lafe called her to him and complimented her on her beauty, telling her how becoming the faint bulge of their child was in her belly. He told her as firmly as he could to take Tui to her house and the two young women, first wife and captive, looked at each other warily. Each wondered what kind of a threat the other would be to their relationship with this Goblin man.

'See to her feeding and bathing, and at all times treat her like a sister,' Lafe ordered, making it plain that he would tolerate no discord in his household. Much chastened and rendered mute with shock, his wife hurried to obey.

The vast amount of stone the party had gathered was put on display and the people settled down to celebration and feasting to mark the great victory over the enemy tribe and the strengthening of their own. Then it was time for the whakatupu tangata that Tama was so keen to encourage, the making of men and warriors to fill the ranks.

Chapter 12

After the raid on the tribe at the greenstone river Lafe settled down to enjoy a spell of domestic life. Contrary to what he had feared, Marama and Tui accepted their roles of senior and junior wives without any signs of ill feeling and soon became very good friends. His house was a model of happiness and order and he was relieved, as no warrior could retain the respect of his fellows if he allowed bickering and discord to take over his family. To be known as a kaka parrot away from his house and a pigeon when he was at home was an insult that he would not tolerate and he was expected to maintain discipline and harmony in his household for fear discord would spread through the village. A husband was not discouraged from applying the rod or supplejack cane if his wife deserved it.

The only change in Lafe's household was the building of a new sleeping hut so his second wife could entertain her husband in privacy and dignity. There was always competition among wives and it was the husband's duty to see that no wife was ill treated or favoured above the other and a good husband was especially careful when it came to sharing his bed so that each of his wives felt that they were welcome and loved accordingly. There were of course the blanket lectures that any husband could choose to listen to and, if he wished, ignore the next day, but on the whole his new family behaved in the moderate and tranquil way expected of them.

The new domestic situation suited Lafe very well and he went about with a new appreciation of life. He wore the nicest clothes and footwear and ate the best food, gathered and cooked to perfection by one or other of his wives. In fact, Tui could hardly have disrupted his household any less. She was wonderfully cheerful and had an even, sunny temperament, and it gave Lafe pleasure to see how carefully and with what pride the two women looked after each other's hair and shared the household chores. Tui was as excited as Marama herself over the senior wife's pregnancy, and kept hoping that one day soon she would be able to announce that she too was with child.

Lafe now sat in council whenever there were important matters to discuss, and it was here that he first learned of the plan to raid up the coast and resettle it by the beginning of winter. This had been the tribe's main ambition since they had been evicted from Murderers' Bay.

'Our raid into the greenstone lake will by now have caught the notice of the more powerful tribes on the east coast,' Tama told the council. 'We have rubbed their noses in the dirt and they will be angry. By autumn they will be ready to cross through the passes and attack us to take utu.

'If we are gone north by then, right out of this area, their strike will fall on an empty village and our tribe will be many miles away by then. They will have to return to their homes before winter sets in. That will give us another year to build up our strength before the eventual battle which must take place between our two tribes.'

The chief indicated that he wished Lafe to complete the rebuilding of the double canoe and take her to sea to find out how well she sailed with the new rig, and after the council meeting was over the warriors began to look to their weapons while the women gathered and prepared food for the days ahead. Militant activity was obvious everywhere in the village from that day as young men clashed with their short, stabbing spears to build up their muscles, hoping to be picked for the next raid. More small scouting parties were formed and sent off, some to watch the passes and others to make raids even deeper into enemy territory looking for trouble. These small ope were successful on several occasions, capturing family groups and marching the women and children back to the village to add to the tribe's population. Tama had his scouts out carefully watching the small villages scattered up the coast on the route he planned to take with his people.

'As long as those northern warriors are scattered about on the fishing and hunting grounds, I know they are not planning anything,' he told the council. Lafe knew it was the power of his muskets that had given Tama the confidence to move from his former defensive position to a mood that now bordered on aggression but it worried him. He was not sure that owning three muskets was enough to sustain this new warlike identity the tribe had adopted.

'Shock value, yes. The musket surely has the power to frighten and confuse inexperienced warriors, but a weapon that takes so long to load and fire will soon be overcome when people are more familiar with them,' he warned the council. 'One day your tribe will run into another that is familiar with muskets or, even worse, have their own, and then we will all get broken heads. The Indians in my own country have found the weakness in the musket, and often prefer their own weapons.

'A good man can run from here to the ocean in the time it takes to load and fire a musket, and hand-to-hand fighting quickly takes away any advantage.' But although he tried his best, his warnings fell on deaf ears.

'All the better that we strike now, before they do,' Tama said, and his argument always carried the day.

As soon as the weather settled and the long, hazy days of summer arrived, Tama sent Lafe to the north in his cutter with three of the fittest scouts in the tribe. They crossed the bar before daylight one morning and headed west into the ocean until the land was just a smear on the horizon. Once they were sure they would not be seen from the shore by any roaming fishermen, they turned and sailed north, careful to maintain a discreet distance from the coastline, and after two days and nights at sea they were able to turn east again and bring the cutter round a long, sandy hook into the waters that divided the two biggest islands of New Zealand.

Further east still, where the distance between the two land masses narrowed, was the strait named after Cook but known by the tribes as the Windpipe Of The Pacific. Lafe still kept well clear of the coast until he was many miles east toward the Windpipe before turning south, on the advice of the keen-eyed scouts, for a direct run into Murderers' Bay.

Lafe let the cutter idle along in the calm seas, anxious not to close the land until after dark. It was a relief to be inside the sandspit and protected from the westerly wind that had given them good but tiring sailing conditions all the way from Okarito. The Tasman was always a lively ocean, stretching as it did all the way uninterrupted from the Antarctic which Lafe knew about from Cook's journals. Now his warrior crewmen were almost as tired as he was and they hoped to find a quiet, hidden creek somewhere in the bay where they could rest up for a few days. Except for small amounts of sleep he had snatched at the helm, Lafe was suffering the most and his eyes felt full of sand and grit. Now and then he found himself slumping over the tiller and wondering how he got there.

They had been sent to Murderers' Bay to look over the place where the tribe hoped to settle. Tama wanted to find out whether the land his people claimed as their own was still held by their enemies and he also needed to know how many allies they might have still living in scattered groups along the coast. If there were any left at all, he had told Lafe, they would be living quietly in the most out-of-the-way places and they could be flighty and hard to approach.

'This is a job for the scouts,' Tama had said. 'Once they get onto the first sign of human habitation they will patiently unravel the tale it tells and follow the signs until they finally run the people who made them to earth. There are few secrets that can be kept from these men.'

Lafe had already seen the men in action during the greenstone raid and, after they had rested, was happy to sleep with his musket in his arms while they went to work. During the day he guarded the cutter where it was hidden away in a little creek and each night he slipped out to sea and moved quietly east to join the scouts as they methodically worked their way along the coast. Every bay, estuary and river mouth on the shoreline was carefully checked for signs of recent human occupation, but the sites of once-thriving villages were deserted now, the grass huts rotted back into the soil and the gardens returned to the scrub they had been cut from.

There was life to be found on the banks of some quiet estuaries and streams where small groups of people still lived. They left signs of their comings and goings although they tried not to; they no longer had villages or gardens to fight for and they had returned to the hunter-gatherer lifestyles of the more distant past. When anyone more powerful than themselves prowled the coast they melted away into the thick forests of the interior where they found caves or dug holes in the earth under dry banks. If weaker people came along they would be absorbed into this nomadic tribe, sometimes through the stomach.

In a morbid sort of way it was quite humorous, Lafe thought, and as much as he abhorred cannibalism he had to see the logic of the scouts. Even the weak who were no use for breeding could still contribute to the strength of the conquerors.

'This reminds me of the tribe in the Bay of Islands, who were so indignant that the black Goblin they had eaten had not lived up to their expectations,' he told his friends. 'The man had spoiled his own flavour by tasting strongly of tobacco.' They laughed delightedly, although they had no idea what tobacco was. This was the sort of story that appealed to their sense of humour very much.

Lafe could see why Tama and his people had such a strong desire to return to their land along this coast. With the mountains protecting it from the cold and boisterous weather of the south and west, this land was as soft, warm and fertile as a beautiful woman. Here the sea rolled gently up onto white and golden sandy beaches in a very different way from the thundering rollers of the west coast which threw themselves onto the rough shingle and shook the very ground the people stood on. Here there were harbours full of finned fish, and on the mudflats and sandy beaches were various types of shellfish in great numbers. It would be possible to build the long nets once again and use them here where a good cast would feed the tribe for weeks and free them from the constant worry of starvation. It was a golden corner of a land that the gods had been generous with, and Lafe desired the land as much as Tama did. He would fight for it if need be.

'This is a powerful force in me,' he told the scouts. 'and for us to succeed in our enterprise it must be the force in all of us, the desire to defend this land against any who would dare take it from us again.'

But though they scouted the coast for many days towards the east, they found no powerful enemy to oppose the building of their new settlement. The scattered families they managed to make contact with would give no undertaking to join the tribe but would simply wait and see. They were used to the shadows and hidden trails now and were as wary of other people as the little native quail that lived in the sand hills.

'Will it be any less painful to be eaten by your Chief Tama than by any other?' one of their spokesmen had asked. Lafe had to admit it was a fair question and one to which he had no answer.

When they had finished the task that Tama had set them, the four warriors sat in the cutter off one of the little bays as the sun slid down the sky toward the mountains. The water was oily calm and they were fishing to fill their empty bellies before they left the coast and headed home. Next to him Lafe had a little pile of shellfish freshly plucked from their shells, and he snagged one onto the hook and lowered it to the bottom of the bay. For the first time it was he who brought the first fish into the boat, then the second and then the third. He was usually the last on any boat to catch a fish and there had been many times when he could catch none at all, competing against Maori who had been fishermen since they were children.

'This is a good omen for me and mine,' he told his companions as he examined the golden red tamure that lay at his feet. Such a beautiful fish, he thought, and looked at his surroundings with a happy appreciation. It was a moment of truth, the moment when he realized that the old world he had known was gone and lost to him forever. Until this moment, his new life had seemed almost like a dream, another part of his existence.

He had often caught himself thinking, this is good, but when I go home, when I return to America…

Now for the first time he realized that he no longer finished his thoughts that way. He tried to tell the scouts what he had discovered and they were pleased that he was happy, even though they didn't entirely understand the reason why.

In the early morning hours before the morepork gave his last call of the night they put to sea and sailed well clear of the land for three days and two nights.

They returned to their village by the lagoon tired but triumphant, and were well satisfied with their homecoming. Tama called a meeting of the tribal council and spoke of his plans, mincing up and down in that strange gait that he adopted at times of great importance, lifting his heels until they nearly touched his buttocks. Lafe now knew this was in imitation of the great white heron of Okarito.

'If we are to go this year then whatever it costs we must be settled in our new home by late summer or early autumn, so we can gather sufficient food for the winter,' the chief said. He asked the scouts to repeat what they had already told him, that the northern people were still scattered in camps at their favourite food gathering areas.

'That is good. They are still not expecting trouble,' Tama chuckled, pleased with the way his plans were unfolding.

When it was his turn to speak, Lafe told the council that the land he had seen was worth all the risk they might take. The people grew misty-eyed at his descriptions of black soil, fine beaches and abundant fish. Their best and fondest memories were of this gentle, warm and fertile land, but the elders no longer had the courage of youth and they were frightened. This was their homeland and they would take the risk, but it was hard to go back after such a crushing defeat. It would be easier to stay where they were. This temptation to remain in exile, as most other tribes did, was very strong. To live as vassals of a more powerful tribe was to surrender food, weapons and women to the overlords year after year, and such an arrangement could last ten generations. The only way to return was to fight for their land and win.

225

Tama ruled only by consensus but he made the decisions and often asked afterwards for the tribe's approval. This great tribal meeting had been called to discuss the move in detail, however, as it was an issue that the chief wanted full support on. To uproot and move the tribe was such a large undertaking it would be easy for the doubters and dissenters to spread fear through the village, so the debate needed to be open and frank. Because of the previous battle there were few people in the tribe who were old and infirm, but those who were did not relish the move at all. They were the survivors who had struggled their way south and now they would have to make the march north again with no spare warriors to guard them. They would simply have to follow the main body of the tribe at the best speed they could manage, and there would be losses among them. All this was accepted and it was agreed that the most important thing was for the living heart of the tribe, the women and children, to arrive safely at their new homeland.

Tui had proudly announced her pregnancy and the news was a great joy to Lafe, who nevertheless ruefully contemplated his own potency. Another of his arrows had found the target, and with the joy and pride came added feelings of responsibility and the strong desire to see his new family secure and settled. If their home was to be in Murderers' Bay he was prepared to go out and kill as many people as it took to ensure a life of relative safety for his wives and children.

Finally the talking was done and the tribe was agreed. 'So be it!' Tama ordered, and the people prepared to travel back to their old home and fight for their land. Once the decision was made the tribe moved fast, and all too soon the last of the war food was packed, the last fastenings on the flax kete checked and double-checked, the boats loaded and everyone settled down to sleep for the last time in the village by the lagoon. It had been a good home and they would be sad to leave it. Well into the night the guards could hear the stifled sobs of the women as the realization of what lay ahead prevented them from sleeping.

All too soon it was morning and the scouts led the way out onto the ancient trail that led northwards. The women sang loud, tearful farewells to the village they were leaving and to the peaceful lagoon of

Okarito that had fed them and sheltered them in difficult times. Then Lafe and the boat crews touched burning sticks to the dry, thatched roofs and watched as the fire jumped from one hut to the next until the whole village was afire. It was a symbolic gesture to show that they would not fail to regain their homeland. Now there could be no turning back.

The boats did not leave the village until the following evening when, as daylight faded and the gloom hid them from any chance sighting by the enemy, Lafe ordered the little fleet out to sea. First over the bar were the two small canoes, each holding five warriors who would scout the rivers ahead, then Lafe took the cutter over the bar with a single crewman to sail with him, and behind them came the big double canoe with an ope of forty warriors all armed to the teeth. Once they were clear of the surf they hoisted their sails and once again the two larger craft travelled far enough out to sea so their sails could no longer be seen before turning north.

The smaller canoes would travel only at night, hiding themselves and their vessels by day. They would pick their way carefully up the coast, entering the Hokitika River on the second night to scout for signs of the enemy before meeting Lafe and the rest of the fleet at the river mouth at dawn. The main party, led by Tama, was walking up the coast, following the shore but carefully avoiding any advance warning of their progress. It was like the two pincers of the crab, Tama explained to Lafe.

'I will be one pincer advancing on the enemy from the land. You will swing in from the sea and be the other.'

The scouts reported only five or six families camped on the south side of the river busily drying sand sharks caught that day. As Lafe's cutter and the big canoe entered the river near dawn on the second day, all that could be heard in the silence was the hiss of the boat hulls through the water and the explosive grunts of the warriors as they drove their paddles with all the power they could muster. In the cold, early light it was a sight that would not be forgotten by any enemy lucky enough to survive that terrible morning.

The three canoes streaked for the group of small shelters on the riverbank and Lafe watched the huts closely. For a time he thought they would be able to run their boats up on the sand and take the people while they slept, but someone must have stepped out and seen them and the alarm was raised. The half-asleep warriors on the bank grabbed their arms and readied themselves for battle while the women and children made off into the forest as fast as their legs would take them. They would not get far, Lafe knew that. Tama's scouts with the main party had by now blocked all the tracks to the south.

As soon as the keels of the canoes touched the sand the fastest young men in the tribe flew in pursuit of the runners, like barracouta after a shoal of smaller fish. Within hours they returned with the first of Tama's scouts and a group of captives, some twenty-odd children and two young men who had been spared to be absorbed into the tribe. There were also six useful-looking women, one a particularly attractive young girl whose breasts showed no signs of having been suckled, Lafe noted. Some of the male prisoners had been made to walk back to their own executions, their hands tied behind their backs until they got to the forest edge where they were killed. They were for the ovens, to give the tribe sustenance for the next stage of the journey.

By nightfall on the day following the raid, Tama and the main party of women and children had arrived at the riverside where enough huts had now been erected to house everybody. The ovens were full to over-flowing and the food was nearly ready to be lifted when the tired walkers came in to the campsite. Marama and Tui were pleased to see Lafe, and he them. They had stood the march well. They were fit and healthy, and though they were both heavy with child they were not too heavy yet to make walking difficult. It was good to have his wives back, Lafe thought, and to see them so happy.

It was a very ancient trail that the tribe followed north, well-worn in places, following the beaches where that was possible. Here the going was easiest on the hard sand, and when the beaches ran out at places where the waves crashed against bluffs the tracks led inland again. They climbed up and over steep cliffs where permanent ladders made from tough vines were fixed to pegs driven into cracks in the rocks. Fast or slow, easy going or hard climbing, the tribe crawled on. This was the greenstone trail that men had followed for centuries, coming down from the north to find the stone and carry it away again. Once upon a time, when the tribes were more peace-loving than now, the stone had moved along this route in a steady flow. War was unheard of in those days and trade flourished from one end of the country to the other, Tama told Lafe.

'Why then did this change from peace to war?' Lafe wanted to know.

'I do not know,' Tama said. 'But I believe that the race of people that ran the trade routes were not Maori. When the Maori came, war broke out and the traders fled. This is what our old people have told us, as their old people told them.'

When the ovens were opened the smell of cooked flesh filled the clearing. Lafe tried to keep his wives from the steaming, succulent human flesh, offering them instead the shark he had gathered from the drying racks, but it would have been easier to hold back the tide than to persuade them to forgo human flesh and eat shark instead. Their hunger for human flesh was beyond normal hunger, he found, and they had spent days talking with their companions of the feast they would have when they got to this place.

Lafe watched with a dreadful fascination as Marama chewed a forearm that still had a hand attached, while Tui was at work with her teeth on the upper arm and shoulder of the same joint.

He could have forbidden them to touch the flesh and they would of course have obeyed him, but he knew that if he made such an issue of it he might draw others of the tribe into the discussion and cause ill feeling among them all. He was still wary of his own position within the tribe and did not want to draw attention to his fastidiousness. He feared that these people had become addicted to human flesh, and developed an unnatural appetite for it far beyond their simple need for survival. He had heard stories among the sailors that this was what happened when people became cannibals.

After a day's rest the men sallied forth to the mother of all greenstone rivers, the Arahura, where they raided several small families and took their stone. Then they moved on to the pa at Taramakau. The fort was deserted, the tribe obviously away on some summer business in a different part of the country, and so they escaped Tama's wrath for the time being. Tama was savage in his disappointment. He had long planned to plunder this tribe's stores of stone, known to be the finest of any in the country, but had to be content with the few pieces that he had taken from the families gathering stone at the river. Spitefully, he burned their village as a warning and a declaration of war, then returned to the coast where the boats and the rest of the tribe waited for the ope. Again they took their ease, fishing for small sharks at the river mouth and drying them for the journey until Tama was satisfied with their food stores and gave the word to move on.

Trail fit now, the tribe moved easily. Relays of warriors ferried the younger children on their backs over the more dangerous parts of the track and through the swamps while a small group of warriors moved ahead of the main party and replaced any of the ladders and ropes that were unsafe. This kept the tribe flowing like water along the trail. Tama was everywhere, seeing that the women's bundles were hoisted to the tops of the bluffs on a relay of ropes so that when they had negotiated the climb they could slip the straps over their shoulders again and move on down the trail. The advance guard not only served as an early warning and protective force, but also chose the campsite at the end of each day's journey and prepared it for the others, so that when the weary women and children arrived at the end of the day there was shelter and food ready for them.

Much of the travel was pleasant, consisting of hours spent walking on the hard sand beaches, and the tribe spent their mostly-fine nights rolled in their cloaks in the sand hills. Lafe and his crews in their small flotilla would sweep ahead of the tribe and set up camp at a major river crossing to await the arrival of the main party. A dozen more families working their summer fishing grounds were taken unaware and captured, and they too were added to the tribe's breeding stock.

It was in one of these raids, on the Kawatere River, that Lafe took another beautiful young woman as his third wife. Though she was very frightened when she was captured she had a certain bearing that marked her out from the rest, and under his careful questioning she admitted to being high-born. For that reason, as well as for her beauty, Lafe took her for himself and he spent two long hot summer days and sultry nights with her while they waited for the rest of the tribe to arrive.

Her name, she told him softly, was Haroto. She was taller and slimmer than his other wives, with fine, silky black hair and high cheekbones and she had a certain reserve that intrigued him. She was neither sulky nor frightened, but she retained an aloofness and dignity that he could not seem to break through. She was not hungry for his body as Marama had been, nor was she as lively and cheerful as Tui, but she submitted without protest, knowing it to be inevitable, and gave in to his demands as he taught her the ways to please him.

The fathering of a child on a high born woman was a great coup; it meant that her mana or spirit was now added to his own, greatly increasing his spiritual power. Her sister was equally high-born as they shared the same mother and their father was a chief, and she was kept under strict guard as a gift for Tama. It was up to him to decide her fate when he arrived, but Lafe guessed that the woman would please him and he was glad to help his new wife by protecting her sister from a much worse fate.

All of the victims were in shock. To find a war party abroad at that time of the year, when every one was striving to put away as much food as they could, was unheard of and their guard had been down. No inkling of Tama's march north had reached their ears, and the last few years of peace had made them careless.

Slowly, day by day and week by week, the tribe put the miles behind them as they moved relentlessly up the coast to their old homeland. The drive to get themselves established and gather their winter food made them impatient and pushed them onwards, but Tama was careful not to move forward while their stocks of food were depleted and made sure they were constantly built up above the level of normal usage.

231

With the women he was even more careful and he made sure they were not pushed to exhaustion. Nearly all of them were pregnant and he was not prepared to jeopardise the fine work his warriors had done through that last winter in building up the tribe. He was proud of their potency, and saw the strength of his tribe growing through its children. He saw that they wanted for nothing that was in his power to supply, and would stand near the track and pat the pregnant women on the stomach as they passed him on the trail.

'Give my warriors a long cold winter's day and they could screw a whale to death,' he was fond of saying with a happy grin.

The summer days were starting to draw in a little when the tribe arrived at the banks of a river called Te Namu, named after the dreaded sandfly that pounced on uncovered flesh in any weather less than a gale. The tribe barely halted to rest as the flies were too numerous even for people used to them. They quickened their steps, hurrying along the sand beach to the mighty Karamea River where they would stay a day or two and rest before they tackled the last part of the journey. It was here that the two parties would separate again, the canoes and cutter heading north to round the sand spit before turning south again and entering Murderers' Bay while the walkers would continue close to the coast before turning inland onto an old trail that would take them over the mountains, through a pass and into the headwaters of a river called Aorere.

'Where this delightful river meets the sea will be our own land,' Tama promised them, 'Here we will build and plant and grow until the tribe is as numerous as the stars in the sky.'

Much of the valuable greenstone they brought with them was now on board the double canoe. It was a risk that had to be taken. The canoe could be captured or sunk, but it was better that the women did not have to carry the heavy stone up over the pass and down the other side. When Lafe's flotilla put to sea again it was as escort for the big canoe as it carried most of the tribe's wealth on this last leg of the great journey. The crews were well rested and they had picked their weather carefully. If the winds were kind the two bigger boats would receive some help from their sails as they sought to claw their way off shore.

It was a coast of high bluffs and reefs and the westerly wind piled the waves high, creating the lee shore that all sailing men were afraid of. There would be no respite for the paddlers of the two smaller canoes who would rely on manpower alone until they rounded the sand spit and left the west coast behind them.

Lafe drove both men and boats hard until they were well out to sea before he allowed them to turn north once again. With the southwesterly to fill their sails the bigger boats made good speed, and the fleet held its course a few degrees east of north all through the night. Lafe searched the northern horizon in the early morning light until he located the perfect snow covered cone that Tama had told him to look for. It was, Tama had explained, arguably the greatest mountain in the northern island. It was regarded as female and his people called it Taranaki, while Lafe knew it from Cook's maps as Mount Egmont. In the cool, clear, autumn air it appeared very close, and was the most perfectly-shaped mountain Lafe had ever seen, climbing from what seemed to be sea level with a lovely and graceful symmetry until it reached a height that allowed it to wear snow in all seasons.

Once the flotilla that made up the tribe's waterborne force rounded the sandspit they saw clearly ahead to the east the large island called Rangitoto, whose mountains showed smoky blue in the distance. This island marked the entrance to Cook's Strait, the Windpipe of the Pacific.

It was like entering another ocean. Once they were inside the long arm of the spit the waves diminished to mere ripples as the boats gained the shelter of the mountains that modified the climate of their former homeland. Soon they were nosing their way into a large shallow estuary called Rua Taniwha, which Lafe translated as Two Dragons. He asked for the origins of the name but was told they were long ago lost in antiquity.

Food was the most immediate priority for the tribe. The hillsides that had been burnt off over the years now had extensive coverings of fern whose roots would keep them alive if all else failed. Fern root

233

was regarded as war food, a dish better eaten with human flesh. It was emergency rations, providing sustenance rather than pleasure, but it was there for the taking and relied on no human hand for its cultivation. The changing seasons, rain or drought did not affect it at all. Below the gentle hill slopes the harbours and estuaries were rich with shellfish, not only the cockles, mussels, oysters and scallops that Lafe had found elsewhere in his travels but also the little pipi that lay just under the sand in the shallows and could fill a hungry stomach with little effort on the part of the gatherer. A delicious flatfish or sole was found and speared in large numbers in these same shallow waters and it could be netted in hundreds on some tides. There were fat red paddle crabs and, best of all, the lovely golden-red tamure or bream that Lafe had caught in the far north inhabited these waters as well. Lafe regarded this as his special fish, and to have caught it so readily on his scouting expedition was to him a good omen for the future.

Almost as soon as the canoes touched the sand, twenty of Lafe's warriors had left for the mountain passes to meet and escort the tribe through the last and most difficult part of their long journey and bring them home. The rest of the ope worked from daylight until dark to build shelters and lay in the enormous stocks of food that would be needed while the marchers recovered from their journey.

Large smoking fires burned night and day as the boat crews harvested food from the sea and laid it out on the drying racks. Green leaves from particular trees were laid on the hot embers, giving off pungent smoke that gave each type of food a different flavour and improved its keeping qualities. As the winter supplies were being processed, great storehouses were erected and the men began to fill them in readiness for the winter that was just around the corner. Already the evening air carried a chill in it, and the long, warm, still days of summer were rapidly becoming only a memory.

Lafe was as anxious as the other men to have his wives off the track and able to rest in secure surroundings before they moved into the last months of their pregnancies. He was looking forward to seeing Marama and Tui again, and also to renewing his dalliance with his newly-acquired third wife Haroto. He planned his household enclave with a growing family in mind, marking out and framing three sleeping huts and picturing in his mind their babies taking their first steps beside his fire.

It was the faint voices of women singing that alerted the men thatching the hut roofs that the tribe was almost in sight. The warriors dropped what they were doing, jumped lightly to the ground and seized their weapons, forming into ranks to answer the women's song with a welcoming haka of their own. Lafe felt his spirits lift as he joined with his friends, stamping his bare feet hard on the ground they had won with such hard, physical effort. He would never perform the haka with the fluid grace of his warrior friends but as he slapped his thighs and roared out the words that now came so easily to him he was filled with emotion, and he realised what a joyful and powerful thing it was to welcome his people home in this way.

From his place in the front row he searched eagerly for his own women. They were at the front of their party, Marama's beautiful voice soaring above the others as she led their heartfelt waiata of homecoming. To Lafe's joy, all three of his wives had travelled together and were well content with each other's company. They were as pleased as he was to be a family once again.

There had been one or two babies born on the journey, and sickness and injury had slowed others among the walkers who would trickle into camp over the next few weeks, but because of Tama's careful leadership and patient progress, few members of the tribe had been lost. A few of the older members of the tribe had not been able to keep up and had fallen behind to fend for themselves and die on the side of the track, but they had not been many. The tribe had arrived at its new home very much stronger and more vigorous than when the original group had left the village on the lagoon. The captured women, Tama's breeding stock, had been assimilated into the tribe with their children and would either become permanent wives or be used as slaves by the single men. Even the young warriors who had been captured en route were safer now than any other time in the journey, because they would now be regarded as slaves rather than just walking food.

235

Chapter 13

The benefits of moving north were obvious during that first wonderful winter at Murderers' Bay. No longer did the tribe have to curl up in their grass nests in a state of semi hibernation for weeks at a time while the southerly and westerly winds or combinations of the two thrashed their village. Now they were several hundred miles further north with a mountain barrier between them and the Tasman Sea, conditions were a lot milder. The ocean was quieter too, and much richer in fish, shellfish and seaweed. They were able to gather a certain amount of food during those first winter months and so avoid outright hunger.

Though they had worked as hard as they could to put sufficient food aside for their winter needs they had arrived late in the autumn, and the amount they had managed to harvest and store was light compared to previous years. Tama grew worried and often inspected the babies, checking their mothers' breasts to see that they were making plenty of milk. Several times during the winter he increased the food rations for nursing women and their children and reduced the amount available to the less fertile members of the tribe.

'We cannot have our next generation of warriors growing up puny, can we, Goblin?' he asked, and the more worried he became the more he drove every able bodied man and woman to scour the countryside for nourishing food for the mothers and their children. 'They cannot suckle their young on fern root alone,' he would mutter. Every day he inspected the food that was brought in to the village and bewailed the tribe's lack of kumara gardens. He would make a good farmer, Lafe thought with amusement as he watched Tama inspecting the tribe's udders, but he had to admit that his father-in-law was a good chief, caring of his people and watchful for their future. He ruled them strictly but always with their best interests to the fore and his primary concern was the collective health and welfare of the tribe.

Through his own ignorance, Lafe broke many of the rules of the tribe. Such indiscretions appalled his wives and there were times when they might have flown from his house in despair but for Tama's intervention. The chief would urge them to forgive their husband for breaking the law of tapu, then would take Lafe aside and explain where he had gone wrong.

'Please try harder not to offend our gods,' he would urge with a stricken look on his face, and he begged Lafe to listen to Marama and learn from her. His mistakes and blunders were sins that any well brought up gentleman would avoid and they often put Tama's Goblin, and therefore the chief himself, in a rather poor light. When Lafe broke a tapu he was made instantly aware of it by his wives or by other villagers, and people would draw back from him as if he had an infectious disease.

At such times Lafe was aware of the tohunga's dark scowl, and Tama himself would avoid his company for a day or two, obviously expecting a bolt of lightning to strike him down and wanting to be far removed when it happened. The people would look on him with pity as if they were mourners looking on the face of the dead. Every morning Tama would carefully enquire as to his health and, after a certain period of time had passed, the astounded chief would realize that the gods had not taken retribution this time.

'It seems that the gods not only excuse the village idiots from the tapu but Goblins as well,' he would whisper in awe. Tama would call the tohunga to perform a cleansing ceremony to drive away any vestiges of bad luck that might still cling to the Goblin and his household. After such a ceremony a piece of Lafe's property would be delivered by his own hand as a gift to Tama, who would accept it with a great show of dignity.

239

Lafe was never sure how such gifts to the chief were expected to please the gods, and he thought it wiser not to ask. It was immaterial anyway, as most of his belongings had already become Tama's property. The chief thought nothing of wandering into his Goblin's hut, picking up any item he thought he might need and wandering off home with it.

'He is a very generous man, my father,' Marama exclaimed one day as she showed off a colourful red blanket Tama had lent to her. In fact it was Lafe's own blanket – one of the three he used to own – but he refrained from pointing that out. Marama would have been genuinely puzzled by his attitude.

Most of the laws that Lafe broke unwittingly were to do with blundering into ancient burial grounds, fishing in forbidden spots or taking foods that were tapu for any one of a thousand reasons. If a chief had died many years earlier after enjoying a meal of pipi from a certain spot, a rahui could be cast on that shellfish bed and woe betide anyone foolish enough to eat from it. If a warrior inadvertently broke a tapu he was immediately shunned by the whole village and not even his wives would allow him to come near them. Within a few days the man's skin would become a sickly grey colour and he would go off a little way in the forest and build a small shelter, wrap himself in his mats and prepare to die. Meanwhile the tohunga wrestled with the gods and cast spells for the throwing off of the tapu. Sometimes he was successful and the warrior returned to his rightful place in the village, but more often the unfortunate sinner was dead within days.

With the help of his wives and his friends Lafe slowly accumulated the knowledge and tribal lore that helped him avoid many of the pitfalls, and it was during that first winter at Murderers' Bay that he became aware of one of the stranger rituals of the tribe. It formed one of the corner posts of village life and it was known as muru. Lafe sought Marama's help in understanding the many twists and turns of this piece of lore.

'Muru is our way of helping an unfortunate member of the tribe,' she explained. 'A man who has lost so much can only appease the gods by losing everything.

'Take Whetu, for example. Whetu was once a very great warrior, but early in the winter his wife lost her baby and the people who were his relations all said, 'Bad luck, Whetu.'

'Now a month later, his eldest son falls into a deep hole in the river and drowns. You remember this?'

Lafe nodded, recalling a confusing incident soon after his arrival at Okarito.

'Now Whetu knows this is no longer just bad luck, so he goes to his hut and sits alone and waits. Soon his relatives swarm into his house and take everything he owns and carry it all away. He is left with nothing. Even his wives are free to go and he will not try to stop them.

'Whetu is thankful and happy. He hopes he has now appeased the gods, and he is honoured that his relatives and friends think so much of him they will help in this way. Now he goes on to live a much more humble life than before, and the gods let him remain with us.'

Lafe sat for a long time wrapped in his cloak staring at the fire, thinking how differently people saw things in different parts of the world. He seldom thought of his home and family in America now, but that night he remembered the death of a baby in his home community, and how the women had baked food and taken gifts to the stricken family. His gentle wife Marama had spoken of Whetu with just as much compassion and concern, and he found he could accept her way of thinking too.

The first of the spring foods so eagerly awaited in this part of the world were the scallops, fan-shaped shellfish with tasty white flesh that lived in the mud of the seabed. This was a food that carried a tapu. It was never taken before it was fat, so the stocks would be preserved, and it was the tohunga's duty to consult with the gods and lift the tapu so the tribe could begin to gather their favourite shellfish. Already the inunga, the little whitefish so familiar on the west coast, was entering the rivers but it would never provide as much food here for the tribe. The rivers were smaller here and the little fish not nearly so plentiful so it was eaten fresh with duck eggs as a seasonal treat rather than being dried as a major winter food.

On the day the scalloping began, every canoe in the village put out into the bay. They were left to drift while the divers, using large stones to take them down twenty-five feet of water to the bottom, filled their flax kits with shellfish. Every man and woman in the tribe could dive and even the children were superb swimmers, their healthy lifestyle giving them well-developed lung capacity. Lafe was a good diver too but it took several attempts before he could get down to the scallop beds, let alone begin filling his kit. Marama was diving with him while Tui and Haroto stayed behind to look after the girls, and she tipped her catch into his kete with a mocking challenge in her eyes before disappearing back into the dancing water.

Soon the canoes were half awash with shellfish and the tired crews scrambled back on board and set off back to the shore. Many of the scallops never made it back to land, the shells prised open and the raw flesh devoured by the paddlers as if they had been starved for most of the winter. These scallops were four to six inches across the shell and were plump, white and fleshy, with a circle of creamy-tasting orange roe. They were the finest shellfish that Lafe had ever eaten and, like most of the other men in the village, he could scarcely stagger away from the fire after he had finished his meal that night. It was quite an achievement to eat as much as the well-known gluttons of the tribe as all warriors were honoured for their capacity.

The preparations for war never stopped. Every year a new crop of young warriors were trained in the military arts, and sooner or later that training brought its own problems.

'They clamour to be led into battle,' Tama complained. 'Any war will do for them. It is a problem we must deal with.' He and Lafe had talked it over many times around the fireside that winter as they came to realise they were under no immediate threat of attack. 'This weapon we have trained and honed for war will become blunt if it is not used,' Tama said.

Lafe had been doing a lot of thinking on his own account. With the spring, a time of plenty had arrived in that benign and fruitful land and Lafe fervently hoped that the culture of cannibalism might fade from the memory of the people, but even amidst the abundance, there were those who hankered for human flesh. Within a few weeks of the lifting of the tapu on the scallop beds, Lafe overheard a group of warriors discussing great feasts. This was a favourite pastimes on wet days, but what he heard dismayed and chilled him.

'I hope Tama organizes a raid soon, I just can't wait to sink my teeth into a nice juicy foot,' one man said.

'Give me a hand any day, or perhaps an elbow,' his friend answered.

'Or the soles of the feet. They are fine eating,' claimed a third.

Lafe was disturbed by the degree of cannibalism in the tribe, most of all by the appetites of his own family. He had himself eaten human flesh on the southern raids but it had sickened him and he viewed it as a last extremity. He had decided not to allow his daughters to taste such meat, but so far he had kept his resolution to himself. These people did not eat human flesh because they were hungry, as he had once supposed, but because they enjoyed it.

He had mused about his two wives, Marama and Tui, and their obvious relish as they had chewed on the hand, arm, and shoulder of the last victim, a member of Haroto's family. They were habitual cannibals, brought up in a culture of cannibalism, and common sense told him he could not just forbid his family from eating such food. The habit was too well ingrained for that, and he had to try to convince them it was wrong. In his heart he believed cannibalism was a barbaric practice that no civilised race would accept.

He remembered someone on the ship, perhaps Matai or Jimmy, talking of Cook's liberation of pigs in this middle island as well as in the north, and he knew from his own reading that the first place in the country where the great navigator had presented a tribe with breeding pigs was on the shores of the Windpipe, not so many days' travel from where he now stood. Although Matai's people in the far north had been used to pigs, his experience with the horse and dog story had told him that Tama's tribe knew nothing of such animals.

'In the spring I will lead an expedition to find the hog and bring it back,' he offered. That would get some of the firebrands off Tama's hands as well, serving the purposes of both men.

Once again he drew pictures in the sand, creating the best picture he could of this strange creature the hog. A large audience watched intently as he scratched out the shape in the smooth, hard sand. In his most serious voice he announced, 'This is a hog.'

'But surely, Goblin, after all this time with us you have come to realize that this creature is really a dog?' Tama spoke with great seriousness, pointing to Salem, and the resulting laughter left many of the tribe slapping each other on the back and quite unable to speak for many minutes. Lafe let the laughter wash over him and almost doubted himself. In this new world of his there was no other animal but dog and rat. There was obviously no such thing as a hog – it had to be a dog.

He persevered, painting such a desirable picture of the hog as a source of food that Tama finally gave in to his desire to hunt it down even though the chief was still convinced it was a dog he was talking about. He allowed Lafe to take his pick of the warriors for the expedition, giving him forty-two men in all. They would penetrate Totaranui, or Queen Charlotte Sound as Cook had named it, in search of the pig that the English sea captain had left behind there.

Though it was a peaceful trading expedition each of the forty-two warriors carried his best weapons and was in superb fighting trim. Lafe would also take two muskets, making the group a hard-hitting force capable of taking what they wanted if they had to.

'There is no such thing as a peaceful expedition nowadays,' Tama cautioned. 'And you will seek two things of great importance to the tribe. First, you will find a tattooist of merit and bring him to me.' It was an instruction, not a request, and Lafe recognised that as always his father-in-law had his own shrewd agenda.

'Secondly,' the chief went on, 'this creature you call the hog will be found and brought home to feed our people.

'Some of my best greenstone will go with you as gifts for the chiefs you may deal with on your journey, but the musket may have more influence than the gift, and you must use it well.

'Hear me. These are the things I say,' he intoned formally, with a ferocious scowl.

Lafe knew that Tama never parted with the tribe's stone unless he absolutely had to, but allies could be useful in the time of war and these people that Lafe was going to trade with were the nearest friendly neighbours they had. It was a reflection of Tama's trust in him, and the place he had earned in the tribe, that he was allowed to go at all, and he was not expected to fail in his task.

Tama spent days choosing the right stone. His was a classic dilemma, Lafe realized. The poorer the gift, the lesser the mana of the giver and no one trusted a man without mana. Now that he knew his people better, Lafe understood that such an emphasis on prestige could in fact impoverish a whole tribe, just as the tribe at Whangaroa had probably beggared itself when it sacrificed the last of the kumara crop to provide a feast for the crew of the *Northern Lights*. As he himself had been beggared by the gifts he had made to Tama, so now he had to borrow his own possessions back, he thought ruefully. To have mana was to have power, respect and chiefly rank, but keeping it was not always easy.

'Have I not given you the greatest gift of all?' Tama would claim if he were challenged. 'Your first wife Marama came from my very own high-born loins.'

Marama, Tui, Haroto and all the other women of the village were there to sing a grand song of farewell as the big double canoe was launched. The tohunga called the blessing of the gods on their journey and Salem, alert in the bow, eagerly sniffed the winds of adventure. Behind him the paddlers began to find their rhythm as they headed out to sea.

Unlike the other expeditions Lafe had been on, this was a voyage of discovery as well as trade. A few of the older warriors had sailed beyond Murderers' Bay into Blind Bay and as far as Rangitoto but never beyond these islands. Lafe still had his copies of Cook's charts, though much of Blind Bay had never been seen by Cook and only the area from Rangitoto to Queen Charlotte Sound was well charted, and he remembered his discussions with Olva as they had navigated down the east coast in what seemed like a lifetime ago. Perhaps Cook had been

245

discouraged by the Dutchman Tasman's experience with the cannibals of Murderers' Bay, they had agreed, and that would account for his lack of desire to enter and chart the waters he named Blind Bay.

'These would have been your ancestors,' Lafe explained to his warriors, who already knew of the killing of the Goblins. Cook's maps were of great interest to them. Although they had not travelled far from home they were a seafaring people and they had a real feel for the size and shape of their country from the endless stories told around their fires at night. Most of his crew had built for themselves a picture of the coastline and much of the interior of the country as well and could have given clear and precise sailing directions to the villages of the North Island. They had learned such things by rote and repetition even though no one alive in the village today had ever been that far afield.

'It is a pity Captain Cook failed to enter Blind Bay, but he will never know what he missed,' Lafe had told them. 'Now we are the explorers.'

'It is the right weather for travel,' the captain of the double canoe agreed politely, 'and it is good to make this voyage into strange lands, to be among strange people and to look for this strange animal the hog.' There was a roar of laughter at this last comment, and the men rolled their eyes towards Salem and grinned at each other. They liked Lafe and trusted him well, but they were keeping open minds on the hog question.

They were all pleased to be back at sea and none more than Lafe, who was delighted to feel the rollers of the open sea under the big canoe. Since they left Rua Taniwha they had followed the coast closely and steadily, travelling eastwards and hoisting the big woven sail whenever they could. They had passed two very pretty little islands and were gliding along off a beach of the most attractive golden sand when Lafe gave the signal to let the anchors go in the clear water. They baited their hooks with shellfish that they had brought with them, tossed the lines over the side and within the hour had enough golden red tamure flapping on the floor to provide a fish for every man's supper. Then they moved closer to shore and sent divers into the water, some swimming to the rocks for mussels while the rest dived for scallops on the sandy bottom.

When Lafe signalled enough they headed for the shore and dragged their big vessel above the high water mark on golden sand that was still warm from the sun. Very soon their fires lit up the sand around them and their supper was grilling on sticks over hot embers. Sentries were posted to patrol the sandhills and guard men and boats, for they were in enemy territory now, and once they had eaten the rest of the crew threw themselves onto the soft sand with their cloaks wrapped tightly around them and fell asleep under the big white moon.

Next morning, with the breeze holding from the south and a clear sky, the big canoe headed northeast and crossed the narrower part of Blind Bay before turning north for Rangitoto Island. On the third day of the voyage they closed with the mighty channel between Rangitoto and the mainland and slipped into a little bay on the island itself, just below the narrow pass. Already Lafe could feel the grip of the current on the two hulls and see large whirlpools in the water ahead, and he was pleased when they hauled up near a sheltered little beach surrounded by jagged rocks. Here they found blue cod that were so keen on keeping their part of the bargain they would almost follow an empty hook to the surface and jump into the boat, ready to be gutted and baked over the fire. Lafe could not remember eating a nicer fish, even down in Dusky Sound. Perhaps it was the setting, but this meal on the little sheltered beach within the sound of the great rushing waters of the pass had an added fine flavour to it.

'Around here the country is so wonderfully quiet, it seems almost completely uninhabited,' Lafe commented to the most widely-travelled of the warriors. He had noticed only the odd bay with a plume of smoke climbing into the blue heavens to show where two or three families might be cooking their evening food.

'It was not like this in the old days, Goblin,' the travelled one replied. 'We once visited many friendly tribes along this coast, and they visited us in return. And at spring high water many tribes used to gather at this very spot, for then the waves coming through the pass were so fierce that they stunned the fish and they could be gathered in boatloads.

'But it is war now, and the tribes are more interested in eating human flesh than fish.'

247

He shrugged his shoulders as Lafe stared at him, trying to decide whether to ask the question. Finally, he did so.

'And are you one who prefers war to peace?' he asked quietly.

'I am one who has always preferred flesh to fish,' was the ingenuous reply.

Lafe thought again how much better it would be if all of the tribes could live in peace again, and men and women could travel from one end of the country to the other without the constant fear of being attacked. But in his heart he also acknowledged the excitement and the savage beauty of war, when the blood raced through a man's veins and rose until it filled his head and his eyes with the madness of battle. War, where the looting and the taking of women were prizes that belonged only to the bold, when to seize an enemy's possessions was to take away his mana forever, leaving your own footprint stamped upon his family tree because the prize awarded to the warrior who struck down the first victim or showed merit in battle was always the pick of the women. War did have a certain appeal, he agreed ruefully.

The next morning they all sat quietly in the big waka fishing and waiting for the hour of dead slack water to arrive at the pass. This was the top of the tide, when the two seas were in balance, and when it finally came the current was stilled and the whirlpools that could drag a canoe and its crew down into the depths of the maelstrom were quiet and subdued. Only then was there safe passage through the pass.

On the other side, the bay gradually widened until they were in open water again and entering for the first time the strait called The Windpipe of the Pacific. Now they could clearly see the shores of the North Island as the gap between the north and south islands narrowed. To the northeast lay Cook's Entry Island that the tribe knew as Kapiti, beyond that the spine of mountains that formed part of the backbone of the great fish of Maui. It was a rugged land.

Conditions were so good that Lafe chose to take advantage of them and sail through the night, as Cook's Strait had an evil reputation for being able to produce a storm at very short notice. Around evening they passed the large entrance of a waterway leading inland, with a large tide running through it that drew them in until it finally lost its grip on the boat. This was not marked on Lafe's map but one of the warriors explained that it was the entrance to a huge inland sea that took three days to paddle from one end to the other. That made it a very large sound and Lafe decided that one day he would travel to the end of it.

The men told him it was inhabited by a warlike tribe of giants, descendants of a completely unknown race, and when he questioned them carefully he found that the story had been passed down around the campfires. No one in the tribe had ever seen one of these giants, but they had known men whose fathers had seen them. Lafe could not shake their story, and it became clear that not only the warriors on board but their whole tribe firmly believed in this race of giants and this was the place where they were known to live.

With the great white moon sailing overhead it was an enchanted voyage across several large bays and past large, brooding headlands made more sinister still by the shadows they cast in the moonlight. The night was fine but cool, with just enough breeze to keep the sails full and pulling steadily and allow the paddlers to rest and doze at their posts, and an hour before daylight Lafe felt the pull of the current drawing them forward toward the sound the Maori called Totaranui.

Once the tide had them in its grip it was simply a matter of keeping the bows square on with the direction the current was running, as it drew them swiftly toward the passage between the rocks and the mainland. They had little control over what was happening and for a mad few minutes the pull grew stronger and stronger until they were among pressure waves that towered above them like giant steps. Though the men received a thorough soaking the canoe took on very little water considering the roughness of the passage, and when the current had finished with them and the boat was under control again they found they had been carried like a piece of driftwood through the wide entrance and into the calm waters of the sound.

Lafe laughed with relief as he looked at the equally relieved faces around him.

'I would not have entered the sound in darkness if I had known it was such a rough ride,' he shouted. It was true – once the current had them in its grip there had been no option but to ride those wild waves all the way through and hope there were no rocks to rip the bottoms out of the hulls.

Lafe signalled for the paddlers to put their backs into it and head deeper into the sound. Everyone was cold and tired, shivering from their icy dunking and they needed somewhere to rest in the warm rays of the sun. He was pleased when he found a beach with high cliffs that would give them protection from a land attack, a flyspeck of a beach really but defendable, and the men nodded approval of his choice. Cook had reported a Maori fort with a sizeable population on a little island several miles further down this sound, and some of Lafe's warriors confirmed the knowledge even though none had personally ventured this far before.

Lafe had learned to respect the collective memory of the tribe. When the people heard a story they had the ability to repeat, learn and store every little detail until some were indeed walking books. He had once listened to a man describe his journey through the mountains almost step by step.

'And then when the sun was on my left shoulder, one hand span above a peak that looked like a warrior's topknot, I came to the forks in the river where stood three rocks, two of them covered in moss,' the man had recited carefully. 'There I rested for the night, and the next day I saw a crooked rata tree whose branch dangled in the water. Here I turned toward the sunrise and followed the stream…'

This story of one warrior's travels had gone on for many hours and had described the man's journey in intricate detail, identifying anything that would catch the eye of whoever was to follow in his tracks. He had repeated it over and over again while his audience checked and memorised every detail until they could almost recite it with him, and thus his knowledge had become theirs. The tribal history was remembered like this and related in the very same accurate detail going back many generations. It was rather like the stories in the Bible, with its long lists of who begat whom, and Lafe had once tried to explain this to Tama but the idea that history could be told in the physical form of a book rather than as stories around the fire was beyond the chief's understanding.

Now they were in another tribe's territory Lafe decided to let them know he was in the sound rather than arriving unexpectedly, which might well cause them to panic and fight. He remembered the last time he had made such a decision, when Matai was dying and these people he had come to know and belong with had been the unknown enemy. The fire he had lit that day had sent the right message, bringing Tama to him, and he hoped the chief whose territory he had entered this time would be as wise. He told his men to build a large fire, knowing the people at the fort would not ignore such a challenge on their doorstep.

'They will come to us when they see the smoke,' he reassured his warriors. 'It is better this way.'

Once the fire had been lit they cooked a quick meal and ate it then dumped armloads of green foliage on the hot coals. Immediately a column of dark smoke spiralled up into the clear blue sky

'Have your weapons ready,' Lafe told his men. Then following his example they lay down in the warm sun, wrapped in their robes, and slept under the watchful eyes of the sentries.

When Lafe felt a touch on his shoulder he was immediately alert again. A quick check of the sun made it around mid-afternoon and he did not need to ask what had caused the alarm to be raised. Four canoes sped like arrows from the island where the fort was reported to be towards the beach where he and his men lay. His pulse quickening, he called his warriors to arms.

The strange canoes were moving fast as they drew into the bay, and with immaculate precision their crews drove their paddles deep into the water on command and back-paddled to bring their vessels to a halt twenty yards from the beach. Lafe noted that each of the canoes carried fifteen warriors, which meant his own party was slightly outnumbered, but they appeared not to have muskets with them. The bay was silent except for the birdsong, suddenly deafening in the absence of any other sound as the two groups of warriors glared at each other across the short stretch of water.

'They are like tied dogs straining to get at each other,' Lafe muttered to one of his lieutenants. 'See that it doesn't happen.'

He motioned to the other musketeer and they both stepped forward, their muskets lying casually across the crooks of their arms where they could be seen clearly by all ranks. Lafe noted that on the visitors' side all eyes had swung to the muskets, which they obviously recognised for what they were, and then back to his own blond hair and bearded but undecorated face. There was a tension in the air that could be cut with a knife.

He waited for the other chief to make the first move and it wasn't long in coming. The leader of the sounds warriors was a big man and he raised his eyes to the sky and bellowed out the traditional challenge, his voice echoing from hill to hill and even shutting the birds up. Lafe answered with the appropriate reply and gestures and the canoes crept warily onto the shore. The chief signalled for the food that had been hastily prepared for these unknown visitors to be unloaded onto the beach and then led his warriors in a spirited haka, thus indicating that he was equally ready for friendship or a fight. Lafe in his turn laid a fine greenstone tiki on the beach as an overture of friendship. It was a gift that made the chief's eyes stick out of his head as he reached for it.

'We have many more pieces of the stone of such quality,' Lafe promised. 'We have come to trade.'

He met the chief's eyes confidently, trying to show strength without fear, and the two men stared at each other for a long minute. Then their host nodded, his decision made.

'My village will welcome you tomorrow, when we have had time to prepare a feast. Then we will talk of trade,' he promised. The canoes sped back across the sound to the fort, the baskets of food left on the beach were opened and everybody fell upon the meal with great heart. Every tribe had a food that was a specialty of its own area. With Tama's people, now they were settled in Murderers' Bay, it was the scallop, but here in the sounds it was the lobster, and the men groaned in noisy appreciation as they sucked the succulent white meat from claws and legs.

'It does not matter whether the food is grown, caught in the forest, or plucked from the sea, it is something that each tribe has that they do better than anyone else,' a warrior remarked, and Lafe had to agree that this tribe did lobster best of all. In the food bags they had been given they found lobster prepared in many different ways and he realized that the tribe must have extraordinary fishermen and very rich waters indeed for them to have put together a meal of such delicacy. One bag, however, smelled so bad that Lafe wondered whether the lobster in it was fit to eat, but the warriors smacked their lips over it with obvious delight. The fish had been deliberately rotted in fresh water for many weeks so that the flesh had become soft, almost liquid, and putrid.

'It smells bad, but we are all very fond of this treat which tastes wonderful,' a man chuckled as the American turned away from a proffered morsel. Lafe was amazed that they didn't drop down dead on the sand poisoned by the food. No sailor would even consider eating fish that smelt so bad.

They spent that night on the sand in the quiet little bay, and it was no hardship because the weather was fine and mild. In the morning, after a decent interval to allow their hosts time to prepare themselves, they launched their waka and set off for the fort. Lafe was looking forward to this feast. Early the previous evening there had been strange sounds floating across the water, sounds that caused great wonderment among his warriors but that he recognised as the squeals and screams of pigs being caught and killed. The men had speculated uneasily on what strange creature made such a noise.

'Perhaps there truly is this creature that the Goblin calls a hog,' one man suggested, and they looked at Lafe with a new respect. He was delighted by what he had heard. It was a long time since he had eaten pork, or meat of any kind except human, and his mouth watered at the thought of it. The noises also gave a good indication that this expedition would be successful in its quest for hogs. Lafe had never really known whether Cook's pigs had survived or been hunted to extinction the moment his ship left the area, and he was pleased to have found a tribe that looked after such a rich food source. He was also looking forward to the reaction of his men to the new food, and fervently hoped it would lessen their constant craving for meat.

As they drew close to the fort, the visitors were impressed with its defensive possibilities. It was built on the top of a tiny steep-sided island with only a single steep narrow path providing the access way. With its high palisades, this pa would be almost impregnable to any tribe with hand-held weapons. Even to take the place with muskets would be

253

difficult, and Lafe knew that the defenders would have to be picked off by marksmen from the boats below. It was a very impressive fort indeed.

'It could be just as hard to leave as it is to get in, so be very careful, my men,' Lafe warned.

They felt many unseen eyes on them as they dropped their anchors into the clear water, signalling that they were ready for the day's proceedings to begin. Immediately a song rose to the heavens from the fort above, followed by a ferocious challenge that was answered from the boats below. Haka, waiata, challenge and response continued in the traditional rituals of welcome and soon the visitors were invited to take the path to the fort above. When they entered the palisade they were seated, according to rank, on flax mats in an open courtyard surrounded by about thirty small grass dwellings.

'Nothing has changed in the thirty years since Captain James Cook himself was here,' Lafe whispered excitedly to his men. 'Some of these people sitting here today might have spoken to the great navigator himself.' He could hardly wait to begin questioning the elders about what they remembered of Cook's visit, but knew it would not be polite to do so until much later in the day. First they must talk of trade.

It wasn't long before their host broached the subject of muskets. Lafe gave the firmest and clearest indication he could manage that he would not consider trading his muskets and his stance was not negotiable. This was clearly a blow to the other tribe and the meeting was silent for a long period of time. Lafe had impressed on his men the importance of showing no fear or weakness and he knew that warriors on both sides were considering the odds on an attempt to take the muskets by force.

He found it interesting that this tribe, which owned no muskets, had encountered them before and could see the advantages of having them and he fervently hoped visiting ship owners would resist the temptation to sell to them. He had no doubt that the moment the Maori tribes got their hands on muskets they would begin killing each other as if there was no tomorrow. To his relief the host tribe conceded the point and the tension eased again. Lafe wanted pigs and the other chief wanted greenstone so a deal would be done, and they both knew that and were happy. There was no haste and the talk flew from subject to subject as the day passed. Lafe was reminded of those longed-for encounters at sea when two ships would meet in the wide ocean and their occupants, from captain to cabin boy, would settle down with their counterparts to have a gam and share news and gossip.

It was agreed that Lafe would be allowed to inspect the tribe's livestock, kept safe on the mainland, on the following day before a price was agreed on. The eastern shore of the sound they were in was in fact another large island that the Maori called Arapawa and there was another type of animal running wild there. From the chief's description it could only be the goat, and Lafe guessed this had been another one of Cook's successful liberations. He would take some goats back to Murderers' Bay with him, not only for eating but so they could be milked to supplement the food for the babies. It was arranged there and then. They would get their hogs and goats from this tribe at Motuara, as the fort was known, and the chief immediately sent men over to Arapawa to capture goats for Tama's people.

Finally great baskets of food were placed before the visitors and Lafe watched his men closely as they encountered pork for the first time in their lives. First they carefully examined the skin of this new flesh, then they sniffed the meat cautiously. Finally they tasted, and their reactions as the rich fat dripped from their chins were all that Lafe had hoped for as they loudly proclaimed it very good food indeed. The hog's head was examined in great detail, with much laughter from their hosts and many exclamations of wonder from the visitors.

'How odd,' Lafe's men said. 'What a strange creature this new kind of dog is.'

'You never know what to expect from these Goblins next.'

Their hosts were delighted with the sensation their food had caused and they vied with each other to describe the pig and tell of its properties. Lafe's mana with his people rose even more.

'You were right, Goblin,' they told him as they gorged themselves until they could hold no more. 'This makes fine eating, this new creature we have come to meet.'

'The taste and the texture remind me of human flesh,' one cannibal warrior confided to him. 'Not quite as good, mind you, but good enough if you were hungry.'

Lafe was a little downhearted when he heard that, but he still had high hopes that once Tama's people had another source of good meat the tribe's appetite for man-flesh would gradually die.

The second part of his mission was one he was much less enthusiastic about, but he knew he had to find a tattooist. He made enquiries and found there was a family of artists at a place called Waikawa, deep in the inner part of this sound Cook had named after King George's wife Queen Charlotte. Lafe laughed aloud as he tried to imagine the English queen's reaction to the sultry, bare-foot and bare-breasted young woman who was at that moment crouched at his side digging the flesh out of a succulent lobster claw for him.

Once he had eaten his fill and business was finished for the day he took the opportunity to examine the fort itself. The logs that made up the palisades were sunk into the soil and in some places into solid rock, and bound together with vines and flax. If an enemy force made it up the steep rock face from their boats they would still have to break through this daunting log barrier in the face of rocks and spears thrown down from above.

But it was the little island itself and its stunning surroundings that impressed Lafe the most. The sea had only the lightest ruffle on its surface from a tiny breeze that caused it to sparkle and dance in the hot summer day. The heat gave the forests that encompassed the bays a smoky blue shade that made them look further away than they really were. Only to the north, the way the party had entered the sound, was there a gap in the vista of beach, forest and mountain, and here there was an uninterrupted view all the way out to The Windpipe and the North Island.

To the west, a short distance from where Lafe stood, were the lovely beaches of Ship Cove where he knew Cook had careened his ships and even planted English gardens. It was an inviting place and Lafe could see immediately why Cook chose to rest and refresh his crews there. To the south, the mountains closed in and the sound became landlocked and narrow, but here there were other islands, thick forests that came down to the water's edge and many bays that gave the southern part of the Sound a sense of mystery and a sense of not knowing what the next bend of the waterway would bring.

Cook had said in his journal that the flow of the tides led him to believe there was another entrance out to the sea, and Lafe now knew this must be so because his hosts had described Arapawa, to the east, as an island. It was long and thin, resembling the top of a mountain ridge that had been overtaken by the sea and drowned, and beyond that was the eastern shore which might, as Cook had believed, not be the mainland at all but another large island.

Though the Erickson clan were Yankees through and through and had no liking for the English in general, Lafe had developed a tremendous respect for the English navigator whose journal he had read and whose charts he had studied daily at sea. He was especially impressed with the man's attitude to the Maori and his attempts to leave every place he visited better off than before. Always, it seemed, Cook had considered those who would follow in his footsteps though he must have known that the rewards might sometimes be poor. His gifts of hogs, or pigs as the English called them, and goats had ensured that he would always be remembered in this part of the world although his attempts to transplant English vegetables into Maori gardens and therefore into their diet had failed.

There were other benefits. Lafe was personally very grateful that he, a white Goblin like Cook and his men, was seen in the same positive light. He could see that the tribes here had developed a great love for the hog in the few short years since the English ship had put boars and breeding sows ashore, and to hear the chief of Motuara extolling the virtues of his own pigs to the newcomers was almost like listening to someone describing a favourite wife. He tried hard not to betray his avid interest. One thing the Maori loved above all else was trading, and already the local chief was aware that he had willing customers. He was no fool, and Lafe told himself he would have to be very sharp in his dealings.

That night, after the many songs and haka had finished, the visitors slept wrapped in their cloaks under the eaves of the huts they had been assigned for the night. They kept their weapons at hand just in case their hosts were tempted to treachery, posted their own sentries and rested rather than slept. Lafe was worried that the greenstone and the muskets they carried might offer too attractive a target for the chief to resist and he had his men lie down in pairs, with only one of the two asleep at any one time. Neither he nor his men slept inside the huts as a favourite trick was to set the hut on fire and club the occupants as they emerged through the low entrance blinded by smoke. Cook himself had regarded the tribes in this vicinity as untrustworthy and had named Cannibal Cove just north of Ship Cove as a sober reminder of the treachery that lost him a boat crew.

The night passed peacefully however and in the morning, after everyone had cleaned up what remained of the previous day's feast for breakfast, the chief invited them to board their big canoe and follow him to Ship Cove to inspect his livestock. What they saw surprised and impressed them. The hogs had flourished well in this new country, with its trees rich in berries and fruit and the slopes dense with fern root. There was pig sign all around the bay and, when they were called, half a dozen large sows and a boar trotted out of the forest with numerous offspring at their heels to feed on scraps cast on the sand.

'These are razorbacks,' Lafe exclaimed. He struggled to find a better explanation, finally telling his hosts, 'Their backs are as skinny as the blade of a knife. These animals are almost a breed of their own. They are very different from the hogs that I knew back home.'

With their extraordinary long snouts, long hairy tails and thick coats, the pigs were extremely ugly and the boars possessed wicked sets of tusks. His own men had retreated to their big canoe at the first sight of them and Lafe could hardly suppress his laughter.

'Come, stand with me, O Great Warriors,' he chided. 'Are you the men sent by Tama?' Aware of their audience they left the boat and joined him, stiff with embarrassment but never once taking their eyes off those strange animals.

Lafe selected his hogs with care. After much discussion the price was agreed and he arranged to pick up the hogs and a pair of goats on his return from the inner sound. The next morning he and his warriors manned the cutter and the canoe and headed south for Waikawa, where they had been told there was quite a large settlement of very friendly people. A fast canoe had already been despatched from Motuara to warn the neighbouring tribe of their coming.

Lafe thought it wise to issue his own warning, and told his men that the tribe they were going to visit suffered from women's sickness or venereal disease. As a sailor he was familiar with the problem and he had delivered lectures on venereal disease before, but he found that to explain it to Tama's warriors called for a lot of careful thought and ingenuity. The tribe had never come in contact with such a disease before, and had never dreamed of a sickness that could attack a warrior's manhood. It shocked them and left them feeling very unhappy and vulnerable.

'Make no mistake,' Lafe told them sternly. 'If you catch the woman sickness your piri piri will rot before your eyes and fall from your body.' When Cook's men had caught the disease and the symptoms had begun to appear they had called it the New Zealand fever, though the tribes in the sounds called it the white man's fever and told Cook they had caught it from a sailing ship that visited the sounds before him. That must have come as a great shock to the British Empire, Lafe mused, as the disease seemed to have been South American in origin.

On their way down that great water highway they searched for a secluded beach where they could rest up and eat. There had been almost no rest at the fort, where they had been alert and watchful for nearly two days now, and Lafe had had the foresight to purchase a good fat hog dressed ready for eating before they left. He knew that his men still had a craving for meat and now they looked for a safe place to cook it. They moved at a leisurely pace, approaching and then passing a beautiful little island that stood guard at the narrowing neck of the sound. Though he was tempted, Lafe would not land on an island because it would be too easy for an enemy to land on the opposite side and launch an overland attack. Instead he chose one of the beaches on the eastern side of the sound, protected by steep cliffs, and they ran their boat up on the beach in the late afternoon sun.

Some of the men dived for shellfish while others searched the nearby forest for their next meal, but soon the smell of wood smoke and roasting pork filled the little bay and called them back to the cooking fire. The hunter-gatherer existence was devoid of any romance. It meant that even before you had finished the meal you were eating you were thinking about the next one and planning where to look for it.

'I know why you all enjoy your food so much,' Lafe shouted, laughing as the men gathered around the fire. 'You never know from one day to the next where your next meal is coming from.'

He was thoroughly enjoying the expedition and knew the pigs and goats would bring about a big improvement to his tribe's way of life. Like the others in the party he was already looking forward to the sensation they would cause when they arrived home in triumph.

They ate and slept well that night, and the next morning made their way past a deep bay whose furthest recesses could not be seen from their boats and whose strong tidal current indicated a connection to another sea. With the help of that incoming tide to make up for the very light breeze, they reached the next settlement by mid-afternoon.

Waikawa came into sight slowly, its steep hills surrounding the deep bay where a village of huts made of the ever handy and warm grasses huddled in a long, shallow valley leading inland. Beyond the forest ridges they could see in the distance, Lafe had been told, there were dry plains and hills and wide, stony riverbeds that sometimes had no rain for half the year. It must have been an amazing contrast to this side of the divide, which was covered in lush forest of almost tropical splendour. The harbour was fine and sheltered, with good clean freshwater streams and ample room on the valley floor for gardens and the raising of hogs.

Again they were welcomed ashore and hogs were killed for the inevitable big feast, but Lafe wondered how much their muskets had to do with the quality of their welcome. There was no doubt in his mind now that the musket was sought by many tribes and the warriors who had them were shown respect way beyond their due.

He waited until everyone had eaten before bringing up the reason for his visit.

'I have come to seek the services of your tattooists who are well known for their skills, even as far as my own tribe,' he told them. He considered a little flattery would not go amiss.

'The faces of our young warriors ache for the want of a tattoo, and the skills of your artists are needed by my people. I have brought greenstone carved by our best craftsmen to buy the services of such a man.'

He let the tension and anticipation build, and when he finally opened his pack and passed around some of the beautiful carved pieces he heard the sucking in of breath over teeth, a sure sign that his audience appreciated the quality of the goods on offer. There was much discussion to follow. There was, it seemed, a young man who had studied under this family who were so skilled in their craft of tattooing. He had reached a standard that would not disgrace them and their tribe's reputation, and for sufficient inducement he would be willing to spend a year or more away from his own village.

'This young man is an artist in his own right. He has the skill and the knowledge that will one day make him more famous than his teachers,' their chief assured Lafe, and several warriors and women were singled out from the crowd and drawn forward to show the fineness and subtlety of the blue-black whorls and spirals that marked them. After much more discussion a deal was struck, and Lafe had purchased the services of this tattooist for a year.

He passed on to the next subject. He wished to purchase a boar and sow from Waikawa to improve the breeding base of the pigs he would take back with him from Ship Cove to Murderers' Bay. Again he and his men had to sit politely and listen to the virtues of the village pigs extolled to the skies before he could put in his opening bid, which was greeted with a show of horror by the opposing chief.

'It is not the done thing to make or accept an honest offer too early,' Tama was fond of saying. 'That takes all the fun out of the game.'

He had taught Lafe well, and the blond sailor looked as sternly as he could on his host's gambits and counter-offers, saying little and warning his men with steely eyes to do the same. Again they rested uneasily under the gables of the village huts, their sentries alert and their muskets loaded with buckshot in case of treachery. There was a smell of greed about this village that made Lafe uneasy. The muskets were a powerful temptation and any tribe might find the urge to get their hands on such weapons overcoming their manners and their natural instincts towards friendship.

At least he did not have to worry about his men slipping off to join the women in their huts. His lecture on venereal disease had hit its targets, and there would be a severe loss of mana for his warriors if the very core of their manhood was attacked by disease. Even worse would be the effect on their own tribe if the disease was brought back with them. The next day Lafe made careful inquiries among his warriors, and was relieved to be satisfied that none of his men had slept with a woman that night. He had the tattooist stripped and he carefully examined the man's piri piri, rolling back the foreskin and checking for any signs of the loathsome disease.

With the help of their hosts they built cages of saplings, woven together with the strong vines that abounded in the nearby hills, for the boar and sow they had bought. Salem did his best to bully the animals into submission as they were loaded on board the big double canoe and Lafe had to call him sharply to heel for fear the big boar would break out and gore him. Then the boats were launched and, with an offshore breeze and the tide to help, they made for Motuara Island on the first leg of their journey home. The next morning they loaded eight smaller sows and two boars into a series of cages and put the pair of goats in a cage of their own. Then they headed north to exit the sound and enter Cook's Strait.

Their voyage home was slow because of the frequent need to gather fish and fern root to feed their animals as well as themselves, but it was largely uneventful and the cargo arrived back in Murderer's Bay in good condition. The only casualty on the voyage was a warrior whose hand and arm were badly ripped when he fell against the biggest boar's pen. As quick as lightning the animal had opened a gash six inches long, and the man lost a good deal of blood before the wound could be staunched.

Their arrival home was all that Lafe and his crew could have wished for. They were welcomed as triumphant warriors and the pigs and goats caused excitement for weeks in the village. To find that the earth was inhabited by other animals beside the rat and the dog was a great revelation to them, as was this proof of Lafe's superior knowledge and wisdom.

'It is true then, Goblin, as you have told us,' Tama said in wonder. 'The world is indeed populated with interesting animals.'

The pigs and goats were moved to large enclosures fenced with tree trunks and the whole tribe spent hours watching every movement they made, bringing them food by the armload and laughing endlessly at the antics of the young hogs as they played in the mud. Now Lafe's own people were involved in this love affair with the hog and he congratulated himself on the success of his plan. He knew that these animals he had brought to the village would make a huge difference to the wellbeing of the tribe, and he firmly believed that under the right circumstances the Maori would become an admirable race of farmers.

Chapter 14

Once again Lafe immersed himself in family life and allowed the peaceful, settled routines of the village to wash over him. He dallied for hours with his wives and children, enjoying their company and delighting in the way his two little girls were growing. He would be considered a very lax husband if he did not give firm orders on how his household should be run and his children brought up, but Marama was an extremely capable senior wife and there were few conflicts. Under his guidance and her management his little family enclave ran smoothly and happily with much singing and laughter.

In the autumn Haroto gave birth to a fine baby boy, his first son, but although she was strong and healthy and nursed him well she seemed even quieter and more reserved after the birth, often lapsing into a melancholy her husband could not shake. Unlike the other two she saw her time with him on the sleeping mat as a duty rather than a pleasure, and her responses were often without spirit but in spite of that he grew fond of her and admired her quiet grace.

He often shared his morning fire and the remains of the last night's meal with Tama before paddling his small canoe out through the waves in the mouth of the estuary to a favourite spot in the bay where he would spend the day fishing for tamure. Or he and the chief might select their longest spears, six or seven yards in length and made from the straightest grained wood, and while away the sunlit hours curled comfortably high up in the forest canopy waiting for a fat pigeon or kaka to arrive. These were days to remember.

Next to them in cages were the tame birds, the Judas parrot and the tui that were tools of trade for a bird hunter. The antics of these call birds were wildly exaggerated and excessive. They were taken when young, most had never successfully mated and the desire was strong in their songs and actions.

'The tui has such a beautiful song she is confident that she needs no other tricks,' Tama chuckled one day, his quiet voice carrying no more than a few feet. 'But the kaka is a parrot and she resorts to female tricks, hanging upside down and showing glimpses of the bright scarlet feathers under her wings. I know a dozen women in our village that she reminds me of.'

Lying draped over the tree limbs and in the shadows, Tama looked like part of the tree itself, Lafe thought. The chief wore a bonnet and cape of dried grasses and leaves and his movements were slow and fluid, his beard appearing neither more nor less than the movement of a streamer of moss in the gentle breeze. Tama loved hunting birds and was very good at it. The call birds he had trained were the best in the village and had brought thousands of their feathered friends to the spear. Lafe appreciated his remark about the behaviour of the parrot and the women in the village, and thought about how true it was, although the chief's next question took him by surprise.

'Are things harmonious in your house, Goblin?' Tama asked.

'Yes, my wives are cheerful and obedient.' Lafe gave the standard reply, wondering what was in the older man's mind.

'And do you get on well with the other members of the tribe?' Tama went on.

'Yes, I get on well with the other members of the tribe,' Lafe answered, unsure now just where the wily chief's questions were leading.

'Then why have you not sought the tattoo?' So that was it. He struggled to find an appropriate answer as Tama went on. 'For every month that goes past that you do not attend the tattooist's couch, I have promised him that I will cut off one of his fingers. So you see, there is a problem. Soon the tribe will not have a tattooist.'

He opened his brown eyes wide and his scarred face creased in a delighted grin as he saw comprehension dawn on Lafe's face. 'I am sure you and he will find a way around this simple problem,' he chuckled, and he turned back to the birds by his side.

Later that day Lafe sat in the afternoon sun surrounded by his wives and pondered on the answer he knew he must give to his chief. They always made the most of this part of the day and ate early because there was no means of artificial lighting in the village. The sun was their lamp, and when the sun went down and darkness settled on the land the people went to bed. His daughters suckled contentedly and Salem lay sleeping at his feet as he looked around the familiar village, seeing his friends not as tattooed savages but as individuals with their own strengths and weaknesses, family relationships and private worries.

Lafe delighted particularly in his children, whose attractive olive skin, brown eyes and lively ways enchanted everyone in the tribe. His wives were fine-looking women and good-natured with it. They were good mothers to his children, showed him proper respect and looked after him well at the cooking fire and during the long, cold nights. Life was good here with the tribe, and there was nowhere else he could go anyway. He no longer thought of himself as a prisoner, and even when he had made the journey to the sounds he had never really considered leaving the tribe. For the last couple of years he had lived for the present, taking each day as it came, but Tama's questions had made him think seriously about his long-term future. He remembered his own people, the father whom he had loved and respected and the country where he had been born and raised, but now he was sure he would never see either again. He was content with his new life and his growing family around him and he felt strongly that he must stay.

'In the end, this is my new life,' he told Tama formally. 'I will choose the tattoo.'

He knew he would be subjecting himself to terrible pain, but he was more worried about the irrevocable changes that the tattoo would bring to his life. He would lose the light brown, smooth skin of his face, which set him apart from the other warriors, and instead have gouged and ridged lines from his forehead to neck. They would be dark blue or black, depending on the way the ink acted under his skin, and though he had already spent hours with the tattooist choosing his design he knew he would never again feel proud of his good looks. He was not a particularly vain man but he had always known he was handsome and this would be an end to the old self he had been.

In the early morning before the dawn light had begun to colour the sky, the tohunga and his helpers came for Lafe and took him to the top of a small hill for prayers and incantations before delivering him to the tattooist. Lafe was now tapu and would remain so until the tattoo was finished. No one could touch him except the artist who worked on his skin, and he would be fed by the tohunga on food impaled on a long thin stick, for he was so tapu that even to touch his own food could endanger his life. The vessel he drank from was carefully burned in case someone mistakenly drank from it afterwards. Such a mistake could result in instant death for the victim.

Lafe's wives had already helped him scrape his beard off, and now his face was scoured clean with rough pumice and any stray hairs carefully removed with a pair of shell tweezers. The tattooist drew his first lines on Lafe's smooth face deftly and confidently, with a feather lightly dipped in ink. Pleased with the line, the young man stooped over Lafe's form where he lay on a mat, his head on a shaped block of wood to hold it firm. In one hand he held his needle, made from the wing bone of an albatross, in the other a small mallet. Lafe felt the prick of the wing-bone needle against his skin and then the blow from the mallet sent pains from his cheek straight into his brain. It was far worse than he had ever believed it could be and he lay half-dazed with the pain. His tongue found the place where the needle had penetrated his cheek and entered his mouth, bringing with it the foul taste of blood and ink.

Summoning all his reserves he managed to respond as a gentleman of breeding would, looking slightly bored and surprised that the tattooist had even begun work yet. He told the tohunga that the pain was so slight he had barely noticed it. The second strike was worse and the third worse still, until he fell into a trance-like state under torture that went on for

267

hour after hour. When the tattooist had finally finished for the day Lafe was carried on a litter to a specially-built hut where he was cared for by the tohunga. His three appointed friends were careful not to have any physical contact with his body as they did their best to keep his spirits up by telling him how beautiful his moko would be.

Lafe was dreamily aware, from what he had been told, that he had reached such a state of holiness he could harm himself just by touching his own body. Some high chiefs, Marama had told him in awe, remained in this state permanently and were so tapu that they could not even touch the food they ate for fear they would poison themselves. Such men had to eat their food off the ground rather than deprive the villagers of every eating utensil it contained.

He spent near every hour of ten long days in the hands of the tattooist before the artist sat back on his haunches and declared himself satisfied. It was done. Lafe was returned to his little hut, the tohunga chanted his prayers and the tapu was lifted.

By now he was running a high fever and knew little of what went on around him except that he had a great and insatiable thirst and his mouth and lips were cracked and swollen. Over the next five days he was fed like a baby and patiently nursed back to health by his three friends.

When he finally became one of the living again, he carefully explored his face with his fingertips. This new mask of his was a mass of swelling, the ridges too painful to touch and he felt sickened by the thought that his features had been irrevocably carved like a lump of meat. He was kept almost a prisoner in his dark hut until he was fit to be shown to the world, and his spirits were low as he lay there and tried to come to terms with what he had done.

Finally he was taken from his hut, which was burned to the ground and the ashes scattered on the sea. His friends led him back to his fireside in triumph, the whole village exclaiming and singing him home as if he had returned from a great battle. Lafe dreaded most of all facing Marama, his first love. Although she had urged him to take the tattoo he could not quite believe in his heart she would still find him handsome and desirable, but when their eyes met he saw only love, pride and admiration. The same emotions were mirrored in Tui's beaming face and Haroto's shy, gentle welcoming smile as all three wives proclaimed that he was the most handsome man in the village.

To his dismay, his children did not know him at first and they turned their faces to hide from him but within hours his gentle, tickling hands and soft voice won them back. The only creature to share his pangs of regret seemed to be Salem. The big dog stayed close by him for days, shadowing his movements, settling at his side and licking at his hands and feet in quiet sympathy.

While his face was healing, Lafe stayed home and had lots of time to think. Now that the hogs were well-established in the village and breeding, he knew he had secured an ongoing supply of meat for the tribe and he began to cast about for other ways to improve their lot. The human population had also increased rapidly over the summer as the people were incredibly fertile and, now they were relaxed and settled in warmer and easier country, everyone was healthy and well-fed. It seemed that the more children there were in the tribe, the happier the village was. The women captured from other tribes over the past two years were now fully absorbed into their new families and they all had children at the breast.

'One of these days you might have to cancel your orders for whakatupu tangata,' Lafe remarked to Tama one morning as they sat watching the children playing in the sand. 'You might even have to separate the men and women or the village will be bursting at the seams.'

Tama thought that was a huge joke. 'My enemies will just have to move over and give me more room then, won't they?' There was a slight touch of menace in his voice that made Lafe look at him sharply. It was too easy to forget, in times of peace and plenty, that this man beside him was a warrior. But there was truth in his words. Lafe calculated that if the tribe kept expanding at its present rate there would be more than three hundred and fifty hungry mouths by the next summer.

That would put tremendous pressure on the fish and bird population in the immediate food-gathering area, up to a twenty mile radius of the village, and would also put a lot more pressure on the able-bodied adults of the tribe as it would be years before the younger children could fend for themselves or help with the hunting, fishing and food preservation.

Not many years earlier the tribe had extensive gardens on this same piece of coast but the invasion had cost them not only their crops but also their precious plants and seeds. In these gardens they had grown the kumara or sweet potato, a gourd and a type of marrow, and from what Lafe had been able to glean from the elders they had been very successful gardeners indeed.

'Why don't we rebuild the gardens and acquire some new plants now, before the tribe exhausts its resources and falls on hard times?' Lafe asked Marama that night. He was in the habit of trying out new ideas on his senior wife before he laid them before her father and he had a lot of respect for her wisdom and knowledge. Tui and Haroto had useful knowledge too from their own different tribal backgrounds.

Many schemes for the tribe's wellbeing were hatched around the village fires over the winter months, only to be discarded when spring came. Mostly these plans were made by young and restless warriors and they nearly always revolved around ambitious attacks on more powerful tribes, motivated by the obvious gains of women and flesh. But Tama was a careful man. He would fight anyone if he thought there was a clear advantage and gain to be had, but he was not prepared to disturb his tribe's prosperity or threaten its welfare for the sake of providing a bit of excitement for his warriors.

His wives were enthusiastic about the idea of establishing gardens, although only Marama had ever seen kumara beds or worked in them, and many hours were spent discussing how such crops would be established. After the success of the expedition he had led to bring back the pig and the goat, Lafe's mana had risen even further and he was sure his latest plan would get a good hearing from Tama. He spent much of the winter thinking the idea through, and when spring came around he laid it before Tama who took it to the council of elders. It was agreed that the Goblin's plans were worthy of discussion, and finally he was given permission to carry them out.

In late spring, when the food supplies had been built up again, Lafe would lead an expedition to the far north in search of the kumara and any other plant he might have the good luck to find. Once again, forty-two warriors would accompany him. It was not a big enough force to terrify the countryside as a large war party would have, but it was enough to put up a good fight if they were attacked.

With spring came the good times once more. The first scallops were gathered to fill eager mouths with their wonderful sweet flesh, and the first scoops of the little silver inanga were mixed with early duck eggs and cooked on hot stones.

'Now this is the food of the gods, made even more delicious by having to wait for it all winter,' Lafe told his wives appreciatively. There was a saying in the tribe, as Marama was fond of telling him,

'How can one enjoy spring, without just having suffered winter to compare it with?'

The pig farming had gone well, the warm fern-covered faces of the hills providing long, tasty roots that put fat on the frames of the animals even through the winter. Now that the herd had grown to a sustainable level pork was available on feast days and the people seemed to enjoy it immensely, although Lafe still heard his wives discussing the merits of human flesh above other food. Pork had not solved the problem but instead seemed to whet their appetites for meat, and he had to be content with knowing cannibalism had at least taken a step backwards. His women had been brought up in a culture where a feast would not be regarded as a proper feast at all without a slave or two cut up and thrown in the oven. The juices of the human body were regarded as the relish or condiments to the more banal vegetable foods such as seaweed and fern root. At least he had so far protected his children from the cannibalistic appetites of their mothers, and he made sure that their first solid foods were of fish.

By the time the spring rains had eased and the sun had browned the scar tissue on his new face, Lafe had chosen his men, put the cutter and the big canoe in good shape for the journey and set the women to drying and preserving enough food to last them several months. He was smugly pleased with himself; he had been busy in the grass huts of this household that winter and he was sure all three of his women were pregnant again. He was sated with domestic affairs and this expedition was just what he needed to put a new spark in his life.

271

Like all expeditions around the dangerous coast of this country, much time was spent choosing the right weather to begin. They would cover hundreds of miles of coastline in short hops, travelling only when the conditions were right. The canoes the tribe used would take on water quickly when any sea got up and although the big double canoe they were taking on this voyage was a lot more seaworthy in that respect, the most comfortable way to travel was still the Maori way, from bay to bay and beach to beach. Time was not important and if a trip took a month, so be it. With the canoes pulled safely up the beach above the level of the waves at night and a good fire to give warmth and light and turn out endless supplies of tasty food, this mode of travel had a lot going for it.

There was nothing to do now but wait for favourable weather. They needed several windless days to allow the boats to clear the Windpipe of the Pacific, then a southerly wind that would last at least three days to take them north past the rocky and inhospitable Wairarapa coast. The first obstacle was always the Windpipe. It was a difficult piece of water and any wind at all made it dangerous, so even those who had lived all their lives with its moods shuddered at the memories of storms they had seen and canoes that had not come home again.

Finally, the day came and the tohunga nodded his approval. All the signs were good.

'To get oneself sunk is bad luck, and perhaps bad seamanship. But to get oneself sunk in enemy territory and therefore to be food for their ovens is worse than bad luck. That is foolishness,' Tama warned Lafe. 'Do not be foolish, Goblin, Do not lose my best men. The tribe might not survive without them.'

He looked searchingly into Lafe's eyes, making sure the message had gone home, then turned his back and strode up onto the sand hills to join Lafe's wives and children and the rest of the villagers in their songs of farewell. For the first time Salem was left behind, as Lafe did not want him to suffer such a long sea voyage in the small cutter, and the big dog hung his head dejectedly as he barked a mournful and rather grumpy farewell. Lafe raised his paddle to his wives and held it aloft for a minute in salute to his chief before giving the signal his men were waiting for.

There was an explosive hiss of expelled breath as they drove their paddles hard into the water in perfect unison and the powerful strokes of forty paddlers sent the double canoe skimming out toward the Windpipe, with the cutter on a short bridle trailing in its wake. The boats would soon feel the strong current beneath their keels as they worked their way east towards the Pacific.

Once they had rounded the headland from Murderers' Bay into Blind Bay and the wind and tide began to work in their favour there was little for the paddlers to do but sit and watch the two islands draw together at the narrowest point of the Windpipe. In the clear early morning air of the third day the mountain ranges of both islands stood out proud and clean, still topped with white from the late spring snowfalls. It was these mountains on either side of the water that forced the killer wind into the ever-narrowing gap of the Windpipe.

The North Island, whose southern shores they were soon navigating, was Te Ika a Maui. Lafe found that he usually thought in Maori instead of English now and he had done so for a while. The names were more colourful and expressive than Cook's English chart notations. Te Ika a Maui, The Great Fish of Maui, honoured the god who had pulled this fish from the ocean away back in the beginning of time so that the great fish lay stunned on the water and turned into land. Lafe had also learned to know the South Island as Te Wai Pounamu, The Waters of Greenstone. It was a pretty name, suiting the low melodious tongues of his women, and the valuable cargo they carried north to trade gave it extra meaning. Tui's family had died chipping some of that very stone out of the river, Lafe mused, and now in this strange and endless cycle of survival it would buy food for her children.

With its great sail set and the help of the current the double canoe fought her way clear of the Windpipe in two days and they entered the Pacific, Lafe's little *Aurora* rising eagerly to meet the waves as he escorted the bigger vessel through. Looking south he could see the same view he had stared at so eagerly from the decks of the *Northern Lights* three years earlier and it dawned on him that after four long years and many adventures he had finally completed a circumnavigation of the South Island. There again were the mountains of Kaikoura and the home of the tribe that Cook had named the Lookers On. As far as Lafe could ascertain, none of the men with him had ever been to any of these places, but many could draw maps of the area and they spoke of it with great familiarity.

Kaikoura was the name given by Maori to the place where the koura, the lobster, was found in abundance, kai being food. Again it was the oral history of the tribe, gleaned and passed down through well-told stories repeated over and over around the night fires of winter, that was the basis of their knowledge of far-off places and peoples.

Lafe was now acknowledged as the best storyteller in all the history of the tribe. Since he had returned home triumphantly with the hogs and goats he had described so many times around the campfires, it had been brought home to his people that there was more to this world than they could possibly imagine.

Lafe enjoyed his role and found he had a natural ability as an actor as well as storyteller. All he needed to do was to select a different animal from the many species he had seen or heard of on his travels. His New England schooling had honed his ability to draw a good picture and with his good actor's sense of mimicry he could hold the tribe in the palm of his hand for hours. He enjoyed telling stories, not only because it increased his mana and entertained his friends but because it allowed him to draw on his memories of another life, memories that were fast fading with the language that was now rusty from disuse.

As the currents of the Windpipe finally lost their grip on the boats they turned north to parallel the coast of that oddly terraced southern cape that Cook had named Palliser. The feel of the ocean began to change as the long, blue evenly spaced swells from the Pacific rolled endlessly under them. To those who were listening those lazy rollers whispered, 'There is no land for many thousands of miles. Stay close to the shore or you will be lost forever in this endless ocean.'

The big canoe rode easily to the swells. She was born of the hand of man but her ancestors had sailed these great seas for many thousands of years. The Pacific was the birthplace of the great ocean-going canoe and she rode atop it like a great seabird with her flaxen sail set taut. On the high platform that bridged the twin hulls was a low grass hut to shelter those who slept off watch, and a small, well-tended charcoal fire inside it to produce hot food for the hungry paddlers at their benches.

Lafe's personal needs were met by his old friend the emoki who rode with him on board the cutter. The slave had asked to come on the expedition to see once again the land where he was born. He cooked and served Lafe's meals and would give his life if needed for Lafe's protection. He was still a fine fighting man even though he was now starting to show much silver in his hair, and it was as a special favour to both that Tama had allowed his personal bodyguard and right-hand man to sail with the expedition. The mokai had been born in Poverty Bay, that much he remembered, and had been enslaved as a small child, whether sold in poverty or taken in war he no longer knew. He had been passed from tribe to tribe till he became Tama's property.

'Look after the Goblin,' Tama had told him, and look after him he would.

On this longer leg of their journey the nights were spent on board and then Lafe and the emoki slept on the canoe with the cutter towed on a bridle of flax ropes between the two hulls. Once the inhospitable two hundred miles of Wairarapa Coast was behind them they would return to the more pleasant routine of sailing by day and sleeping on the beach at night, but here where the coast was nothing but rocks and large kelp beds for as far as the eye could see they would not risk attempting to land. They knew there was good fishing among the rocks but it was safer to stay well clear for the two days and two nights it would take to reach better land to the north.

The weather held calm with light winds, allowing the canoe to land on a small beach just south of Heretaunga, at Cook's Cape Kidnappers. Here they moved quietly and with stealth, raiding the gannet colony for the fat young birds and any eggs they could find before putting to sea again to avoid a tribe that lived not far away. These east coast tribes were known to be powerful and ferocious, ever ready to protect their beautiful beaches and food sources against anyone foolish enough to land there.

Invigorated by the fresh food they headed across the bay to Mahia, a large peninsula, and on up the coast to the place Cook had called Poverty Bay. On this coast Lafe made them all sleep in the most secluded bays by day and sail only by night, well out of sight of suspicious eyes on the land. Moving anywhere at night was not popular in the Maori world as the darkness was inhabited by many ghosts and spirits and by the souls of dead people who came out in the dark to prowl. But there seemed fewer ghosts at sea and the men considered the risk worth taking.

As they passed across Poverty Bay the emoki watched the shore keenly, sobbing a waiata of longing and greeting to the land he could no longer remember or call his own, but his voice was muted and he posed no threat.

After weeks of travel they finally slipped quietly around East Cape in the dark and set their course for a great smoking volcano on the horizon. The men called the island mountain Whakaari and Lafe knew that this was Cook's Bay of Plenty with its gentle climate, prolific native villages and fertile gardens. When they reached the island they would rest there and fish for a few days as it was thought to be uninhabited. It had a bad reputation, the emoki told them. The volcano brooded and smoked for years and then it would awaken and toss rocks and flaming pumice into the water in a wide arc around its shores. It was a day's journey by canoe from the mainland so it was rarely visited by the local tribes who were somewhat in awe of its reputation.

Once the canoe had eased itself through the rocky outcrops to nestle on a tiny sandy beach against the steep sides of the island, the fishing began. Lafe took the emoki and several warriors to the south side of the island so they could climb up through the desolate pumice-strewn landscape to the rim of the crater. Peering warily over the edge they could see right down into the eye of molten lava below and smell the foul breath of the mountain. The emoki declared that if there was a home on earth where the devil lived, it was in that great hole. He was afraid and wished to return to the boat but it was a rare thing to see inside a living volcano and Lafe climbed further around the rim trying to find better places to view it from. At last he realised he was causing the others in the party a lot of anguish. The slave was showing the whites of his eyes and looked ready to scramble up to the rim again to drag Lafe away. He was frightened of the hole, but much more frightened of Tama and was terrified he might have to report that because of his carelessness he had let the Goblin fall into a crater full of fire.

While they were away the fishermen had found a place to drop their lines and were bringing up a type of tamure that Lafe had never seen before. They were a pure, brilliant red colour with long gossamer-thin fins, a fish far too pretty to eat unless you were a hungry man. There seemed to be many different types of fish around the island, many unknown to the men from Murderers' Bay, and they guessed that the waters warmed by the volcano might have something to do it. Four or five mighty hapuku were hauled to the surface, to the great excitement of the crew who loved nothing better than this fat tasty fish. It certainly was a bay of plenty and Cook would have smiled to have seen such abundance.

From Whakaari their course was due north, taking their boats far from land until they could see the great white cliffs of the island some still called Hawaiki. The meaning of this name, Lafe was told, was our old home or the land we once came from but there seemed to have been more than one Hawaiki as far as he could ascertain. As the great canoes made their way down through the islands in the Pacific over the centuries, many stopping places became old homelands. Most tribes it seemed traced their lineage back to one or more of these great canoes that had landed intermittently at scattered sites throughout the country, and parts of the very old chants that Lafe heard at the fireside were verbal sailing directions handed down from the great navigators. Such knowledge still existed in the memories of tribal elders.

Slowly the smoking crater of Whaakari sank below the horizon as the boats headed north on a sunny, playful sea. Despite having no navigation tools of any kind and no one on board who had ever travelled this route before, the seafarers were never in any doubt as to the course they were following.

'The song of journeys has never been wrong before so why would it be wrong this time, Goblin?' the emoki asked when Lafe voiced his doubts. 'Our ancestors sailed for many weeks out of sight of land and they were not lost.'

'This is a very small voyage by comparison,' the captain of the double canoe agreed. 'We have the volcano in sight still, and soon we will have the stars.

'On a long voyage, the tohunga or senior navigator sat like this,' the navigator said, and he lowered his buttocks until his testicles dangled free in the bilge water in the bottom of the canoe. 'Then he could feel from the swing of his bag how the currents were affecting the course of his canoe.'

Lafe was fascinated, and the other warriors nodded in approval as the older man continued the lesson. 'Know your course, which you take from the stars at night, and know how the currents affect the path of your canoe. That is the way it has always been.'

'But how would you navigate in the seas to the far south where the sea was full of great lumps of ice?' Lafe challenged with a twinkle in his eye. 'Your piri piri would fall off!'

The warriors roared with laughter and the man's eyes grew wide as he contemplated this new idea.

'Eh!' he said finally. 'That is a hard question for me to answer.'

'A story! A story!' the men cried out, sensing new wonders to marvel at. Although Lafe had never seen the great ice of the southern seas he had been in the northern Atlantic and Greenland as a young whaler, and he was able to tell a credible story which had his audience sucking their teeth with wonder. He described the icebergs he had seen floating far out to sea where men hunted the great whale, and the ships that had died after hitting them in the dark. He told them about the pack ice and its inhabitants the seals and the polar bear. Seals these paddlers knew well, but the bear was a new creature even in a story and Lafe described it as a large white hog with long hair that lived on the ice and fed on the seals it encountered.

All else was forgotten as the crew became absorbed in Lafe's description of the large long-haired hog. Now they had seen pigs in the flesh their new experience gave them many questions of comparison and Lafe had to strive to remember everything he had ever seen, read or heard about the bear. He was forced to answer a hundred questions that taxed his knowledge, from the size and shape of the droppings to how it was possible for two large hogs to mate on such a slippery surface as the ice that they lived on, and when he told them the animal could walk and even fight on its hind legs alone their imaginations ran riot.

'This is surely a wonderful world that we live in,' said the emoki thoughtfully. There was a long silence as they thought over what they had heard. They all agreed that the Goblin told a good story.

'But how we would navigate our canoes in this ice water I do not know,' the captain concluded. 'A man's piri piri would not last long in such an ocean.'

As the stars appeared overhead one by one they were checked by the navigator and the course adjusted accordingly. Many of the paddlers wrapped themselves in their robes and crept into the grass cabin to sleep, knowing they would be needed by dawn if the islands were near. Lafe lay wrapped in his blankets near the mighty sail and watched as the stars made their slow way across the heaven, thinking about this journey and the others made centuries ago. These people's ancestors had set off for an unknown destination, far out across the Pacific, in canoes similar to the one he was now on, and they had not known what was waiting for them at the end of their journey. He shared his thoughts with the emoki who was settled nearby.

'Not just men, but women and children too,' he said in wonder. 'You brought your families with you on the canoes, and the tools, seeds, everything you needed for a new life. What a journey. What faith your people had to follow a bird, a cuckoo that laid its eggs in another bird's nest.'

'When it departed the islands every year in spring and headed south, our people said, 'There is land down there' and they came to find it,' the emoki agreed.

'To follow a bird and discover a country, that is a good story,' Lafe told the older man sleepily. 'That is one of the best stories I have ever heard.'

He drifted off to sleep with the rocking of the canoe rising to the long easy swells and the creaking of the flax ropes and pegs that held her cunningly together.

He was woken by the watchman before daylight and found that the wind had dropped away during the last hour. The watchman had also raised the paddlers who shivered as they pissed over the side and took their places on the benches, and after a little good-natured pushing and shoving the canoe singer gave them the beat. Soon the canoe was moving fast again as the paddlers shook the kinks out of their muscles and warmed to the task of driving her forward. As the sun rose above the horizon its rays struck the great cliffs ahead and turned them pink in the early morning light.

These cliffs were on the main island of the small group called Ahuahu. They were deliberately approaching in daylight from the open sea with the sun behind them, as friends would come, not in the gloom and shadows of the mainland like a stinking raider. Lafe knew that already the conch war horns would be blowing on the island ahead, the warriors would be looking to their weapons and their women and children would be heading for the safest place on the island where the men would gather to protect them if they failed to evict these raiders at the water's edge.

There were several larger islands to the north of this group. Lafe recognised Barrier Island from Cook's chart, and as Ahuahu drew closer they passed a smaller island of very red soil that appeared almost pink in the early light. The islands were bush clad and seemed to be inhabited by millions of birds, their chorus quite deafening as the paddlers passed close by. There were so many jagged rocks protruding from the sea that any sailing ship would be forced to stand well clear of the place, Lafe noted, but the waters were warm and from the numbers of seabirds diving on schools of fish it was obviously a rich fishing ground. On the mainland, three or four little trickles of smoke climbed into the breathless sky to show the locations of small family groups and sub tribes who lived on the beaches.

While they were still at sea the cutter was unbridled and Lafe, the emoki and One Eye the musket carrier stepped aboard and ran up the sails to catch what breeze was available. He would approach the people on this island as a white man, Lafe decided, a Goblin armed with muskets and authority, as very few of the tribes had any faith left in the good intentions of their own race. But then his hand went up to touch his cheek. He had quite forgotten he had a new face – he still saw himself as he had been before the tattoo.

'Never mind, a Goblin is expected to be full of tricks,' he told One Eye with a smile. He enjoyed these meetings with strange tribes, always with the whiff of danger sufficient to add spice to the day, and he sang a few bars of a half-forgotten sea shanty as he steadied the tiller and led the big canoe through the rocks and into sheltered water. It was almost like being in a lagoon, surrounded by a gleaming white sand beach. The tall white cliffs that could be seen so far out to sea dominated the coast a little further south of their landfall, the sunlight picking them out in great detail and showing every fissure and crack on their surface.

They had expected a reception committee and they got one. Lafe counted about eighty warriors lined up in fighting formation on the beach, nearly twice the strength of his own men, but they did not look as if they were ready to attack. He signalled the canoe to stay in the centre of the lagoon while he ran the cutter up on the beach and leapt nimbly on to the sand, his musket at his shoulder. He strode toward the elderly man who was obviously the warrior chief, and as the man stepped forward to meet him Lafe saw his eyes nearly bulge from their sockets. A tattooed Goblin? He had obviously never seen anything like this before, and there was uncertainty in his eyes. Was he being tricked? He cast wary glances at the great double-hulled canoe.

Lafe reached inside his robe to where a greenstone hei tiki swung on a thong close to his chest. Carefully he lifted it over his head, holding the eye contact, and laid it on the sand at the chief's feet. The older man stared at him for a long time, then he picked up the gift and ran his finger over the exquisitely carved surfaces of the little grinning god. He looked at Lafe in awe, tears forming in his eyes.

'In all my long life on this island I have never seen such a treasure, let alone been presented with one as a gift,' he told Lafe. They pressed noses in the hongi, and the welcoming haka began as the big double canoe sped across the lagoon and up on to the beach where willing helpers ran it safely beyond the reach of the waves. For an hour or more the two groups performed the rituals of greeting, each in turn displaying their military prowess with powerful war dances. They were soon joined by the women who sang their own welcome before they got busy fanning the fires into flames and preparing a feast.

The old chief and Lafe sat and talked for many hours that night, long after the rest of the village had crawled into their sleeping huts and contented snores rose from the emoki sleeping nearby. The chief longed to hear the stories of the greenstone trails of the middle island, and in return he told Lafe of his own tribe's wonderful history. When the great canoe fleet had arrived at this country they called The Long White Cloud many generations before, a handful of his ancestors had settled on this island called Ahuahu. These people had brought with them the very best plants from their own islands in the Pacific, every one that they thought would be useful in their new home, but to the dismay of the small group of people who made it to the end of their journey they found they had travelled so far south that the plants would not grow in the colder climate and most of them died in the first year.'

The chief waved an arm towards the hillside where the tribe's great gardens were just visible in the moonlight. 'Here on Ahuahu, where the great white cliffs reflect the sun back down on the gardens, the little kumara struggled to stay alive. Our people cared for them tenderly, they sprinkled sand around the plants to warm them even more and very slowly the kumara began to adapt to its new home.

'Many generations of people were born, many grew up and died without ever tasting this sweet potato. Still the people tended the plants, but they ate only fish and fern root. Then one day this precious kumara produced its first tiny edible roots.'

By now all the other tribes had forgotten how to be gardeners and lived as hunter-gatherers, he explained, roaming from one place to the other, chasing and killing that great bird the moa. Once it was gone from the land, every last one killed and eaten, then the hungry hordes descended on the shellfish beds until they too failed.

The old man nodded his head soberly, re-living the story as he told it. 'Many tribes knew hunger and starvation. Then they came to us and begged for the kumara, and we gave it to them.

'Do you understand this, Goblin? By now twenty or more generations had passed by, on this island of Ahuahu, and not once did we make war. We never went to battle, so our only meat was the odd seal we killed and the whales that sometimes washed up on the shore. Our children eat no meat. We are the keepers of the gardens.'

But once the other tribes had settled in favoured spots and built their own gardens, he told Lafe, they suddenly found that they could no longer fade into the forest when a more powerful tribe raided in their lands. They had crops to protect, so they had to stay and fight. Soon large forts were built in every district, and great battles began to break out all over the land.

'A famous chief once said, 'what is kumara without relish? Such a dish is not fit for a chief.' He was referring, of course, to the flesh of man for that was his relish.'

The old man sighed deeply. 'Now we have wars everywhere and we call them the kumara wars,' he told Lafe sadly. 'So far we here on Ahuahu have survived all the strife but for how long? For how long? I tell you this, Goblin, I know in my heart that it will not be for long. Very soon they will forget that we were once the keepers of the gardens.' And there the old chief ended his story and they sat for a long time in silence, each reflecting on the folly of his fellow man.

The next day Lafe was shown proudly over the gardens that covered many acres of gently sloping hillside. Each little plot was surrounded by waist high stone walls that kept the cold winds from the plants. In the winter and early spring, slight breezes moved from one body of water to the other across the low waist of the island and stopped the frost from settling on the tender plants.

'It is a very pleasant place to live, this beautiful island of yours among the fishing grounds,' Lafe told the old chief. 'Perhaps I will return one day with the hog so you can have meat.'

'No, no,' the old chief said, laughing as he rolled his eyes in mock horror. 'I have heard of this animal you call the hog and others call pig, and I know that he and our kumara gardens cannot ever share the same island. We do not wish to be keepers of the pig.'

Lafe completed his purchases of tubers and young plants and made preparations to head north, arranging for the plants to be ready on his return. His warriors would settle here for a couple of weeks and already they had made themselves comfortable, making eyes at the girls who made eyes at them in return. There were ample supplies of kumara in the storehouses and Lafe made sure he paid for the food his crew would eat, knowing also that they were skilled fishermen who could catch their own weight in fish any day in these waters.

That evening he slipped out of the lagoon in the cutter, accompanied only by the mokai and One Eye. It was safer to travel at night as many parties of warriors travelled by canoe up and down this coast in daylight and they could be as dangerous as wild beasts. By dawn the cutter had been hidden among the rocks on the southern tip of the largest of the Barrier Islands and its occupants slept away the daylight hours rolled in their robes in the shade of the rocks. Every night for the next six nights they crept from island to island in this fashion until early one morning they slipped through the entrance of Whangaroa and into the harbour.

This was the harbour that Lafe had sailed into four years before on his arrival in Aotearoa and it was a bittersweet return. His mind was full of memories of Olva and his shipmates on the *Northern Lights* and also of the mission that had brought him back. Chief Kaitoke came to meet him and was very pleased to see him, but he recoiled at the tattooed face, a clear sign that someone else had laid claim to his Goblin.

There was no easy way to break the sad news, and as gently as he could Lafe told Kaitoke of the death of his son Matai at the beautiful lake near the tail of the fish. The old chief staggered a few paces in the sand and seated himself on a piece of driftwood with his thoughts. He would hear no more that day, and it was not until the following afternoon that he sent for Lafe and bade him continue his story. Lafe talked of their sealing adventures, praising Matai's courage and skill in fishing, and assured the old chief that his son had been steadfast in his task of

284

passing on the language and traditions of his people. The memories came back to him vividly as he described how Matai had been buried in the dunes above the sea, and how he had recited the words he had been taught and the people with him had paid tribute and honour to this chief's son.

Then he explained how he had been captured by the tribe to which he now belonged. Chief Kaitoke was indignant that anyone should dare to take his Goblin and offered to lead a war party south at that very moment to teach Tama a lesson. Finally, Lafe broached the subject of the chief's granddaughter, the second reason for his visit. All through the last four years the vision of this woman had stayed alive in his mind and now he was here to claim her.

'I have come back as I said I would,' he told Kaitoke. 'You promised her to me in marriage and I have come to keep my part of the bargain.'

The young woman was sent for, even though a thin grass wall was all that separated them and the words that passed between the chief and Lafe had been clearly heard by her and the women with her. She came proudly and willingly. As soon as she had seen the cutter enter the harbour mouth she had known he had come for her and now she stood before him with her head bowed and her eyes cast down in dignified modesty.

Lafe took a little greenstone tiki from beneath his shirt and placed the thong around her neck. The cheeky little green god was still warm from his body as he settled it between her breasts, and she raised her head and smiled shyly at him.

'My name is Miri,' she said simply, 'and I have waited a long time for you to come.'

He smiled back at her, admiring her full, voluptuous body. She had yet to reach her sixteenth birthday, and yet she had counted the months and weeks since she was promised as a bride to a stranger from across the sea. To these people a promise was indeed a promise, he thought, and wondered what would have become of the poor woman if he had not come back for her.

Lafe had his gift for Kaitoke brought from the cutter and taken from its finely woven sheath. It was a patu, made from the best greenstone the country could produce. It had been finely polished and shaped to fit the hand of a chief as if the gods themselves had fashioned it, and it was by far the finest fighting weapon that had ever been seen up there in the far north of this northern island, hundreds of miles from the greenstone rivers it had come from. The gift somewhat mollified the old chief, who had hoped Lafe would settle with his own tribe but now had to reconcile himself to his granddaughter heading south with her new husband.

'She will be greatly missed by her people, as she is one of the bright stars in the tribe,' he told Lafe. In his secret thoughts he hoped that this granddaughter would be able to persuade her husband to come back to his tribe one day.

'As our people say, when you marry the woman you marry the tribe after all,' he chuckled. 'And there is now a great deal more competition between the tribes to acquire a Goblin. Most of the tribes see you people as a way of increasing trade.'

He explained that most years now a ship was seen sailing up or down the coast, and they nearly always stopped at the Bay of Islands, where there were two very lower class Goblins living.

'But they are nearly always drunk from your firewater and they break many laws of tapu,' he said contemptuously. 'Someone will probably kill them one day soon.'

For a long time now Lafe had contemplated leaving a letter behind for any ship that might call, so that his father could be informed of his fate. By now his family would think he was dead, and it would ease the old man's mind to know that he was still alive even though he could never leave the country. It had crossed his mind too, that he could help the tribe if his father sent a ship to their country, bringing a selection of goods from the factories of America and trading for pigs and kumara to sell at Sydney Cove. But he had neither paper, pen, nor ink to his name, and the risk of entering the Bay of Islands to communicate with a couple of drunken white men was too great to contemplate.

Once the marriage ceremony was over and he had thoroughly bedded his new wife, the cutter was loaded for the return journey. Miri brought with her a certain amount of luggage that Lafe had noticed a wife never travelled without, and the vessel was heavier in the water as they left just on dusk, the tearful farewells and lamentations of her people fading into stillness as they picked up the wind in their sails. Once again they slipped from island to island, travelling only at night.

The cutter entered the lagoon of Ahuahu carrying three tired passengers and an even more weary skipper, and while they slept the big double canoe was made ready to sail. The grass sleeping hut was loaded with its precious cargo of young kumara plants and tubers, all carefully wrapped in moss to protect them from the salt air, and as much dried fish and other food as they had room for. The farewells were brief and that evening the two boats sped eastward on the first stage of their journey back to Murderers' Bay.

Lafe would have liked to enter the large bay just to the south of Ahuahu where Cook and his crew had spent several months observing the transit of Mercury. The British captain had called the place Mercury Bay and spoke very favourably of it. But the longer Tama's best fighting men were away, the greater the risk of attack on the tribe they had left so poorly defended and there was a strong sense of urgency on board the big canoe. It was time to head for home.

Chapter 15

The stars were brightening as the big double canoe headed out into the rolling swells far off the coast, with the cutter snug on its bridle following in a silver wake. They were relieved when they reached the deep ocean. The greatest risk in the whole expedition was always going to be this return journey; word would have travelled and a cunning enemy may have already guessed they would be returning that same way. As long as the weather allowed it Lafe planned to stay at sea, well out of sight from the land, for as much of the journey as possible. Only bad weather would bring them close to shore for shelter, and then they would try to replenish their supplies of fish and shellfish.

It was a hard way to travel. The fickle winds that blew contrary to their set course could not be avoided and the boat's motion allowed for little proper sleep. The paddlers spent hour after hour at their benches, cold, tired and uncomfortable, mechanically following the canoe singer's remorseless beat.

Lafe's new wife, along with many of the crew, suffered from debilitating attacks of seasickness brought on mainly from the fear of losing sight of their land. In the first minutes of a new day, many an anxious look was cast in the direction of where they hoped land would be and there were sighs of relief when they could still see the long cloud that cloaked their country. The island group had a mountain spine running from near the top of the north island to the very bottom of the south.

Moisture-laden air from the sea was lifted higher and higher up the faces of the mountains until it turned to dew, and from far out to sea all that was visible for many days of the year was this cloud that gave New Zealand its name of Aotearoa, Land Of The Long White Cloud.

For the first five days of the trip the weather held and they made good progress, but on the sixth day the heartbeat of the ocean changed and the new rhythm of the sea sent them toward shore seeking shelter. They had rounded both the East Cape and the peninsula called Mahia and were faced with the long, hostile coast of Wairarapa ahead of them. Lafe kept them out to sea as long as he dared but in the late afternoon he set the big canoe creeping into the great bight of a bay a little north of Kidnappers, looking for a quiet, sheltered harbour to rest up and wait out the storm. They paddled wide of the canoe to avoid the knock of wood against wood, and moved parallel to the coast while he carefully searched a river mouth with his glass to see that the Heretaunga people did not inhabit it already. It was a dangerous place to spend the night, but there were no other good resting spots for a hundred miles or more to the south and they had to find shelter.

The other attraction of this beach was that it was not far from the gannet colony that they had raided on the voyage north. They needed food badly and planned to raid the colony again if they could. It was early enough in the breeding season for the adult birds to have laid new clutches of eggs and with luck there would be another crop of fat chicks waiting. Lafe's mouth watered at the thought of a meal of fresh eggs. But more than anything else they all longed to climb out of the damp, cramped canoe and sleep for a night on good firm sand again.

There was a cry from one of the paddlers and Lafe pulled the glass from his eye as the man pointed desperately along the shoreline. Two canoes darted out of the reeds just inside the mouth of a little side stream and streaked like arrows after them. For a split second everyone on board was frozen to the spot. It was a near-perfect ambush, but the ambushers had become impatient as they watched the big double canoe dawdle past their hideout and they had struck too soon.

Lafe and the emoki leaped to the sail and let it fall while the paddlers dug deep in the water, picking up speed as they drove the canoe with all the desperation of doomed and frightened men. Lafe watched their tired muscles ripple under dark skins and knew they could not keep it up for long. He glanced behind them, calculating angles and boat speeds, and with a pang of anguish he knew what he had to do next. In one movement he reached down with his knife and slashed the bridle, letting the cutter go. It was a hard thing to do but his beloved *Aurora* was slowing them down and in a few minutes they would be caught. Sadly he watched the little unmanned craft fall away and dance across the waves. It was one of the few possessions left from the old days, and he was thankful he had emptied it of stores so it would tow better.

The danger was not over by a long way as the two following canoes deftly avoided the little boat and came on, determinedly racing each other to be first to the kill. Lafe called for muskets, powder and ball from inside the little hut and while the others leaned their backs to the paddles he studied the enemy and planned his next move. The two single hull canoes charging at them held nearly thirty warriors apiece so there was no future in trying to make a fight of it. Even with two muskets he knew sixty warriors would soon overcome his forty-two. The two chasing canoes would catch them eventually because his men were tired, and he knew they would not fight well because of the gannet colony.

Long ago he had learned that the Maori would sometimes give up too easily, for reasons that a white man could not always fathom but he put down to guilty conscience. His people would not fight well today because they had robbed another tribe's larder, though if the boot had been on the other foot his forty-two warriors would have chased and probably killed all sixty of the enemy in a fit of righteous rage. To blatantly plunder another tribe's food supply was an aggressive and criminal act, a great coup if you got away with it, but if you were caught the retribution was a just one and the penalty was certain death. In such circumstances his people were quite capable of giving in far too easily.

He had only two chances, both of them slim. They could run out to sea and take their chances in the storm, hoping that the less seaworthy single canoes would give up the chase, or they could try to hold them off with the muskets until it was dark and then lose them with a few rapid changes of course during the night. He knew that the Heretaunga people would be hard to shake. This was their coast and they would have spent days working themselves up into a murderous rage as they watched and waited for the raiders to return. That someone would plunder their food supplies under their very noses was too much to bear and now utu was more important than anything else. They had been wronged and they would travel to the ends of the earth for revenge.

One Eye, the young man whose eye Lafe had knocked out with a pellet of birdshot in that first battle against Tama's tribe, was on board as the second musket man and he had become a fair shot but in this situation Lafe knew every ball would count. He decided to do the shooting himself and have One Eye load the muskets for him as fast and as accurately as he could.

'Drive the canoe hard and straight, my warriors, while I brush these flies from our tail,' he called to the paddlers to keep their courage up. Deliberately he kept his voice light and cheerful for the sake of his crew, though he was feeling far from confident. 'I will give them a taste of the thunderstick before very long, and we will see how they like it,' he shouted, so loudly that even the farthest paddler could hear him.

This was the most dangerous time in the pursuit, and he urged the canoe singer to call more loudly. Like the whale chases of old, if the crew began looking over their shoulders now they would lose the rhythm and the power and strength of their paddles would leave them quickly. If that happened, they would be run down and killed in seconds. It was only pride in their skills as the boat people and the many hours that Tama had kept them at their paddles that had allowed them to keep the slender lead they still held.

Lafe made a rest for the musket barrel from kumara bags and he lay down to take up his sight of the enemy. It was frightening how quickly they were coming on and he suspected that his own paddlers were close to losing heart. They had already been at their paddles for weary hours as they ran towards the land to beat the storm, and though they had spent weeks at sea and were fit and hardened to their work they would only be able to keep up this terrific pace for a short time.

The oily sweat on his palms made it hard to hold the musket as he poured a measure of power down the barrel, rammed a patched lead ball after it and primed the flash pan with a little fine powder he carried in a smaller flask. He had deliberately kept his canoe in the calmer water close to the shore as they raced south so that he could use his musket to greatest accuracy without the waves throwing him off his target. Now he wondered if he had made the right choice as the enemy canoes closed steadily in. Perhaps he would have given his people more of a chance if they had headed directly out to sea and chanced the storm, but it was too late now. If they slowed to change direction they would be caught before they had completed the turn.

'Face the front and ply your blade like a warrior,' he snapped when one of the men dared to look over his shoulder. He was relieved to see there was no sign of Miri who had wisely retreated into the grass hut. Carefully he aimed his musket at the front paddler in the nearest of the two approaching canoes. He could see the man's tattoo clearly in the dull light and could almost read the expression on his face. He waited until his own canoe began to lift in the swell and, as the pip of the foresight crossed the warrior's chest, he touched off the trigger. The musket kicked hard against his shoulder and there were shouts of rage and shock from the pursuers as their leading paddler fell backwards from sight. When the smoke cleared Lafe could see that he had missed his target, but the canoe had dropped back a few yards before taking up the pursuit with even more vigour.

He felt his own canoe leap forward, the men finding new energy now that the battle had begun. The warrior he had fired at was back at his paddle but he showed the whites of his eyes in fright, knowing that he was the target of the weapon that he had heard so much about. Lafe guessed that this enemy tribe had not yet managed to trade with the white man and secure their own muskets.

His third shot went home, and when the smoke cleared he could see that the lead paddler had been punched flat by the ball which had passed through his chest and hit a second man on the bench behind him. The wounded man had let out a loud yelp and dropped his paddle, upsetting the stroke on that side of the canoe.

'I have struck the first blow,' Lafe yelled triumphantly as the enemy canoe slewed sideways, offering a larger target. He grabbed the freshly-loaded second musket out of One Eye's hands and fired again, knocking another warrior out of the middle of the row of paddlers. The man fell across the gunwales and his blood poured down the side of the canoe, staining it a rich red. Lafe switched his attention to the other canoe which was coming on fast. It had picked up speed while he was firing at the leader and was now very close.

He glared across the water at the enemy chief who stood impassively amidships with his arms folded beneath a much-decorated cloak as he directed the battle. They were close enough now to lock eyes and, like two savage dogs confronting one another, the two men each showed their primitive desire to fall on the other. Lafe felt the madness of battle on him and knew that he was ready to kill and keep on killing until there wasn't an enemy left standing.

Under the urging of the chief the enemy canoe ran in close with the obvious intention of ramming the bigger vessel and boarding her. Desperately Lafe grabbed the next loaded musket and fired it directly into the man's tattooed face, sending him sprawling on his back among the paddlers with his brains splattering over them. The empty skull, still attached to the kicking body, landed in the lap of one of the paddlers who let out a fearful howl as the head of any chief or tohunga was tapu. The pursuers sheered away, the sudden silence broken only by the roar of wind and waves. Then a man cried out an incantation, and a mournful dirge floated across the water as the strange tribe grasped the fact that they had lost their leader.

There was a hiss of released tension and the paddlers in the double canoe faltered in their stroke but Lafe barked at them to keep going, directing the bows of the big canoe towards the deep ocean away from the hostile shore. They would have to take their chances with the storm. The two strange canoes shadowed them till dark, hoping for an opportunity to attack but never coming close enough for Lafe to use his musket again.

The muskets were re-loaded, primed and wrapped carefully in waterproof mats and stored in the little hut amidships with the kumara plants. To Lafe's delight his new wife Miri showed her mettle by emerging with gourds of fresh water which were carefully passed down the rows of exhausted paddlers. He ordered her back to the safety of the hut, and the emoki brought food to the benches while One Eye and Lafe took up a paddle apiece, one at the head of each row, and led the crew in singing every song that the tribe had ever known. Hour by hour through that pitch-dark night they struggled against tiredness that seeped into their bones to keep the canoe head on to the building waves that threatened to sink her.

By now the men were exhausted. Some fell asleep and were slapped awake again as the canoe punched through the rising face of each wave and careered down the slope into the troughs on the other side. The swoops were hair-raising and frightening; as their bodies fell their guts were left behind still hanging somewhere near the top of the wave and the smell of vomit was strong in the wind. It was very black and wet, there were no stars and they steered by feel alone. There was fear in the wind too – no one wanted to think about the consequences of heading out into the storm, but they could not turn back.

The two hulls of the great double canoe and the platform between them were held together with ropes and wooden pegs. Sharp chips of stone had been used to drill holes through the wood of the hulls and strong, plaited flax ropes had been threaded through to bind the platform into place. To increase the freeboard, planks had been lashed into place along the tops of each great hollowed-out hull and then smeared with sticky tree gum to make them waterproof. The canoe had been lovingly built by skilled craftsmen and was as strong and sturdy as she could be, yet she flexed and twisted alarmingly as she rode the waves, her lashings creaking and groaning as if in mortal pain.

'Courage, my warriors. We are the boat people, the tangata bola. Have we not just defeated a superior enemy? Is that not a sign that the gods have shown us great favour? We are one with the sea and our ancestors watch over us.' So Lafe cajoled them through the long night, drawing on every ounce of endurance and seamanship he possessed. Were his own ancestors not boat people too? He felt his father and Olva at his shoulder as he drove his men through the storm, yelling defiance at the howling wind and waves.

Towards morning the wind backed right around the compass, leaving the sea confused but not so dangerous as before. It drove the canoe south and east with the tiniest scrap of sail to steady her and still the paddlers could not leave their positions but they slept like the dead, huddled under their cloaks to avoid the wind while their buttocks were rubbed raw from contact with the wet benches.

For two days they fled from the land, until Lafe began to worry that they might be swept so far out into the Pacific that they would not have the strength to beat the wind and return. But on the third day the wind started to ease and went around a few more points, which allowed Lafe to sail a course parallel, as far as he could judge, to the coast and the next morning they woke tired and cold to be greeted by the sun in a cloudless sky. A stiff breeze began to blow from the south. Then a man cried out and they all turned to where he pointed far to the west. There on the horizon were the faint outlines of snow-covered peaks, the Kaikoura mountains, the Lookers On.

The canoe was far to the south of where it should be, Lafe realized, and well into an area of another sworn enemy, the Ngai Tahu. He cursed his tired crew until they made quick work of turning the canoe onto a new course. They dared not close with the coast until they could reach the Windpipe and slip through it into friendlier waters.

The southerly was strong and nearly cold enough to freeze the poor paddlers to death, but it allowed them to close the shores of the Windpipe and seek the shelter of the high land there. They found a sheltered sandy bay where they could spend the days fishing, gathering shellfish and resting to rebuild their strength. This was familiar territory to many on board. It was the island of Arapawa, home of the goats, and it was rich in fish and shellfish. They kept their presence quiet and their cooking fires low, and the people of nearby Motuara never knew of their return.

It was here on Arapawa that Lafe learned that his lively young wife Miri, who had nearly died of seasickness on the perilous journey south, could dive and swim like a seal. She was far better at it than any man he had ever seen, except perhaps for Matai who had been her kinsman, and he lived like a king because she always kept the best of her catch for her husband. Lafe spent many long hours lying on the sun-warmed rocks watching her pretty, brown pointed breasts as they bobbed in the water whenever she surfaced to throw her catch to his side.

'Here, my husband,' she would say, smiling enticingly into his face. 'Do you think this lobster is big enough and fat enough for your dinner?'

How beautiful and charming these women of the South Pacific were, Lafe thought to himself. The world would be a very much poorer place without them. And he whispered his thanks to the gods many times over for delivering him safely to such a place. Miri was his fourth, youngest and most beautiful wife, fresh from childhood, and she pleased him immensely. I will not need another, he told himself, although I still have to explain this one to Tama. It was his greenstone that paid for her, and he is very touchy about his greenstone.

The weather had settled down after the storm and it remained fine and hot for days on end, the crew revelling in the familiar surroundings as they picked their way home along the coast.

'To visit other lands is good, but there is no finer place than our own village here at Murderers' Bay,' One Eye said as they stroked their way towards home, and he spoke for them all. Their spirits were lifted with the joy of homecoming even before the first cries of welcome were heard across the water and their reception, and the feast that followed, was worthy of their endeavours and left them swollen with pride and satisfaction.

Early the next spring they performed the most sacred duty of the year, the planting of the kumara, and although the ceremony had not been performed for many years there were enough old people in the village to remember the proper way to do it. They had planted kumara before, in the good years when the tribe had good gardens, before the raids that drove them off their lands. And before the hogs.

After several gardens had been ravaged by the creatures, Tama announced tough new rules.

'If anyone's hog is found in the kumara gardens, both they and their hog will go into the ovens together,' he threatened, and cleverly-built fences sprang up round the village. The pigs were much prized and beloved animals, but it was painfully obvious that wherever there were pigs and gardens together there would be trouble. The gardens were a community enterprise and labour was divided among the families. The men were the main force when it came to the breaking up of the soil before planting, or the harvesting of the kumara, but they wisely kept to their digging and transferred the care and propagation of the delicate plants to the women.

By now the population had grown, just as Lafe had predicted, and Tama allowed several smaller groups to split from his tribe and form their own sub tribes further east along the coast. Such things did not happen quickly. A group of warriors and their wives would choose a piece of land for its beauty or its productivity and would visit it and sigh over it for many years. They would have to petition their chief many times before permission to move was forthcoming. It was understood that they would at all times regard Tama as their sovereign chief, and in times of war they were expected to fight their way back to the main village stronghold and help in its defence.

Lafe's own family was growing fast too, and his children were easily distinguished from the rest as they ran and tumbled among the waves where all the children in the tribe spent much of the summer.

'Wherever I look, I see Goblin children,' Tama would say, laughing at him. 'No one took my order of whakatupu tangata more seriously than you did, Goblin.'

Lafe had seven children now, four boys and three girls, and more were on the way. The firstborn of each of his older two wives were female, and now Miri was pregnant too he wondered whether she would follow the pattern. It was a pleasing mixture of races, he thought. His children all had the brown eyes of their mothers and their hair varied in colour from near-black to a reddish gold, while their lighter skins tanned to the colour of dark honey in the sun. They had puppies to play with too, a litter of black and brindle puppies that had come from a skinny brown bitch brought into the village by refugees from the north. She was not much of a dog by Lafe's standards but she had come off a whaler and seemed to have some British bulldog in her breeding. Salem had covered her eagerly and she had whelped a litter that ensured the big black Labrador's genes would survive even though his muzzle was grey now and his days were numbered.

Tama still came to visit often, at times almost overcome by the sheer beauty of these half Maori, half European children.

'The bloodlines of your people and mine have combined to produce the most beautiful children on earth,' he said one day after many hours of thought. 'Your people of the northern country and our people of the Pacific, two races at opposite end of the worlds. But we must truly share the same gods that they have smiled on these children so much.

'When these grandchildren of mine are grown they will make marriage alliances with other royal bloodlines from all over the country and bind other tribes to our own with ties stronger than we have ever seen before. They will give us power and protection from our enemies.

He sighed heavily. 'But first we have to survive the next ten years, and that will be the hardest thing yet.'

Several small canoes with families on board had turned up on his shores lately, all from the northern island and their occupants had thrown themselves at his feet to ask for mercy and permission to stay. An endless war was causing even the most peaceful tribes to take up their weapons in order to fight for survival, and many had given up their own lands in answer to pressure from the north. As such people were dispossessed they moved south, found a tribe weaker than themselves and took over new territory in place of what they had to give up, and the end result was these refugees who had been pushed from the island altogether. In the highly charged atmosphere of the north the law of utu, for real or imagined insults, was enough to pit neighbour against neighbour and tribe against tribe, shattering the bonds that had held alliances together since the very first canoes had landed.

Only once during these troubled years did Tama lead his tribe into war. After much discussion with the tribal council he decided to seize a fort on the other side of the large bay to the east of his land. It was a clever tactical move, calculated to install a friendlier regime that would act as a buffer on the logical invasion route into his own territory.

Lafe was a full member of the tribal council now and was aware of the problems that Tama faced. His young army had never been tested, as many of the boisterous young warriors now filling its ranks were only children when the tribe undertook the long march from their lagoon home on the west coast.

These young men had learned to build beautiful canoes which they sailed and raced against each other, and could hunt, fish and run as well as their fathers had done before them, but they had trained in the arts of war without ever believing that their skills would be needed. For the good of the tribe they must be hardened in battle, the council agreed. How else could they test themselves and build new military traditions? How else could they add their new fund of stories and deeds of valour to the history of the tribes, and how else could they plant their seed in new bloodlines and breed the warriors of the future?

'Send out the runners to summon the tribe to war,' Tama ordered.

For days the village swelled in size and a frantic chaos reigned as the people from the outlying settlements marched in and each new group was greeted with singing, feasting and the glorious war dances, the warriors grunting and stomping until a dust pall hung over the village. Children ran in every direction howling for their mothers while dozens of pigs uttered their death screams as they were butchered to feed the newcomers.

'For us it is not just the glory of the tribe, but the women and the feasting that we fight for,' Lafe heard the warriors boast to one another around the fires at night. They were all in high spirits as they ate their way through mountains of food prepared for them, and he knew that the feasting they talked of was the traditional cannibal feast to celebrate victory. He was still uncomfortable with cannibalism, but he worried that the supplies of pig and kumara the tribe had put aside for the winter were being depleted at an alarming rate by all the extra mouths. He brought the subject up with Tama, who appeared unconcerned.

'Never mind, Goblin, this is war. This is the way it is always done,' he claimed cheerfully. 'We will soon be eating the enemy's kumara, and his meat too.'

The enemy fort was on top of a small, steep island with a little rock causeway linking it to the mainland. It would be a tough defensive position to take at any time, but Tama's spies had reported that very few of the fighting men slept in the fort. Most had taken to sleeping in huts built near their hogs and crops on the mainland to avoid the tiresome trek back and forward across the causeway.

'They have become careless,' Tama sneered. 'Now they will pay the price. Great tribes grow greater. Careless tribes get swallowed by the sharks!' He shouted his words into the darkness where his three-hundred-strong war party had gathered, their numerous small fires winking in the darkness as they listened to the battle plan.

Tama chose a series of foggy autumn mornings to cross the bay in great stealth and position his warriors for the strike. By day he hid his canoes and men in the forest above the sandhills as the little army closed in on their unsuspecting victims, and the sands were swept with branches to erase their tracks. Scouts trotted in regularly to report that the enemy was still unprepared and suspected nothing, and in the hour just before dawn, when man's spirit is at its lowest, the tribe struck out of the fog.

They came at the causeway in their canoes, and the half-asleep sentry had only a few seconds to become aware of a new sound that had crept ever so softly into his consciousness. It was a regular, sibilant hiss like a gentle waterfall and it came from the open sea. Soon he was properly awake and he listened hard as the noise grew louder and he realized it came from a wider front than where he first heard it.

'Shisss….Shisss…Shisss…'

Perhaps it was one of those sea serpents the old people talked about, he told himself. The first twinges of fear began to pucker his scrotum as a new thought seeped into his brain, that the noise could also sound like many hundreds of paddles being dipped and withdrawn in unison from the water. Then the first canoe swept out of the fog and for a split second the sentry was frozen in fear as the great double canoe drew a straight line for the very stone he stood on. He opened his mouth and screamed in despair, knowing even then that he was too late and he was doomed.

The first of Tama's men leapt from the canoe onto the causeway, dashed the young sentry's brains out with his patu and set off at a run for the grass huts. Canoe after canoe disgorged their crews in the shallow water and they charged up the beach and attacked the sleeping village. Lafe and his muskets had been ordered to remain behind with the canoes, and even though he could see nothing from where he was he could hear the frightful sounds of battle carried through the fog. The thud of patu against skull and the screams of the dying and the injured carried easily through the damp air, and worst of all was the keening of the women and children as they ran from place to place trying to find somewhere to hide from the madness that had suddenly sprung out of nowhere.

The women were hit on the head with the flat of the patu to fall stunned, so they would be easy to round up after the battle, and meanwhile the killing went on and on. Lafe thought how easily these women and children could have been his own but there was nothing he could do to save them. It was more than his own life was worth to interfere in such a serious thing as war.

He had killed many times in the past years, and such killing had come easily. But a battle with warrior against warrior was different. To attack or defend with honour was one thing, but this senseless killing of hundreds of people was damaging his spirit and for the first time in many moons he felt himself draw apart from his tribe. The battle raged for an hour or more then quietened, then raged again as more of the enemy were rooted out from where they had hidden. The excited yips of the warriors as they ran down yet another man or woman told its own tale. Lafe's ears had heard enough and as the fog cleared he tried to shut out the sounds of murder by moving closer to the sea.

After a long period without much sound except for the wailing of women and children, Tama and most of his warriors staggered down to the beach again, their striking arms bloodied with gore to the elbows. They rested on the sand for a while and then trotted over the causeway to investigate the fort and make sure that no one escaped.

It was a strong fort even now, when it was only held by a small force. Saplings sunk deep into the ground and woven together with ropes made a formidable barrier with their sharp pointed tops. A fighting platform ran around the top of the wall on the inside, and darts and rocks were already being thrown down on the heads of the attackers. This fort had been safe until the arrival of the musket, Lafe realized sadly. Now twenty of Tama's best men advanced toward the main gate, carrying Lafe's old axe and tomahawk.

Close behind them came Lafe, Tama and One Eye with the muskets loaded and ready. When one of the defenders stood up to dart a spear at the attackers Lafe raised his musket, picked a patch of sky above the man's head and fired. Tama fired too, and his shot took the defending warrior in the belly so that he fell groaning back onto the platform. Lafe reloaded slowly and steadily, so that when another enemy warrior jumped to his feet it was One Eye who killed him cleanly with a shot to the chest. None of the defenders would risk musket fire after that, they had been properly cowed by it.

Tama's warriors chopped through the lashings that held the gate and tied ropes to the posts, and a hundred men tore it from its opening and stormed inside. Nearly a hundred men and women were inside the fort, but they gave up without another blow being struck. Lafe had seen this behaviour before but it still amazed him that, knowing the consequences, they did not fight to the last man.

'It's as if they say to themselves, I have lost so now I will go willingly to the ovens,' he said to One Eye. 'No one from my race would surrender so easily if he knew such a death awaited him.'

'There is no shame in being eaten, it happens to everyone, just the same as there is no shame in being killed in battle,' Tama said as he overheard this remark. 'But your shooting was very poor today, Goblin. Perhaps you are not getting enough practice?'

Lafe said nothing, but he felt Tama's shrewd eyes on him as they walked back across the causeway together. The warriors were leading their prisoners away, their hands tied and linked to a long flax rope. Some of them would be taken back across the bay and kept as slaves.

Lafe walked through the ruined village to where a small party of Tama's men held the women prisoners together. There was a sickening stench of blood and death in the air and bodies were strewn on either side of the paths and around the small grass huts. The old people had all gone, killed with blows to the head or allowed to escape into the forest where they would not survive for long on their own.

All that remained of the three hundred villagers were the younger and more attractive women, most of the children and a few of the men, no more than a hundred and fifty souls altogether. He knew many of them would end up in the ovens.

For four days the ope feasted on the victims and lay with the women. Lafe declined to make a choice for his own sleeping mat, as his rank allowed him to do, and was gently chafed by Tama for his lack of tribal duty. Some of the young, single warriors would stay behind with the women of their choosing and Tama would send more men and their wives from the village to populate the place again under the leader of his choice. The uneaten bodies and the prisoners, the spoils of war, were loaded into the canoes and they set off once again to their village across the bay. But there was no triumph in Lafe's heart at this homecoming. Something within him had changed.

Chapter 16

Some time in the early 1820s Lafe began to take stock of his life. As near as he could work out, he had spent more than twenty years with the tangata bola, the boat people as they now called themselves. The years had slipped away on gossamer wings and, without quite knowing how it had happened, he had settled in and become a single strand in the fabric of the tribe.

Now I could be truly be described as a native, he mused. As tangata bola I have allowed the years to pass by without a care for the future. I only have to look around me to see how time has slipped through my hands like grains of sand through an hourglass. Time has been counted in the Maori way, in seasons and events.

He remembered back over the outstanding events since he had been with the tribe, and the things that had meant most to him. First was the loss of Matai, whose death he always associated with that last glimpse of his fellow whalers rowing for their lives and the meeting with Tama who had taken him captive so long ago. Then he had lost his fine sailing cutter the *Aurora*, whose rope he had cut in frantic haste to save the lives of the ope he had led north to get the kumara. He still shivered when he remembered that desperate flight into the eye of the storm to escape from the Heretaunga war party.

Then came the death of his loyal friend Salem the dog, who had grown old and grey and finally died among people who loved him, but his progeny lived on and there were now fine, strong hunting dogs in almost every household in the village.

Lafe's wives had lost the first flush of youth now, in this country where young girls blossomed early. His grandchildren were too numerous to count any more and his father-in-law was an old man with white hair. Tama was still the hereditary chief of the tribe and his mana was unchallenged, but now more than ever he ruled through a council of lesser chiefs and elders. It was a successful system, but it gave the long winded their chance to take the floor.

And there never was a more long-winded creature on earth than a minor Maori chief, Lafe chuckled to himself one fine morning as he closed his eyes to the sun's rays and let the warmth wash over him. For days he had sat nearly cross-eyed with boredom and sleepiness, forced to listen to such men discussing obscure points of Maori protocol. They stalked back and forth outside the meeting house with their great carved sticks, shaking them savagely to emphasize each point of their argument. There was not a lot of good to be said about democracy, Lafe decided, remembering the days when a leader gave orders and his men obeyed without question.

In the twenty years or more he had been with the tribe it had flourished, cleverly avoiding the wars that flashed through the country like bush fires. Strategic alliances had been made with other tribes and they helped to keep the peace, but it was vigilance, a well-trained force of warriors and their three muskets that had saved his people. Now there was increasing evidence that the old disciplines would not be enough to protect them. The musket wars had come.

Some tribes had gained access to muskets through the whalers who used their harbours, trading pigs, potatoes, kumara and women. Their desire for the thunderstick was so great that tribes beggared and starved themselves to acquire the new weapons then as soon as they had sufficient muskets, powder and ball, and could think up a good enough reason, they attacked their old neighbours. The effect of such actions spread outwards like ripples from a stone dropped in a still pond and tribe after tribe went under, wiped from the face of the earth as if they had never existed.

The tribes of the far north got their hands on the musket first, from traders at the Bay of Islands and Hokianga. Almost as soon as they had armed themselves they attacked southwards, causing a domino effect that toppled many of the tribes in the North Island to a greater or lesser extent. Scattered fragments of families began washing up on the beaches of Murderers' Bay like wounded birds to tell their stories and seek sanctuary. It was only a matter of time before the spark of war crossed the Windpipe and engulfed the tribes of the South Island, and when that fire broke out it would remove whole tribes from the land, leaving it as empty as it was before the first man set foot on it.

All the casualties from the previous wars, since Maori had landed in the country many centuries ago, were as nothing compared to now. Tribes of more than a thousand members were taken in an afternoon, the warriors killed where they stood and six or eight hundred women and children dragged off to the cooking fires or to slavery. Crops were not planted or were never harvested and cannibalism now ruled the northern tribes. These were no longer kumara wars, these were musket wars and even a peaceful tribe had to have the musket for its own protection. The very act of owning it, however, could attract a pre-emptive strike against them for fear they would grow too strong.

It was during this period of great conflict in the north that Ngai Tahu, the traditional enemies of Lafe's tribe, got their hands on enough muskets to begin an ambitious invasion of the lands to the south from their great fortress at Kaiapoi. These lands were inhabited by their own near relations who also had muskets, and furious battles broke out. This was a war that would be known as the Eat Relations War.

While Ngai Tahu fought in the south the surviving tribes watched each other closely in the north. There was a general in the making, a ruthless chief named Te Rauparaha who broke out of his homeland near the centre of Te Ika a Maui and fought his way down the coast mopping up all the tribes he encountered along the way. The coastal route he chose was well populated so the carnage was great, lowering the population on the island dramatically. Te Rauparaha's people were the Ngati Toa, and soon they were poised near the southern tip of the island, dangerously near the narrowest point of the Windpipe.

On fine days the North Island could be seen from Murderers' Bay. It was far in the distance but the great mountain they called Taranaki would stand on the horizon like a guardian, her perfect shape outlined in the clear morning air. She was a reminder to the tribe of the unrest they knew was happening and some days Tama would look at the blue smudge of land on the horizon and remark, 'Rohe the spirit woman is very busy on that island lately, with all the lost spirits roaming about after the killings.'

His people believed each spirit that left the body of the dead travelled to the very tip of the North Island to gather with others in a tree that overhung the sea. This place was called Spirits Bay, and when the time was right each spirit would slide down the tree roots and enter an underwater cave to travel on through to the underworld. Rohe was the ferry woman of the underworld whose task was to carry the spirits across to the other side, and once they ate of the food that she offered they could never return to the real world of the living. This was known because anyone who recovered from a trance or returned from unconsciousness had obviously refused the food Rohe offered.

Tama would have been happier if the fighting tribes of the north had wiped each other out or at least seriously weakened each other in their battles, but this was not so. Some tribes grew hugely powerful, spreading like the octopus from the alliances they forced upon weaker tribes. Others were like the shark, swallowing smaller fish whole. Te Rauparaha was one such shark. It was rumoured he could raise a fighting force of one hundred warriors armed with muskets and five hundred more with conventional weapons, and that his ope ate only human flesh.

'This Te Rauparaha alone would provide full-time work for Rohe the ferry woman,' Tama offered, and Lafe could see that day by day, as the war clouds gathered over the land, the old chief became more and more worried about the safety of his tribe.

'All that will be left in the end will be the sharks,' Tama fretted. 'In other wars we, the smaller fish, found ways to survive. But not any more. Now all of the big fish are going to eat up all of the little fish.'

The tribe had never been able to increase its stock of muskets beyond the three that were with Lafe when he was captured. They were worn out and unreliable now and it was only Lafe's skill with file and hammer that had kept them operating for so long. There was but a handful of powder left in the keg, and small stones had been used for many years in place of musket balls. At every meeting of the tribal council the men wrestled with the problem of how to find a new supply of muskets. Even if the cost beggared them they would have to pay it because the need had become desperate.

For more than a year now, Lafe had been planning to leave the tribe. He didn't know how but he was sure that the coming war would provide a way. It was through no fault of Tama's that he had come to this decision; this was a well-ordered tribe and he had made good friends among the people. But as his children had grown up and left the village to make their own homes elsewhere, so the value he felt in himself had diminished and he had felt his life begin a slow slide towards irrelevance. His daughters had been married to make the valuable alliances Tama had prophesied, his sons had their own women now and belonged to the many warrior fraternities responsible for guarding those same villages, and although there were grandchildren he saw little of them. His four wives had grown older with him and were now far more interested in food than lovemaking, and he had to admit that over the last few years he had become less interested in the nubile younger women of the tribe.

As he sat on the sand hills contemplating the lack of intellectual stimulation in his world, his attention sharpened suddenly as he realised that the sun was reflected from the sails of a beautiful three-masted ship. She had ghosted into view from out of the Tasman and was now shaping her course for the Windpipe.

Lafe jumped to his feet. He had seen sails on the horizon but there had been none for several years now, and none had affected him like this one.

'A whaler!' he called to Tama. 'It's a whaler, and by God I can almost smell her from here!'

Tama came running and they both stood silently and watched the ship tack her way up against the awkward breeze and finally disappear towards Rangitoto. Lafe sighed, stirred by deep longings and deeper loneliness. After so many years as a solitary Goblin among the Maori he was homesick and felt the need to mix with his own people again.

To read books once again, now that would be something, he decided, and to talk of the great things happening in the world, with people who spoke the language he was raised with, would be a truly great thing. He had grown accustomed to being a leader whose word was law, but he promised himself that he would even be prepared to work his passage home to America as a deckhand if he had to.

One thing that he had never become reconciled to was the Maori attitude to life, an attitude he secretly called 'always never mind'.

'Never mind tomorrow, for today the sun is shining and we have food enough in our bellies,' they would answer to one of his queries, and his wives would be astonished when he ordered some longer-term task.

'Too lazy to even brush the flies off their dinner, some of these people,' Lafe would mutter under his breath, but he too had seen how easy it was to slide into that state where the languid brain produced just enough activity to get its owner safely through the day. He had seen the signs in himself, the same disease creeping up on him until he had made a pledge to set mental problems for his lazy brain to wrestle with every day. Only the threat of imminent war could shake the people out of the lethargy they had grown into over the easy years.

Once the crops were established and hogs and goats had multiplied the tribe settled in to enjoy the good life that always came with times of plenty. Their wooden stockades still bulged with nursing sows and young weaners, but over the years a number of animals had escaped into the hills where they had thrived on berries and fern root. The forests were so full of wild pork that as long as the tribe was able to hunt they would never lack meat again, and Lafe seldom heard anyone cry over the lack of human flesh to eat with their kumara.

Tama had grown old now, and the fire had gone from his eyes. It was partly this land of plenty that was to blame.

'No one hunts better than the hungry hunter,' he had been fond of saying when he was younger, but few people in the village could even remember those far-off hungry days.

'It is the fault of this place we have come back to, Goblin,' he would complain. 'It is too good, too beautiful and too fertile. Life has been too easy here for too long, and our people have grown soft.'

In the end it was Tama who came to Lafe with a plan. He must have long suspected that his Goblin had a secret desire to rejoin his own people, because he began his argument with the words that echoed what was already in Lafe's heart.

'I think you must rejoin your people again, Goblin.' He paused to let his words sink in. 'We must somehow get our hands on one hundred thundersticks, or our tribe is as good as meat in someone's oven. Never have we been in so much danger and the answer is in your hands now.'

Lafe was taken unawares and tried to keep his joy from showing as he listened carefully to the old chief's words.

'You must go and find a ship that will trade with us,' Tama marshalled his arguments. 'We have hogs, kumara and greenstone to barter with, so you must find the ships and persuade them to come here and trade. Perhaps your own good father, if he is still alive, will send a ship full of guns to ensure the survival of his grandchildren,' he added cunningly.

'Oh how I wish that small matter away back in our history had never happened here. That was when this place earned the name of Murderers' Bay, and of course that is why the ships do not come.

'You must stop being our Goblin and become our Pakeha-Maori, to open up trade between your people and our tribe.'

It was an order, not a suggestion, and Lafe realized the old chief had been thinking these thoughts for many months.

'Do you have a plan?'

'We will place sentries on the sandspit where they can watch far out to sea,' Tama replied. 'When they see a ship heading for the Windpipe they will light a signal fire and we will have time to intercept the ship before it gets too far away. I think, Goblin, that this is a very good plan. We will put you on board the ship and then the rest will be up to you. You will tell the captain that we are peaceful, loving people, and you will bring him here to trade with us. If this captain has guns, tell him to bring them and his soldiers too. When we conquer Rauparaha and eat him this captain can come to the feast and I will give him the head.' Tama finished triumphantly, pleased with the way he had thought it through.

As he had spent much of the winter thinking more than half-seriously of different ways to escape from the tribe, Lafe was surprised to say the least that he was being given permission to leave it. In fact, as Tama was the chief his plan was not negotiable and Lafe was being ordered to go. He was aware that if it had not been for the immediate threat of war from Ngai Tahu and this Ngati Toa upstart Te Rauparaha, he would not be leaving at all.

Tama had always gained enormous mana from having a Goblin, and now there were more white men in the country there was even more status to be gained by any tribe which had its own Pakeha-Maori, usually a trader who owed his loyalty through having chosen a wife from that particular tribe. To the Maori, blood was always thicker than water and it was taken for granted that you would favour your wife's tribe above all others. Even if there were strangers of your own race, your wife's tribe would have precedence above them, and the position of a Pakeha-Maori was at times a precarious one as he could not afford to transgress the rules of his chief and the laws of his people.

Lafe knew that his value was like that of a prize pig. For Tama to relinquish the ownership of his Pakeha-Maori was a great thing and there was little that Lafe could give Tama in return except his agreement to go and the promise to do his best to find a ship or trader and bring him to the tribe. The plan to put him on board a ship was a good one, but he had to insist that it was not wise for him to go aboard any other ship except a Yankee whaler. There was always the chance that the British and the Americans were at war again and if this was the case he was damned sure he did not want to rot in chains as a prisoner of the British. He tried to explain this to Tama who eventually accepted that if Lafe was put aboard a ship from the wrong tribe he might be eaten and therefore rendered unable to carry out his task. But as a good proportion of the whaling fleet operating around the globe was made up of American ships, or at least it had been when Lafe last set foot in a whaling port, intercepting one seemed to be a feasible idea.

Lafe was careful to show no outward sign of his emotions in front of the chief. It would not have been polite to look pleased to be going back to his own people, but in his heart he was overcome with

311

emotion and after Tama had left him he spent many hours alone on the dunes, staring out at the sea that was finally to be his escape route. Then he went down among his wives to tell them of the decision that had been made that day.

'We are not happy, but then we are not sad either,' Marama said dutifully. As the senior wife it was her place to speak for the others on such an occasion and she addressed her husband formally. 'You have been away often before and have always returned. This time you may be away longer but we will still care for the children and your possessions as before.'

Lafe was careful to give no hint that he may not come back at all. Such an idea would cause discord and unhappiness in his household and might even make Tama rethink his plan in some way. Over the next few weeks he visited his many sons and daughters and their children up and down the coastline, inspecting their households and enquiring after their welfare as he had done before. He spoke casually of his going away, leaving them with the impression that he would one day return. They were fine people, these children of his, handsome and clean-limbed, and from the number of babies they nursed and the toddlers around their dwellings they were obviously as fertile as their parents had been.

Late one evening when Lafe had returned from his wanderings he sat staring into the coals of the fire and pondering his future. The morepork called from the graveyard and he shivered. The village was long asleep and so was his own household.

Where was I when the years were so swiftly flying by? he asked himself. Is this how life must be in these Pacific islands? He had never really noticed how the time had been wasted, the years had simply slipped away until they were nearly all gone. Perhaps in the future a benevolent god would give his Pacific Island children two lives, one to be given up to toil and trouble, the other to be dreamed away in the sun. That would be so much fairer, he decided.

He was now around forty years of age as near as he could figure it. Once he had been meticulous in his date keeping, until one day he realized that it was possible two years had slipped by instead of just one since his last calculations, and from then on it just hadn't seemed to matter any more. Time had been measured in tides and seasons, the days and months had passed with the waxing and waning of the moon and the fattening of his wives' bellies and there had been no reason to know more than these signs. Tribal life had wrapped him in its warm embrace and he had forgotten for a time that there was any other life, but the one he was leading. Lafe knew now that it was too late for any recriminations, he had loved these people and their ways and belonging to a big family with four women of his own had many advantages. But now he began to shake off the slothful native thought patterns he had fallen into, trying to remember the English names for things and rehearsing in his mind the words he would speak to other white men.

It was many weeks before the signal fire sent its greasy smoke trail up into the sky to alert the tribe that a ship was squaring away and would soon be heading toward the Windpipe. Lafe ran for his few belongings, wrapped them hurriedly in a flax mat and had time only to raise his hand in farewell to his wives before the warriors sent their three best canoes shooting like arrows across the bay and out into the ocean. The tribe had built these three huge double sailing canoes in recent years, combining the best of their traditional crafts with their newly-won sailing skills in keeping with the spirit of the boat people, and their crab-claw sails made a grand show.

'This is the pride of our fleet that we taking to intercept this foreign ship,' Lafe told the captain of his canoe. 'Make sure that every man understands his task in this thing we are about to do. If we make one single mistake the ship will use her big guns on us and escape, and we will probably be killed into the bargain.'

For weeks he and Tama had drilled the boat crews until they were sure everyone understood what was wanted of them. The warriors were prone to over-excitement, and all it would take would be an impromptu haka, which was no different in a sailor's mind from a war dance, or an attempt to pursue the sailing ship and she was likely to fire on them. More than one ship had been boarded and her crew slain by Maori and they would be wary. Lafe dimly remembered his own father warning Olva, as ship owners no doubt still warned their captains, 'Take care, trust nobody if you want to see your homeland again.'

313

He had borrowed his old glass back from the unwilling Tama with some difficulty and now he used it to search the tops of the masts for the ship's flag, taking care to look for guns as well. She was a Yankee all right, and he gave a little yip of delight when he found the old familiar ensign in his glass. He signalled for the three canoes to spread out and lie across the approaching ship's path, lowering their sails and doing their best to look as friendly as possible. The day was warm and the breeze light, so it was easy to let the playful waves have their way with the canoes while the paddlers slouched at their benches.

Lafe knew that by now there would be action on board the whaler. By now they would have run out and loaded what cannon they had on board and armed every sailor with a musket and what ever else they carried, such as swords, knives and even flensing tools.

The three big canoes would make her captain mighty suspicious and he realized he had to get the ship to come close enough to recognize him as a white man. As he watched the big vessel creep forward across the waves he remembered his father quoting an old saying.

'There are old sailors and bold sailors, but there are no old, bold sailors.'

He lay back in the canoe and pretended to fish, watching the three-master through his fingers as she edged her way towards them. When she was close enough he got casually to his feet, feeling the eyes of everybody on board the sailing ship on him. He took off his cloak and shook out the long, blond hair that he usually wore woven into a topknot on the top of his head. The ship had not stopped, but she tacked away across the breeze until she was at a safe distance from the canoes before turning into the wind to lie becalmed with her sails aback, waiting for him to make the next move.

Lafe and the emoki clambered into a small two-man fishing canoe that they had brought with them and paddled across to the ship while the big canoes drifted away downwind. As Lafe closed with the ship he allowed his long hair to obscure most of his face so the sailors would not see the tattoo. As he drew near to the high, planked sides he could smell the ship, rich with oil. Only a whaler could love that smell and he breathed it deeply, filled with a sudden excitement.

314

'That is the smell of money,' he heard Olva's voice telling him as he had heard it so many times so long ago. A rope ladder was thrown over the side and a rough voice ordered him to grab it. Already the ship's sails had been hauled tight and were starting to fill and the ship was once again underway.

'Goodbye, emoki,' he said in a voice suddenly thick with emotion as he touched the old slave's shoulder. 'I am going home.'

He caught the ladder and pulled himself onto it, leaving the small canoe and its solitary paddler to be picked up by one of the double canoes. Then he climbed slowly up to the deck, aware of a circle of strange, silent faces that stared down from above as he hauled himself hand over hand with his best woven flax robe flapping around his knees. He clambered over the rail and turned to pull the ladder up, giving himself time to think. These men surrounding him were a very different type from those he remembered. Their faces seemed somehow naked and unfinished without the tattoo, he thought as he stared back at the ring of silent sailors, all the while desperately trying to remember the words of the sentence he had practiced for just this day.

He looked again into the eyes that surrounded him and realised there was no welcome to be seen there, only horror and revulsion. In some of their faces he even saw fear. This was not what he had hoped for. In his dreams he had seen himself being welcomed by his own people, and now the words he had memorized so carefully slipped away from his tongue and the tears began to fall down his face instead. These looks of disgust had chased the words he wanted to say right out of his mind and all that came out of his mouth instead was a miserable howling noise that made no sense even to himself.

A sailor with obvious authority stepped forward and touched his shoulder, indicating that Lafe should follow him, and led the way below. There a much older man that Lafe took to be the ship's doctor mixed him a strong drink and he recognized the main ingredient as rum. Waipiro, stink water was the Maori name for it and it was no wonder. His nose curled up in disgust as he sipped a little from the jar. He had drunk nothing stronger than mountain water for close to twenty years now and his taste buds revolted at the spirits, but the drink calmed him a little and

315

gave him strength. He soon managed to convey to the first mate that he was Lafe Erickson, one time second mate of the whaler *Northern Lights* out of New Bedford in America.

The captain was sent for and Lafe was coaxed to tell as much of the story as he could manage. It was difficult for him. His tongue had grown clumsy as there were many sounds in the English language that the Maori did not use, and his mind was struggling because he now thought in Maori and had to translate those thoughts into English in his head. Many of the words he needed had gone from his memory completely but he felt better after his story was told and apparently accepted. He swept his long hair behind his head and tied it in place with a piece of flax from his robe. To hell with the white race, he decided. If they did not like his face then there was nothing he could do about it.

They gave him a hammock and a blanket but he hardly slept that night, his mind racing with the strange, new smells and noises that were all around him. The next morning when he went up on deck the ship was making a sweeping turn to enter a spacious harbour on the northern tip of Rangitoto. Deeper and deeper inland they sailed, passing through a narrow entrance into a place where they floated serenely in quiet water. On either side the tall forest towered higher than her masts. Lafe thought it one of the finest sheltered harbours that he had ever entered, and wondered why his people had never talked of it.

It was plain it was not the first time this ship had been here. He saw several young Maori among the crew, and when the men launched the boats and headed back out the entrance to fish he was sure they were regular visitors to this coast. His nose told him that the ship had been working the whaling grounds until very recently, and he guessed that she had been to Sydney to unload her cargo of oil and was returning for more whales.

For a week the *Mary Elizabeth*, for that was her name, rested at anchor while a severe storm blasted its way through the Windpipe, and during that week Lafe told his story to her interested officers. Parts of it he had to repeat many times as he haltingly found his way into the English language once again. He listened carefully to the words as he

316

spoke them, often substituting Maori words for English until he had a sentence that was understood by his listeners. They were Nantucket whalers on their second trip to New Zealand, he found out, and they were headed for Kapiti Island to pick up fresh food and discharge their Maori crewmen before cruising for whales off the southern and east coast. They had already discharged a cargo of oil in Sydney and when they were full again they would sail for America via Cape Horn.

They had no news of the *Northern Lights*. Whether she was still working the fisheries or long ago sunk to the bottom of the ocean they could not tell him, and no one on board knew of the Ericksons. These people of the islands of Nantucket were Quakers and were interested only in the affairs of other Quakers and their ships.

The Mary Elizabeth's captain was willing to sign Lafe on as a crew member, though he thought he might have a troublemaker on his hands until he heard how the American had received his tattoo. Fortunately this captain had enough understanding of the country to have some idea of the pressures his passenger had been subject to. It was a shock to Lafe to realize just how much his tattooed face coloured the way that he was received by his own people. In the minds of the more civilised nations the tattooed face of a savage conjured up all sorts of unspeakable acts of grossness and deviation, and on the face of a supposedly civilised white man it seemed to be far worse, an abomination to all who beheld it. This was worse than all his worst fears.

When the captain of the *Mary Elizabeth* took Lafe below to his cabin and stood him in front of a mirror he received another shock. Looking at himself in the still waters of a stream had not told him the whole truth. On the darker skin tones of the Maori the blue, black lines of the tattoo blended a little better, but on his own face they were a travesty, a human countenance that jumped out with startling aggressiveness, and he knew he would have to get used to this different vision of himself. He could only hope that the people of his race, when he met them, would make an effort to find the man beyond the tattoo. Most would not bother, that was the way of the world and he knew that, but the thought of their reactions sickened him.

When the norwesters eased and a more moderate southwesterly wind came into play, the *Mary Elizabeth* made her way out of the bay and into the Windpipe. The captain set her bowsprit pointing to Kapiti Island and she gamely rolled her way through the aftermath of the storm that had just blown through.

Lafe was interested to see Kapiti, this steep-sided little island on the wild western coast of the North Island which had recently become the stronghold of Chief Te Rauparaha. This was a man whose exploits had come to the notice of the whole country, who in a very short time had become the paramount war chief and one of the most powerful and feared men in the land. He was a good fighting man but his reputation for slyness and treachery was unsurpassed and every success made him just that much more formidable as the years went by. The southern tribes knew that he was already looking across the Windpipe for new conquests, and they knew that after he had subdued some of his more fractious neighbours in the north they would be his next victims.

Lafe studied the island carefully as the ship crept around the rocky southern coast and up the more sheltered east coast channel that divided Kapiti from the mainland. He wanted to learn as much as possible about the home of his tribe's enemy. This island of Te Rauparaha's was a great defensive position. Its steep sides left an attacking force no choice but to attack straight uphill, and it would take a large, well-trained army with muskets to evict the Ngati Toa chief from there.

The *Mary Elizabeth* dropped anchor beneath a palisaded fort in a small bay called Rangatira, or Great Chief Bay. The fort was on a terrace above the channel and had extensive earthworks, the first that Lafe had ever seen in this country, to guard against musket fire.

'This Te Rauparaha takes no chances at all,' Lafe remarked to the captain. 'He will be a dangerous man one day.'

As soon as the captain and the Maori crew had gone ashore, canoes slipped out into the channel and began to ply back and forth bringing pigs and potatoes out to the ship. The great pots that cooked the whale blubber were set over the fires to boil water to scald the bristles off the pigs and the work of killing and salting them down began. After the pork had been stowed in barrels, great canoe loads of firewood were

318

brought aboard and stored below decks, all paid for by muskets Lafe thought as he watched one of the ship's boats take five muskets, several barrels of powder and a large bag of shot ashore.

'I hope the captain is aware of the danger of supplying muskets to people like this,' he commented to the mate. 'I would like to speak to him about it when he returns.'

'Waste of time,' the other man grunted. 'The only trade these natives will accept is muskets and we've got to have food and firewood.'

When the captain came on board he ordered the ship made ready for sea, and signalled for Lafe to follow him below to his cabin. He seemed uncomfortable and Lafe tensed.

'I have bad news for you,' the man said bluntly. 'We are leaving on the tide, but Te Rauparaha is coming on board to take you off the ship. One of the Maori sailors must have told him about you and he demands you be handed over to him.'

'And you would do this?' Lafe asked him, aghast.

'He said that by your tattoo you have chosen to be Maori, so you belong to this country, and here you will stay.'

Lafe tasted the metallic tang of fear in the back of his throat. He tried to speak, but the captain raised his hand and forestalled him.

'There is nothing I can do. I have already tried, God knows that I tried, but there is no turning that devil from his course once he has made up his mind, and I have my men to consider.'

Lafe knew that what the captain said was true. Rauparaha would have the ship seized and the entire crew killed rather than show any weakness in front of his own people. A war chief never gave an order twice, and Te Rauparaha would have his life snuffed out, like killing an insect, if he was thwarted.'

'I have told him that you are the best I have ever seen at fixing muskets, so I believe that at the very least he will keep you alive,' the captain said sympathetically. 'Good luck is about all I can offer you, Lafe Erickson.' He left the cabin, and Lafe cursed his bad luck as he headed back up on deck. Choosing a ship that was heading for Te Rauparaha's den had not been a wise decision, he concluded. The captain signalled to Lafe to attend him again.

319

'I have sent for paper and pen. Write to any relatives you might still have living and I will see that the letters are delivered. That is all I can do.'

The crew quickly heard what was to be Lafe's fate and got together a bag full of small gifts for him. Lafe was overwhelmed by this outpouring of pity and touched that they would give of their own few possessions to a stranger. A quick look in the bag showed a shirt and trousers, a clasp knife, and numerous other useful small items that would make his life a little more comfortable. Lafe's letter, written with the mate's help, was in the captain's hands before Te Rauparaha came on board an hour later with his bodyguard of fifty or sixty warriors.

At first glance Lafe did not think much of this Napoleon of the South Pacific, as some people were beginning to call him, although after he had watched for a while he had to admit the warrior chief had a certain presence about him. He moved and acted like a king.

When Rauparaha had made his farewell speech he signalled for his warriors to perform their war dance, which was skilful and well practiced. Lafe watched with critical interest as the warriors raised their knees and brought them crashing down on the deck timbers with one solid thump, as they beat time with their open palms on their biceps, rolling their eyes in the most ferocious expressions. He was well-skilled at judging such things now, Lafe thought wryly. He tensed as Te Rauparaha rose at the end of the ceremonies, adjusted his robe and stepped toward the ladder. For a wild moment he hoped that he might be forgotten, but then the chief gave the most casual flick of his eyes in Lafe's direction. A warrior trotted over to where Lafe stood hoping to remain unnoticed among the sailors, and touched his shoulder.

'You! Come with me to your new home,' he said, and his quiet, sibilant voice raised the hackles on the back of Lafe's neck. He smiled as bravely as he could, nodding to the captain and crew and mustered all his dignity as he left the Yankee whaler for whatever fate had in store for him. From his place in the Ngati Toa canoe he heard the steady clack of the ratchet on the windlass as the whaler began to lift its anchor from the mud and the crack of the sails as they caught the wind. She was putting to sea without him and Lafe would not look back.

For a few days the *Mary Elizabeth* had been a wonderful dream, but it was a dream that was not for him.

Now he knew he was in very bad trouble, perhaps worse than he had ever been in his life before. When they got to shore he was taken to a small, rough grass hut on the edge of the clearing and told by his escort that this was the place where he would live. He entered the mean hut to find two miserable pieces of humanity already in residence, sailors who had for some misguided reason deserted from an English whaler. They told Lafe that Te Rauparaha had them chased down and caught and brought back to his island where they lay in this filthy hut more dead than alive, doomed to a far worse fate than had been theirs on board ship even under the cruellest captain.

The men had been forcibly tattooed, and Te Rauparaha had sent word to them that if they wanted to become Maori he had done his part to help them. Now they should always be happy because they were his white Maori. They had both been very ill but they were still forced to work harder in the gardens than all the other common slaves on the island, they told Lafe.

'If you do not work, you will not eat,' their captors had told them. 'And if you do not eat you are useless. Skinny, useless slaves are simply flung from the cliffs near the gardens onto the rocks below. Food for the fish,' their captors had said, rolling their eyes with glee.

Lafe listened to their story and recognized their type. These two sailors had obviously thought the Maori a lazy race who spent their time lying in the sun so they had run from their ship to join them and live a life of ease, hoping they would never have to do more than raise a fingernail to scratch themselves again for the rest of their lives. But the Ngati Toa chief had shrewdly recognized them for what they were, and had them tattooed for the sheer delight of himself and his tribe. He would probably work them to death for the same reason.

'Born lazy,' Lafe said aloud as he looked at the two pathetic specimens lying on their filthy grass bedding. He turned on his heel and went to fetch a gourd full of water from a nearby spring. Curtly he ordered them both to wash themselves while he cut fresh bedding. The dried scabs and pus on their faces made him feel sick and when one of

321

them argued that he was too unwell to move, Lafe dragged him from his bed by the arm and spun him around. Sinking his boot into the sailor's arse he sent him flying from the hut.

The next morning he was shown into a hut full of broken and rusty muskets salvaged from the recent battles the tribe had been involved in. 'Make them good again,' he was told roughly.

Left to his own devices, he surveyed the contents of the little hut in despair, but the instinct for survival was strong and he knew he could do something to make himself valuable to his captors. There were a handful of poor tools stored with the muskets, and from scraps of steel he set out to make a few more that he desperately needed.

Soon his little workshop and the dirty little hut he had to share with the sailors had become his whole world. From the first call of the bellbird in the morning until his eyes could no longer see the work in front of him, Lafe laboured to produce usable muskets from the pile of flotsam left over from other wars. His status was little better than the lowest slave on the island, but another nameless slave supplied all his food and basic wants and he was left unmolested and unharmed. He did the work he was told to do, and as he worked he dreamed of another tribe in another time and of friends he should never have left.

Chapter 17

Kapiti Island was very different from the relatively sleepy village where Lafe had been living with the tribe. This was the base from where the Napoleon of the Pacific ran his affairs, planned his wars and smashed his great ambitious fist into the underbelly of the country. Many canoes crossed the Windpipe or crept down the coast carrying chiefs from other tribes to confer with Te Rauparaha. Some came looking for peace, some for war, but they all wanted the Ngati Toa chief's advice or help in achieving these things.

Every couple of months a sail from one of the great white man's canoes would be seen approaching the Windpipe and Te Rauparaha would send out his canoes to lure it to Kapiti to trade. Their numbers seemed to increase at a very steady rate and Lafe soon realized that Rauparaha had captured all but the tiniest bit of trade that was available at any one time near his domain. He had an insatiable appetite for ordinance, muskets and even small cannon, and with every ship that called the crates of muskets, powder and ball continued to pour into his storehouses while his own men and women scoured the swamps of the mainland for loads of flax to pay for these weapons. There were of course many other ways to pay – potatoes, pigs, kumara and women were all part of Te Rauparaha's trade for muskets.

None of these great goings-on had any direct effect on Lafe. His voice was no longer listened to and his words had no more power now than the words of the two white-Maori whose dwelling he shared. The status of the lowest slave in the village was enviable by comparison to his own, he realised. He had lost all his mana because he had willingly turned his back on his own tribe, something no Maori would ever do.

In hindsight his reasons for doing so had not been as well thought out as they might have been. He was like the man who cried because he had no shoes, until one day he met a man who had no feet. The old proverb certainly described his own predicament well, and he mentally flagellated himself for his stupidity. He spoke only when he was spoken to, using as few syllables as possible, and the work he did was no more nor less than what was required to escape punishment and keep his usefulness to the tribe intact.

He maintained his own personal standards though, and refused to accept the squalor that the two white-Maori regarded as normal in the hovel he shared with them. He bullied them without mercy, carrying a thin sliver of sharpened metal from one of the broken muskets tucked into the seam of his cloak and using it to terrorize his bunkmates into some semblance of cleanliness. Though his actions might be judged by others as cruel, it was the cruelty of authority which was the only law that these sailors understood. They were already brutalized by the system that sent them to sea as little more than children, and in the rough, often cruel world of whaling ships and whaling men a bad captain or mate controlled his men with threats and violence.

Any victim that achieved power over others would perpetuate that same cycle endlessly, for ever and ever. Lafe was physically and mentally stronger than his hut mates and did not carry too heavy a burden on his conscience when he pricked the throat of one of these vile pieces of humanity with his makeshift knife, not quite enough to permanently scar the man but enough to make him realize that there was another force under the heavens that had to be obeyed.

Their Maori masters had put these two on the hardest task on the island, stumping the ground for a new garden. Noting their plain laziness, the overseers decided to forcibly extract every last bit of energy that they were capable of producing so life for these two runaways had descended to the lower levels of hell itself. To have deserted their ship

324

for this was their fatal mistake. Now all they had to look forward to was the most strenuous toil they had ever undertaken, under their new captain Te Rauparaha.

Lafe was amazed that the wily old chief had so quickly sized up these two sailors, and at his sheer vindictiveness and cruelty. The men had run from their ship and professed the desire to become Maori out of total ignorance and for no other reason than to avoid hard work, and Te Rauparaha was shrewd enough to recognise this. Now their only function on earth was to provide a little temporary amusement for a savage chief, and the small amount of land they cleared would be only a short-lived memorial. The rough tattoo that had been forcibly applied to their cheeks was all part of the subtle joke that their captor enjoyed. Te Rauparaha took time every day to come to watch the two at their work, and every week he increased their workload slightly. The pair regarded him as the devil himself, while he slowly, deliberately and ever so subtly worked them to death.

Te Rauparaha found his new captive harder to read. Often when Lafe was rebuilding a musket he would look up to find the chief's restless dark brown eyes watching him, but he never spoke, and when he had seen enough he always left as quietly as he had come. He never commanded more muskets so Lafe carried on steadily disassembling the broken and destroyed weapons and rebuilding serviceable ones from the parts. More than once he was allowed to go aboard a ship to procure a tool he needed, but he was well-guarded and the opportunity for escape never came. Even if he had been less carefully watched he was a marked man because of his tattoo; the sailors treated him with deep suspicion and he knew it would take time to break down their distrust before he could even think of planning an escape on any of their ships.

Much of the time he listened without speaking, until most of those around him forgot that he spoke both English and Maori. Because of that his ears picked up many things that were filed away for later consideration. This was how he kept up with the goings-on around him, the news of wars and intrigues that swirled around the island like whirlwinds. Such snippets related to the whole dominion of Kapiti Island, the lower North Island and the top of the South, and he listened especially for news of his own tribe but the pickings were sparse. Reports from the southwest where Tama's people lived were few and far between.

In Te Rauparaha's long migration from the north he had gathered together many smaller tribes and groups under his very able leadership. Trouble began as they chose new areas of land to settle on, and there was constant bickering and fighting among them. Much of the chief's time was taken up in the settlement of these disputes, and war parties were often dispatched from Kapiti to settle such quarrels and bring reluctant minor chiefs to heel again so the island seethed and bubbled with intrigue, rumour and plans for war. The constant arrivals of freshly-captured slaves, and canoe loads of flesh consigned to the ovens after a battle, added their own sense of drama to the morbid excitement of the island.

Te Rauparaha had close to two hundred slaves to see to his comfort and personal wants alone, Lafe had noted, and the chief was also a lusty man who chose widely from the ranks of women and retired early most nights. The men, women and children who came fresh to the island as slaves came with their own stories and tales of lives in far away places. Often they came from tribes who once flourished and lived and loved in some little bay in the sunshine and were now annihilated.

'Now we are no more,' they told Lafe sadly. 'Our own lives, loved ones and hopes of the future are gone forever.' They would shudder as they talked of the flash of paddles in the early morning light and the ripple of flame from the muskets, their best warriors shot down and killed while they were still wielding their age-old stone weapons. These were the years when the musket was king in all the lands of the Maori, and gluttony sat at the king's right hand.

During this period Lafe found only one person to talk with. Most of the island's population stayed well away from the white-Maori, unwilling to risk the displeasure of those in high places, but the exception was a garrulous old and fairly useless slave called Rua. He told Lafe that every morning he awoke astounded that no one had taken up a patu and dashed out his brains or tossed him from the top of the cliffs near the gardens where he worked. He did not like work and preferred to talk, which made his survival even more remarkable. But after fearing for his life for so many years, he told Lafe, he had suddenly found that the fear of death had left him and it was not so easy to leave this life after all. Now no one could be bothered killing off the old slave.

He had been a warrior in his day, from a tribe that lived at Totaranui in Queen Charlotte Sound quite near to where Lafe had secured the first pigs for his tribe. Rua's people had insulted Te Rauparaha by offering to play a tune on his skull with the club used to beat the edible pith from the fern root.

'We hear that this grievous insult had put old Te Rauparaha in a terrible state of temper,' the old man cackled. 'But what worries did we have? We had our forts in good condition, one on each of the islands that protected the entrances to the sound.

'When our spies told us Rauparaha was out, we warriors left our village and manned our forts. We were keen for battle, we were not afraid,' he assured Lafe.

'For weeks we waited, and nothing happened, until early one morning in the mist we heard the rhythmic hiss…hss…hss of the water falling back to the ocean from his paddles. There were many hundreds of paddles. Then we realized the sound was coming from behind us.

'Yes, Goblin.' The old man seized Lafe's arm and rolled his eyes at the memory. 'The canoes were coming from the direction of our village, where we had left our women and children protected only by a few old men. Yes, it was from that direction that it came, the hiss of the paddles. It was then that we knew we had lost all that was worth fighting for. And there was no fighting that day. We were led away without any fight left in us.' There were tears in the old man's voice as he relived that terrible time.

'Rauparaha had gone south, then doubled back at the Wairau River and returned to the big harbour north of the river at Kanae Bay. He dragged his canoes through a low pass in the mountains and re-launched his warriors into the sound behind our forces. Now who could have thought he would do such a thing?' He sought an answer from Lafe even now, as if the answer would bring back all his missing people.

'I am still alive but I don't know why. Many hundreds perished that day, and I am the last of my line. Yes, the last of my people,' Rua

327

said sadly. 'And to my dying day I will never forget the sound, the hiss of the paddles breaking the water, that sound that came from out of the mist.'

He always had a story ready when Lafe passed by at the end of the day, and that way Lafe got to hear much of the gossip of the island and many of the stories that were important in the top part of Te Wai Pounamu. There were stories of the very earliest people of the land, those who now lived only in the remotest parts of both islands. There were the little fairy people who lived in the deepest forest, a race of giants that inhabited the further reaches of the western sound where Lafe had been sealing, and that strange and gentle race called the Moriori who had inhabited the whole of the country when Maori had first settled it. These Moriori people, according to Rua, knew only peace and did not even have a word in their language for war. They were a very different race from the Maori. They lived in earthen burrows, lined with warm, dry stripped flax, on the driest parts of well-drained ridges throughout the land.

'We are people who live in the earth, we are not rats. Why do you treat us like rats?' they cried to the invaders in despair, but these were their last words as they retreated far out into the Eastern Pacific.

'Some still live on specks of land out there,' Rua said, waving his hand eastward toward the vast reaches of the ocean. 'They have gone back to where they originated from, near the beginning of time when these shores were young, soon after the great Maui hauled his fish up from under the sea.'

That Maui had indeed fished the North Island up from under the sea was never in doubt, Lafe had noticed. Where another race might treat a story of a man-god fishing a whole country up from under the sea with scepticism, Maori could point to rocks high on the mountain tops with perfect seashells embedded in them as proof that this thing had so obviously happened. Lafe found it very hard to think up a convincing or better reason to explain the presence of seashells so far from the sea.

One morning as Lafe passed the gardens he was hailed by the old slave Rua, his nut-brown wrinkled face wreathed in smiles of excitement.

'Well!' he said. 'They have done it now. The fat is really on the fire.'

'Done what?' Lafe demanded.

'Wiki and his brother have run off with their heads,' Rua told him. 'Mark my words, there will be a big fuss over this. I hear that Te Rauparaha is very angry. A war party has gone after them already and any tribe that harbours them will regret doing so when that ope arrives.'

Apparently these two slaves had taken off during the night and swum to the mainland with gourds tied around their bellies. Lafe wished them luck but at the same time fell to laughing at the thought of Te Rauparaha's rage and frustration. The old chief was angry enough to chew up his own sleeping mat in a fit of rage, just because two of his slaves had run away with their own heads.

It was the habit of Te Rauparaha to select slaves who had pleasing head shapes and strong features, then to have them tattooed by the best tattoo artist on the island. These slaves were then exhibited to all the traders and if one of them agreed to the purchase price the Ngati Toa chief would have the finely-tattooed head chopped off the slave's shoulders, smoked and preserved for the sale. These two heads that were now missing represented quite an outlay in time and were worth muskets, so it was no wonder their owner was in a filthy mood.

Lafe knew Wiki and his brother. They were mokomokai. Moko was the tattoo and mokai meant pet slave, so they were Rauparaha's tattooed pets and they spent much of their time walking around the village looking down their noses at all the other slaves because their handsomely-decorated heads were worth the unbelievable price of one musket each.

To run off with your own head and deprive the rightful owner of what was considered his well-deserved profit struck Lafe as a very funny joke indeed, and he was still laughing as he pushed on to his workplace. In due course it was reported back that Rauparaha was very angry indeed with his ungrateful slaves. He had the island searched thoroughly several times for them, at the same time as his war parties scoured the mainland.

As the weeks became months and Lafe continued to toil at the armoury, he became aware from the gossip among the slaves that Te

Rauparaha was about to put to sea with a large war party aiming to subdue parts of the east coast of the southern island. Over the next few weeks the preparations became more obvious as food was preserved and packed and weapons were made ready. It did not occur to Lafe that he himself would be involved, but one day a warrior came to him and ordered him to prepare for battle. He was a trained musket man and was expected to use his skills in the coming war. His reputation with a musket had spread over the years and it now appeared that Te Rauparaha had known of this ability when he had Lafe taken from the ship.

Six large canoes left Kapiti Island to cross the Windpipe. The fighting men on board numbered close to three hundred and Lafe was among them. A small contingent of slaves went with them to do the menial work around the camp or to provide a back up source of food in case it was needed. The fleet made easy time down the coast to Mana Island where the tohunga would decide what the weather gods had in store for them that day. Lafe's heart lifted as he felt the movement of the sea under him again and watched the well-oiled muscles of the warriors sliding easily beneath their skins. It seemed that the gods were kind, and soon the tempo changed and the warriors began to dip their paddles with the powerful, easy strokes that they could keep up for hours at a time.

Once the canoes were committed to crossing the Windpipe it could be fatal if a storm rose and caught them in the middle as there was very little chance of being able to turn back. The tohunga navigators, who spent much of their life sniffing the wind and studying the weather patterns, could be relied on to get the canoes safely to the other side.

When they entered Totaranui it was a very different sound to the one Lafe had visited years earlier. This time the canoes paddled up the centre of the sound with the arrogance of conquerors. The village on the very steep-sided island called Motuara, in that beautiful bay Cook had named Ship Cove, was gone, the fortified pa no longer existed and the whole area was in the process of returning back to forest. Lafe could see where the tree-trunk barricades that had once barred the passage to the fort had fallen or been toppled, and the fires that had once burned continuously to feed the people had gone out forever.

No longer would their smoke be seen against the blue sky as a welcome to travellers when they passed from the tempestuous waters of the Windpipe into the tranquil waters of the sounds. Whether they were friends or strangers, men had stopped and rested on their paddles as they passed by the little fort on Motuara Island, and when they had picked up their paddles again they had felt refreshed by the beauty of the place. Many had wondered how it would be to live in such a village, but now, Lafe thought, as he looked up to the broken, deserted fort, those people who had once lived there were no more than well-gnawed bones. The taste of disgust was strong on his tongue.

Canoes no longer stopped at Motuara but hurried on, afraid of the ghosts that now inhabited the place. When the sun sank behind the nearby hills the air around the old fort seemed to have a certain chill to it.

'Perhaps what we feel is a little breeze stirred up by the passing of many ghosts,' Lafe muttered to himself. The pens on the mainland that once held hogs and where Lafe had chosen his own tribe's stock were gone too, he saw, and he guessed that those pigs not eaten by the invaders had gone wild in the forest. They would have lived well there on the abundance of ground-living birds, the fern root and other vegetation and the host of berries and seeds dropped by the fecund forest. He looked at the warriors in the canoes around him and wondered how many of them had helped to bring about the destruction of these people, who had lived in this part of the country so blessed by the gods.

As they moved on up the sound the faces of the warriors were stoic and impassive, as befitted a war party. They were the bringers of death, with no feelings at all for the centuries of struggle that had brought this village to the richness and beauty it enjoyed before it died, or for the hundreds of years it had taken for a people to build themselves from a handful of hunter-gatherers squatting under a damp bank to a vibrant village that owned pigs and had the ability to build a fort on such a beautiful island.

That the gods would allow the faltering steps of human progress in this large and nearly empty country to be wiped from the face of the earth was surely an abomination. Lafe had asked himself many times in the last few years whether the one God he had been brought up to believe in or the many gods he had adopted from the Maori could possibly be aware of what was happening to their people. All the way on that long canoe trip from the outer sound along the middle reaches to the inner waterway it was the same. Where smoke from cooking fires had once smudged the skies, now there was none.

Even Waikawa, the place of the calm and peaceful waters where the ope beached the canoes, was deserted. The vigorous little village that had once thrived there was gone and the forest was already beginning to stretch its shade across the land that had once known the voices of children at play. Lafe hoped that the tattooist he had borrowed from this village would never return to see the fate of his people.

They carried the canoes into the forests and covered them with branches. Then, when the war party had rested for several days and the warriors had feasted to their hearts' content, scouts were sent ahead while the rest of the group skirted the great swamps of Koromiko. The ancient old tracks that took them inland were worn deep into the land from the many people that had used this old route to get to the east coast, and Lafe wondered who would need such tracks in the future.

Te Rauparaha's warriors were superbly trained and very fit and they could keep up a murderous pace for hours at a time. They travelled at a gait that could only be described as a trot, and they ate up the miles without effort. The scouts acted as the great wings of the advance, and when they reached the open plain they swept forward holding tight to their victims until the main host arrived to crush them. No one survived the depredations of the ope.

The flying fish that breaks across the bows of the canoe is doomed, Matai had told Lafe so many years ago, and it was certainly true on that raid. In the torrid little battles that they fought Lafe dutifully fired his musket and reloaded as fast as any other warrior, but he was careful to fire into the air a scant few inches above his intended victims' heads. This was not his tribe he was fighting for, and he would not add to the already considerable number of Maori deaths that had stained his hands and whose ghosts threatened his sleep at night.

They took two small villages along the course of the river they followed, before they reached their destination at the great lagoon where the river finally met the sea. Lafe was astounded at the speed they travelled. They burst from the swamps onto the dry, scrub-covered plains faster than any warning of their coming could have travelled. He wondered if any other army on earth could move so fast. The food to sustain the little army each day was chosen from among the recent captives, or from leftovers from the day before. This walking food, the most expendable of the people from the conquered villages, travelled at a trot behind the warriors all the way to the ovens they were forced to dig for themselves each evening, and in this way they supplied the sustenance that kept the warriors' bellies full. So Te Rauparaha's ope was able to keep moving through the country at great speed.

The captives astounded Lafe by showing very little emotion at their fate and giving their captors very little trouble. Once they had been taken in battle it seemed almost a matter of honour among them to go to the ovens without complaint or fuss. Lafe would sit quietly at his fire feeling sick while his stomach fought to digest the large chunks of greasy human flesh. He had no option but to take his cannibal meals when they were offered because there was nothing else to eat, and without this food he would soon tire and fall behind. It was all he could do now to keep up the killing pace that the warriors set, and they never waited for stragglers or wounded slaves. If a man fell behind he was soon taken care of by the surviving villagers who had managed to hide in the forest when the ope came through, and to fall into such hands was the last thing that anyone would want to happen.

'There are a hundred and one ways to die,' the slaves told Lafe, 'but to fall into the hands of the widows must be the worst fate of all.'

In late afternoon of the fourth day the war party reached the sea, and several hundred warriors and their slaves stood on the dunes and stared out over the huge rollers breaking on the beach. This was the end of a journey of thousands of miles for these waves, which had come all the way across the Pacific from South America, and Lafe was moved by the sight. The men he was with had no way of sharing his knowledge but they stared at the waves in fascination and whispered to each other that this sea had come from another place far away. The idea appealed to their seafaring blood.

This place where they stood was called Kauraripe but already they were starting to use the English name of Cloudy Bay that the whalers had given it.

That evening Te Rauparaha swept into the bay in a fleet of canoes that rode the whitecap rollers right up and into the mouth of the river. Great was the excitement of both parties. The chief was greeted with a dramatic haka and a fresh lot of corpses went into the oven for the feasting, but that night Lafe sat at his own fire and roasted a flapper duck for his tea. Te Rauparaha had led a successful raid on a village further up the coast and he was now able to declare the Wairau totally under his control. He had brought with him many prisoners, some for the ovens and some younger women for the beds of his warriors.

That night great blazing fires of driftwood reflected off the waters of the lagoon, periodically sending great clouds of sparks into the heavens. They lit up the scene like beacons and shone their warning for many miles around.

For Lafe there was no escaping the sounds of death as the killing and eating of the prisoners continued. Thuds and death rattles could be heard from right around the lagoon and many of the women were forced to watch as their fathers, brothers and lovers were slaughtered and thrown into the ovens. The women were used repeatedly throughout the night, while the boasting and singing went on around the fires until late.

The two war parties settled in and built their small huts on the banks of the lagoon. This was to be their summer camp, Lafe realized as they began the task of catching and preserving the many thousands of flapper ducks on the lagoon. These were the young of both the teal and the paradise ducks, flappers because they had yet to grow their flight feathers and were still bound to the lake.

Each day the canoes were paddled out into the lagoon towing great long nets to surround the huge rafts of flightless ducks, sometimes catching as many as a thousand in a single cast. Their necks were quickly wrung and they were plucked, cooked and preserved in their own fat, stored in gourds ready to be taken back to Kapiti for the winter. Many more thousands of ducks were split down the breastbone, flattened and smoked over manuka fires. They were very tasty and could be stored for many months in the raised storehouses of the village. Te Rauparaha was very fond of duck, so it made sense for him to acquire the hunting rights to the best duck lagoon in the country. Lafe suspected that he had coveted this lagoon and the ducks that lived on it for many years.

Lafe found life at the lagoon very pleasant. There was a much more relaxed atmosphere during this duck hunting on the lagoon than there had been on the island of Kapiti, and he did not miss the long hours that he had been forced to work at his bench fixing muskets. Here the days were full of laughter as the canoes sped around the lagoon netting large numbers of ducks.

Such days often began seriously with the business of hunting but later became days of competition with swimming races and diving, the older warriors always on the lookout for new ways to deflate the fragile egos of the new recruits to their ranks. For many of the younger ones this was their first war party, and some of the captured women had been handed over to these young men for their first experience of lovemaking.

'Now look at them. They are like dogs trying to piss on every tuft of grass on the river flat,' the older warriors laughed at them. Cunningly the old hands conspired to tip over the young warriors' canoes at least once a day, leaving them floundering in the mud and much deflated, and most days finished with the men lying around the fires idly chewing a smoked duck or a limb off one of the steadily-diminishing ranks of slaves while stories of the tribe's history were told and retold.

As a non-person Lafe sat well back in the shadows. For a Pakeha slave like him to even think of taking part in such conversations would probably lead directly to his death.

'The oven is gaping for you, slave!' was the constant threat thrown in the face of such captives, reminding them that for even the slightest infraction of the rules or for forgetting their place there was only one end. Even the unhappy could exit the world only through the ovens. When they were happy the Maori were good masters, none better as far as Lafe was concerned, but when they were not happy they were as cruel as the worst child that does not yet even understand the meaning of the word. Cruelty was a game they played, always with the intention to insult and degrade their enemies. Lafe had learned that these people were capable of the basest types of behaviour, the worst types of torture and brutality known to man.

The chief himself would hand his special enemies over to the widows of the tribe and they would make incisions in their victims' necks and suck the blood from them while they still lived, taunting them until their eyes closed for the last time. Lafe had long ago decided to shoot himself rather than fall into the hands of that particular bunch of torturers and he began seriously searching for some way to escape.

If he did manage to escape he had only two choices; to try to rejoin his own tribe or to board a whaler with the risk that its captain could be blackmailed into handing him over to Te Rauparaha again. Nearly all the ships trading or whaling off the New Zealand coast had Maori sailors in their crews now, and the first loyalty of these men was to their own tribal chiefs. Besides that, Lafe had to consider the Maori love of gossip; if he did manage to board a ship word would quickly spread.

He knew that no other tribe would risk giving him shelter. He was Te Rauparaha's personal property and wars were started over far lesser crimes than stealing another man's slave. This Goblin was too well-known now to get away that easily. There was very little likelihood that Te Rauparaha would ever willingly release him, he knew that. The chief seemed to get a perverse sort of satisfaction from keeping a stable of white Maori prisoners. They gave him mana among his peers and that was a great satisfaction to him.

Lafe decided that sooner or later he would have to try to escape whatever the risk. He was not sure if he could survive another war party.

Finally all of the surviving young ducks had grown their wing feathers, and one day they departed the lagoon with a great whistle of wings in the misty morning light. The month of the ducks was over for another year. Many canoe loads of preserved duck had already left the lagoon to cross the Windpipe for Kapiti and now it was time for the warriors to leave the lagoon too. Some trotted inland to retrieve the canoes they had left at Waikawa while the rest shepherded the most heavily-laden craft up the coast to the point where the Windpipe was narrowest and where they would cross.

In the early morning light of that fine autumn day they could see the first snows crawling down the slopes of the great mountains that stood to the south. High above the bay they stood, these mountains that Cook had named the Lookers On. Their white capes signalled to the tribe that winter would soon be upon them, that any food they had not yet gathered would be spoiled by the frosts and was better left in the forests for seed. The birds that had escaped the nets and spears were better left in peace now to provide the next generation of ducks and pigeons so there would be plenty again in the following summer.

Chapter 18

'**It was so much easier** to survive the winter when I had wives,' Lafe moaned. There was no one to listen to his complaints but he was in the habit of talking to himself now. He been shut up inside his little hut for nearly a week while the wind tore at the walls and roof from all points of the compass, carrying away so much of the roof that during a lull in the storm he could see a star through the thin thatch that was left. He had spent a lot of winters in this country now, but he could not remember enduring a worse one than this. Te Rauparaha's damned island was so near the Windpipe of the Pacific and so exposed that it was hit by every bit of bad weather that happened to be passing.

For days he had slept until he could sleep no more. Then he spent hours staring at the roof, listening to the wind and rain as the storm tried to tear his hut apart. Even when he had first been taken prisoner by Tama all those years ago he had had the big black dog Salem for company, and later there had been his women to comfort and amuse him during the long nights. Now he was a prisoner on Kapiti the winters seemed to last a lot longer than ever before and, with nothing to distract him from the aches and pains of middle age, the hours and days dragged relentlessly.

Most of the work that he did on the muskets was finished now until after the next war, and no one seemed to mind that he did very little these days. It seemed to be enough that he was around when his overlords needed him.

The two other white Maori shared a hovel down by the gardens now, to get as far away from Lafe as possible, and when he saw them he could tell from their condition they were still being worked slowly to death. He felt sorry for them but did not miss them. He could cheerfully exist without their company, he told himself, though to be worked to death was an extreme form punishment even for trash like them.

Old Rua the slave spent many an hour in front of Lafe's fire, and sometimes Lafe went to sit by his fire to pass the time. When Rua talked he talked of better times, of long, sunny days when neither of them were slaves, as if with his own tongue he could shorten the grip that winter had on the land. Lafe would shut his eyes and let the old man's eloquence transport him back to the village at Murderers' Bay, reliving the endless summers and hearing once again the laughter of his children tumbling in the shallow waves. They talked of their wives and agreed that a woman was a great help in getting through the winter. As he cleaned and dressed his own long hair or plucked the hairs from his beard Lafe would sometimes feel Tui's hands on his cheeks or smell Marama's sweet breath. He often thought of Haroto, the sad one, and young Miri who was probably a grandmother by now, wondering how they were getting on.

Mentally he whipped himself every night for trading the comfort and security of his own tribe for the dream that had led to the predicament he was now in. He knew that by letting himself be taken he had also put his people in danger, although he did not dwell on that. Every day they would look for his return with the muskets and trade goods they had sent him to find, and with each passing year their trust in him would fade. He had wrestled for many hours in the darkness of winter with this problem of why he had become disenchanted with his tribe. Their adherence to the disgusting habit of cannibalism had angered him, though he conceded that perhaps he had expected too much.

For a time, with the coming of the hog, he had convinced himself they had given the habit up but it was not to be. As soon as the tribe went into battle and took enemy casualties or captives they went back to eating human flesh and Lafe cursed them for it. He had tried to impose his will on his own family but it was like trying to hold back the tide with his hands.

339

What he required was too far outside their cultural experience.
He had never managed to get used to their casual cruelty either.

'Why are you killing the slave?' he would ask Tama or one of the warriors, and always he got the same, slightly puzzled answer.

'But he is to be eaten.'

Old Rua was an habitual cannibal from a long line of cannibals, and the flesh of man was the food he loved above all others. Much of the time he bemoaned the fact that he was too old to go out with the war parties any more, and thus missed out on such delicacies. Human flesh was often brought back to Kapiti with the other food that was gathered for the storehouses, but it was considered prime fare and was never wasted on mere slaves.

Rua could never understand why Lafe had left his tribe, and when he put it into words neither could Lafe.

'One day I began to miss my own people in America, just as I had in the first few years, and I then became critical of all I saw and heard around me. Then I began to suspect that my wives did not appreciate me as much as they once did, and I could not be made happy again'. It sounded petulant and feeble, even to his own ears.

'I had it all once,' he told Rua bitterly. 'When Tama died I would have taken over as chief, but I gave it all away to become a slave of Te Rauparaha. My God, how I am suffering now for my stupidity!'

Ships came and went from the island, some flying the American flag and, by the smell of them, Yankee whalers. Lafe had to watch them setting their sails to catch the wind, never daring to go closer than the garden terrace. A slave like him could never hope to take part in any of the affairs that went on between the officers on board and Te Rauparaha's men. To approach an officer or even a sailor would mean instant death for any slave who could be so forgetful of his station in life, and it seemed that Te Rauparaha had learned enough English that he had no need of an interpreter.

Lafe harboured a secret dream that his father was still alive, that the letter he had sent home had reached its destination and that one day a rescue party would arrive to set him free, but such a hope was so far-fetched he dared not dwell on it for fear it would send him mad.

340

All that winter he racked his brains for a way to escape but none presented itself and it began to seem that he was to stay on the island for the term of his natural life, or at least until he no longer cared whether he lived of died. But right now, Lafe decided, he still cared. The blood still coursed strongly in his veins and with it the instinct for survival. He hoped to see many more years out yet.

During the long winter days he thought often of his children and his grandchildren, now scattered up and down the coast on the island across the Windpipe. They were quite close and on clear days he could see their mountains, but they were as far away as the moon under the circumstances. Always he found himself regretting the fact that he had never spent as much time with them as he might have. He could always identify his children and even his grandchildren at a glance among the dozens of other children playing in the river or rolling in the dirt, involved in the many games that the Maori children played. His children were different, set apart by the soft, honey colour of their skins. He smiled many times over when he remembered Tama's proud words.

'When I ordered the tribe to engage in whakatupu tangata, no one went about it quite as vigorously as our Goblin.'

Why, oh why had he stopped loving his wives and children enough to stay with the tribe? They had given him everything they could possibly give, and more. He and his family were part of this rough, fighting, squalling, terribly beautiful country, and yet at the time he had not quite grasped the fact. It seemed very clear to him now. His blood, the blood of the Swedish Ericksons, ran through the veins of these people, and the men and women who were his descendants would bring the beauty and intelligence of the Swedes to the Maori race. Who would have thought, when he stepped off his ship to hunt seals in the great southern fiords in the summer of 1801, that such things would come to pass?

Lafe spent much of that winter patiently filing pieces of metal to make new locks for the muskets in the armoury. It was no longer urgent or even necessary work but he did it to stop himself from going mad, and when the cluster of stars known as Mata Ariki rose in the east to denote the shortest day of the year and it was time to break up the sod ready for planting, he willingly joined the ranks of slaves with their digging

341

sticks. They toiled their way across the fields in one long line, driving their sticks into the moist earth and turning the soil while the tohunga sang the planting songs. The women worked their way along the fields behind the slaves, breaking up the clods with smaller sharpened sticks. Lafe liked the gardens and found working in the soil very satisfying after the long months of near solitary confinement in his little hut and workshop.

Te Rauparaha was fond of his gardens, and personally supervised much of the work done there. He took a renewed interest in his other two white Maori, the unfortunate sailors whom Lafe had kicked out of his hut, and set them to pulling the toughest weeds and to digging out all the tree stumps. He drove them every minute of the day, literally breathing down their necks so they were afraid to stop long enough to dash the sweat from their eyes. But for the rest of the slaves, including Lafe, the pace was much easier and there was a surprising amount of laughter and singing in the fields.

Lafe wondered if the old Ngati Toa chief was attempting to teach the two deserters that there was indeed merit in hard physical labour, a certain uplifting of the spirit in contemplating a well-turned out garden, but he knew that was unlikely and would anyway have been a waste of time.

The fate of the two sailors was watched with great interest by everyone on the island. What Te Rauparaha was doing was regarded as right and proper, and it appealed to the Maori sense of justice. This pair with their long, matted beards, foul-smelling bodies and stinking hut had long ago lost the respect of even the lowest slave. They were the worst examples of the lower class in any race, Lafe believed, and he hoped that not too many such sailors would be let loose to breed with the Maori in this unsophisticated new country. What a race of hellions they would produce between them, he reckoned. For the good of the country he hoped it would be settled by honest, strong people from the west rather than the convicts of Sydney Town or Van Diemen's Land. He believed that the interbreeding of Maori and convicts would be disastrous.

Since his father and Olva had first conceived their brave plan to come whaling down into the southern ocean, many others had followed. From May to October, when the right whale began its migrations down the west coast of the Northern Island and through the Windpipe to the colder breeding grounds, the pods were hunted by American, British and sometimes even French whalers. Lafe had yet to see a French flag, but Rua told him that a whaling ship had once come to Kapiti with a crew of 'Wi Wi', as they were known to the Maori. For weeks now that the season was in full swing there had been occasional sails on the horizon, and Lafe's heart lurched with hope each time he saw one. These were the ships that sometimes called to barter for supplies at the beginning or end of the season.

'Though they remain always as far away and as unattainable as the moon for this slave,' he told Rua. 'Sometimes I am so lonely and sad I have almost considered taking another wife from among the slave women on the island, but I have remembered just in time the promise I made myself not to take another Maori wife.'

'Not ever?' Rua opened his eyes wide, and Lafe chuckled.

'Though I do find myself making calf's eyes at the women here at times. I well remember what it is like to tumble a woman on the flax mat.'

'Then you should do it again, Goblin, to see if your memory plays tricks on you. Or perhaps you have forgotten how to do it at all?'

Rua had offered many times to be the go-between if Lafe wanted a woman on the island, but he was resolute. When the time came to make his escape he did not need the complications of a family, and until then it was best that he did not share his little hut with anyone. The less others knew of his plans the better.

Because there were so many slaves on the island Te Rauparaha did not have to wait for his men to gather the harvest before forming a war party. That was what slaves were for. All year round he sent men off to scout for victims on the edges of his far-flung domain. He would not make war in the winter though, unless he himself was attacked. The weather was too bad in winter, but Lafe suspected the real reason was that it was often a time of hunger for the tribes and his victims would be too thin. As soon as the spring crops were in the ground, however, Lafe was tapped on the shoulder and told to prepare his tools and make ready to accompany the next ope.

343

Again they crossed the Windpipe to Te Wai Pounamu and entered the great drowned mountain valley of Queen Charlotte Sound to paddle its reaches, stopping at each bay and checking for traces of human life. If they found signs of recent occupation the scouts sprang away into the forest in pursuit of these scraps of humanity. Sometimes if the refugees had sufficient warning they got clean away, but at other times whole families were driven back to the canoes in a state of profound shock. They might have survived other Ngati Toa raids in recent years, but now they were the walking food.

The war party combed the country before them thoroughly until they reached the very head of the sound, and here they crossed the waterway to a little bay they called Torea. Lafe realized that they were about to make a portage, and this was a place where they had crossed the land before. Ropes were made ready on the yellow quartz sand and fastened to the unloaded canoes and some of the party went into the forest to cut smooth, round logs to use as rollers. Others gathered shellfish or surrounded and speared the numerous stingrays in the clear waters of the bay, and that night they ate well. Before the sun was up in the morning the journey up the slope had begun.

Close to fifty men were on each of the two ropes attached to the first canoe, and when the rollers were in place the canoe singer began his song. At the end of each line he brought his foot crashing down on the forest floor, letting out a loud grunt that came from the bottom of his large belly. The men on the ropes threw their backs into the weight at this signal and the canoe surged forward and upward, several yards at a time. Slaves retrieved the rollers from the back of the canoe and ran to the front to place them under the keel again. Steadily the great canoe travelled up the slope under the canopy of huge trees, grinding small ferns and shrubs beneath its massive keel.

One of the slaves, perhaps because of his own carelessness or because someone tripped him, got his leg caught and fell under the sharp prow. The great canoe did not falter or slow on its passage through the forest. There was a brief scream, and in due course the crushed and bloody carcase rolled out from under the stern covered in dirt and leaves. The canoe singer, who had climbed a tree stump to look down on the canoe's progress, struggled manfully to maintain the cadence and beat of his song, but in the end the sight of the slave's mangled body was to much for him and he fell from his perch choked with laughter.

The canoe surged forward a few ineffectual feet before the warriors dropped their ropes and fell about laughing too, hanging on to vines and shrubs while they pounded each other on the back. They laughed until they could no longer speak, and when somebody regained his voice it was only to mimic the squeal of the unfortunate slave and that set them all off laughing once again. When the canoe singer managed to regain his composure again, after much coughing and spitting, he ordered another slave to drag the battered corpse into the bush and leave it for the pigs.

'He had no right to do that. Now he is not even fit to eat,' the singer growled in disgust. Lafe just stood back and watched, careful to keep his face impassive and noncommittal.

He could see that the path they were dragging the canoe over was well worn into the forest floor, obviously from the many other canoes that had used this same route over many years. It was a viable alternative to the long paddle all the way back to the Windpipe. He knew from his expeditions with his own tribe that there was another great arm of the sea leading inland, although he had never explored it, and remembered following the coastline from Totaranui almost to the island of Rangitoto to pass the entrance. The weather patterns in the Windpipe were an obvious reason for this route to have been used regularly, but he knew that would not be the only reason. This war party was entering the other sound by the back door, so to speak. Surprise was their weapon of choice, and their reason for this portage.

The trip through the low saddle between the two hills and down the other side was easier but more dangerous than the trip up had been, as the canoe threatened to get away on them and crush more of the slaves. The ropes were now tied to the stern of the canoe and the men fought to hold it steady on the steep slope. Woe betide any man whose clumsiness caused the great carved prow to be damaged by ramming it into a tree. It was likely that Te Rauparaha would have the whole crew killed and eaten for such a crime, not just the slaves, and it was known that he had

345

done worse for far less reason. These great, carved war canoes of Ngati Toa were the tribe's most important possessions and each had its own name. They were revered by every man, woman and child, and among the first words learned by a Ngati Toa child was likely to be the name of a canoe.

It took four days to hoist the four canoes up through the saddle and down the other side, and to launch them into the still, calm waters of the Kenepuru. This body of water was the second of two great drowned mountain valleys which lay side by side, separated by a mountain ridge that was low in places and narrow enough for a single sentry to watch large stretches of water on both sides. These two sounds together formed an easily-followed route into the guts of the country, Lafe mused. There were endless bays and beaches with timber and fish abounding, and there was enough flat land for a settler to grow crops and farm animals one day.

The quiet reaches of deep water between each bay enchanted him. In the sunlight the waters sparkled and shimmered as the light breeze touched the surface in the middle of the reach. The colour of this water so far in from the sea was a light powder blue, almost the colour of the alpine lakes high in the mountains and, like those lakes, its surface carried the reflections of the mountains that surrounded it.

Dark green forest crept right down to the water's edge, a forest so dense it could hide an army of lost tribes, and the song of the birds was almost deafening as they fed on seeds and berries in the upper canopy. On the forest floor were other birds that had never learned to fly or, because they never needed to, had slowly forgotten how. There had been no mammals here in Aotearoa except the bat until man arrived, and the birds had filled the spaces that would elsewhere in the world have been occupied by mammals. Now there were rats, dogs, goats, pigs and men, and the last were the greatest predators of them all.

Here in Kenepuru there was a great deal of pig sign. They had rooted and overturned ground on the beaches and through the forest floor, and Lafe wondered how the weka, the kiwi, the kakapo and other ground-nesting birds would survive.

346

The ope was back on the water now, checking all the beaches and the old village sites for signs of human occupation. This was Te Rauparaha's land, taken by conquest, and the only people who could safely live here were those he sent to populate it. It did not matter to him that the people he had scattered and whose tribal structures he had destroyed had nowhere else to go. Those hunter-gatherers who scratched out a precarious existence would never concern him because they were not of his tribe. They were the enemy.

'In this world, all of the big fish eat all of the little fish,' Tama had said, and so the Ngati Toa chief would have told his victims if he had bothered to explain. But they were only slaves and food, and why would he justify himself to them?

The beauty of the waterways they were travelling reminded Lafe that his own tribe lived not so far away, within a falcon flight across the mountains, and though his own land at Murderers' Bay was quite different from Kenepuru it had the same quiet serenity. Even as one of fifty paddlers on the big canoe he enjoyed travelling through the peaceful sound and thought with distaste of the noise and desolation of Kapiti, the landscape cleared and the birds silenced by the comings and goings of the several thousand people that lived on and around the island.

This was a very bountiful and beautiful part of the country, but without people it was so very lonely, Lafe thought. Surely such beauty was wasted without the human spirit to enjoy it?

'I will escape one day.' he promised himself, whispering in time with the stroke of his paddle. 'Even if it is just to enjoy for a short time the peace and quiet of a place like this one. It would be worth the risk.'

He looked for any signs of the race of giants he had been told lived there. It was the sort of country that could hold many mysteries but there was no sign of giants, and in the deserted villages the dimensions of the huts were no different from those in other places. He overheard the tohunga, who was a wise old bird, telling his warriors that this race of giants had left the area perhaps a generation or two before.

'They were a people that hunted the many species of moa,' the tohunga said. 'When the moa left these waterways so did the giant moa-hunters, and nobody knows where they went.'

Lafe had seen the bones of these large moa birds at the middens by the lagoon at Wairau. It was a giant bird indeed. Its leg bones looked far more suited to a large mammal and Lafe estimated its height to have been twice that of a man. The Maori talked much of these birds and there appeared to be many species, ranging from the size of a dog to the huge bird whose bones Lafe had seen. The tribes spoke of the moa as if they had known them intimately, but when he questioned them it seemed that it was always someone else's aunty's cousin who knew someone who had been kicked by one many years before. Everyone believed that in some parts of the country the giant birds still roamed, but no one quite knew any more where they were.

The canoes drew their paths like arrows along the quiet calm reaches, travelling fast in the twilight, always aiming to position themselves for the strike in the first few minutes of the dawn's early light. The warriors slept cold and hard on the sandy beaches without a fire and they needed no waking in the mornings because the cold, damp air saw to that. They were always gathered at the canoes before the tohunga gave the word, anxious to move off and shake the stiffness out of their muscles. Lafe had noticed that the cold was never as unpleasant to the Maori as when they were unable to light fires. Fire made them brave and cheerful, driving away the real and personal devils that inhabited their night world.

Faster than a sentry could climb a hill to his lookout, the canoes would sweep around the corner of the bay and slither up on some quiet beach where a solitary trail of smoke was beginning to climb its way to the heavens. Seldom did any of the villages hear even the whisper of paddles before Te Rauparaha's warriors were on them like mad dogs. There was no serious fighting. The shock of the sudden arrival of the Ngati Toa ope was enough to send the poor villagers into shock and they always gave up very quickly.

After each raid Lafe salvaged any muskets that were usable from among the motley collection that were captured, removing the locks and flints from those that were not. He kept anything that could add to Te Rauparaha's armoury and threw the rest of the junk into the sea. A motley collection of smaller canoes now travelled with the war party, paddled by the captives themselves who seemed to Lafe to be strangely subdued. They hung their heads like whipped dogs and seemed to give no thought to escape. Although Lafe had seen this reaction many times he never got used to it.

'If it was me or any sailor I ever knew who was faced with the oven, we would try to escape and die trying,' he muttered. He was damned sure that if and when his own turn came he would not go quietly.

After a month or more in the inland waterways he noticed that Titi Island was off their bow and the blue water of the open sea lay ahead. Another day and they were back in the Windpipe again at the entrance of Queen Charlotte Sound, shepherding the ungainly fleet of captives to the point where they could safely cross to Kapiti. Lafe did not care to think about what would happen to these captives when they were landed on the island, and when the fleet arrived home in triumph and his services were no longer required he crept back to his little hut and did his best to shut out the sounds of violent and agonising death.

The ope had not long been back on Kapiti when the island sprang into feverish activity once again. War horns were blown to summon the fighting troops from far and wide, and canoes darted from the mainland to the island and back again. The big war canoes were launched and manned with the tribe's best fighting men, armed to the teeth and ready to do battle, but when the canoes returned the warriors were black with musket smoke and there were gaps in their ranks. Many of the survivors had head wounds and broken limbs, and they limped from the canoes with none of the bravado of returning conquerors.

The slaves were agog at such goings-on, and Lafe kept his ears open and gleaned what information he could. It seemed that civil war had broken out among the various tribes on the mainland. These had not been good years for weaker tribes and many had been swallowed up so completely that history would not even record their passing. All that survived owed allegiance to Te Rauparaha and it was only with his consent that they had settled on the land he held power over. Many of these tribes and sub tribes were related in some way to each other, and most were linked to Ngati Toa as well. They had come to live under the protection of Te Rauparaha's muskets and enjoyed the fruits of association with such a powerful friend, but now the musket wars had reached new levels of violence and it seemed that everyone was on the march.

These tribes that settled on the mainland near Kapiti paid their dues by supplying fighting men for Te Rauparaha's formidable army but they fought and squabbled among themselves, raided each other's food supplies, stole each other's women and, like all bad relatives, created their own type of hell and discord. When things got out of hand they were punished by Ngati Toa warriors and for a while a sulky type of peace would be maintained. Then the demand for utu would start them all off in a new round of killing.

As another summer passed and another winter approached, Lafe once more considered taking a wife. He feared the loneliness and perhaps even the madness of the dark months ahead. Soon there would be twelve long hours of darkness in each twenty-four, and often he would lie in his hut and think about sharing his nights with a woman. There would be no shortage of offers, he knew that. Though he was a slave he was healthy, with no broken or diseased limbs, and he was still capable of trotting all day with a war party. He had all of his hair, his teeth were still good and he was certainly capable of siring the beautiful, light-skinned half-breed children many women wanted to bear. But he did nothing more than dream about it.

That autumn he travelled once again with the tribe to the big lagoon on the Wairau to spend a month hunting ducks. The exercise strengthened him and the change refreshed him, and by the time he returned he was reconciled to spending another winter alone and more determined than ever to escape in the following year. He would go in the spring when the weather would be better, food would be easier to find and the ground would be warmer, he decided. It worried him that he was getting on in age and would soon start to lose his fitness and stamina. Then he would have no choice but to stay.

He had given his age much thought of late. As far as he could figure he was around forty-five years old, not yet an old man but not young either. He was ten years older than Tama had been when they first met, and he had spent nearly thirty of his years among the Maori, although it didn't seem that long since he had come ashore with the sealing party in Dusky Sound. Often as he drifted off to sleep in the darkness of his little hut he thought of his first wife Marama, remembering their first wonderful days and nights together. He wondered if she was well and if she still thought of her Goblin husband.

He was woken suddenly one morning by whoops and screams and the clash of weapons. In the few seconds that he lay and listened before he leapt for the musket by his side he realized that, unbelievable though it seemed, the island was under attack. He ducked through the low door of his hut and worked his way down to the edge of a terrace overlooking the beach. In the dim grey light he could just make out a swirl of fighting bodies on the sand. He could not distinguish between friend and foe, but among the howls and screams of the fighters he distinctly heard the thud of stone on bone and skull.

A canoe swooped in from the open sea and ran up onto the beach. He quickly realized that the warriors pouring over the side of the canoe were attacking the island and almost without thinking he threw his musket to his shoulder and blew one of the invaders clear off his feet to land dead in the shallow water. He had already reloaded before the warrior's heels stopped drumming on the side of his canoe. With the ease of long practice his hands flew through the tasks – powder, ball, ramrod, priming, cock the action and fire. It was smooth and mechanical and when his weapon flashed again another warrior dropped his patu and spun like a top with a fountain of blood gushing from his chest.

Lafe loaded, chose another target and fired, again and again until he seemed to have gone on for most of the morning. The battle ebbed and flowed across the beach, at times the attackers appearing almost to reach the village before they were pushed back to the water's edge. Sometimes a musket ball would penetrate two warriors at once in the tightly-packed ranks of the enemy.

Finally he saw that the tide had turned and the surviving invaders were trying to re-launch their canoes. Some in their despair began swimming out to sea in the direction of the mainland while the fighting continued on the beach. Above the shrieks, groans and thuds of battle Te Rauparaha's voice rang out as he ordered his canoes out to take up the pursuit of those trying to escape. Lafe moved down to the beach with his musket and bayonet to join the fray, and soon the last of the attackers was dispatched to the land of ghosts.

The beach was covered in bodies of friend and foe alike, locked together in the great dance of death while the survivors staggered like drunken men leaning on each other for support. When the bodies of his enemy were all laid out in rows an angry Te Rauparaha marched up and down swearing and cursing them. He clicked his tongue with approval when he saw the toll of enemy warriors killed by Lafe's musket. His men had been woken so suddenly that they had instinctively seized their patu and any other weapons at hand and leapt into the fray, leaving their unloaded muskets hanging back in their huts.

Lafe stared at all the bodies and thought of the blood he had shed once again when he had promised himself he would not fire at another man. He would not berate himself too harshly, however, because he had fought only for his own survival. Te Rauparaha's enemies would have shown no mercy towards the Goblin who kept the Ngati Toa armoury functioning.

'My hands are red with blood once more,' he told old Rua sombrely, 'but I had no thought to stop shooting until the last one was dead. I have never loaded so cleanly and fired so swiftly in all my life.'

'If you had not, we might all be lying dead on the beach instead of them,' Rua replied. He had watched the battle from the terrace when all the rest of the slaves had fled. It would be talked about around the fires of the country for years, this battle on the beach at Kapiti. It was said that early that morning the great chief Te Rauparaha himself had been woken by a dream, and in his dream he was swooped on by a great black hawk. He caught it and broke its neck and this was what had woken him from his dream, this premonition that he was about to be attacked by a real enemy.

He had already begun to muster his warriors when the attack began and so he was almost ready and had managed to beat off the first wave of attackers. But for those few minutes of warning the battle would have been lost.

His attackers were his own allies who had become afraid of his ever-growing power and had gathered their war party in secret on the mainland.

'Now they will know my anger!' Te Rauparaha told his gathered people. When the canoes returned from pursuing the enemy they related the slaughter that had taken place on the sea and reported that the fish would dine well for weeks. Many of their attackers had abandoned their canoes and taken to the water, attempting to swim to the mainland or drown rather than be taken, for they knew that if they fell into Te Rauparaha's hands their lives would be long and filled with pain.

Because of his actions that day Lafe was no longer treated as a slave. His status had changed and he was no longer required to work in the gardens although he would still fix the muskets as there was no one on the island who could do it better. The greatest honour of all was one he would rather have forgone. He was invited to join the cannibal feast that night and offered the best titbits of human flesh from the cooked bodies of their enemies. He forced himself to nibble on what was offered, keeping his expression bland and his feelings of disgust to himself.

Things were looking up.

Chapter 19

When spring came Lafe went back to work in the gardens. He liked the peace and quiet of the terraced plots and the smell of the earth and he was sharpening a metal hoe, one of the few the tribe now owned, when he saw one of the minor war chiefs making in his direction. He knew what was coming and his heart lurched. For the last week he had watched the preparations going on all over the island as food was sorted and packed and the war canoes were refurbished. Now the young chief stood before him and touched him on the shoulder.

'Be ready!' he ordered roughly. 'In two days we go to war.'

'This is an honour I can do without,' Lafe muttered under his breath as he watched the warrior stride away down the rows of the garden without a backward glance. But now that he knew he was included in the ope he could begin to put his own plans into action. He hated the thought of more killing but in the last few days he had begun to fear that he would be left behind after all.

He had spent all that winter planning his escape, choosing first one plan and then discarding it as too risky and working out another. Instead of spending most of the winter in his bed as the others did, he had spent the long hours walking and climbing all over the island. His new status as almost a warrior and the freedom he enjoyed as a result had helped, and although his strange new habits had raised eyebrows, nobody had told him to stop. As a consequence he had greeted the spring as a healthier, fitter and happier man than he had been since he was first taken to the island. Now the moment he had been preparing for had come, he was as ready as he would ever be.

He went home to his hut and began to pack the items he had carefully fashioned or stolen and stored for this day. He had a warm cloak, fishing lines and iron hooks, extra powder and shot and, last of all, a good knife and a small axe he had made during the winter. All he needed now was the food he would have to steal in the last few days before he made his break.

They were going to war against his old foe Ngai Tahu, the only really powerful tribe left on Te Wai Pounamu, although even Ngai Tahu's forces were not as powerful as they had been in the years before the Eat Relations War that had set faction against faction, family against family. Apparently Te Rauparaha had decided to attack the northern-most enclave of the Ngai Tahu at Kaikoura. Word had come to his ears that a chief called Rerewhaka had made a rash threat against him, threatening to gut the Ngati Toa chief with a shark's tooth if he ever passed that way. Such an insult could not be ignored and so the war trumpets, fashioned from huge seashells, began to wail.

Soon the excitement of the choosing of the warriors was over and the canoes were packed and ready to leave. Thirty or more slaves were ordered into the canoes as well. Just in case we run out of vittles, Lafe guessed. This time he was determined to escape, but he would wait for the confusion of the homeward voyage as the best time to make his break for freedom. Despite the danger that lay ahead he made up his mind he would never return to Kapiti.

The war fleet crossed the Windpipe and crept down the east coast, never quite able to trust the spring weather, until they reached the great lagoon at Wairau. They rested there for a few weeks, building up their food reserves by catching eels and fish and collecting the eggs of the many wildfowl around the lagoon. Finally they set off again towards the south. Lafe studied the coastline and the mountains as the canoes passed by, remembering them from that long ago voyage of the *Northern Lights* and wondered if he would ever pass that way again.

Not many other places on earth had such wonderful mountains, he decided as the canoes glided along the coast. From the bench where he swung his paddle he could crane his neck to see the snowy tops that pierced the clouds, and when he brought his eyes down he could follow the forest-covered slopes that ran all the way down to the white sand beaches where the land was swallowed up by the deep blue Pacific. This chief who had so rashly insulted the war lord of the Windpipe was, Lafe presumed, from that same tribe that Cook had seen sitting in their canoes in the shadow of that beautiful mountain range. It would be a pity to shatter the peace and beauty of such a spot, but he knew that soon the fighting would start and the peace would be over.

From well up the coast they could see the location of the enemy village. Ngai Tahu were not prepared for war. Smoke rose into the still air from cooking fires burning behind the great wooden palisade that had protected this tribe for many years, and looking up at the fort Lafe saw that it was well built and powerful. It was also big enough to hold a lot of fighting men and he suspected that it would take many weeks to take it.

The canoes formed into a fan that spread out over the ocean and headed directly for the small beach below the fort where already the enemy had gathered to oppose their landing. As he watched, Lafe saw more and more fighting men race to the beach and he could not understand why they did not fight from within the palisade. There was a splatter of musket fire that fell among the canoes but no paddler missed a single stroke as the attackers sped towards the beach at a tremendous pace, and as they hit the sand and leapt from their canoes more and more warriors poured out of the fort and joined the fighting. The battle ebbed and flowed along the shore, and Lafe loaded and fired his musket as quickly as ever although he was sure he never hit a target and was happy with that.

The two warlords, Te Rauparaha and Rerewhaka, faced each other in personal hand-to-hand combat and finally the Ngati Toa chief laid his enemy low. Then the enemy retreat began and the battle turned into a massacre, the Ngai Tahu warriors chopped down like corn as they tried to retreat. By noon the fighting was over and all that could be heard was the wailing of the widows and children.

Lafe walked the shores and the hillside where most of the fighting had taken place and saw huge numbers of dead. He guessed that the village had once held nearly a thousand people, and nearly all of them had been killed. The few who survived and escaped would never come back to this place again after such a defeat, their unhappy memories and fear of unquiet spirits keeping them away as surely as a physical barrier. Soon the fort would begin to decay, logs falling from the great palisade year by year until it resembled a gap-toothed old woman and was just as powerless.

'Hundreds of years of human progress gone in a morning,' Lafe murmured sadly to himself.

'We have made this fort fit only for the ghosts and its gardens for the wild pig to root in,' one of the victors boasted and Lafe could only agree with him. It was so true. This didn't feel like a victory to him, more like a murder. The defenders had lost the battle in the first hour as they had not been able to stand against the well- practised and confident Ngati Toa army. As far as the eye could see groups of warriors were spread out across the hillside, still killing people they flushed from the scrub and rocks where they had hidden. It took a long time to murder a village full of people, Lafe realized as he waited for it to finish.

'When the battle has finished, the murder has just begun,' Lafe said to the boastful warrior, whose only reply was a look of puzzled incomprehension tinged with suspicion. The words were too subtle for him to grasp. 'I mean that I hope you are very happy with this day's work,' Lafe said dryly.

'Oh yes, it is a very good day indeed.' The man grinned, showing a mouthful of perfectly white teeth that looked very very sharp to Lafe. He shuddered and looked away quickly, only to see two slave women carving great lumps of red meat from the buttocks of a dead warrior.

He began looking for the enemy muskets that would be part of the spoils, remembering an old saying from his past life. To the victor go the spoils of war. He had never truly considered the words in all their ramifications.

By evening some order had fallen over the battlefield and the great fires were lit near the beach, throwing a garish light over the whole

357

scene. Then the real celebrations began and for several days and nights the carousing and woman-taking went on until the whole camp was exhausted and slept the sleep of the victorious. After fifteen or eighteen hours of sleep Te Rauparaha and a group of his best warriors shook themselves back into a state of alertness and headed south to trade for greenstone. The rest of the ope prepared for the journey home, gathering together the captured canoes and loading them with the fittest looking young men and the most attractive young girls among the prisoners.

Were these the lucky ones, Lafe wondered? They were spared the killing that followed the fall of their village but instead, still suffering from the shock of defeat and the deaths of their loved ones, they faced the indignities of slavery and he felt very sorry for them.

It was a large fleet that began the journey back to Kapiti, the jubilant and happy warriors already looking forward to a heroes' welcome. They camped once again at the lagoon on the Wairau River to catch and gather food and wait for Te Rauparaha, who would rejoin them before they continued the voyage north to the Windpipe.

During these days of waiting Lafe sat near the trail that led to the lagoon. He pretended to work on the locks of several damaged muskets that he had salvaged, but really he was watching the newly-captured women and girls as they passed along the trail to fetch water from the lagoon. Often they would steal a few minutes at the water's edge to bathe themselves after being badly handled by their captors, and he saw that most of them took the trail with their heads down. These were women who had already given up the fight and taken on the mental burden of slavery, and he discarded them in his mind as soon as he saw the defeat in them.

Finally the one he was looking for came down the trail. She was still a young woman and the way she held her body showed she had spirit. She held her head high and looked ready to spit in his eye, but he was prepared to bet his life that she was even more ready to escape the indignity she was suffering in the hands of Te Rauparaha's hard, lusty warriors. He watched from a distance as several men claimed her favours during the day, taking her one after the other to their chosen hut. She did not flinch or cower when she was taken, but Lafe could sense the build

358

up of anger in her every time she walked past him and down the path to the lagoon to bathe again.

.   That evening, while the feasting and dancing went on and the great driftwood fires blazed, he gathered the last of the food supplies he needed. He stored them in two flax kits complete with pack straps that he had stolen from a couple of slaves and hidden deep in the straw in one of the huts.

Later while food was still being served and eaten by the fire he removed his two kits from their hiding place, crept down to the lagoon and hid them under the leaves of a flax bush. Next he retrieved a paddle that he had stolen from a carefully- guarded hut earlier that day. There were two small fishing canoes on the lagoon, floating next to the bank and tied bow-on to stakes driven into the soft sand, and he had earlier made the decision to take them both. He would paddle one and tow the other to the centre of the lagoon then cast it adrift to delay the pursuit.

For a long time he crouched silently in the scrub watching the trail back to the village, waiting to see if he had been followed, but finally he accepted that everything was as it should be. He checked the sky and saw that the moon would be up in another two hours. Then he melted back into the shadows, circling until he reached the back of the huts again. He crouched there, watching the woman he had picked and reviewing all the plans he had made so far. This was a moment of uncertainty, for he was not yet sure that taking the woman with him was a good idea.

There were things both for and against the plan. On the one hand she would slow him down. She might even refuse to walk at all and then he would have to kill her to protect himself. On the other hand though, two pairs of hands and eyes made the finding of food much more certain. Maori women were trained from the time they could walk to find the foods they could rely on for survival and she would have other skills like the making of sandals and clothing and the preparation of certain foods and medicines that they would need to stay healthy. The most basic reason of all was that two people wrapped up in a cloak generated a lot more heat than one, and in the mountains where he was heading that was important.

His musket lay near at hand, his knife was in his belt and his tomahawk was in his hand. He hefted it, practising a few swings at an imaginary head while he waited. It was necessary to his plans that a warrior would choose the girl for the night and take her to his bed. As he watched, a group of men rose from their meal and looked towards the captive women. She was one of the first chosen and a big man dragged her by the hand towards his hut. Lafe followed them quietly into the darkness, staying in the shadows thrown by the little huts.

He sat outside and waited again, listening without wanting to, hearing the grunts and groans of the warrior's vigorous mating through the thin grass wall that separated them. It seemed to take a long time for the warrior to reach a noisy climax and then fall asleep, his belly full of flesh and lovemaking. Through the thatch Lafe heard the man's soft breathing change to snores as the used and discarded girl wept quietly in the farthest corner of the hut.

With an unexpected suddenness the moon hauled itself over the horizon and bathed the village in the soft light that Lafe was waiting for. He rose quickly and crouched as he stepped carefully through the door of the little hut. He heard the catch in the girl's breathing and knew she had seen him but was frozen into silence, hoping against hope that he was not another warrior come to stake a claim on her bruised body.

A little shaft of moonlight filtered through the hole in the wall that let the stale odours out of the hut, and when his eyes adjusted to the gloom he could make out the sleeping man's head. In his heightened state of excitement at the danger he was in, Lafe was almost overwhelmed by the smell of stale sweat and the rank smell of semen in the air. He raised the tomahawk, reversing the blade, and without a single qualm he used it like a hammer and struck the warrior firmly on the temple. Then he dropped the weapon, jumped quickly to the girl's side and clamped his hand over her mouth. Briefly he felt a scream build up against his hand but only a small squeal escaped as he began talking to her urgently, telling her that he was a friend and would do her no harm if she behaved.

'Do not fear me,' he whispered into her hair. 'If you remain quiet when I take my hand away from your mouth, I will help you to escape from this place. But if you do not I will have to kill you. Do you understand?'.

He gave her a minute to feel the power of his will.

'Nod your head if you agree not to cry out,' he urged her. Thankfully, he felt the nod of her head and gently removed his hands but let them linger on her throat as he listened for any sound of alarm outside the hut. He could feel her nakedness under his hands and the knowledge sent a jolt of hot blood right through his loins.

'Put on your robe. Quickly now!' he told her, straining to hear any sounds of alarm or disturbance. He need not have worried. All he could hear from the little huts nearby were the rich sounds of sex, the groans, howls, moans and weeping which made this night ideal for his plans.   He held the girl by the wrist as he reached out his other hand and touched the warrior's temple where he had struck him. There was a large depression where the skull was broken and, though loud snoring noises came out of the man's mouth and his feet kicked ineffectually on the grass floor, he was done for, Lafe decided. He was never sure just how thick a warrior's skull was and he had seen many recover from serious knocks.

'Will you walk to the lagoon or do I have to tie you and carry you?' he asked the girl. To his relief she agreed she would walk, and with a firm grip of her hand he stepped out into the moonlight. He let her see the wicked blade of the tomahawk before he slipped it into his belt, and with his spare hand he snatched up his musket from where it leaned against the side of a hut. He hoped that anyone seeing them in the bright moonlight would think it was just a warrior and a woman out for a stroll. People living in such close little villages learned to see many things without actually seeing them and to listen without hearing what they were not supposed to hear.

No one tried to stop them or demanded to know where they were going as they walked hand in hand down the trail to the lagoon. At the water's edge Lafe moved quietly but awkwardly, holding the girl's hand tight in his own while he used his other hand to put his belongings in the canoe. All the time he strained his ears to hear if anyone was following them down the track in the dark.

They were lucky. Only one sentry had been posted to guard the paddles, and from where he stood outside one of the huts he could not see the trail down to the lagoon. Te Rauparaha and his war party had successfully defeated all of the major tribes for many days' walk in any direction, and they had become complacent about any risk of attack.

Lafe eased the girl into the canoe and clambered in beside her, and they paddled away from the shore with the second canoe following in their wake. He was alarmed at how dangerous their situation had become. Once they were a little way from the shore the lagoon was lit up as bright as day by the moon and he could see every detail of the little village on the bank. Someone had only to glance out from the village and they couldn't help but see the two captives making their escape. This crossing of the lagoon was the most dangerous part of the plan but, although the hairs on the back of Lafe's neck stood straight up on end and every fibre of his being was tensed in anticipation, no alarm was raised. He cast off the second canoe in the middle of the lagoon for the errant breeze to take it where it wished.

Once they were out of earshot of the village he told the girl in a quiet but urgent voice that he would take her to the mountains where they would hide for perhaps a year, and then he would take her to try and find the rest of her people.

'You have to trust me and I you, because we are now both orphans in this part of the country,' he told her. 'Without a tribe to protect us, every man's hand will be against us.'

He could see she was puzzled by him. There would have been whispers about the tattooed Goblin who had left his own people.

'Why do you wear the tattoo of another tribe?' she asked suspiciously.

'Because I was a slave too,' Lafe told her. He had no time to explain further. He had done what he could to gain her confidence in the short time he had while they crossed the lagoon, and it was up to her now. If this girl decided to make trouble when they got to the other shore he would have to leave her or kill her, and neither option was a good one. He decided he needed to risk everything to gain her confidence.

'When the canoe touches the far shore I will climb out first, and for the time it takes to have ten breaths you will be free to escape if you wish,' he told her. 'But if you want to run, look first at what you have just come from and think what the rest of your life will be like. Think of the lives of the children you will certainly bear to those warriors whose slave you will be.

'Then look at the mountains in the distance where we are heading and think of this promise I give you. I promise you freedom.' He could not look at her, nor she at him, but as he whispered these words he tried desperately to convey in his voice a sense of hope.

When the canoe gently nudged into the far bank, Lafe looked steadily at the girl and reached for his pack and musket.

'Stay,' she said softly. She stood up and in one fluid movement dropped her robe in the bottom of the canoe, slipped quietly over the side into the waist deep water and guided the canoe into an old dried riverbed. Lafe waited quietly on the bank as she gathered a handful of soft fern and scrubbed the smell and the semen of her tormentors from her body, dabbing tenderly at her painful loins before climbing out of the water and putting on her cloak again. Then between them they cast the canoe out into the lagoon and began to climb up an old dry riverbed, carefully placing each foot on the smooth river rocks that would leave no track for the scouts to follow.

The moon was well up, and as they climbed the low foothills they could look back on the camp that still slumbered quietly down below them. The moon that had so recently been their greatest danger was now a big help, allowing Lafe to choose a place to leave the stream bed, and they were careful to leave no trace of their exit when they jumped across from the rocks onto the grass.

Lafe knew that when his escape was discovered Te Rauparaha's men would expect him to have gone north or west, back to the country where his tribe lived, and that was where they would send their fastest scouts after him. Instead he turned south, using the stars of the Southern Cross that hung in the sky before him. These were the stars so loved by navigators when they crossed the equator, and by the boat people when

363

they journeyed around the coast, and now they would be his guides. The girl was a good walker even with the spare kit strapped to her back, and soon the lagoon was left far behind as they climbed steadily into the dry, grass-covered hills.

As they climbed Lafe tried to put himself into the minds of the scouts who would be on his trail by morning. They would fan out, climbing to the tops of the highest points around the valley, and then wait for their quarry to make the next move. The scouts were chosen for their abilities to move fast in hard country for weeks if need be, and in the end few people ever escaped them. They were truly a terrifying force and he cringed when he thought of those men on his trail and of what it would mean if he and the girl fell into their hands.

His plan was to climb and keep on climbing, always hoping to remain above the scouts, and to move only at night to take away the advantage the open grasslands gave to their pursuers. In the distance he could see the snow covered peaks of a range of mountains that dominated the skyline and the highest was Tapuaenuku. That was where he was heading, and if he had to he would take the girl with him right up to the snow line. For sheer dominance none of the other mountains came near to Tapuaenuku, none of her brothers or sisters had such a lofty crown, and she carried a year-round coating of snow that slid down her shoulders into the upper valleys. The route Lafe chose that night was a long, steady climb to a range of hilltops that were not quite mountains, and with every step they moved higher and closer to their destination.

He watched the girl closely and when she showed signs of tiring he called a halt so they could lie on the dry grass and rest the twitching muscles in their legs. They sipped good water from a gourd and nibbled some of the dried eel that Lafe had lifted from the drying racks that day before forcing themselves to move on again. For the first time they dared to talk while they rested, and Lafe had his chance to ask her name and briefly tell her of his plans. He explained how a Goblin like himself had come to the country, spoke of the people he called his own in Murderers' Bay and explained how he came to be with the Ngati Toa from Kapiti. She had never seen a white man before but her tribe knew of the Goblins who lived with Maori in the north.

364

'Now you must tell me of yourself,' he urged.

'I am Rima,' she said simply, 'because I was my father's fifth daughter. My family were of high birth and my father was a warrior of importance in our tribe.' Her eyes filled with tears and he guessed that she had watched her father die on the beach that day. The time would come for her to mourn her family, but it was not yet. Survival was their first priority.

'I will do anything to escape the degradation that was my lot with those dogs back at the lagoon.' she told Lafe softly. 'I will follow you gladly and be grateful. I have spent much of my life in hills such as these, collecting the wild roots and berries that my people relied on.'

Lafe was relieved that he had made such a good choice. Her time in the hills had given her body strength and suppleness, her long legs carried her well in this hard country and although she was tiring she had not begun to stumble or fall. When the first lightening of the sky in the east promised that dawn was not far away, he let her rest more often. They had conquered the first range of hills and could no longer look back on the lagoon. Though he was tiring too he urged her on after each brief stop, calculating that it would be at least midday before the scouts could gain sufficient height to make further travel dangerous.

The dry hills of the Wairau were almost a desert at this time of the year, the short dry grass brown and brittle underfoot and dusty to the touch. All there was to relieve the browns and greys of the countryside they were travelling through were the small pieces of dark green forest tucked away in the dampness of the stream beds. The girl stumbled more often as the sun climbed across the sky, but she still put many more miles under her feet before Lafe chose a place to lie up.

Several times he looked closely at a possible hideout and there were many such places, little stream beds stretching down the hillside in the distance with good stands of native forest on either bank, but he stayed well away from them, searching instead until he found a very nondescript, ugly little gully a little way off the main ridge. It contained only a jumble of large rocks and a few scrubby trees and he chose it for the very good reason that nobody else would have done so. It did not have water, sheltering trees or any other desirable features for a man on the run. Those devils of scouts who would be following could almost see into their quarry's minds, and he knew that a frightened man would always choose the best and safest-looking place to hide.

He and Rima moved in a wide circle around the patch of scrub he had chosen and entered it at its lower edge where the sign of their entry would not be seen from the ridge above. Carefully he stood all the grass back up again to hide the gap, adding little pieces of dead scrub until he was satisfied that it would pass all but the closest attention of the scouts. Crawling along under the scrub toward the centre of the gully he found a large tree with the wickedest mass of thorns on it that he had ever seen on any growing thing. He suspected that it was the matagouri that the Maori talked of, and he had to admit he had never seen a more lethal looking thorn in his whole life.

'All barefooted people have to have immense respect for this thorn, is that not so, Rima?' he asked. He held up one of the thorns, full four inches long and barbed. His own feet were as hard as leather, as he had been barefoot nearly as long as he had been in the country, but he feared those thorns. They could lame a man.

Beyond the thorn tree was a large rock, one side looking as if it had been sliced with a knife to form an overhang that gave shade and a little cover from the weather. The canopy of the thorn nearly completely covered the rock, making it a formidable place for any enemy to approach except by crawling in along the same path as Lafe had come, and between the trunk of the thorn and the rock was a small piece of level ground that would allow the two of them to stretch out in the shade of the rock.

He crawled to the rock, carefully picking the thorns out of his path, and used a small piece of scrub to sweep the space clear. Then he jammed the water gourd, refilled a few miles back at a tarn left by the last rains, into a deep fissure in the rock. Rima crawled into the shade and joined him, too tired even to chew the piece of fish he offered. All she wanted was to take a sip of water and close her eyes.

It was a relief to be off their feet and in the shade. Even the earth was deliciously cool under the rock while out in the open the hot, breathless day continued to burn the remaining life out of the grass hills. With good water not far away and plenty of dried fish in their packs,

Lafe was for the moment, quite content to play the waiting game. They allowed themselves another piece of dried eel and a few sips of water each, then rolled themselves in their robes and they were soon deep in exhausted sleep. He woke near evening and listened for an hour, but nothing disturbed the evening song of the birds in the nearby forest and he knew they were safe for this night anyway. He slept again, waking on and off until the sky started to pale in the east and he could sleep no more. Tama's people had taught him that sleep could be hoarded, a little put aside each day against times to come when sleep might be in very short supply.

The girl began to wake, and out of the corner of his eye he watched her leave the gentler world of dreams and come to grips with the reality of where she was and how she had got there. He saw the sadness wash over her face as the memories of the last week came flooding back into her mind, and he felt her despair. He wished that he had the magic the tohunga claimed for themselves so he could place her back in her village and return it all to the way it had been before the attack, but he did not have those powers so he set out to try with a little kindness to make her burdens lighter. He passed her the water and some dried fish.

'Did you sleep well, Rima?' he whispered.

'I did,' she replied, slowly chewing a little of the fish and looking about her. 'Thank you.' Her robe fell from her shoulders as she ate and beneath it she wore only a short kilt of flax and grasses around her waist. Lafe looked at her well-formed breasts and tried to guess her age. Maori never bothered to count their years on earth so he did not ask her.

'Were you taken to wife before the attack on your village?' he asked her politely.

'No.' There was a deep hurt behind the word. Her first mating had been every woman's nightmare, brutal and terrifying. There were four different stages of development for women in the tribes; a girl child grew up to be a girl awaiting marriage, then a married woman and finally an elder. As an unmarried girl Rima would be between fourteen and sixteen years of age and she was lucky in many ways, Lafe decided. She would get over her losses far quicker than a woman who had lost her husband and children in battle. She was young, resilient and healthy, but that was why he had chosen her from among the rest of the women anyway. She was also pleasing to look at, he decided, and she seemed to have a disposition to match. Perhaps they had both been lucky.

He told her that he was planning to cross the valley of the Awatere when he felt it was safe and then to climb Tapuaenuku. The girl admitted that she was afraid of this mountain, which was sacred to her people, but she did not say that she would not follow.

'We will travel again tonight,' he told her. 'Again we will have the moon to guide us, and that will put us within reach of the river in two more nights.'

They left as soon as the moon was up, picking a ridge that took them in the direction they wished to travel. After several hours Lafe realized that he had chosen one of the main ridges heading out of the hills toward the southwest, a good route as far as ease of travel went, but it was much more dangerous and he knew he should have chosen a much lesser ridge to follow. Quitting the ridge top now would be too difficult as the sides became progressively covered in forest and scrub and it was as black under the canopy of the forest as the inside of a cave. The soft snow grass muffled their footsteps and the moonlight allowed them to make good progress so they travelled in near complete silence, with only a touch of the hand here and there to reassure each other that they were all right.

Lafe smelt the scout before he heard or saw him, but in the few heartbeats that it took for his nose to recognize the smells of fat and smoke that clung to the scout's clothing it was nearly too late. The man exploded from his nest in the lee of a large rock like a wild boar from his den, his patu stabbing for Lafe's temple. There was no time to cock and fire his musket so in pure reflex Lafe jabbed at the black mass of the other man's body with the barrel, gouging a path across his ribcage with enough force to deflect the blow that would have ended his travels on this earth then and there. But the scout still had the power to knock Lafe off his feet and he blindly grabbed for the other man's robe as they both rolled down the incline locked together. Lafe lost his musket in the tumble and now he didn't dare let go of his attacker. He stabbed for his enemy's eyes with both thumbs, felt the patu crash against his face as they rolled together and knew it still dangled from its thong on the warrior's wrist. His only chance was to stay in too close for his opponent to use it. They were brought up against a large rock and for a few seconds Lafe managed to finish up on top but the younger man was very strong and oily and with a massive heave he rolled Lafe over and pinned him to the ground.

This was to be his undoing. His hands sought the soft part of Lafe's neck while his thumbs sunk deeply into the folds under his victim's jawbone and he squeezed until Lafe's eyes started from his head. But Rima had scrambled down after them and found a good footing and just at that moment she measured the distance to the back of the warrior's neck with her eye and swung the digging stick she had carved out of a root, wielding it like an axe to strike a double handed blow.

Lafe felt the hit through the scout's fingers, still deeply imbedded in his neck, and felt his opponent's power start to weaken. Rima struck another blow and when Lafe managed to struggle free and drag some air back into his empty lungs she finished their attacker off by bashing his brains out with a large stone. Lafe sat panting helplessly, while Rima gave him little sips of water to ease his tortured throat. Apart from some bruising he seemed to have been lucky, and he quickly established that his working parts were all functioning again.

'I am obliged to you for your help, Rima,' he told the girl quietly. 'Nobody could have chosen a better friend than you.'

Together they climbed back up to the ridge top and examined their ambusher's bed. It was plain that they had stumbled upon him while he was still asleep as his robe still lay on a bed of soft snow grass in the lee of a boulder that broke the night breezes. This ridge, as Lafe had suspected, was one of the main routes out of the area and the scout had watched it by day and slept close enough to it during the night so that no one would pass without him knowing.

'It seems he slept a little too deeply tonight,' Rima said, answering the question that was on both their minds. 'We were fortunate.'

They dragged the dead man into the thick undergrowth and hid his body, taking only his food and weapons. They were anxious to cover some distance before first light, as they knew that they had knocked a hole in the cordon around them and now had a good chance of slipping through. But the scout had shown unerring ability when he managed to pick the exact route that they had chose to escape by, and where there was one there would be others. They had to keep moving fast.

After two nights of picking their way across the grass hills and two days of resting without incident, Lafe chose a ridge that began to lose height and take them down towards the river in the valley below. From the heights he had been able to study the country where they were heading. This fast-flowing Awatere drained a large area of upland grass and tussock. Barren looking hills stretched away into the distance, and beyond were the dark blue snow-capped ranges he hoped to reach.

That night they waded the river, threw their belongings onto the bank and had a thoroughly good bath, though a hurried one. The water was stingingly cold but it cleaned and refreshed them before they climbed again, wanting to get as high up the far side of the valley as they could before sunrise. It was harder going now as they picked their way through scrub and a lethal sort of spiny plant whose leaves hardened in the sun to form a dangerous spear.

Once the river was behind them Lafe started to breathe easier. He knew the scouts would pursue an enemy to the ends of the earth and they had Te Rauparaha to face if they returned empty-handed, but every night's march made the search area that much larger.

Once they began to sidle the faces of the mountains again he felt safer and started to think about finding more food. They would soon have to travel in the daylight hours so that they could forage for birds and whatever else the country offered. Lafe was delighted to find that even in these dry grasslands that there were signs of pigs passing through. They were so far from the place where Cook had first turned them free and yet here they were, busy turning over the soil and raising their families.

'Food of the gods and food for hungry travellers,' he told Rima happily. 'Soon we will be able to stop running and have a fire again.' The thought of being able to hunt again and even eat pork fat and skin crisped over a fire spurred them both on and they moved fast and easily across the vast landscape.

370

They found the courage to move in daylight, setting their sights on a little patch of forest in the headwaters of a stream high on the shoulder of Tapuaenuku. They spotted it first in the early afternoon and Lafe decided they would build a camp there and have a fire to cook their first hot food in nearly a week. There was a little of the fish left and during the day Rima had proved her skills at snaring weka. She had unfastened a few feathers from her cloak and fastened them to the end of a long, thin stick, one of two she had been carrying from the river crossing for just that purpose. At the tip of the other stick she fastened a little running noose made out of a piece of cord. When she was in position she blew across a blade of flax held between her two thumbs and the squark she made brought two curious weka along to investigate. They stalked into view with their beady eyes darting all around, intent on doing battle with this strange bird that had taken up residence on their land, and their supercilious expressions left no doubt about who owned this patch of bush.

When Rima held the stick with the bunch of feathers on the end and shook it in their direction, the birds became infuriated and began to attack it. She held the noose in front of the feathers and kept both sticks dancing in front of them, and it was only a matter of time before one weka put its head in the noose. Quickly she dragged it in and wrung its neck, handing it to Lafe to deal with while she manipulated her sticks again. The second bird retreated only a few paces, and when the flax whistle was blown and the lure shaken in its face it threw caution to the winds and attacked the feathers again. It was just as quickly caught and dispatched into Lafe's food pack.

Lafe had eaten many weka since he had come to this country and it was as good as any chicken he could remember from his other life. The poor weka could never learn to keep his head out of trouble, a trait that all Maori were grateful for. Just when the supply of food at a traveller's camp was at its lowest point this little brown bird would stalk in, stare at every person and every new thing as if it had never seen anything so odd in its life, then pick up any object that caught its fancy and carry it off to the forest. This curiosity would bring the weka fearlessly within reach of its own cooking fire and right under the noses of people who considered it delicious eating, but no matter how many thousands of weka were roasted on the fires there never seemed to be any less in the forest.

Just before dark the two travellers climbed the last slope to the campsite they had chosen on a sheltered terrace under the forest canopy. While Lafe cut grass for their roof and beds, Rima quickly lashed saplings together and bent them into a frame for the hut. They lit their fire under the trees so the smoke would waft through the branches and not leave a column that could be seen for miles, and before long the plucked and gutted weka were braising over the embers.

There had been more than a week of fine, hot weather, but now the cirrus clouds Lafe knew as mares' tails streaked the sky overhead, telling them that soon the weather would change. They would sit out the bad weather here and rest up while it lasted.

'To sit again in front of a fire that banishes the chill from the air, and stare into its embers is one of life's great pleasures, don't you think?' he asked Rima. 'And to turn a goodly-sized weka slowly over that fire is another,' he added grandly. He was in a fine mood. Now that he was sure their pursuit was far behind them they could travel at their own speed and enjoy the countryside as they passed through it. They would continue to be watchful, however. He knew Te Rauparaha would be angry and vengeful and that he was a marked man as far as Ngati Toa and their allies were concerned, but he guessed that the old chief was shrewd enough to let him keep. Right now the warlord from Kapiti had bigger fish to fry.

When the storm had passed, he and Rima chose without haste a direction of travel and began their wanderings. These were the high alpine grasslands they travelled over, with tall yellow grasses and tussock that came up to the hunter's knees and reflected the heat of the sun back onto his body. It was hot, dry country here in the middle of summer and any breeze set the hill faces alive with movement as the sun-dried grasses danced and swayed with each gust. The only shade in this country was by the huge, lonely boulders left behind by the sea, or perhaps a glacier, and sometimes in a day's march they passed very small stands of forest clinging to the damp gullies where they had been spared by the fires had swept across the hills many times in the past. Why they had been spared Lafe did not know, but each of these patches of forest contained a family or two of weka and so the couple travelled, as had the tribes before them for many generations, from weka to weka.

'It is his extreme misfortune that the gods made him so good to eat, and at the same time gave him his wicked curiosity and that sense that somehow he lives as an equal with the human race,' Rima chuckled as they snared another fine bird.

It was good country to travel through, with ample water, and the great golden meadows allowed the man and woman to put good miles beneath their feet. They moved only when the food was finished in an area where they had camped and they went wherever the search for food took them but the trend was always westward, still climbing toward the head of the Awatere and the great range that was the backbone of the island.

Every morning Tapuaenuku was there to greet them, and as they got higher and began to stalk across her northern slopes they travelled only on the best days when her tops were clear. There were many wonderful mountains in constant view as they travelled, none more impressive than this one but they all tried to outdo each other in their splendour. Each day the travellers sought nothing more than to make a little distance to the west and to find enough food to sustain themselves for another day. If they were successful in both endeavours they went to sleep happy, and if not they consoled themselves that better times were ahead. It was seldom that they lay down with completely empty bellies; the country always provided something for their evening meal but it was not always enough.

This was the high grass country, eyes-wide-open country where they could not afford to miss the smallest sign of food. The behaviour of a bird could lead to its nest and every bend of a stream or bank of a small pond was searched diligently. Often the bird or fish they needed turned up in the last hour of the day just when they had became certain that they would be curled up in their robes with sunken bellies that night. The food supply was seldom large enough to warrant building a hut and staying, so if the night looked fine they made a soft grass bed and covered it with Lafe's cloak. It was old now but was still a good cloak, and they spread Rima's cloak over the top of them. This was newer, beautiful and warm with the feathers of many birds woven into its fabric, and they went to sleep each night huddled in each other's arms. They had become lovers easily and naturally, growing close during the long days they spent together travelling, hunting and helping each other. Now they comforted and sustained each other through the long nights and were very pleased with themselves.

All too soon it was the month of the duck, when every patch of water had fat, flightless waterfowl on it. The food was more plentiful but there was also a warning in the air; as surely as spring followed winter, so would winter follow on the heels of autumn.

'We must quit this country soon, husband, and find a place to winter over,' Rima said one day. 'Soon there will not be enough food for us, and when the ducks fly, so must we.'

Lafe knew she was right and they must move soon, but he had put the idea out of his mind from day to day because life was so good up there on the slopes of the mountain. When they descended to the warmer valleys there would be other people to deal with, and therefore much more risk of being attacked. He had enjoyed the summer and did not want to leave the mountains, but they began to look wider and make their plans.

Chapter 20

The river they followed began as a drop of dew quivering on a leaf high on the tussock shoulder of the mountain. When Lafe and Rima joined the river it was a tiny stream, a mere trickle that wound its way between the stones and tussocks at the very beginning of its long journey. Its waters were icy cold and clear from its passage through the limestone rock that had filtered and released it to flow again further down the mountain. This was the same great river that joined the sea at Cloudy Bay as a full grown, kicking rambunctious waterway, a river subject to great floods, the same river that had formed the lagoon where Lafe stole Rima away from Te Rauparaha's warriors. Only a few days' journey from where they found it the river would grow in force, no longer flowing around obstacles but slowly grinding them to powder and spitting them into the sea as fine silt. But at that first meeting the little silver trickle gave no indication of what it would become.

'Why, even a duck could drink up all the water in this little stream,' Rima laughed.

To travel with this river would be to complete a large semicircle before they reached the ocean, Lafe knew. The Wairau chose her route through valleys between mountain ranges, each valley feeding her with other streams adding their own share of water to swell her flanks. In places the mountains squeezed her hard and for a distance she was fast and noisy and in a hurry to get through. In other places the valleys allowed

375

her to spread out again, and here her waters slowed and she moved more sedately on her way. When this great river reached the plains she began to lose her way, breaking into many little rivulets that travelled side by side, sometimes joining together only to split again. So the wise people began to call her a braided river because she reminded them of the many strands of hair brought together at a woman's neck.

Because the river headed roughly north, the direction they wished to travel, Lafe and Rima followed her. Slowly and steadily they lost height until once again they were below the snow line and among the forest, the trees growing larger and more robust for every hour's journey. Day after day they followed the river until one morning Lafe noticed a more easterly set to her course and they left her, for she was leading them back into Te Rauparaha's land. They climbed out of the riverbed and followed an extensive valley that climbed gently toward the west and the setting sun.

The knowledge came to him so slowly that part of the morning slipped by before Lafe realized they were following an ancient human trail. Many of the main valleys of Te Wai Pounamu still had the remains of these old trails left over from the peaceful days when trade and not war ruled the land. Thousands of feet had flattened and worn the earth over centuries to form this trail and it flowed along the valley like a stream, always picking the easiest route around the rocks and trees in its path. Lafe suspected that this was an important route, perhaps from when trade flowed from the east to the west coast and back again. It was part of the greenstone trail.

'One day these trails that we are following will be gone,' he said to Rima. 'What will happen then? Will we have to wait another thousand years until new explorers begin to follow new routes and the feet of thousands of travellers pound out trails again?'

'There is no real answer to that question,' she admitted. 'War has its time, then peace has its time.' It was as close an explanation as she could make for the strife that her country was in. Lafe pondered past and future as they followed the ancient trail, sensing other footsteps where his own bare feet trod. Men, women and children from a vastly different age had taken this path before him, perhaps passing these very trees as it flitted through high forest, across grass flats and around patches of swampy ground. The trail climbed, always choosing the gentlest gradient until it led through a mixture of alpine forest and back up into tussock and grasslands again.

They passed slowly along the foot of a range of high rugged peaks on the southern side of the valley, peaks that already carried the ominous signs of the first autumn snows. These mountains rose so steeply from the valley floor that Lafe suffered a strained neck from looking up at them and Rima had to cheer him up by promising to pound his neck muscles when they made camp that night.

They knew that somewhere ahead was a lake, though neither had been this way before. They had heard of this lake in the way that all such knowledge was passed on through the tribes, through the stories told and repeated so many times around the village fires at night that it was placed forever on the maps they carried in their heads, and Lafe marvelled that though their two tribes had lived so far apart each had learned the same detail. The lake was called Rotoiti, the little lake, and it featured in the history stories of all the northern tribes of Te Wai Pounamu.

When the trail finally led them to the edge of this high mountain lake it was as if the gods had rewarded them well for having travelled such a long way. It appeared so suddenly in front of them that they both instinctively shrank into the bushes at the side of the track. Surrounded by mountains all touched with snow, Rotoiti gleamed like a jewel in her setting of dark green forest that swooped from the snow line right to the water's edge. She was so deep and clear that they could count the grains of sand in her shallow bays, and her waters were a deep blue-black that mirrored the mood of the sky above. Lafe and his wife stood and gazed out over the water in awe. His hand lay lightly across her shoulders and their faces were full of wonder as they drank in the sight.

'So this is what these mountains hide from us mere mortals,' Lafe said finally. His voice was low and hushed so as not to shatter the peace of the valley.

'I wonder if the eels are fat?' Rima was always the practical one, and he laughed. This lithe and lovely fifth wife of his was good for his soul.

The sun was still hot and the fine stones were warm under their feet, feeling good after all the pounding they had taken over the rocks and tree roots of the trail. As Lafe gazed out over the lake and breathed in its exciting damp smells, the hand that rested on Rima's shoulder seemed to develop a mind all of its own. Down her backbone it slid, softly, softly, until it touched the waistband of her small grass skirt. With a flick of his wrist it was gone, fluttering down to land on the sand at her feet and the hair below her belly sprang free and stood forth boldly, ruffling slightly in the coolness of a breeze. His hand cupped one of her plump buttocks firmly and she gave a small shiver of anticipation and turned her face to him. Then with a heave of his hand he sent her pitching from the low bank into the near-freezing waters of the lake. She shrieked as her head went under and she came up blowing like a porpoise.

Lafe laughed so hard at his own joke, stamping his feet and leaping along the bank to avoid the cold water splashed at him, that he nearly lost his footing and fell into the water himself, but Rima just smiled sweetly, lazily swam across the little inlet and settled herself on the sand of a little peninsula. She stretched herself out to warm in the sun, ignoring him so he had no choice but to climb high around the bluff or plunge into the freezing water and swim across to join her.

Quickly, before he lost his courage, he stepped out of his loincloth and hit the freezing water in a low, flat dive. Gasping at its coldness he stroked quickly across to where Rima lay and scrambled out on the sand. They made love slowly and gently, both exulting at the giving and taking of the act of love and its affirmation that the gossamer-thin web binding them together was daily growing stronger.

Afterwards Lafe lay in the warm sand with his eyes half closed, and in the rosy glow of post-coital pleasure he thought how lucky he was to be exploring such wonderful country and to be in love once more. He thought of all the winters he had spent on Kapiti as a slave without a woman to warm his nights and care for him. He had almost given up hope that he might find love again, and he thanked the gods for the young girl by his side. Rima, who had been her father's fifth daughter, was now his fifth and most precious wife. She made him feel young again. Once again in the twelve hours between daylight and dark his testicles had filled so he was ready for the flax mat, and on that beautiful, lonely lakeside he had not needed to wait for the darkness.

'I am a stallion,' he chuckled to himself. This brought a smile to his wife's face as she heard his quiet laughter and guessed his thoughts. Rima had slowly begun to forget the horror of the attack on her village and her treatment in the hands of her captors. The demands of their journey, with the need to be constantly alert and active and to search vigorously for food, had helped her to forget and the beauty of the country had soothed and renewed her bruised spirit.

It also helped that she now had a husband, perhaps not one she would have chosen for herself but she was happy with him. Her station in life meant that her father would have chosen a husband for her among the warriors of her tribe, but this man she had as her companion was a good man. She knew that after being the plaything of an enemy tribe she was lucky to have a man who wanted her as his wife and who had given her back her honour. By asking, rather than taking her like a slave, he had given her something more important than even her life. Yes, he was a good man, she decided, and she would follow him now for as long as the gods allowed it.

They built a little grass hut down at the end of the lake where in the evenings the long, drawn-out whistle of the kiwi reached their ears from every gully in the watershed. They hunted and ate this kiwi, a fat, nocturnal ground-living bird whose shape and habits were more suited to those of a mammal. It lived in burrows beneath the roots of trees or under rocks in a most un-birdlike fashion. Its nostrils were near the tip of its long beak and it had strong, thick legs and the longest silky feathers in the bird world, very suitable for the making of cloaks.

Rima began to make Lafe a glorious cloak, a garment that would also cover their bed at night, so they ate lots of kiwi. They were fat and delicious at this time of the year and they were easily dug out of their holes in the damp, dark valleys. Any hole in the ground that did not have a spider web woven across its entrance was fairly likely to be the home of a kiwi, and Rima would put her nose to the opening and sniff it out. If she decided the bird was home they began with their digging sticks and dug it out.

Finally one morning they decided to move on from the southern end of the lake. They followed an old trail that led them through the forest to another lake, bigger and even more beautiful than Rotoiti, that they knew from the old stories was her sister Rotoroa, the long lake, and there they built a new hut and settled again. But they did not linger long. The year was passing quickly and the air had a bite to it in the early mornings. Sometimes mist hung over the lake shutting out the sun, and they knew it was wiser to quit the high country for the long winter that was coming.

They travelled north once again until they reached a river that ran determinedly out toward the west. Lafe believed that they were moving across the top of a main divide as on either hand he saw a major river that headed to the sea, one to the east and another to the west. They moved north along the ridges and dropped into yet another river system, this time flowing in the direction they wished to travel, so they followed it and slowly lost altitude day by day until the nights were decidedly warmer than before.

One day as they walked down the river's edge looking in every pool for a fat eel, Lafe idly glanced at the soft sand ahead of him and jumped as if stung by a bee. For the first time in many months he was looking at the footprints of another man and they were fresh, pressed into the sand as clearly as if a big warrior had just stepped out of them. The travellers left the river in haste and climbed up into the ridges, every sense alert as they crept noiselessly back into the shadows of the trees. They lit no fire that night and took turns to sleep and they did not relax again until once more they swung west on a new course.

A few days later they were traversing a ridge that was cut steeply away on one side, and they got an unexpected vista to the north through a hole that a large fallen giant of the forest had made in the canopy. There in the distance below them was the ocean. Lafe stood for a long time transfixed by the sight. He recognized instantly that there laid out before him was Cook's Blind Bay, the very piece of ocean he had travelled so many times in the big double canoe. To the west, still hidden by the mountains, was Murderers' Bay where his people lived.

They travelled on, staying in the mountains away from the coast where they might encounter unfriendly people. Now their route was across the grain of the country and they were constantly dropping down to cross a stream only to have to climb once again. They travelled even more slowly than before, always from food source to food source. If they came across a good food source like the raupo, a type of reed that grew in the little lakes that dotted these hills, they built a little grass hut and stayed for days diving to the muddy bottoms of the lakes to pull the edible raupo roots and gorging themselves on the fat eels that always lurked in such places.

They always found it hard to move on from such a camp and when they did they carried as much food with them as they could, often enough smoked eel to last them several weeks or more. With winter upon them they were afraid to have less than several weeks' food in reserve, for they never knew what might lie ahead. When the cold winds whipped the trees and sheets of rain slid down from the mountains like a grey curtain, all manner of birds, fish and insects seemed to disappear from the face of the earth leaving empty bellies and fear behind them. It was a diet with very little starch or fat in it, and in such harsh country to lose strength was to die.

Now the country was overlaid with cap rock and seemed to grow only hungry scrub. Springs of the purest water bubbled up from holes in the rock, but water does not fill empty bellies. They found caves to explore here, gloomy caverns full of insects that glowed in the night and dripping water that formed huge pillars like ancient dragons' teeth. They spent several nights in different caves because the weather chased them in to seek cover, but they hurried from the area as soon as they could. No damp, draughty cavern would ever be as comfortable as the warm, dry, little grass huts they were adept at building for themselves. Besides, according to Rima, the caves were the home of the taniwha, a dragon that in the minds of Maori still lived and roamed the earth, and Rima didn't like sharing a dragon's home.

Lafe had never met a living soul who had ever seen a taniwha, but everyone he had ever met in Te Wai Pounamu had an uncle whose mother-in-law had a cousin who had been eaten by a taniwha. Many things that went wrong in the Maori world were laid at a taniwha's door. If a cross-eyed child was born, its mother was thought to have been scared by a taniwha during pregnancy. There seemed no end to the mischief caused by this dragon. Ferns that grew in swamps and in dark shady caverns had names that denoted that they were food of the taniwha and though Lafe tried many times to convince Rima that such a beast did not exist, it was to no avail.

'One day you will meet a taniwha face to face and you will be the worse off for speaking of them so disrespectfully,' Rima warned him.

'I will have my musket ready and it is he that will have to watch out then,' Lafe would tease.

'Pah! What harm would your puny thunder stick do to the taniwha?' she would scoff. But then she grew serious. 'Husband, you must not talk like this, especially near the homes of the taniwha. You must learn to speak more politely,' she would beg him. 'Or we will both suffer for your insolence.'

Further west they travelled into a much richer forest, where the floor among the roots was littered with berries and seeds that had dropped in the autumn just past. They encountered many more signs of pig in these places. Now they were passing through the mountains inland from Murderers' Bay and sometimes the high ridges would reward them with a glimpse of the great sandspit that ran many miles out to sea and a promise that they were nearing the end of their journey.

Up there in the mountains they built a comfortable hut of more permanent materials. They were tired of travelling and the food supply looked more promising than in many other places they had passed through. They made their winter home under a dry rock ledge well up on the side of a hill, away from the valley floor where an enemy could stumble on them. When the hut was finished, Lafe was satisfied that it was so well hidden that no one would find it unless they were lucky enough to stumble directly on it. The ledge could only be approached along a single narrow track between large rocks, easily defended by musket fire and bayonet.

It was good to hunt pig again, Lafe decided as he slipped down to the valley floor where the soil was rich and deep. Quietly he loaded his musket, his ears tuned to the faint sounds that came to him from out of one of the little gullies. Once in awhile he would stop where the pig rooting was freshest and flip a sod over with his bare toes, checking the colour of the grass where it lay against the earth the way the pig's nose had left it. He moved slowly up to the head of the valley checking the pig sign all the way, and there the grass adhering to the clods showed that he was moving in the right direction. It was still very fresh and his body began to tremble with excitement. He moved steadily now, gliding through the forest on his bare feet, feeling the ground under his soles before his weight went down so that the sharp snap of a twig would not betray him. His ears told him the pigs were near long before he saw them, as he could hear them using their strong jaws to crack the kernels of the tawa berries that littered the forest floor.

He checked for the twentieth time that the breeze was still blowing softly into his face, then crept closer to the sound. He rested his musket on a tree root and waited as the pigs fed downhill towards him. The first one he saw was a slab-sided old sow with drooping udders and he ignored her as being very poor eating, but before long twenty more pigs fed their way into view and stood with their muzzles elevated skyward, cracking kernels as fast as their jaws would work.

Lafe picked a solid looking young boar and sighted quickly on the section of its rib cage that hid the vitals of heart and lung. Quietly he stroked the trigger and the musket exploded. The noise was shattering and in less than a heartbeat there wasn't a pig to be seen except the young boar kicking his life away on the fallen leaves. Lafe carefully loaded and primed the musket again before he went up to the pig. This was the part that he enjoyed, the quiet examination of the prize before he began butchering it. It had been a good shot; the musket ball had punched several ribs out on either side of the pig, smashing its lungs to pink foam without damaging any of the meat. This had been a beautiful animal, glossy-coated and fat with the pure black hair and long tapered snout of the true Captain Cooker. There was no question that it was a descendant

383

of the pigs he himself had brought to Murderers' Bay many years before, and the thought made him very happy. He had always remembered that voyage fondly, but had never dreamt at the time that one day he would need the food quite this badly.

He built a fire, and when it burnt down to the coals he heaped an armload of fern onto the embers. He laid the pig on top and let the steam from the fern loosen the bristles so that they came clean out of the hide when he scraped it with his sharpened knife. The heat curled and blackened the longer bristles, leaving the nut-brown skin that would taste deliciously of smoke. When he had finished cleaning the hide he gutted the pig, hid all traces of his fire and the offal then slung the carcass on his back and carried it back up to the camp under the overhang.

'Ho, Rima!' he hailed the camp. 'What do you think of this pig? What a pity it was not a taniwha!'

He laughed as she ran her hands admiringly over the smooth skin of the carcass. Like all Maori, Rima loved a fat pig almost more than anything on earth and already she was planning the series of feasts she would prepare. In such damp conditions meat would only keep if it was thoroughly smoked over a fire and hung on racks in the breeze underneath the overhanging rock.

'If only we had a supply of salt, I would make the best bacon in the world,' Lafe would boast. 'Still, the valley produces the odd bird and sometimes a fat eel and we have that old standby the fern root. We shall not starve, even if the pigs leave.'

Now that they had a good warm hut and it seemed that there were enough pigs in the valley to keep them fed through the winter, Lafe began to turn his mind to the problem of making contact with his tribe. The winter was well advanced and the storms rolled in one after another from the Tasman Sea, and the pair spent much of their time wrapped in their great kiwi feather cloak and burrowed deep into their loose grass mattress to keep warm as they dozed away the days and nights and waited for spring.

'The question is, how do we make contact with the tribe?'

Rima had not liked the idea of rejoining Lafe's tribe right from the start and had said so. 'They are not my people. Why would they be kind to me?' she argued. Her experience with Ngati Toa had given her no reason to trust any other tribe but her own, and Lafe spent many nights wrestling with this problem.

He tried to remember how many winters he had spent on Kapiti and thought it had been eight years or more since Te Rauparaha had taken him off the *Mary Elizabeth*. Like the Maori he had fallen into the habit of no longer counting or caring and now had only the vaguest idea of his own age. The great chief Tama who had also been his friend and father-in-law might well have died by now or at least lost his power to support Lafe, and the politics of the tribe could have changed a great deal. Lafe might even be seen as an unwelcome rival to a new chief. He was aware that not everyone had liked the privileged position held by Tama's Goblin.

Another problem was the young warriors they might meet in the forest, whose job it was to protect the village. These men would have been mere children when Lafe left the village, and they were just as likely to kill two strangers they found wandering on their land as they were to recognize and welcome him, he was sure of that. One thing would not happen, he promised himself. He and Rima would not be taken as slaves again. He had already promised his new wife that he would save the last shot in his musket for her rather than let her be taken captive.

The long days of winter ran smoothly and seamlessly on towards spring. Nothing new or different imposed itself on their lives and they were happy with their lot. No one entered their valley or left a footprint to disturb the tenure of their days and the only slight cloud that marred the horizon was when Rima began to believe she was with child. This was an event they would normally have welcomed, as no child in the world is more happily received than in a Maori family, but now it meant their the time of dreaming and slothfulness had to come to an end.

A plan was made. Lafe prepared his belongings and a store of food to take with them, and he left a good supply of dried meat to hang in the breeze under the ledge in case they had to run again. When the weather settled and promised to remain fine for a period they started for the coast, moving more carefully and warily than any creature of the forest. At each stage of the journey Lafe would scout ahead and then return to collect Rima before they covered the next few miles together. They circled through the hills to come down on Lafe's village from the forest behind it. After so long it would have been good to travel the beaches again but the chance of meeting an enemy was too great and they kept to the trees.

When they reached the hills directly above the village Lafe excavated a small cave in a sandy bank, just big enough to hide Rima and their possessions, and promised that nothing would stop him from returning for her in two days. Then he set off, lightly loaded with his fighting weapons, cloak and a little food, to find his people again.

As he closed on the village he picked up an old familiar trail that lead to a favourite set of hills where he had spent the summers bird hunting. But as he walked the excitement that had been building in him for days was replaced by the slimy taste of fear of what might be waiting ahead. Something was not right; something had changed. Here and there he began to notice the trail that he followed was starting to grow over from lack of use. Where the path had been worn to bare earth by many feet over the years, it now had long curled tendrils of fern emerging from the soil and even the slow growing moss was beginning to cover the ground again. The busy and thriving village he had left had a network of well-used trails leading away from it like the spokes of a wheel but now where this trail crossed wet, swampy ground there were no footprints, only the cloven-footed tracks and overturned earth of the wild pig.

The trail sidled around the face of the hill, crossing several watercourses before it swooped down to the estuary where the village stood. There was a vantage point here where the village could always be seen laid out below at the foot of the hill, curling around the shore of the estuary. Lafe had often stopped to rest on just this spot and gaze down at goings-on in the village below. In the early days, when Tama had first led his people back up from Okarito to settle on this spot they had carried much of the timber for the fort down this trail and it was here that the men had stopped to rest and to see how quickly the village was growing.

Now when Lafe reached the spot his heart was filled with dread. For the last hour he had been following a disused trail and he already knew what he was going to see below him, he had seen it so many times before. But there was no power on earth that could stop his eyes from looking over the escarpment at the sight that would scar his soul.

It was far worse than he believed it could be and the shock of seeing his own village destroyed caused him to fall to his knees. It was the same in so many places now, nothing but old embers, piles of well-gnawed bones and ruined gardens that the pigs claimed as their own. But this had been his village, these were his people and he wept for the family he had lost, and more. He sat for a long time on that hill above the village, watching as the playful breeze chased dead leaves through the gaps in the palisade that had not lived up to its promise of keeping the enemy out. Dust swirled up and down the empty rows where the huts had once stood, where he had found human love and laughter and toil and dreams.

'Auie!' he lamented. 'Auie! Oh my poor wives and my children, all gone, and their lives just begun. Oh Marama, Tui, Haroto, Miri!' All had borne his seed and he named his children aloud into the wind, all sixteen of them. For each name he found a face in his memory, a head of golden curls, strong coffee-collared limbs, a particular smile or a cadence in the voice. Then there were the grandchildren, those he knew and remembered and those he had never met who came afterwards.

'It is the saddest thing on earth when a parent has to bury his own children,' Lafe whispered, but only the gods could hear him. 'It is against all that I was brought up to believe. I became Maori, I took the tattoo and I accepted their gods as my own, but this I cannot accept.'

The gap-toothed palisade told its own story. A section of it was charred and burnt right away and earthworks showed how the attackers had driven a sap on an angle up to the wall. Under cover of the earth wall the enemy had set dry wood alight, thrown it against the palisade wall and let it burn. Lafe knew that in time he would find out who had attacked his village and there might well be a day for utu but that day was not yet come. Now it was the time for mourning.

For many hours he sat on the hillside with his head in his hands, touching neither food nor drink, and when the evening came he rolled himself in his cloak and slept fitfully on the side of the trail.

In the morning, before the mist had lifted from the hills, he entered the fort through a gap in the palisade. His footsteps were weary and his heart was heavy. There before him were the smudged patches of blackened earth that were all that remained of the neat rows of little thatched huts that once stood there. The stone circles remained where the fires used to be lit on cold nights, and the blackened remains of corner posts protruded from the earth like rotten teeth. There was so little to show for what had once been a young and vigorous tribe of many hundreds of people. Lafe hissed his anger fiercely at the gods just in case they were listening, though his faith had taken a severe shaking.

'These people trusted you,' he told the empty heavens. 'We practised art here to glorify our gods. What did our song mean to you? What is art if it is not of the spirit?'

He did not receive an answer, nor did he expect one. On this fine winter's morning the gods were too busy for the problems of mere mortal man.

He found the ovens on a sandy terrace above the estuary. They were depressions in the soil full of blackened rocks and bones, many, many bones, and not one set was intact. Even before the pigs had come the bones were intermingled, thrown carelessly to land where they would. But the pigs had come, and those animals so dearly beloved by the tribe had turned their bones again and again, mixing them together so thoroughly that even the gods would not know who was who any more.

Lafe stared in horror. 'I cannot leave you here like this, my people,' he cried to the bones in an anguished voice. He found a flat piece of driftwood and began to scrape a large hole in the sand as a burial pit, his tears falling on the sand as he worked. For hours he laboured like some wild creature, throwing the soft sand out in an arc to land around the edge of the hole. Several times he was satisfied that the hole was deep enough, but each time he surveyed the volume of bones again and went back to his digging. He smoothed the sides and bottom of the grave until he was satisfied with its shape and then he lined it with fern gathered from the forest. Finally he began to collect the bones, armload after armload, these bones of the men, women and children he had loved, and he laid them gently in the bed of fern. With each armload he wondered if he was carrying the bones of his own family, and each time he shut his mind against these possibilities and worked on.

He gave no thought to food or drink, and as the day wore on he began to talk with the spirits of the bones, oppressed almost beyond endurance by the sadness and futility of his task. When he finally lifted his head to the sky he saw the sun descending behind the hills in the west and he smoothed the sand over the mound knowing that in a short few weeks the wind and the drifting sand would obliterate all signs of the grave. He knew that one day far into the future when the wind uncovered these bones people would say, 'Here lies a great cemetery,' but that would not be true, and only he would ever know the truth.

'Here lie the bones of my people, all that remain after the feast. That is the truth!' he cried. He could only hope that what he had done would allow the spirits of his people to rest easier knowing that the right prayers had been sung over their burial place. He stood with his head bowed, saying his farewells as Matai had taught him so very long ago.

That night Lafe lay wrapped in his cloak inside the outline of the hut he had once shared with his first wife. He had scraped away the charcoal and ash and rolled in his cloak on the clean white sand, needing to feel close to her more than anyone, and here he continued his fast. He had not eaten for two days and a night and he was becoming light-headed and dreamy.

When he did sleep his dreams were very vivid and disturbing. He saw Tama's people again, his people, as real as if they still lived, winding their way through the forests of the northern island in single file. They did not speak and they walked with their hands held out in front of them, fingers hanging like the blind people. Many hundreds walked this way, making up a line that stretched back through the mists of the gloomy forest. Once or twice he thought he recognized, in the set of the shoulders or the carriage of their body, someone he had known. Women carried children still strapped to their backs or were followed fearlessly by their other children in a line, their hands too held out in front like the blind.

389

Lafe knew in his half-sleeping, half-waking state that the people he saw in his dream were not the living. They were the spirits that once belonged to the bones he had buried this day, and they were making their way to Spirits Bay to jump into the underworld.

With a sinking heart Lafe recognized Marama in the line. He called to her and she turned briefly and waved him away, then shuffled onwards as if to show that he had no claim to her any longer.

'Oh, Marama! You were the great love of my life,' he cried out, but the effort woke him fully and the contact was broken. He lay still, his heart racing with fear, not sure for a moment whether he was in this world or the next. It was all too easy to be invited into the spirit world and if you fasted and reached the right mental state you were allowed a brief glimpse into what lay beyond death. But if you ate of the food offered by Rohe the Ferry Woman you were unable to return. It was a dangerous undertaking and usually only the tohunga of the tribe dared to venture into these realms.

But the vision of Marama turning to wave him away was so very real. Lafe could tell from her gesture that she was sending him back, telling him he had much of his life still before him and he should not venture into the world she now inhabited. He could see her still when he closed his eyes, her head thrown back, the beautiful cloak draped over her shoulders open at the throat and the broken string where her personal tiki had hung between her breasts.

Lafe had never ever once seen her without her little god ornament and this memory of the broken string at her throat disturbed him. Marama's tiki with its protruding tongue was an image, half-lizard and half-god, made from the finest piece of greenstone the land could produce and it was the size of a man's hand. As it had absorbed the oils from each previous owner's skin it had also absorbed their essence and, it was believed, their spirit as well. Her plump little stone god had always been warm and alive to touch and as smooth as the skin of a baby. It held great power for the wearer and for the tribe in general, and was so powerful and valuable that it was a tribal heirloom.

This tiki was possibly many hundreds of years old and had always been worn by one of Marama's family. It had been given to her as a child when her mother died, and she had worn it every day of her life since. In the normal course of events she would have chosen in time to pass the treasure on to her eldest daughter, so Lafe was sure the broken string that hung from her neck was some sort of message.

'But where is the tiki, Marama? And what is your message?' Once more he passed into the sleep of the dead and this time he slept through the night without dreams. When the morning light coloured the sky he took water and food. He was weak after his two day fast but his spirit was easier now and he sat with his cloak wrapped around him and thought deeply of what he had dreamed. At the head of her sleeping mat his senior wife had always kept the beautiful little carved box that held her most valuable possessions. Lafe was suddenly alert and his heart raced as he measured with his eyes where the head of her mat would have been.

'I wonder?' he thought aloud. 'She was always a clever girl and she had plenty of warning before the enemy broke through the palisade?'

He plunged his hands into the soft sand and dug down to the depth of his elbows. Soon his fingers touched a hard, unyielding surface and he knew what it was before he dragged it from its hiding place and shook the loose sand from its lid. The box was long and flat with a finely-fitted inlaid lid, its rich brown timber showing the delicate toes and markings of the tuatara lizard, the oldest living creature on earth, whose likeness had been carved into it, and two sparkling buttons of iridescent paua shell still marked its eyes. The box was treasure enough in its own right but when Lafe slid open the lid there, nestled in the plumes of kotuku the great white heron, were not one but two hei tiki.

He laid the two greenstone figures gently side by side on the flax mat and studied them. They were nearly identical, both cut from beautiful stone, but only one had the patina of age on it. Lafe picked up this older of the two little green gods and ran his fingers along its surface. It was as smooth to the touch as the skin of a baby. He sniffed it and it still smelt faintly of his wife's skin. He examined the finely woven human hair cord carefully before putting it over his head, and the little god lay comfortably against his chest as if it had always been there.

391

He examined the other tiki closely. It was a copy of the first, greener and more translucent, and the stone looked as if it had more recently been cut from the earth. The thong was freshly woven from human hair and showed no signs of having been worn. After much thought he came to the conclusion that this tiki was to have been a gift for him when he rejoined the tribe and that his wife had never lost faith that one day he would return to her. Every night she would have coaxed and cajoled her little god into returning her husband to her safe and well.

He rolled the little box containing the tiki in his cloak and prepared to leave. He had cared for the dead and now the living required his attention. As he climbed the hill he stopped once more to look back. He touched Marama's tiki that was now his for reassurance and addressed the gods out loud.

'They respected their gods! They were fine artists who brought honour to you! They were the boat people, they built the great double-hulled ocean-going canoes whose bow and stern post were so finely carved, not for their own vanity but for the spirit that you, their gods, breathed into their souls.

'So I command you, you gods, to care for the dead! Help those taken as slaves and make their life bearable! These were fine people!'

Lafe knew that any Maori hearing him talking to the gods in such a fashion would have been shocked and frightened, but he was angry and decided that direct communication was necessary. These Maori gods had altogether too many human failings. They were vain, boastful, vindictive and sometimes even forgetful and their people all too often suffered.

Many of the tribe had died in the defence of their village, but some would have survived in the forests and some would be slaves. The living would be scattered like seeds to the wind, and his seed and his blood was scattered with them. He had done what he could for his people but in the end it had not been enough.

Chapter 21

It was four days before Lafe returned to the little burrow under the bank. He found Rima frantic with worry and fearful for his safety but when she saw his face she knew at once he had undergone a terrible experience and it was she who assisted him back to their hut in the mountains. Her husband had changed; he had not returned on the day he had promised, and now that he was back he was quiet and withdrawn and seemed to have lost all his strength. She feared that the gods were angry with him.

For a long period he did little but lie on his sleeping mat staring at the thatch above him. He ate only sparingly of the food she spent many hours finding and preparing, and she feared for his health. At times he cursed her race and said things that hurt her.

Rima guessed what might have happened at the village. It was not an uncommon thing with the whole country at war, tribe against tribe. It had happened to her own village and her own people, and she felt her own grief again as she watched Lafe mourn his friends and family. It was a country of sorrow now, and until he had done his grieving she must be strong for both of them.

Her husband frightened her by spending his days on the mat running his fingers over the tiki and cursing the gods so furiously that she begged him to stop before they were killed by a lightning bolt or worse. He spoke little to her and seldom even bothered to answer her questions, and for a long time he lost interest in the life they had once shared.

Every morning she rose with the birds and went out to scour the valley for food to supplement the supply of pork that still hung from the racks, and every day she worried more as the racks emptied and their supply of food dwindled. But she did not complain; that was not in her nature. When she found a weka and enticed its head into her noose it was cause for rejoicing, and sometimes she dug up a kiwi, but the valley had been well worked over and it was long past time for them to move on. If she had been able to kill a pig that would have been enough to sustain them but she could not, and so she just had to wait until the gods decided her and her husband's fate.

Sometimes when she felt tired and overwhelmed by their troubles she climbed to a warm rock above the hut and exposed her belly to the rays of the sun so the baby within could feel its warmth. She talked to her unborn child and told him what she could see of the great world from her rock. She had no doubt that her child was a boy; certain signs and omens had confirmed that already.

'One day soon you will see what I see,' she told him. 'From this rock I can see the great ocean where you will spend much of your life. Already I feel you stir when I look at the ocean. You will be a great sailor like your father who came to this country from far across the sea.'

Rima shuddered when she thought of the challenges her son would face as a man of two races. Her child would not even have the support of his tribe and that was a worry to her.

She spent much of her time on the big warm rock petitioning the gods to cure her husband. Rima knew that if he had broken a very powerful tapu, as she had first feared, he would be dead by now and she believed instead that he was affected by a sickness of the mind. She had heard of such a sickness and hoped that with time and a little help from the gods he would eventually be cured of what ailed him. There was little more she could do in the circumstances, and nowhere else to go.

'If my husband dies, so to will I and my unborn child die,' Rima whispered to her gods. 'Do we deserve that?'

Her desperation grew until one day she summoned all her courage and spoke sharply to Lafe, as she never had before. She told him that the child growing inside her would need a father to protect and provide for him, not a grandfather who lay around the hut all day doing nothing. Her remarks were brutal but successful and the next morning Lafe rose from the mat, picked up his musket and went out to hunt. He never knew how thankfully she wept when he was gone.

He came back empty-handed that night but her heart was lighter. Day by day his strength returned and he travelled further and further from the hut hunting for food. Then one day he stalked and shot a pig and the food crisis was over. With the return of his strength, the smile came back to his face and his joy of life returned. Soon things were as good as they had been before Lafe went to the village and found it destroyed. A chapter of his life had closed, as it had for Rima when her own village was sacked by the invaders, but their life together went on.

One evening as they sat by their fire after they had eaten, Lafe fell silent for a long time staring into its flames. Then he rose and went to the back of their hut, returning with the carved wooden box he had found in the village. He took the second tiki and placed the thong around Rima's neck, settling the god between her breasts. He had never spoken of the hei tiki around his own neck, nor of the carved box and she had never enquired, but her eyes widened when she saw this second greenstone figure. She began to protest, but he quietened her with a gentle finger on her lips.

'This tiki was fashioned by a master craftsman as a special gift for me. I now give it to you, my wife. You will wear it and after you your children will wear it and their children, down through time for ever and ever. The tiki that I wear will one day find its way to my eldest living daughter, Marama's child, as it was always intended.

'This is the way it will be,' he told her firmly, and as was expected of a good wife she dropped her eyes and obeyed. Never in all her dreams had Rima believed she would own and wear such a valuable and exquisite piece of jewellery. This little grinning god belonged around the neck of a chief, and although such treasures were sometimes worn by their first and most senior wives they were not for people like her. Tribes would go to war and brave warriors would die for such a tiki, and all Rima could do was hold the glowing greenstone figure up to the weak winter sun and gaze at it in delight.

She shed many tears when she thought of how the little god had come into her possession. Lafe had no doubt that his tribe's greenstone had caused envy among other tribes and so led to the attack. Tama with his wisdom and skill had built up their considerable wealth, and Marama's action in hiding it from the enemy had been the bravery of a high chief's daughter. It would be forever part of the story of the tiki now, and Rima felt blessed by the senior wife she would never meet but whose hands had smoothed the stone. For all these reasons and more, this gift her husband had given her was beyond all price.

For the rest of the winter they stayed in their hut under the ledge. The valley still produced enough food and now there really was nowhere else to go. At least it was safe in this valley; it seemed that no one lived within many miles of the destroyed village with its bones and ghosts. Several times Lafe and Rima crept down to the seashore and came back with their kits full of shellfish, improving their diets for a few days at least and providing a welcome change from birds, pork, grubs and fern root. But as the weather began to settle and the warmer days of spring arrived, they decided to move on. For nearly a year they had not met or spoken to anyone else, and life had become little more than the daily grind of finding sufficient food, cooking it and eating it. Now there was a child coming, food and shelter alone were no longer enough and they longed for other people to share the triumphs and successes of each day.

They decided to travel back across the country to the great inland waters of Queen Charlotte Sound and to look for the scattered groups of people who still lived there. Perhaps one of those small family groups living in the thick forest near the waterways might allow them to join their tribe. They would be taking a risk because Lafe's description would be well-known and Te Rauparaha's arm had a long reach, but in the end it would be better than just existing the way they were. It was worth the journey anyway, they agreed. Loneliness was never so bad when you were on the move.

Rima's belly was just starting to show a little fullness when they moved away from Murderers' Bay and, keeping to the hills, began to travel slowly eastwards back through the country they knew so well.

Travelling in the lower country was easier as spring slowly gained her grip on the land over winter. Food was plentiful and it was delightful just to be on the trail again. It was so good in fact that although neither knew exactly where they were headed it really did not matter. At least the days had a purpose, for they were on the move and there was a lightness in their steps.

In these lowland forests they travelled through the birding was good, the very air full with the songs of the birds in the canopy above and the constant rustle and flapping overhead never ceased. The calls of the bellbird dropped like liquid honey into the air that surrounded them as the birds fed on flowers high above them. They ate eggs from a dozen species, and to their joy they were in time to see the rivers run with silver and to catch the little translucent white fish that was their favourite spring food.

'Now we really know that spring is here,' Lafe murmured as he filled his mouth with yet another rock-baked omelette. 'Isn't it easy now to forget the hungry times of winter? Everywhere you look the hills and valleys quiver and pulsate with life.'

Rima laughed as he cocked a comical eyebrow at her thickened waistline.

'Are you calling me a hill or a valley, husband?' she teased him. 'We humans are not so much different from the trees and the birds, after all. We grow fat when spring is here.'

Again they wandered where the food was best, but this time their general direction was always eastwards until once more they touched the inland waterways and followed the little bays north into Kenepuru Sound. This was Te Rauparaha's dominion and Lafe stayed on the alert, his senses sharp as he watched and listened for the sinister sounds of a war party, but common sense told him that the sweep Ngati Toa had made through this country was unlikely to be repeated for some years. As they travelled they looked for signs that others might have left behind them and once in a while they would follow a set of human prints in the sand, always old and indistinct, only to lose them again by the end of the day. They found the hill where the great canoes had been portaged over from the other sound but saw no sign that such a feat had been repeated. The ferns had grown back and young saplings already blocked the track.

They lived on oysters and love, tinged always with loneliness for other people. If there were refugees and survivors still living near the waterways they were few and very flighty. Their tracks told the story. They never left any sign of their passing if it could be avoided and when the chance came to jump onto a rock surface that did not show any tracks at all they took it. Sometimes tracks would appear from a stream bed where someone had walked in the flowing water rather than leave footprints an enemy could follow.

Lafe and Rima travelled slowly, enjoying the ease of life once again near the sea but always alert, always watchful, hoping to find friends. Once they realized that there was no one actually living on the shores of Kenepuru they set off across the high ridges of a small mountain range that separated it from Queen Charlotte Sound. They took their time and spent a night on the tops before finding their way down a stream that led down to a little beach.

One afternoon when Lafe helped Rima down from a rocky headland onto yet another yellow quartz sand beach he realized how heavy she was becoming and knew they would have to settle somewhere soon. He had hoped she could be with other women when her time came, but now that seemed less certain. He eyed each of the beaches and its surrounding country not only for its food supply but for the potential escape routes that would take them back across the low mountain saddles and into the hinterland. One day very soon he would have to make the decision, he knew that, but for the time being the countryside still beckoned them onwards.

For weeks now they had been in Queen Charlotte Sound, climbing up and over headland after headland and dropping into yet another sheltered beach or cove. They had fallen into the habit of climbing from rock to rock, choosing places where they could step in and out of the water without leaving their own tracks on the sandy beach. This method of travel had become second nature. Where they stepped onto the sand it was close to the water's edge so that the tide would turn within a few hours and wash away any trace of their passing, leaving the beach once more as it was when the gods with infinite loving care laid it down.

They had spent so long watching for the sign that when they found it they were taken by surprise. Lafe jumped down from a rock and his feet had scarcely touched the water when he saw human footprints on the tide line. He dived back into the undergrowth like a startled weka and Rima froze in her tracks and dropped to the ground. After so many months of sharing their world with no one but each other, the surprise and shock of this discovery unnerved them.

They examined the tracks cautiously, comparing them with their own footprints, and decided it was a family group without any men attached. This was not unexpected or unusual. The wars had accounted for most of the male population in the area. When a village was attacked its warriors would more often than not fight long and hard to give their women and children time to escape. Some did not, of course, and actually outran kith and kin to vanish into the forest, but these footprints belonged to the sort of group that Lafe had sought for many months, a group without men to lead them. Men were far more dangerous and unpredictable than women and children on their own would be.

Checking his musket, he left Rima hidden on the forest edge and melted into the gloom of the deeper forest until his eyes adjusted to the light. He circled through the forest until he hit the little freshwater stream that drained out onto the beach. Every beach was blessed with such a stream and he followed it down, its babbling waters covering any small sounds he made as he crept close to his quarry. Before he could even see their camp his nose picked up the smell of wet charcoal and the lingering smell of smoke that clung to the damp forest, and he guessed that they had cooked their food before daylight and doused the fire for fear that the smoke would give away their position. He crept closer until he could hear their low voices and the sound of someone snoring in a very small grass hut. Then he went back to fetch Rima.

They had discussed this moment and how they would deal with it. Both knew that the sight of a large blond tattooed Goblin would send the people scuttling off into the deepest forest in terror and he would not be able to stop them, so it was Rima who crept in close to the source of the voices and then showed herself, speaking softly and smiling. A heavily-pregnant woman is one of the least threatening creatures on earth and after their initial fright the wanderers were asking question as fast as they could think them up.

Soon Rima called for Lafe to join them and he stepped out of his hiding place into the little clearing next to the stream. There was not much to see; a single grass hut, a fireplace and next to it several racks of smoked fish drying. The camp belonged to three women and a young boy, all with their eyes sticking out of their heads with shock at the sight of a Goblin with a musket. Two of the women were older but one was a very lovely young girl of about Rima's age or slightly older, perhaps sixteen or eighteen winters, and the boy looked to be around eight. For a long moment they all stared at Lafe, and he at them.

When you have not seen another face except that of your own woman for so long, it is amazing how interesting the faces of humans are, he thought as he watched the play of emotions on the faces of the strangers.

The older woman was the first to find her tongue. 'Ehhh! You did not tell us your husband was a Goblin. They are far uglier than I ever believed.'

'Don't speak foolish words, old woman,' Rima warned her. 'This one talks our talk.' She waved her hand in Lafe's direction and he chuckled. One of the things he had missed in the last year was the robust conversation of Maori women. Food was brought and offered and he relaxed and leaned his musket against a tree. There was a marked easing of the tension as Rima told them of their escapes and travels since running from Te Rauparaha.

'Yes, he is a savage dog that one,' the older woman offered. 'You'll find no spies of his here.'

Her small group consisted of herself and her sister, each with one of their children. They had lived as primitive hunter-gatherers in the forest for a number of years since war had come to the sounds and destroyed their village.

'So this creature is the father of the child you are carrying, Rima?' their leader asked politely. 'Does this mean they make babies the same way that our men do? I have always wondered about that.' She spoke so innocently, rolling her eyes in Lafe's direction, that all four women burst out laughing. 'I have never seen one of these Goblins close up, only their ships far out on the ocean.'

She and Rima chattered on, bringing a smile to Lafe's face. It was good to be back among people again. He formally asked if they could join their groups together and was welcomed with genuine joy.

'To have a man in the group with one of the dreaded thundersticks is an advantage not to be denied,' the two sisters agreed.

'And if you can kill the pig with your thunderstick you will indeed be welcome,' the older one added. 'I have not forgotten the taste of pork though it is years since I have had any.'

Next morning the women banded together to build another hut and Lafe was sent away to hunt for a fat pig. Although there were plenty in the vicinity the little family had never been successful at killing one and had not eaten meat of any kind for many years. They assured the newcomers that nothing would impress them more than a piece of roast pork set before them.

Lafe climbed high up to the mountain faces above the bay and searched the horizon carefully before risking a shot. He killed a nice fat young boar which had hesitated a fraction of a second too long to look over its shoulder before making an escape. The soft lead ball took it behind the shoulder and killed it before it hit the ground, and Lafe singed and cleaned the carcass under the high trees in a breeze that allowed the smoke to disperse before it reached the sky.

Knowing the love that Maori had for fat he stripped the rich white fat from the pig's entrails, wrapped it in leaves and stored it inside the rib cage, then left the pig to cool in a place that would be easy to find on his return journey. He had decided to climb on up to the top of the range that divided the two sounds. He found a rocky knob where no trees could gain a foothold, which allowed him to climb out and above the extraordinarily thick forest that carpeted the slopes beneath him. From there he could see the whole panorama of Queen Charlotte Sound laid out at his feet, with only a few twists and turns of its waterways hidden from view.

'If we were to settle permanently in the little bay below, how safe would we be?' he wondered aloud. His eye travelled up one side of the sound and down the other. No one moved on the beaches, no smoke rose into the sky. Not a sail, not a canoe cast their shadow on the still, blue water below. There was nothing to attract strangers or war parties to this particular bay. It was only one of a hundred similar bays thereabouts and as beautiful as he found it to be it was in no way unique.

Far to the north was the entrance to the sound and to the Windpipe of the Pacific, from whence the enemy had always come. Along the eastern shore he could see a second opening to the waterway that was the sounds, and he realized it was Arapawa Island that divided them. The two white sailors on Kapiti had told him of this entrance and he had travelled past it and on down the east coast several times on Te Rauparaha's war canoes but he had never yet ventured into that second channel. Who knew what enemy might live in that stretch of water? Was there anywhere that was safe in this country any more? That was the big question, and to that there was no answer. He decided that his little band of women and children would be as safe where they were now as anywhere else in the country.

As the sun sped across the sky he heaved himself to his feet and set off back to pick up his pig. He was welcomed as a hero should be, and there was song and dance that night to celebrate the return of pork to the food baskets that went into the earth ovens.

'If we are careful and don't become too complacent we might survive here,' he told Rima and the other women. 'No fires during the day, no tracks worn in the forest and no more than one shot from the musket every eight or ten days, and we might be able to stay right through to next spring.'

Life settled down to an amicable pace with lots of good food and a comfortable style to it that allowed the days to fly past. The women showed Lafe their most precious possessions, two small canoes that they kept hidden in the forest. When the moon was up they would launch the canoes and paddle to the fishing grounds off the headlands, fishing for cod and setting lobster traps to pick up the following evening. They never ventured out of the forest by day and always took care that their footsteps on the sand were below the tide line.

Rima did not travel far now and spent much of her time making cloaks and mats which she was very skilled at. Lafe found himself spending more and more time with the boy, who dogged his footsteps and was hungry to learn the ways of men, and with the girl whose name was Moana. She was always ready to accompany him wherever he went and was obviously attracted to him although he was careful not to give her too much encouragement. She was of an age where under normal circumstances she would already have been married with two or three children. Rima said nothing as the days passed and Moana spent more and more time by her husband's side but Lafe was aware that things could not progress long in this fashion. Finally he was approached by the girl's own mother.

'Will you take her as your wife?' she begged him 'She pines for the pleasures of the sleeping mat and for children of her own and she knows she will never find a husband living as we do.'

Lafe was unsure how to respond, but she guessed the cause of his hesitation and reassured him.

'We women have already discussed this with your wife and she agrees that it is the proper thing to do,' she told Lafe. 'As your senior wife she will welcome my daughter to your household.'

Lafe could do nothing else but agree. It was hardly an onerous or difficult duty, after all, and he decided that he should try not to take too much pleasure from it but he was glad he could help. So it was arranged, and one fine evening after enjoying a feast and the symbolic wearing of new cloaks he found himself sharing a sleeping mat with a very lively young sixth wife. Her vast enjoyment in the pleasures of the flesh threatened to wear him out, however, and he privately swore he would take no more wives under any circumstances. It was this way for weeks and every night he found himself less ready to rise to the challenge until finally one of his arrows found its mark and the girl was with child.

'A wonderfully fertile race, these Maori, and I will take some of the credit for the Ericksons,' he chortled with genuine relief. 'I only have to hang my cloak in any of my wives' huts and they become pregnant.'

During this busy month Rima, to the delight of the whole camp, was delivered of a healthy boy child. The mood of the little group changed once again, and after the relief of having a man with a musket to protect and provide for them their spirits were lifted even higher by this baby among them. He was the best tonic they could have had and it made them feel their little band was a tribe once more.

Lafe felt the strong bonds of family wrapping themselves around him again as he looked at his new son.

'When a man has lost his home and family and a new child comes along, this is truly a gift beyond price,' he whispered to Rima. 'What will we name the boy?'

'I have been thinking that we might call this child after your friend that you buried at the tail of the fish,' Rima said shyly. 'I have heard you speak of him many times. With your permission I would like to call our son Matai.'

'It is a fine name,' Lafe agreed, and in his heart he was very glad. With this name the chief Kaitoke, his friend Matai and his fourth wife Miri would all be honoured and remembered, as would Tama who had helped him bury his first Maori friend. So it was done, and Matai became part of the new tribe. He nursed well and grew fat and contented, loved and cared for by all his aunts.

One day when Lafe was hunting high on the mountain he was surprised by the sight of a small cutter-rigged sailboat entering the sound from the open sea. His eyes drank in all he could see of her, the line of her sail and the way she heeled to the breeze. The little boat tacked, picking up the breeze again on her other side, and steered towards the channel on the other side of Arapawa Island where she slowly drew out of sight. Seeing the cutter stirred up all sorts of emotions in Lafe's breast and with the pig on his back he fairly flew down the ridge to the beach below. Somewhere tucked up in a small bay in this labyrinth of waterways must be the mother ship, he reasoned. He told the women what he had seen and discovered that they had seen the little white ship several times during the previous winter. They had seen it coming from and returning to the other side of Arapawa and they guessed that the Goblins might have a village somewhere in the channel.

'You should have told me this thing before now,' Lafe told his new mother-in-law.

'Who am I to know what strange things you Goblins get up to,' the woman retorted, shrugging her shoulders. She was angry with Lafe now. 'Goblins come, Goblins go. You are not real people like us, you know. Even if my daughter does stick up for you.' She spat at his feet to emphasize her point.

'Be careful what you say, old woman,' Lafe growled. 'Don't forget you have a Goblin grandchild on the way.'

For ten days Lafe watched for the cutter before he saw it again. It came around the corner of the island and sailed for the main entrance of Queen Charlotte Sound and he watched all day until it was just a speck on the horizon. Three days later it returned and he watched it enter the channel. In a stiff breeze and running with the tide it was soon lost to sight but he was even more sure now that somewhere down the east side of Arapawa was a settlement of Maori or Pakeha who had some sort of regular contact with the outside world. He was chillingly aware, however, that a three-day journey could easily have taken the little cutter across the Windpipe to Kapiti Island and back.

'I must somehow make contact with them,' he told his little band as they sat around their fire in the darkness that night. 'Though life is good here on this beach, we can only survive like this as long as we remain undiscovered and sooner or later we will be found.

'Look at us. One man, four women, a boy and a baby. Almost everybody is stronger than we are, and we will not last long when they do find us. We must find a stronger group that will accept us and we must join them,' he urged.

The two older women were frightened by his words. They had been by themselves for so long now they trusted no other people. Rima's fears were different though, and she alone shared Lafe's deepest concern. He was a marked man and as soon as word got back to Te Rauparaha, as it inevitably would, that he was alive and in the sounds he and the people around him would be in grave danger. In her heart she already knew what Lafe had not said to her, that he could never be part of the new tribe.

It took time to persuade the two older women but they accepted that the future of their children depended on going along with what the rest wanted, so Lafe and his new wife began preparing for an expedition. On the first night with a useful moon they launched the bigger of the two canoes and paddled for most of the night across Queen Charlotte and into the channel that separated Arapawa from the mainland. Here they were able to rest their aching arms and travel with the tide that pushed them far up the channel. The tide was strong here in this narrow channel, far stronger than the two paddlers could manage. When slack water came they had to work hard for every small gain in distance and when the tide began to run against them they quickly sought a quiet little bush-clad bay to lie up for the rest of the night and the following day.

They were prepared to move cautiously. They carried enough dried fish and cooked pork to last them a week or two and they could see from the empty shells cast up on the beaches that there was plenty of shellfish.

The next night when the tide turned in their favour they slipped the canoe back into the channel and travelled on at a fine speed, plying their paddles in a deep steady rhythm. They passed many attractive bays outlined by the moon on both sides of the channel, but they hugged the northern bank for fear that the strong tide would carry them out to sea if they came upon the entrance unexpectedly. Just as Lafe began to suspect from the feel of the current that they were approaching the open sea they smelled the first tang of smoke on the air. It was a smell to quicken the pulses, the unmistakable scent on the wind of a whale being cooked down for its oil.

The paddlers looked for and found a little cove on the northern side of the channel and turned the canoe into it before they could be swept out into the ocean. Quickly they beached the little boat, dragged it into the forest and carefully brushed away their tracks with a leafy branch. Lafe managed by a huge effort of will to curb his impatience and doze through most of the following day, although his mind was racing so madly he did not get a lot of rest. That night he made sure Moana understood his instructions and knew how to follow them, ordering her not to move from her hiding place for at least two nights.

It was twilight when he left her, with still enough light in the sky to find his way through the forest before the moon came up, and crept towards a place where he could see what the whalers were doing. He was filled with excitement. The well-remembered smell conjured up long-forgotten sounds and images and the thought of his own people working on a whale on the beach below made him want to fly through the forest and join them. But once before he had been too hasty and for his trouble he had been handed over to Te Rauparaha as a slave. This time he must be very patient and regard men of all races as his enemy, he told himself. His nose had taken him through the forest and down to where he could see the glow of the fires on the shore below, and now the smell of whale was a rich and heady aroma in his nostrils. Once in a while the fires sent up clouds of sparks into the sky, a sure sign that there was a watchman tending the trypots as they boiled the oil from the blubber. The smell had spread to the next bay and well up the side of the mountain, making the air nearly thick enough to eat.

Lafe sought a place where he would be able to see everything that happened below and yet not be surprised by anyone stumbling upon his hiding place. Not far from where the fires blazed he could make out the shapes of nearly a dozen huts in the darkness. They sat on plots cut from the forest on one of the few level pieces of land in the bay and the cleared area around them ran a little way up the slope to where there seemed to be a rough enclosure on the edge of the forest. He could hear hogs moving about and fighting, and now and then a dog barked. As the moon rose he feasted his senses on the sights, smells and sounds of his own people, each new discovery stimulating his memory and his starved brain. Finally he grew tired and, selecting a little knoll where he could quickly retreat to an ugly, bush-choked gully if he was disturbed, he rolled himself up in his cloak and slept till dawn.

When the first rays of light touched the little village below it came to life. Hogs and children squealed and the dogs began barking. He roused himself and sat shivering in his cloak as he watched the little chimneys below begin to smoke. After the men had breakfasted they came out from their huts, gathered around the large whale beached on the foreshore and began carving off the long strips of blubber.

407

This was a shore whaling station, he could see that now. To his disappointment no great ship rested here in the harbour, only the two whaleboats on the beach and the cutter which floated on the quiet waters of the bay. While he waited for the light to strengthen he used his fingers to estimate the numbers of people living at the station. Each whaleboat required a crew of seven, one man would be up the hill on lookout, there would be a boss and one or two others to tend the fires, cut wood and cook. Probably twenty men, their wives and as many children, Lafe thought from the noise, about sixty people in all.

Among the men working on the whale was a tall, raw-boned white man with a startling black beard who was obviously in charge. He worked as hard as any of them but he gave the orders and the others deferred to him. There were other Europeans too, and several with lighter skins who might have been half-breeds while the rest of the crew were Maori. The station itself was simply a thatched shed and Lafe could see that it held barrels for the oil and a quantity of whalebone. Coils of rope and a few tools lay about and the place had a look of permanence about it. There was a large block and tackle that was used to pull the whale carcasses up onto the shore, and the whalers were using an assortment of blubber knives and other tools.

Two large trypots with fires burning under them gave off the odour that no whale man would ever forget. A set of sheerlegs sat on the level ground above the pots for lowering the blubber in, and as Lafe watched another piece of blubber was snatched from the ground and the men hauled on ropes to lower it into the pots. He could almost hear the voice of Olva, the captain of the *Northern Lights*.

'The smell of money, that is, Never forget that, Lafe.'

This would be a cheap station to run, he could see that, and if they took twenty whales in a season there would be quite a profit in it for the owner. He had been out of the trade for many years, but from the number of ships he knew had been visiting the coast he suspected that whale oil had become even more valuable than before, and was worth a lot more money. He was fascinated and enthralled by the scene below and would have left his lookout and joined the men if he had not been wary of being handed over to Te Rauparaha once again.

408

This was Ngati Toa territory and unless someone had killed off the old scoundrel he still held sway over all who lived and breathed on it. This whaler could only operate with the benevolence and good will of Te Rauparaha, and Lafe knew if he was seen by any of the men or women on the station, word would soon reach the ears of the warlord at Kapiti. He shuddered at the thought. From where he was concealed he could look out to sea through the narrow entrance and see the hills of Te Ika a Maui, the North Island. Te Rauparaha's stronghold with its legions of warriors was less than thirty sea miles from where he was sitting.

When he tired of watching the men work he drank in the beauty of the scene around him. The deep blue waters of the channel changed suddenly as they flowed out to meet the white rollers that stormed through the entrance from the Windpipe. It would take brave men to row a whaleboat out through that turbulent funnel to hunt whale in the open waters of the strait and then to tow their catch all the way back into the channel through those rollers, he decided, and his admiration of the black-bearded whaler grew by the hour. From the sea entrance to the whaling station the air was thick with birds diving on the fish that caused the waters below to bulge upwards from the pressure of the schools beneath the surface. Lafe could see that the channel was rich with fish that were attracted to the blood and particles of flesh and blubber that found their way down the slipway into the water.

'Big fish always eat little fish.' The saying reminded him of Te Rauparaha, who always used it to justify his attacks on other tribes. Perhaps it would do the old warlord good to come and see the whalers in action, Lafe thought. Here little fish often ate bigger fish.

The settlement had been there at least two summers, he decided. Extensive gardens held rows of what looked like root vegetables and cabbages, and the mere thought of eating carrots and turnips again made his mouth water. He vowed that as soon as it was dark he would take a taste of each of them and he began to mark in his mind where the village dogs lay.

He had chosen a sunny little spot for his vigil, and he chewed his pork and fish and lay down for a sleep, comforted by the voices and the activity below and the smell of whale grease in the air. He woke after

409

an hour or two, feeling unwell and fusty from having slept too long in the sun, and staggered to a little stream to drink and wash his face in its cold waters. It was never a good idea to go to sleep in the sun but he reckoned on being up most of the night and the water from the mountain stream soon brought him back to life. Once again he sat watching the men below him at work, chewing another piece of fish and impatient now for the long day to end.

He had already marked out the timber house at the end of the row of huts on a little terrace. It was not a lot bigger or grander than the grass huts the workers lived in and it still had a thatched roof. Just before dark the big black-bearded man strode off towards it, obviously expecting that his dinner would be nearly ready, and Lafe could see the glow of candles from within when the big man opened the door and entered the dwelling, shutting it behind him.

He waited until darkness had spread its blanket over the little row of huts then crept to the veranda and tapped lightly on a window of real glass, the first he had seen in New Zealand. There was silence in the house for a spell and he waited with every nerve in his body tensed. Then a powerful and confident voice urged him to enter. Quickly, before he lost his courage altogether, he opened the door and stepped into the light, shutting the door behind him.

For a moment he was blinded. His eyes were not used to the strong light anymore, but when he could see a little better he realized that his host stood in front of him with a British sailor's sabre held loosely in his hand. Lafe had the clear impression that if he made any trouble this man would hack the head off his shoulders with the greatest of enjoyment. A woman and several children hugged the wall, rooted to the spot but well clear of any violence should it break out in the room.

Lafe searched his mind for the right words. They came to him in the Maori language but his tongue became tangled with the English words and several times he backtracked to find the thread of what he wanted to say. The black-bearded man went to a keg that stood in the corner of the room, poured a mug of rum and handed it to Lafe who sipped it. It was unbelievably foul but it did jolt his thinking processes back into some sort of order.

'So, you are the Goblin we have heard so much about?' Blackbeard asked with a smile, and Lafe agreed that he was such a person.

'I am known by the name of Jackie Guard of Tar White,' the whaler told him. 'This is the place we call Tar White. Be seated at the table and my wife will feed us both.'

It had been many years since Lafe sat on a chair and ate at a table, but any fears of clumsiness were quickly allayed by the kindness of his host and the simple hospitality of his family. While they ate Lafe laid out most of his story, in a mixture of English and Maori, from the time he arrived in the country. It was a long tale, but there had been rumour and gossip about him already and with a lot of prompting and prodding from his listener he finished his story. When Jackie was certain that he had the bones of the tale he sat for a long time saying nothing while his unexpected guest enjoyed the whale meat and vegetables set before him.

'And what would you be expecting of me then, Lafe Erickson?' Jackie asked in a quiet voice.

'I would like to bring my people here to live,' Lafe told him simply.

'I live and run my station only as Te Rauparaha allows,' the whaler replied warily. 'Your women and children could mix with my lot and he would not be bothered with a few extras around the place, but if he heard that I had sheltered you here at the station there is no telling what he might do.

'You must never be seen near the station again or I will take you prisoner and hand you over to Te Rauparaha myself. My woman will not talk, but be warned that if any of my men or any of their families ever see you here I will do what I have to do to protect myself and my people.'

It was what Lafe had expected, but the big man's next words filled him with sudden hope.

'I could get you on a Yankee whaler, they are as thick as fleas on a dog's back around the coast this year. But that will be your decision to make when the time comes for you to make it.'

They talked on long into the night, finding common ground and enjoying each other's company.

'I was one of those travellers that arrived in Australia without paying my passage – a convict in other words,' Jackie told him. 'When my time was finished I went to sea and after a few years I saw this Tar White and recognized it as a grand spot to set up shore whaling.'

Slowly and with a lot of hard work, Guard was building a future for himself and his men, and Lafe realized that here lay his biggest danger yet. This man would ruthlessly eliminate anyone who endangered his prospects there on that part of the coast. Finally his host called their talk to an end.

'I must sleep,' he said. 'There's a lot of whale still to boil down, come tomorrow. Sleep here on the floor and go before daylight.'

He brushed off Lafe's thanks and said bluntly, 'If you come back to ask my help again, be sure you know what it is that you want.'

Lafe slipped through the door of the small hut before the first of the birds began to tune its voice, and was gone to the safety of the forest before anyone stirred in the huts. It took several days for him and Moana to rejoin their own little band, and he took a few days more to rest and marshal his thoughts before he began the difficult task of convincing his women that they should leave their camp.

'Hear me now. People cannot live without other people,' he told them. 'We are not strong enough to survive on our own out here, and if we do not move we will wither and die.'

At first they refused to consider his suggestion at all, then for days they argued against leaving their quiet little bay. There was food and shelter there, they had his thunderstick and there were pigs in the forest. And their little band was growing, with another baby on the way. The four women were all skilled at catching fish and snaring birds, and the boy would soon grow strong enough to do his share. His voice shaking with anger, Lafe explained to them for the tenth time what he thought they should do.

Finally, he left them to make the decision. But they were Maori, without the structure and support of a tribe, so in the end they would go. It was much easier under a chief who would simply say, 'We go', and they would never think to challenge his decision. Lafe had been that kind of husband too and he knew that if he ordered his wives they would go, but this was their future now and he would have no part in it.

Neither of his wives would accompany him back to his homeland. They were firm on their decision about this. They could not live the rest of their lives among Goblins and there was no way he could change their minds.

'We will be happy to wait for our husband to return, but we will not sail out on the ocean in one of those strange ships full of Goblins,' Rima told him firmly. The thought of living in a land where people rode dogs to visit neighbouring tribes was impossible for her to contemplate and from what little her husband had told her it appeared very strange and different in his far-off land. The customs of his people sounded frightening. Lafe knew he could order them to accompany him and they would, but he also knew they were likely to die of unhappiness or one of those other diseases that appeared to lay their race low so quickly.

For days they discussed what they should do. First they swung this way, then that, but in the end it was the fact that they were a tribal people that won them over. For the women it was the children, the singing and the dancing and the day-to-day pleasures of village life that called them back, and in the end they would take any risk to become part of that culture again. For the younger women especially, to be attractive without seeing that attraction mirrored in the eyes of another was a soul destroying thing, and the seasons of a young girl's attractiveness were not unlimited.

Lafe found that he too was drawn back to his own culture and away from this land he had learned to love. His thoughts now were of three-masted Yankee whalers and the big fish they chased, and of a little town on the shores of Chesapeake Bay. He felt no disloyalty to his wives or the country that had adopted him, but after so many years had passed he had a very strong urge to return to his roots. These people were his friends and he loved them, but his family was elsewhere.

The little family used their two canoes to ferry themselves across the Queen Charlotte Sound to a deep bay on the near side of Arapawa. The big island climbed straight up from the sea to its high backbone, a

413

range of hills mostly covered in forest, and Tar White was on the other side of these hills. It could be reached by an old foot trail that ran along a series of ridges and saddles, Jackie Guard had told Lafe, and once they had thrown up a little hut on a hidden terrace the new arrivals explored the bay for food and escape routes in case they were discovered. They were in a large, rather shallow bay with an abundant supply of shellfish, especially the juicy succulent scallop they all loved. But there were many other types of seafood there in the bay and at the headlands. In the space of time a man could hold his breath he could catch a lobster weighing many pounds. There were finfish and rays and several species of small shark or dogfish that were good eating too, and they all jumped willingly onto a baited hook. Lafe shot a couple of pigs and smoked their flesh, and the younger women and the boy caught several young goats when they came down to the beaches to feed on the seaweed tossed up by the waves. Everyone knew the time was fast approaching when Lafe would leave, but they did not dwell on it.

'Today is today, and tomorrow will look after itself,' they said. Because they did not comprehend the great distance between their own country and the rest of the world they did not really believe he would be gone for long.

'He will be back to give us more babies next winter,' Rima and Moana told each other, and on this matter they were quite confident. In their own society the men always returned to make babies with their wives in winter. And why would he not? They were attractive women and they looked after him well.

One morning they heard the smack of a porpoise tail on the water out in the bay and slipped out to watch. It was as if they had been summoned as an audience for the performance. One porpoise left the pod and sped the length of the bay, leaping from the water and crashing back on to the surface on its belly, and by the time everyone had gathered on the beach there were nearly fifty porpoises putting on a display of acrobatics across the width of the bay. They sped through the water with flicks of their tails and launched themselves into the air, crossing each other's paths without collision to bellyflop back into the water with a noise that could be heard in the farthest corner of the bay.

The two older woman slapped the water with the flats of their hands to show the porpoises they were welcome, and the fish darted in to run past their legs and cavort in the shallows.

'See how they have come to welcome us to their bay,' Moana enthused. When they saw that Lafe was a little sceptical of the idea, the women were hurt.

'But don't you understand? They are the people of the sea, the same as we are the people of the land,' the elder woman told him seriously. 'We are very close and understand each other. Who knows, but these might be our ancestors in the bodies of these very fish.'

They all nodded seriously to Lafe, willing him to believe as they did, and he gazed at them with tears in his eyes. After all these years these people were not his people and their beliefs were not his beliefs. It was time to leave. For many hours that day he sat with Rima while she nursed young Matai, and felt again the heaviness in his heart at the thought of leaving them both. This was the wife with whom he had shared many adventures. He had saved her life and she had saved his, and theirs was a very special bond.

'Will you and Matai not come with me to America, Rima?' he begged for the last time, already knowing the answer in his heart. 'Do you have to stay? I would guard you both and care for you, and though things would be strange at first we would be together.'

'No, my husband,' Rima said quietly. 'As surely as you know you must go, I know my child and I must stay. We are people of this country, my son and I.'

He heard the steel in her voice, and would ask no more.

That afternoon he sought out Moana and asked her too, but her answer was the same and that night he said goodbye to each of his wives, giving them instructions on how his children were to be brought up. This was expected of him and they did not question his plans or his ideas. That would not be a proper thing to do.

In the early light of the new day Lafe touched noses with his family in a long and lingering way, shouldered his pack and his musket and began slowly to climb the hill above the beach. He looked back once before the trees swallowed him up and he saw Rima still standing where he had left her, the beautiful green tiki around her neck picked out by the strengthening light. He raised his hand once then ducked his head and entered the cool shadowy forest.

By midday he had climbed through the saddle and begun to work his way down the steep ridge to the whaling station far below. The rest of his family would follow him over this same track in the same number of days as the fingers on their hands, and he knew they would soon be absorbed into the tribe that had sprung up around the whaling station. Te Rauparaha would take revenge against him if the opportunity arose but it would be beneath his dignity to notice women and children, and two more babies with straight hair and honey-coloured skin would be neither here nor there on a whaling station.

That night he crept into Jackie Guard's house to make his final arrangements and he spent the next day hidden in the forest. The following evening before the moon rose he was smuggled onto Guard's cutter and it put to sea with one of the whaler's trusted lieutenants at the helm.

Chapter 22

1832

The lively little ship climbed up and over the swells and picked up speed going down the other side with a gut-swooping action that made Lafe's heart sing. As they shaped up to clear the channel on the outgoing tide and enter the Windpipe all he could make out in the blackness was a series of sinister high rock walls with necklaces of foam at their base. He could sense the walls pressed close on either side of the narrow entrance as the flow of water out of the channel met the sea and set up currents and back flows that could be felt through the keel. The boatman strove to keep them in the middle of the stream and keep the bow of the cutter head on to the swells that rushed at them out of the darkness.

'This place must give you a wild ride when you are bringing in a whale,' Lafe yelled over the noise of the sea. He spoke in Maori but received only a flash of white teeth in reply, and guessed the man had been told not to talk to him. That was safer for everybody and his respect for Jackie Guard rose even more.

He was pleased to be back at sea again and he loved the action of the little cutter under sail. She was not so greatly different from the one he had built and owned himself and had been forced to abandon to the Heretaunga war party. He wondered where the *Aurora* was now.

'Such a lot of sad memories,' he whispered, and his thoughts turned to his family in Murderers' Bay as he watched the land behind the cutter merge into the darkness. Soon only the white spume thrown up by the rollers was visible as the cutter forced its way into the Windpipe.

'Don't even think of coming back!' Jackie Guard's words rang in his ears still. 'Point your nose in the direction of America and stay there, otherwise Te Rauparaha will have you.'

Lafe knew he was right. The desire for utu or revenge bubbled just beneath the surface of any tribe in this land, and to cross a man as powerful as Te Rauparaha was an action that demanded utu. As a man and a chief he would be obliged to take revenge or lose the respect of his followers. Lafe thought of the two wives he had left on Arapawa and hoped that they would have a home at Tar White. Guard had assured him that he would look out for them and ease their way through life as best he could, and Lafe had sold his musket to provide a few small things for the little family when they came in. It was all he had to give them, but he felt particularly lonely and helpless without it.

At the end of his long years in this country he owned very little more than what he came into the world with. The kiwi feather cloak Rima had made for him hung from his shoulders, and the cheerful little greenstone god that had been Marama's dying gift hung around his neck. He could have sold that to Guard for a pretty penny, but in the end he had not been able to part with it.

'Well, I have had the experience of being rich and poor now, such is life,' he told himself. There was no bitterness at the thought but his smile had a wry twist to it. 'But I can say that I have led an adventure filled life, which is worth all the gold in the world.' He spoke these sentences out loud to practice his English. To him the words sounded all right and he was pleased that he could form and understand the words that came out in this rusty native language of his. He sensed the boatman's head come up at the sound of the words and he felt the man watching him for a few minutes without saying anything. This young man was a half-breed, Lafe thought, like his own children, most probably fathered by a sailor. They were a new race of people and he hoped they would be able to save what was left of the country.

The cutter carried her sail well as the man bent her course to the southeast and trimmed the boat so she travelled easily along the swells, taking them comfortably at an angle. It was a good evening to escape the country. The moon was late rising so the night was dark, and a good breeze filled the sail from the beam.

He knew he had to rest and he did not know what the next day would bring, so he lay down as best he could in the cramped space and covered himself with an old sail. For a long time he lay on his back and watched as the tip of the mast carved a lazy course across the heavens. He saw a lone wandering star that streaked across the sky, and realized he was as alone with his thoughts and fears now as he had ever been in his life. Once in a while he turned his head to see the white of a breaking roller on the cliffs of the east. But for that he could have been a hundred miles out to sea.

By daylight they would be off a wide and expansive harbour in the north of Cloudy Bay, not far from the lagoon on the Wairau river mouth where he had run from Te Rauparaha more than a year before.

'How strange life is,' he told the boatman. 'Sometimes you run and run and in the end you are back where you started from.' But he doubted that the man's grasp of English was good enough to understand what he was trying to say. He could have repeated his thoughts in Maori, but he wanted to exercise his lazy tongue in his own language. What would it be like to live among his own people again, he wondered. Even Guard had frightened him a little with his ability to make quick decisions and carry them out. On board a ship it would be the same; decisions made, orders given and carried out in an instant.

These were things he still remembered well, but in the life he had been leading even the smallest thing was discussed for many nights around the fire before a decision was made. Then the tribe was so easily distracted. Fish might come on the bite, a large lobster might be caught in a trap or the footprint of a big pig might be discovered and such things would take priority so that in a few hours everyone had forgotten that a decision had been made about anything. It had been an easy way of life to fall into and he remembered the countless hot afternoons that he had dallied away with his wives, never thinking further ahead than the next hour of pleasure. No wonder the years had passed so quickly that he scarcely saw them go by.

419

He made a great effort to put aside his memories before they rose up and swamped him, and tried instead to think about what was going to happen to him next. Chances were that one day soon he would be dumped in a seaport somewhere on the eastern seaboard of America with a few dollars in his pocket if he was lucky and not a friend on earth. It was quite possible that he could starve to death unless he quickly found out how to make his way in this new world.

His father was dead now, nothing surer. The Swede had already been an old man when Lafe left the shores of his home country. Had he died thinking that his only child had perished in the hands of the Maori, or had someone from the ship found the messages Lafe had left carved into the trunks of trees near all the good landing spots on the west coast? And had the letter sent from Kapiti on the whaler *Mary Elizabeth* reached America and found its way into the right hands? Lafe certainly hoped so, because the answers to these questions would have a large bearing on what happened when he reached the end of his journey.

He had few relatives, only one uncle that he remembered, and two cousins who were a little older than he was. Those two were probably his only living kin now and he wondered if they had inherited the Erickson wealth. Or had his father's enterprise failed when the *Northern Lights* ran onto an uncharted reef somewhere, or perhaps like many other ships simply failed to return to her home port at the end of her journey.

There had been a fortune in sealskins alone awaiting the *Northern Lights* in Dusky Sound and there would also have been many barrels of oil from the whales she had killed. If the ship had managed to pick them up, Lafe calculated, and it had not all been lost in the devilish game of dice that life really was. But there was a positive side of the ledger to balance those losses. There was the fruit of his loins, the seventeen children his wives had born him and the eighteenth still to come. As each of his children had grown old enough to understand, he had taught them the name Erickson.

'This is your name, Son of Erik,' he had told these solemn little sons and daughters, 'and don't you ever forget it.'

Those who were too young to learn the name from him would learn it from their mothers, and even Rima and Moana had been carefully instructed to tell their children about the name of Erickson when they were old enough to understand its meaning.

'Enough Ericksons to go spinning through the next century like a cannonball,' Lafe chuckled to the stars above him. If they were as fertile as their mothers and father, and some had already proved that they were, then there would be enough Ericksons to populate one of the main islands by themselves in a few more years. Many of his children and grandchildren must have died in the massacre at the village and in the tribal wars that raged through Te Wai Pounamu, but he would not let his mind dwell on that. Instead he saw his strong sons and attractive daughters as they had been when he knew them, striding forth to meet life and the challenges ahead of them.

He slept for a stretch, woke up refreshed and offered to take the helm. He soon had the feel of the little ship and, after watching him for a while to make sure the little cutter was well-handled, the boatman wrapped himself in the same piece of sail and was soon snoring fit to wake the dead. Lafe was still at the helm when they swept around the headland at dawn and into the commodious harbour, and there before him lay the most beautiful sight he had ever seen. Three big whalers sat on their anchors, tucked in a little bay surrounded by forest, on water as still as a lake. He nudged the boatman with his foot and the man came awake and quickly took the tiller, tacking to bring the bow around to point at one of the ships. She was a large three-master carrying an American flag on her crosstrees. The other two ships were whalers too, but the flags they flew were British.

The boatman spoke for the first time, telling Lafe in his own English language that the whalers had been very successful sallying out from this harbour to ambush the whales as they swam down the coast to the southern waters. Lafe wondered if this sudden friendliness was because daylight had revealed his tattoos and the man knew who he was, but he expected that Guard knew who he could trust and who he could not.

The cutter made directly for the side of the American ship hidden from view of the others in the bay, a ladder was thrown down and as soon as Lafe had stepped onto the ladder and begun to climb, the little boat paid off. Catching the breeze again it fled back the way it had come and Lafe turned to watch it go. He guessed the boatman was under strict orders but he felt very lonely as he climbed slowly up to the level of the deck. Guard had told him that a runner had been sent south to notify the Yankee that a new crew member would be joining them before they left the bay. A first glance at the faces of the officers confirmed that they had not expected what they saw.

'Good morning,' he said, but the words did not sound right even to him and the looks on their faces told him that his greeting had not made sense to them either. As they continued to stare he sensed the exasperation of the captain, but he could not help him. Being aboard a whaler and amongst his own people had unmanned him once again and he began to cry, overcome with the emotion of the moment.

The captain finally showed his kindly side and Lafe was helped below and out of sight until he managed to compose himself. Then he was fitted out with clothing and taken to the mess for the breakfast he badly needed after the long night at sea. The cook produced pancakes and syrup but the food was so strange and sweet after what he was used to he could barely do justice to it. After he had eaten he was shown to a bunk in a quiet part of the ship and left there. He lay and listened to the activity on deck as the men made ready to sail. He could hear the water kegs being rolled over the side so they could be towed ashore and filled. The ship had a tempo and a rhythm that told Lafe she would not be in the country much longer and he could only hope that this time he would survive those last critical hours.

He took off the cloak his wife had spent so many days making for him from kiwi feathers fitted so cunningly into the weave, and he rolled it and stored it carefully in a canvas bag he had been given. That and the tiki around his neck were the only things he would take away from this country, unless of course he counted his memories. They were far too many and too valuable to be weighted in any equation. Such riches would tip the scales in favour of everyone following in his footsteps and risking the same fate, he thought. Had he been unlucky to become separated from his sailors and taken prisoner by the Maori? In fairness and in truth he would have to answer no to that question, he decided.

422

The man who stays close to the hearth and never adventures can just as easily die of a heart seizure at the sudden rustle of a mouse, he told himself with a frown of disgust at the thought. He had known many in the old world who would never venture far from the farm or the shop, under the delusion that the world would come to a complete stop if they were not there to watch over their tiny corners of it. Soon he would be back among those people once again and he wondered how they would see him. Would they be able to look past his tattoo and find the real person underneath?

He had been disappointed at his reception on the deck that morning. Once again the stunned silence and the eyes that stared at his face had unnerved him, taking the words out of his mouth before he could even utter them. He would have to get used to the staring eyes, he told himself. For the rest of his life everyone he met would stare at him.

He went up on deck to watch what was happening, listening carefully to the words and to the way they came out of each speaker's mouth. Where he could be useful he helped and received tentative smiles in return for his trouble. The kegs of fresh water were swung on board and sent down below by the noisy crew and he saw that there were not many of them. He guessed that this whaler was full of oil, and that even these last kegs that were now full of fresh water would be filled with oil by the time the ship reached her next port. He knew it was a whaler's proud ambition to return with every vessel filled that could possibly hold oil, including the chamber pot under the captain's bed.

That evening he was shown to the little cuddy where the officers ate their meals. He could see that he caused them a problem in that they did not quite know which part of the ship he best fitted into so for the time being, because he had once been a ship's officer they let him join their little group. He could not join in the general conversation but he listened hard, picking up words and fitting the sentences together as best he could. This was a happy ship, that was soon obvious by the good spirits and respect the sailors showed toward each other. Successful and happy both, and near the end of her voyage too, he decided. The second mate, who said he had much to do with Indians, took unofficial charge of Lafe and took the trouble to speak slowly and directly to his face, and in this way managed to convey some of the conversation that swirled rapidly around him.

An hour after daylight the next morning the tide turned and began to run out of the bay, and the ship plucked her anchor out of the sandy bottom of the snug harbour and went with the tide. Right up to that moment when they began to pick up way Lafe still expected Te Rauparaha's war canoes to come around the corner and pluck him off the deck, and when the ship began to feel the power of the Pacific Ocean under her keel he felt a huge weight come off his shoulders. It was strange, but somehow he had never really believed that he would leave this lovely, warlike land.

He had no specific duties on the ship but helped where he could, and when they found he had the sensitive hands and the instinct to achieve that fine balance between wind and water he became a helmsman. In this way he began to get to know the ship's officers. At first they spoke so fast the words ran from their mouths like a waterfall and appeared to swirl around in the air with no meaning while he strove desperately to catch enough of them to make a sentence, but gradually he attuned his ear to their speech and the half-remembered patterns of the language became clearer.

Although they carried a man in the crow's nest they were not hunting but making their way across the Pacific at their best speed for Cape Horn. Then they would sail up the South Atlantic to the ship's home port on the east coast. Lafe had found out the ship's name now, and a pretty name it was too. She was the *Jane Rhodes* from New Bedford, Massachusetts, two years out from her home port and now full of oil and heading home at her best speed. He heard that Jackie Guard had sent a message to the ship telling them that a ship's officer kidnapped by the Maori some years earlier wished to sign on for the voyage back to America. This had suited the captain, as a whaler was always short of crew after two years at sea.

'We did not expect a tattooed savage who could not speak English to be delivered on board instead,' the captain told Lafe bluntly. He was not an unkind man, this John Blake, and his remarks were not taken as such, but he made it clear he considered that Jackie Guard had got the

424

better of him in this matter. After a few days, however, he realized that Lafe's loss of speech was a temporary thing and he began to change his mind. His curiosity grew and he sensed that a great story lay behind the tattooed face.

The captain was prepared to pay for his story in the currency of the ship, a few tasty preserves hidden away for such a moment, a bottle or two of wine, and if need be enough rum to float a man's tonsils. On most nights the officers off watch would gather to listen and would question Lafe about his time in the land of the cannibals. With time and patience they coaxed the story out of him and enjoyed the food and drink their captain supplied. Their questioning was gentle though, and John Blake only allowed the story to be extracted at a pace that Lafe was comfortable with. When his audience had left the cabin to go to their watches or their bunks it was the captain's turn to talk, and he did his best to answer the many questions that Lafe plied him with. In this way Lafe began to understand that the world had galloped forward at breakneck speed while his own mind remained locked in the first few months of the beginning of the century. There were so many things that he wanted to know, half a lifetime of knowledge he now sought to catch up on. Even whaling had changed, though not greatly.

He gathered that the New England that had spawned him had left its kicking, sprawling infancy behind and was moving to achieve a respectable young adulthood as a country. With its infinite supply of land and its resources, America now held unlimited promise for the many people who came to live there, and its civilization was slowly pushing westwards. There was big money being made in shipping and whaling, though the seals were now scarce due to over-fishing. This was the second trip the *Jane Rhodes* had made to this southern fishery and both trips had been successful. This was a full ship with happy investors and a contented crew who would kill one or two more whales on the journey home so they could arrive in triumph.

John Blake could afford to be generous so Lafe was signed on the ship's books and would have a few dollars in his pocket when the ship paid off at the end of her voyage. Now that his story was known around the ship he was no longer looked upon as a renegade or a white man gone bad, and curiosity drove the sailors to his side. He was asked many questions about his way of life among the Maori and he found a growing knowledge and interest in the peoples of the South Pacific. The sailors had their own stories of the islands, passing them from ship to ship and seeking confirmation of the way life was lived in such places. When word went around the ship that he had six wives and had fathered eighteen children it reinforced the popular belief that he had spent his time lying around in the sun in dalliance with dusky maidens. He found it easier to smile knowingly than to disillusion them.

In time it seemed that the tattoo was not so important any more. The sailors got used to it when they got to know the man behind the face, but he knew it would never be like that with strangers. The tattoo was designed to shock and intimidate people, and that was its purpose in the Maori world. It was a face to take to war, to strike fear into the heart of the enemy, and to a white man seeing it for the first time it spoke of savagery, dark secrets and black magic, things scarcely understood in more civilized countries.

Many warriors added to their tattoo every year, using designs that told of the wars they had fought and the enemy they had killed until every bit of space was taken up and their faces were as black as the soot they used for their ink. Lafe was glad that his own tattoo was simpler, carrying the scrolls and elaborate spirals of the particular tribe he belonged to. Tama's people had been reluctant fighters, preferring to celebrate the shapes and forms of the bush and sea coast that sustained them. But in the society of his own people, such distinctions were irrelevant. To them Lafe's face was grotesquely carved and stained. And the tattoo could never be undone. This was the face he had now, and somehow he had to learn to live with it.

By the time the *Jane Rhodes* set her course for the coast of Chile they had been at sea for several weeks, his English was more or less usable and he began to ask about his relatives in Norfolk, Virginia. Several officers remembered the Erickson name and some had heard of the *Northern Lights*, but the general opinion was that the family was no longer in the shipping business.

426

'The shipping and whaling game is not so large that we would not have heard of them,' John Blake told him. 'But no one has sighted your old ship for many years now. There was talk that a ship of that name once came back from the South Pacific with a fortune in whale oil and seal skins, but that was a long time ago.'

With the power of the roaring forties pushing the ship to the limit of her worn sails and rigging they made good time across the Pacific, stopping only to kill and process a whale off the coast of Chile before squaring up to round Cape Horn. The ship was full to the gunwales now and the sailors could boast that even the cook had to give up his pots to store oil in. Such a trip was a matter of great pride for all aboard, and many a good story in a seaport alehouse began with the words,

'I remember such and such a ship, whenever she came into port the crew were like skeletons because the cook had to give up his pots to store the oil.' True or not, such talk meant the company that ran such a ship had the pick of the crews because their voyages were known to be profitable.

Lafe thrived on life aboard ship and found that his mind, grown rusty over the years from the lack of stimulation, slowly began to catch up with the world again. The constant challenge of new ideas and the need to plan for what lay ahead when he stepped ashore in his own country made his head cry out for help some days and then he became despondent and wished the voyage would just go on forever. He began to doubt that he was up to facing life with the handicaps that he suffered, but John Blake calmed him and set him more difficult tasks to take his mind off the future. He grew to respect his strange crewman's seamanship, and promised his support.

'While you are ashore you will always have a friend,' he told Lafe. 'And no ship that I command will ever leave the coast without my offering you a berth on board her.'

Cape Horn provided no more excitement than a rough ride and a taste of the cold that awaited them at home. There were minor problems of broken gear and ripped sails that slowed them, but soon they were out of the Horn's influence and heading north up the South American coast towards their destination.

Some days the wind did not blow at all and only a handful of miles were recorded in a twenty-four hour period. For a ship homeward bound these were the hardest and most frustrating of days and the sailors became moody and prone to outbreaks of fighting. During the long weeks Lafe studied maps, took his turn at shooting the sun at noon and the stars at night and pored over the ship's books. He studied every aspect of shipboard life and took his turn at every sailor's task until he was nearly as good a seaman as he had once been. He no longer found himself thinking in Maori and painfully converting his thoughts into English and he planned ahead now rather than taking each day as it came.

At some stage during the long trip up the centre of the Atlantic through the doldrums, he was aware he had crossed his outward-bound path and so completed the full circle of the globe. For many of the sailors on board it was the same. Their ship had followed the same course to the fishing grounds that the *Northern Lights* had followed thirty or more years before. For some of the older hands this was their second circumnavigation, for this ship had been to the southern oceans before.

According to the ship's log the year was 1832 so Lafe was fifty-one years old. So much time had gone and he scarcely knew how or where. Many times during the voyage he lamented the passing of those years of his youth and vigour, and at such times a song would come unbidden into his mind. It was a song that his first wife Marama had chanted when the mood took her.

'Soon I will be lost to sight, carried away on the swirling currents, Carried far away, going out onto the ocean where the whale swims. All that is left to me is to spout endlessly.'

The way she had spoken these words in her lilting language had been very poetic and beautiful and he was reminded of the singing of the whales. All whalers knew of the whale's song, though the concept was far too strange for any landsman to understand, and Lafe had heard it himself when their ship was lying quiet in the water. The song of the humpback whale was by all votes superior to any other, and the thought of this great creature sending its voice through the deep gave Lafe a strange feeling up and down his spine. Some would have it that it was the song of the mermaid, but it was not.

428

The crossing of the Equator had come and gone now and as the weeks slowly passed the days grew cooler and coats and jackets began to appear on deck. They were coming into the northern hemisphere winter, which promised a cool welcome after the temperatures they had grown used to. One night Lafe realized that the Southern Cross whose stars had been his companions for thirty-two years had dropped below the horizon. Soon they were at the same latitude as the Azores and they were nearly home. When the lookout called land from the masthead they knew that somewhere behind the islands on the horizon was New Bedford, the home port of the *Jane Rhodes*.

Lafe leaned on the rails, well wrapped against the cold and determined not to miss a thing as the ship entered the bustling, commodious harbour with only her topsails set in the stiff breeze that had a touch of sleet in it. It was a frightening thing to see so many people going about their business in such a determined fashion. On one side men teemed like ants over the wharves loading and unloading ships, while across the harbour other ships were being built and fitted out as if there was not a moment to spare. The workers barely took time from their tasks to give the incoming ship a wave and a cheer. Such an arrival would be a gala event among Maori and no work would be done that day or for several days afterwards, Lafe reflected. How had a race of people become so well organized that they did nothing but toil from daybreak to nightfall? These people of his homeland were so different from the people of the South Pacific, and already he was finding it hard to like them as well.

The ship anchored in the roadstead until she could be towed to the wharf, but it was only a short respite. Unloading began immediately she was secured, the mate began to pay off her crew and soon the deck was quiet, the sailors dispersed to their homes or to the bars and shanties where they found willing hands to help them spend the money they had accumulated over their two years at sea.

Lafe was not yet ready to leave the security of the ship and, thanks to John Blake's compassion and understanding, remained on board as a watchman. Brief sorties ashore had proved to be a trial. The traffic, the buildings and the hustle that had become the way of life for everybody in this vigorous young country were very disconcerting to the newcomer. John Blake came once or twice a week with his wife in a carriage to take Lafe to their home and there they helped him to broaden his experience of his native country. There were trains to ride, horses to master again and the social etiquette of drawing room and dining table to learn and practise.

Young Mrs Guard of Tar White had been the first white woman Lafe had met in thirty years and she had been a mere girl from the slums of Sydney. Mrs Blake was the second and her gentility, kindness and courtesy went a long way to restoring his confidence.

There were also the curious and the downright rude to confront every day. New Bedford was a sailor's town and it had seen many strange sights but she could not take Lafe in her stride and before long his tattooed face was perhaps the best known in the town. His tales were told and retold wherever people met, and his life among the women of the South Seas was whispered about until the stories were exaggerated beyond belief. The resulting notoriety was not welcome, but as he became more familiar with his new world his confidence grew day by day until at last he was ready to go ashore.

For many years he had been plagued with doubts about the fate of the remaining sealers from the *Northern Lights*. The last he had seen of the men in his shore party they had been rowing vigorously in the direction of Dusky Sound, he had almost rammed Tama's big sailing canoe to help them escape and he was subsequently captured by the tribe. He had never heard of his shipmates or the *Northern Lights* again.

'Somewhere, someone in this town will know of Captain Olva,' he said, and so he began his search. The *Northern Lights* had recruited her crew from New Bedford so it was more than probable that somewhere among the little houses still lived an old shipmate. He haunted the taverns frequented by sailors, picking up titbits of information that eventually led him to a very old sailor who lived in a rundown boarding house not far from the docks. The old man eyed him suspiciously, from his tattooed face to the seaman's boots he wore.

'Who are you?' he demanded. 'I don't know you.' He had been a big man in his day but time and a hard life at sea had taken its toll and now his back was bent with age and his flesh hung from his bony frame. Lafe studied the weathered face and body and caught a vague glimpse of someone he had known thirty or more years back.

'I have come to talk with you about the time you served in the *Northern Lights* and went whaling in the waters around New Zealand,' Lafe said quietly.

'Aye, that's true,' the man agreed, his interest quickening. 'A harpooner I was then, Sam the harpooner. Sam, no second name, that's how I was known. The best harpooner that ever sailed the Pacific.' His old face wrinkled with pleasure at the memory of those far-off days.

'Lafe Erickson, second mate,' Lafe said, touching his breast.

'You don't look like the Lafe Erickson I knew,' the old harpooner said suspiciously. 'Besides, he is dead.'

'I am very much alive, I can assure you, Sam,' Lafe growled, 'and under these scars is the face of the same Lafe Erickson you went awhaling with.'

Once Sam was convinced that he was truly an old shipmate the memories came back clear and lucid. That same storm that had forced Lafe and his sick friend Matai to seek shelter near Kakapo Lake had driven the *Northern Lights* far to the south of New Zealand, nearly to the ice, Sam recalled with a shudder. When she had swept into Dusky Sound near three weeks late it was to find the remains of Lafe's sealing party in a state of siege and very frightened. They had been attacked by Maori and the three men missing from their party, a sailor, the second mate and the Maori called Matai, had all been killed by the savages.

Sam remembered very well that the second mate who had been killed was Lafe Erickson, the son of the ship's owner. Captain Olva had retrieved the caches of sealskins and had the coast searched as far north as he dared go, but no sign of the missing men was ever found. Sam sat for a while thinking, as old men do.

'I remember now, we still had one of the Maori guides on board and we stopped to drop him where we had picked him up from. Okatoo, or some such?'

'Otaakou. That was the name of the place the guide came from,' Lafe agreed. 'His name was Jimmy.'

431

'A nice man for a native,' Sam said. 'I remember him now.'

He also remembered the big black dog, Salem, and that more than anything convinced him that he was indeed talking to the onetime second mate on his old whaler. The *Northern Lights* had returned to New Bedford with the richest cargo that had ever been brought into the port. Sam was paid off then, and with such a large amount of money in his pocket that he had stayed ashore ever since. He remembered little else but the rumour the ship had been lost some time ago in the slave trade.

'And what of Captain Olva?' Lafe asked, but there was nothing to be learned of his old mentor and his father's friend. He spent the whole afternoon with the old harpooner, reliving their days on the ship and enjoying shared memories of Olva and the other men they had known. He returned to the *Jane Rhodes* with a full heart and sought the quiet of his hammock to go over and over their talk, fitting together these new pieces of the puzzle that had tormented him for so many years.

John Blake had meanwhile written to various sources in the shipping town of Norfolk seeking information on any of Lafe's or his father's surviving relatives, or any firm that had conducted business with the house of Erickson. Like Lafe, he knew that someone, somewhere would hold the key to the missing years and it was only a matter of time before they found it.

Chapter 23

When the letter arrived from Norfolk Lafe read it a little sadly. It was from a small firm that had been factors to Erickson senior for many years and it confirmed that their client had died ten years earlier. If John Blake could provide some positive identification of the man on whose behalf he had made enquiries, the writer held information of interest and desired a meeting as soon as possible.

'This is very promising, don't you think?' the sea captain asked. Lafe took his time over rereading the letter until he was sure he had digested its contents thoroughly. In the months at sea he had spent a lot of time over his books but still some phrases in the English language eluded him.

'So my poor father is dead, though I have known it in my own mind for many years,' he answered finally. 'And he died not ever knowing whether his only child had preceded him to the grave or not.'

For a father to bury his only child, even with no body and no real surety, must be the cruellest fate, he thought, and he wondered yet again about his own children. He knew he had buried at least some of them that terrible day in the village by the sea, but he had left a living son and by now Moana would have delivered her child too. Which of the eighteen were dead or alive only time would tell and he might never know. With an effort he switched his mind back to the problem in hand.

'What of these factors and what do you think they want?' he asked John Blake.

The other man considered his answer. 'Factors live and die by their reputation,' he said slowly. 'To the shipowner who is often away at sea or in another country they act as banker, solicitor and agent. I have heard of this firm and I wager that you can trust them with your money and your life, as your father obviously did. The best thing we can do is travel to Norfolk to see them.'

He thought for another moment or two. 'I still have time to fill before my ship needs me, why don't we go by road? It will give you a chance to see some of your country again.'

Lafe looked at him in surprise. He had expected that if he went at all, he would travel on a coastal ship. But the captain sensed his leeriness and went on quickly, marshalling all his arguments, and before Lafe could think of a good reason not to go the plans were made.

'I want to see you settled properly before I take my next ship awhaling,' his friend told him bluntly. 'And I don't want to see your great tattooed face every morning of my life.'

Lafe felt badly hurt by this but he sensed that for his own good John Blake was going to cast him loose into the current again. Would he sink or swim, he wondered. He supposed he might manage a few ineffectual strokes before he sank to the bottom for good. He touched the great tiki around his neck, a gesture that had become a habit now, and thought of Marama waving him back from the spirit world to this one. It gave him courage.

'Remember you were destined to be a chief one day, did you not tell me that yourself?' John Blake said. He knew he had hurt Lafe and his voice was gentle. 'Let the dogs snap at your heels, as I have seen them do. There are plenty of them around and you cannot fight them all. Instead we are going to claim your inheritance if there is any. Remember that this is the money that you yourself earned on the whaling and sealing grounds. You father sent you to sea to earn that money and you took great risks to do it. People died filling those casks with oil and nobody in this world has more right to your father's money than you do.'

Within a couple of days they were off. They travelled by coach to New York, a huge bustling seaport town where there were more people thronging the streets than Lafe thought existed on the whole earth.

434

From New York to Philadelphia they travelled again by coach, but from Baltimore to Washington they rode the railroad. Lafe felt this noisy, jolting, smoke-belching machine was a very strange way to be conveyed from one place to another. He thought it might be all right for freight goods but he doubted that it would ever become popular with men.

He gradually became more used to being stared at and he learned to ignore the looks of distaste on the faces of some of the people they travelled with or met at their lodgings. Sometimes a man came up to talk to him out of curiosity and Lafe found that human nature in America was not so different after all from anywhere else, though he found the natives of New Zealand a lot more open and easier to read. Some of the people he met were so interesting that he quite forgot it was the sight of his own face that had begun the conversation in the first place. Soon he was instigating conversations of his own, and he began to grow more fond of his fellow man when he realized they suffered more at the sight of his tattoo than he did. He found woman were easier to talk to because they sensed that he was more vulnerable than a wounded bird beneath that skin of his and they felt his need for human contact.

He and the captain left Washington by coach for Richmond and travelled on from there to Norfolk in Virginia. By now Lafe had gained an insight into the great possibilities of his country. The farms were green and orderly, the animals fine, handsome and well-kept. He was impressed by the industries of Philadelphia and Baltimore and felt that here America seemed to have a sense of its own destiny.

The seaport of Norfolk had grown so big that Lafe no longer recognized it as his own town. The river was full of boats and ships putting out into the bay, and the bigger ships were preparing to leave the bay and head across the oceans to who knew where. Other ships had recently arrived and were unloading and the sheer volume of produce crossing the wharves was staggering. It was mostly manhandled by Negroes, many of them slaves, and he looked at them with sympathetic eyes. He too had been a slave and he knew how it felt. He was interested to see that this town had visitors with skin colours of various hues, from the coal black of the Africans to the yellow skin of the Orientals and every shade in between.

435

They took up lodgings in a quiet part of town not so far from the wharves, but far enough away that their nights were not disturbed by the sailors' revelry. Lafe spent a lot of his time worrying about money. The problem was that he didn't have any and he had to rely on John Blake for the roof over his head and the food on his plate. It was not easy to accept and he began to realize that the more civilized the country, the more the likelihood of a man being chewed up and spat out into the gutters if he didn't have this most important of all commodities. If it was not for his benefactor he himself would be in the gutter by now. But John Blake was an unfailing friend who believed in what was right, and when he saw Lafe about to stumble he put out a hand to steady him again. Every day now the tattooed Swede became mentally stronger. One day soon he would be able to stand on his own again, and for that he was thankful.

When the factors heard that Lafe and John Blake were in town, arrangements were made for them to come to their chambers and at the agreed time the two whalers arrived at an old but gracious building that overlooked the river. It was a morning of spring showers and a cold wind that blew right down from the Allegheny Mountains, still carrying their winter covering of snow. Lafe's blood had become thin in the South Pacific and he didn't care much for the winters in his homeland anymore.

They were shown into a room full of well-stuffed easy chairs and polished furniture that smelt of money. There was a cheerful fire burning in the grate and they found a gentleman of indeterminate age waiting for them. Lafe guessed by his wrinkled face and silver hair that he might have been in his seventies. He was flanked by two younger men, possibly his sons.

None of them showed the normal reaction to his scarred face, which told Lafe that they had been warned of his tattoo. They might have had their spies out watching him or perhaps they were simply too well-trained and experienced to show surprise at anything. Whatever it was, Lafe was impressed when he stepped close to shake hands, almost eyeball to eyeball, and all he could detect was a polite and dignified interest.

When everyone was seated and comfortable the old man began.

436

'We are a family firm and we have been in business in this town almost since it began. We have been factors all this time and our interests are the buying and selling of ships' cargo.' The old man looked closely at Lafe before he carried on. 'For many years we have handled the cargoes of Erickson ships, and much other business beside that. Both families have found it a profitable arrangement to date, and over the years considerable trust was built up between us.' Once again he paused before carrying on, and Lafe could see he was feeling his way.

'Ahead of us I see shoal water. It is in the interests of both parties that we proceed with caution.

'I will ask you, Lafe Erickson, to tell us your story from the time the *Northern Lights* left Norfolk in 1800 until the time you stepped onto the wharf at New Bedford in 1832. It will take time, we know, but do not worry. We will not be interrupted and we have all day if necessary.'

He smiled encouragingly at Lafe and said quietly, 'You may begin when you are ready.'

Lafe sat for nearly a minute, saying nothing as he turned his mind back all those years. He rose and went to the window where he could look down on the very same river he had sailed so confidently in the little cutter he had built as a lad. What a story it was to tell, with a scope and breadth that covered half the oceans of the world. For a minute longer he looked to where the river joined Chesapeake Bay. Here the wind whipped up sheets of spray where the current from the river opposed the waves blown in by the spring winds, and he remembered those last precious hours he had spent with his father. With his back still turned to the room, he began to speak.

Part of the way through his story, he realized that the factors had his father's journal in front of them, and from time to time they stopped the flow of his story to ask questions and clarify certain points. Lunch came and went and the sun crept across the sky. The old man started to look weary and his sons finally called a halt, anxious not to tire him too much. They asked Lafe to return the next day and begin where he had left off. When the two sailors returned to their rooms Lafe was exhausted from the mental strain of trying to find the right words to convey what had actually happened since he had left their port.

437

'Do you think they believed what I had to say?' he asked bluntly.

'It is the damnedest story I ever heard in my life,' the captain replied. 'I have had months to get used to it, but to hear you tell it today, nobody could ever disbelieve you.'

The next day they gathered again in the room of the factors and he continued his story right up to the time the *Jane Rhodes* had reached her home port. When he finished there was a long silence in the room and he reached out to warm his hands at the little fire burning in the grate, seeing in its flames a thousand campfires and those he had shared them with.

'Will you excuse us for a few minutes, Mr Erickson?' the old man finally asked. 'We wish to talk alone with Captain Blake to clear up a few minor points.'

Lafe took a walk along the river while the sun struggled to take the chill from the air. He knew that his fate hung in the balance in some way, but he felt strangely removed from the decisions that were being made in that quiet office. When he returned to the building his steps were slow and weary, but he found a different atmosphere when he re-entered the room.

'Welcome back, Mr Erickson,' the old factor said quietly. 'You understand, I hope, that there was a great need for caution on our part. Your father never gave up hope of your eventual return and he invested a substantial amount of money with us. We are now satisfied with your credentials and this is your money.'

Lafe leaned forward slightly in his seat but he was careful to let nothing show on his face as the old man smiled and continued in his dry voice. 'Under our careful stewardship you will be pleased to know that this sum has grown to sixty-eight thousand dollars. We congratulate you on your good fortune.'

Lafe felt a small glow of happiness in the pit of his stomach. He would not end up on the streets after all. He knew John Blake would always find him a berth but the way people had turned away from him had been like a dagger in the guts and he had never fully recovered from it. In his dreams he paced the docks from ship to ship, hungry and looking for a berth, and every face was turned away from him.

'I am afraid the rest of my news is not so good,' the old man told his guests. 'Your father left his ship, warehouses and his considerable property to you and your uncle, his brother, on an equal basis. While he was alive your uncle remitted your share of the profits, as an honest man would, to this firm to hold on your behalf.'

He paused to reorganize his thoughts, and he squared his frail shoulders as he delivered his bombshell.

'But since your uncle died, God rest his soul, his two sons have seen fit to dispute your father's arrangements.' The words were fairly spat out, Lafe noticed. 'All of the assets held by your uncle have since been sold except for your father's ship the *Northern Lights*, and she was lost slaving off the coast of Africa.'

The old man looked at Lafe over the top of his glasses, taking the measure of his reaction. 'I must warn you that the recovery of any of these assets would be extremely difficult.'

'One question,' Lafe cut in. 'Did my father at any time consider that I was dead?'

'No, there were the marks you have told us you carved on the trees in certain bays. Those marks were found and reported back to him, and because of that he never lost faith that you would return. And there was the letter brought home by the whaler *Mary Elizabeth*. That arrived at the time of your uncle's death. It was too late for your father to know the good news, but your cousins knew of its contents.'

Lafe thought for a minute, struggling to find the right words, and when he spoke again his voice was hard.

'So I am right to think that these two cousins of mine have knowingly and deliberately set out to steal what is rightfully mine?'

The other men stared at him, noting now the steel-blue eyes that they had not noticed before.

'Yes.' the old man spoke for all three factors. 'We do believe that is what they have done.' He was anxious to finish the interview now and go home to his fireside. Just for a moment he had seen behind the tattooed mask that this son of his old friend the Swede wore. What he saw was more than the ruthlessness of a hard businessman, and it chilled him to the core. What he saw was the cruel anger of a savage.

Later that night the two whalers returned to their lodgings to discuss the day's happenings over a bottle of wine. John Blake was happy for his friend and congratulated him on becoming a rich man.

'What does the future hold for you now?' he asked

'I will buy a ship and become a sailor again,' Lafe told him seriously. 'For months now I have worried about how I will make a living. With a face like mine it would not have been easy. Sometimes I dream that the whole of humanity has turned its face from me and I will end up in the gutter as I have seen so many sailors do here and elsewhere. When you can no longer get a berth on a ship and you have no other skills to offer and no kinfolk to take you in, then what is left but a slow undignified death?'

He spat into the fire and added grimly, 'And from what I heard today I don't expect that my precious cousins would extend much of a helping hand in my direction. Do you believe that a bad deed can be done to help the cause of humanity, John Blake?'

'If you mean that the end can sometimes justify the means even if those ends are met by crime or wickedness, then perhaps I could see an argument, although no cases spring immediately to mind,' the other man said cautiously. Lafe filled their glasses again and began to explain the Maori concept of mana as he had come to know it.

'It is a matter of honour, but honour can be seen in more than one way. Among the people I have been living with it is seen in this way. When a man does you a bad turn, his mana goes up by the same amount as yours goes down. It is like looking at a sight glass. You can see the loss or gain to your mana in increments. At least, the Maori can and I have come to see it that way too.

'And this is where that lovely word utu comes in. If a man steals your hog, his mana has gone up and yours has gone down by an equal amount. But if you steal it back again you are both level and a lot of energy has been expended for no gain at all. Then there is the risk that this taking of your hog could happen again and so interfere with your normal pleasures in life. So a wise man kills the thief and takes all his pigs, and that makes his gain and the thief's losses permanent. And this is utu.'

440

The word was harsh on his tongue as he repeated it, and his face was a mask of strength and hatred.

'I see,' said John Blake thoughtfully, and indeed he did see, and was deeply troubled by what he saw in that tattooed face.

The next day the captain returned to his ship in New Bedford, and that same day Lafe began his utu. For weeks he walked the town, the bars, and the brothels, watching and listening. Wherever the sailors congregated he spent his money and listened, always listened. At last his strategy was rewarded, his cousins were pointed out to him and he watched them as a cat would a mouse. They were plump from good living and carried the conceit on their faces of those who do well from the efforts of others.

That was true in more ways than one, as Lafe soon discovered. The brothers had lost the *Northern Lights* on a slaving run and now their real wealth came from the prostitutes and the brothels of the town. Lafe thought many times about what Rima and her sisters had suffered at the hands of the Ngati Toa warriors and as he looked at the pale, consumptive drabs of the back streets and the lives they were forced to lead he began to despise these relatives of his even more.

Many times during the weeks that followed he was aware of shifty figures in the shadows and he was sure his cousins were having him watched as well, but he didn't let that worry him too much. His face made him the best-known man in town anyway. He hired a couple of robust, well-armed sailors to watch his back and then began to frequent the places that his cousins were in the habit of visiting.

Soon a little bird whispered in his ear that every night his cousins visited the opium den in the slums outside the town. They had become slaves to the tears of the poppy. Lafe filed this away in the back of his mind. He knew the nature of the world that these Erickson brothers inhabited, and knew too that such men made enemies wherever they did business. Now he made it his job to find these enemies and set them one by one against his cousins. He became reckless with confidence and sent the rumour flying from tavern to tavern that there were people in town that were looking to balance the ledger. The message was clear. His poor cousins did not have long to enjoy this world.

And now that I have done what I have done, I will wait to see if my cousins flush from the bushes and come within gunshot range, he told himself. With his money it would not be hard to arrange to have them dumped in the river with a cannonball tied to their legs, and he knew that they knew it. But he had better plans than that. For a few more weeks he spread himself and his money around the town. He was popular wherever he went now as people had grown used to his face and he had built a reputation as a generous man. He had heard some of the stories about himself, and was particularly amused by the one that told how for the price of having his face tattooed he was allowed to choose from the tribe more wives than he could count. It did not hurt the reputation that he was trying to cultivate.

One day a letter arrived at his lodgings asking for a meeting, and he knew he had flushed out his birds. But were they in range yet? He arranged to have the meeting on neutral ground at a hotel, and several days before the set date he bought up all the opium for miles around, though it cost him a pretty penny. He arranged for the Chinaman who ran the den to run out of product. The man did not care why, and for good money he would deny entrance to those two forever if that was what Lafe wanted. He did not like them or what they did to women, and he sensed that their power around town was on the wane anyway. There had been stories circulating over the past few weeks that made him feel his establishment would be better off without such clients.

'Disgusting, that women should be made to do what they do to make such men rich,' he agreed. It was good to have money, Lafe thought, and he had certainly spread enough of it around that week to make his factors cringe. He had caused half a dozen of his cousins' best prostitutes to flee their stables and take up life in another town far, far away, and he knew his relatives were starting to feel the hurt.

He arranged with the hotel for food to be prepared, sent up and served when he called for it. He dressed in a fine suit with his long hair carefully washed and combed back, tied with a black ribbon at the nape of his neck. For some strange reason his fine clothes and flaxen hair seemed to accentuate his tattoo rather than subdue it.

The cousins were shown into the private room and with a brief touch of hands they were escorted to their places at the table, where Lafe sat watching them without moving a muscle. He let the silence drag on until all three could feel the tension in the room. These cousins of his had pale, sallow skins and they lacked the muscle tone that a sailor or a man of the land would have developed. Some would call them clever, Lafe thought, but it was a common human failing to confuse cunning with clever.

As the centrepiece of the table he had laid out a water pipe, commonly used for the taking of opium, with its little acorn shaped cup to hold the piece of resin. He had been shown how it was used, and next to it and close enough for his guests to smell he had placed a tiny ball of almost black opium on a little silver tray. It had cost him a sailor's wages for a week, and he watched with well-hidden contempt as both men's eyes darted from his face to the silver tray and back again.

'As much as I enjoy the silence, you two have asked for this meeting,' he reminded them quietly. 'May I ask what is on your minds?'

'What do you want?' the elder of the two spoke, trying without success to keep the belligerent tone from his voice. 'We have come to find out what it is you want from us.'

'I want a ship, a good one and a cargo to take back with me to the Pacific,' Lafe told them quietly.

'So what do you expect us to do about it?'

'Money,' Lafe said. 'I expect money from you. But first, let me tell you a story.' As he began, he mentally thanked the tribe for the hours they had spent telling stories, and the ability he had developed to see the country clearly in his mind as he described it to these men who were his only living relatives. He told them of New Zealand, its people and its climate, of how a man could grow almost anything he desired there and of the land rush that would one day take place. He spoke of the unlimited supplies of timber, spars and masts enough to fit out every navy in the world, and of the great pods of whales that travelled their ancient routes from the tropics to the ice every year, most of their journey within sight of land. He told them of the valuable trade in food between New Zealand and the penal colony at Sydney Cove, and he talked of minerals, of jade

443

such as that he wore at his throat, more valuable than gold in the Orient. There was enough flax to establish a strategic supply of rope for all the ships in every fleet of the world, and there were thousands of acres of prime land to be acquired cheaply for the price of a few blankets and muskets and such things.

He told them that the lack of any real British control over the land made for great opportunities for enterprising people. But mostly he dwelt on the value of whale oil at the current price it was bringing on the markets, and of the fortunes that were being made by bold and adventurous men in the South Pacific. When he finally finished he thought his old chief Tama, who had been long-winded himself, would have been proud of such a spiel.

'But why have you come to us?' the elder cousin asked.

'Because I have not sufficient funds of my own. And with a face like this,' and Lafe gestured airily at his own cheeks, 'it is not as easy to obtain the money I need as you might think.'

During the dinner which followed he noted a sense of relief on the faces and in the manner of these Erickson cousins, overlaid by a touch of contempt than oozed out at times during the conversation that followed. They had seen him as a threat since he had come to their town, and might even have been frightened by him but in the end he had come to them like any other man might, looking for money. This they understood, for money was the god they worshipped too.

When the dinner was over Lafe kept his guests' glasses topped up with wine and watched as their eyes darted more and more frequently to the pipe and the little ball of opium. Their tongues darted like lizards around their lips in involuntary reaction to their desires, and when he thought it was time he put them out of their misery.

'Do you gentlemen indulge?' he asked casually, picking up the pipe and giving it an appreciative sniff. 'Help yourselves.'

He watched closely as one of them took a piece of the black sticky opium the size of a small pea and placed it in the pipe. Holding a small burning taper above the little ball he hungrily dragged the smoke down and across the cooling water into his lungs. The little ball bubbled and spread until it looked like a spot of very expensive tar, then it vanished completely, leaving a tiny spot of residue behind. Its sweet, cloying smell filled the cabin. Lafe took the pipe in his turn and cut a sliver of the gum, placed it in the cup and breathed deeply. The smoke had a strange, sweet taste as it was drawn into his lungs. The Chinaman had explained the effects that he would experience next, so Lafe stretched out and waited for the dreams to come.

Slowly the colours of the room grew more vivid, the little dust motes that hung in a sunbeam that crossed the room from the lowering sun held him entranced. Soon he felt his spirit becoming lighter and detaching itself from his physical body and then he was able to look down upon himself lying upon the couch. His spirit became restless and roamed, touching as lightly as a butterfly upon many things but never resting long enough in one place for him to capture it again. Thoughts streaked across his mind and were more difficult to capture than quicksilver, each bursting into tiny pieces and re-forming into another, all different but really the same.

Several times during the next couple of hours his two bodyguards entered the room according to the instructions they had been given, and the last time they came they removed the comatose forms of the two brothers and transported them gently by coach to their own home. Lafe awoke much later, aware that it was now dark and he was alone.

He tried to recapture parts of a dream he had experienced, remembering that it was about the cuckoo that arrived in New Zealand in the springtime. To the Maori the birdcalls had been cries of hunger, but by autumn the notes had changed and the cuckoo called 'All is well'. Somehow in his dream Lafe had seen the bird fly north into the Pacific to spend the winter roosting on the backs of whales. He had seen that quite clearly, the rows of cuckoos sitting with their wings folded on the vast backs of right whales. Now he remembered the many times he had chafed Marama about her funny little beliefs.

'But what if the whale should dive? What would happen to your birds then?' he had asked.

'Then you would be right and I would be wrong and there would be no birds,' had been her light reply. 'But you watch, next spring the birds will come again and you will see that I am right after all.'

445

'Such strange dreams,' Lafe told himself now. 'Such strange dreams.'

The next meeting began with hard negotiations between the cousins, neither side giving an inch unless they had to. Frederick and Günter Erickson were on one side of the table, Lafe on the other. Though we are cousins, you would not know it from listening to us, he reckoned to himself. And I wonder how my father would enjoy this meeting? In the beginning, he knew, his cousins were fighting for a quittance. They had expected at some time in the future to be brought before the judge by Lafe and his factors, and now they could see a way out.

That way was to put money into what should prove to be a profitable voyage for both parties. In that case they would expect Lafe to sign an affidavit stating that he had received fair payment and had no further claims against them or any of their descendants, and in return they would finance half of the ship and the cargo of trade goods she would carry and receive half of the profit of the voyage when costs and crew had been paid.

Lawyers were consulted and agreements drawn up until the brothers were convinced Lafe had been bound by red tape and could not wriggle free. But Lafe had learned the facts of life on the very first ship he had sailed on, and one of the things the sailors had taught him was that no one was more suspicious or mistrustful of his fellow man than a thief himself.

Now that he had a signed agreement with his cousins, he began to look for his ship. Many good ships had come away from the northern fisheries with poor cargoes, as there had been few whales there now for many years, and some owners were ready to sell their ships rather than outfit them and send them south around the world. So it was not long before Lafe found what he wanted and began to negotiate. He had set his sights on a solid three-master of six hundred tons, built on the Chesapeake.

She had done only three seasons whaling and her name was *Venus*. Lafe liked the name. His first wife Marama had been named for the moon and she used to laugh and say, 'When you look at the sky you will always be reminded of me.'

Now Lafe knew when he looked at the sky he would not only look for the moon, as he always did, but for that bright and friendly planet *Venus* beloved by all sailors. She was first out in the evening and last to go to bed in the morning, and many a night he had steered by her.

A letter arrived from his factors desiring a meeting, and this time they came to see him. The two sons were led by the old man himself who wasted no time in telling Lafe that his business partnership with his Erickson cousins had scandalized all who knew about it.

'Frederick and Günter Erickson are not to be trusted,' he said with venom, his old eyes fairly popping out of his skull in emphasis. 'They deal in slaves and young women and their debauchery is known throughout the state. Your father would be disappointed in you.'

'As you trusted my father and my father trusted you, so you can trust me,' Lafe replied, and that was all he would say to them.

There were more meetings with the cousins and there was more smoke and there were more dreams. Lafe continued to supply them with just enough of the tears of the poppy to keep them under his control. He spread his money shrewdly and totally controlled the only supplies of opium that came into the port. It was a damned expensive habit and a dangerous one at that, he concluded. It did not take him long to realize how easily a man could be captured by the subtle promises of the drug and its stealthy invasion of body and mind.

'Heaven to live with and hell to live without,' the Chinaman had warned him, and Lafe had to summon all his strength of will to control his own use of the opium he supplied to his cousins and business partners.

He was glad of the distraction of his new ship. After her sea trials he moved her to a berth on the wharf and had his possessions moved into the captain's cabin, pleased to feel the sea beneath his feet again. Within days her rigging swarmed with workmen and a warehouse began to fill with the trade goods that would be her cargo. Case upon case of muskets piled up until they made up the bulk of the stock.

Lafe faced no moral dilemma about the sale of muskets to the natives. He had believed in the policy that whalers followed when he first set foot in the country and muskets were not sold to natives, but now that some tribes had become well armed the others faced extinction if they

447

did not have access to their own supply of firearms. His own tribe had perished because they had not found a way to arm themselves against the threat from the north.

Finding a crew for his ship posed few problems. His tattooed face was well known now and so was his reputation as a resourceful man who had lived for more than thirty years among the natives of the country where the ship was headed. Neither had done him any harm. The romance of the South Pacific was now firmly established from the many books that were in circulation and, in the sailors' case, the stories passed from ship to ship. Tahiti was more talked of and better known among sailors than London or even England would ever be. Big, strong intelligent boys and men came on board looking for berths and were sent down to Lafe's cabin to be questioned and, if they met his standards, signed on. Those with more than one voyage behind them had the pick of the positions as there was no substitute for experience on a whaler.

Lafe was impressed most of all by the young men no older than he had been when he first went to sea. They had come out of the hills and the valleys with an unquenchable thirst for adventure and he signed on as many as he could. These were the vigorous youths of the world, the best the human race could produce and they would carry their bloodlines to the farthest corners of the earth.

They were in sharp contract to Lafe's cousins who had never moved more than a few miles from where they were born. Something was lacking in such men and they proved the old adage right, that the weakest of the litter always stayed closest to the nest.

His cousins continued to put much pressure on him to sign the quittance that they had drawn up but Lafe would not have it. Not until the last trade item was stacked in the warehouse, the ship was ready for sea and all the bills were paid, he told them. It was not a hard thing to refuse and he thought that they would not have been surprised if he went back on his word and tried to extract more concessions from them. As a man of his word he would sign their quittance when all their affairs where in order and satisfactorily squared away, he told them bluntly, though he knew that was more than they would have said in his shoes.

Thanks to their joint arrangements much of his fortune remained intact and he left the care of it with the factors who had proved such canny investors over the years. He would write to them using a simple code if he required the release of any funds in the future, and they would also handle any cargo he might send or bring to the port and handle all affairs pertaining to his ship.

The weeks sped past and the sailing date rapidly approached. Now Lafe scarcely saw his bed before midnight and was the first on deck every morning. When they were three days short of sailing, he gave the order to begin loading the cargo and stores and he sent for his cousins to come aboard.

The first of the cargo was two large barrels that had once held rum. They were lowered below decks and manoeuvred into the main cabin that Lafe had made his own, fitting it out in a style that suited him as both owner and captain, and he had the ship's carpenter measure and cut circles out of the solid oak floor so his men could lower the butt ends of the barrels into them and fix them firmly. Under no circumstanced did he want them to work loose in a storm and destroy the cabin. Across the top of the barrels sat a large piece of mahogany that would serve as a table. One of the younger sailors had spent a week polishing this piece to Lafe's satisfaction and it only awaited the attention of the carpenter to bolt it into position.

Lafe spent most of each day behind this table now, dealing with the endless paperwork that running a ship required. He was thankful he had a good grounding in the rudiments of ship's paperwork under his old master, Olva, on the *Northern Lights*. Everything on board seemed to require a list, from the muster list of men who had shipped aboard her to the list showing every barrel of pork and where it was stored. Every single barrel that was slung down into the hold had its place and was loaded to a plan so that during the two-years voyage each could be located and retrieved from the hold exactly when it was needed. As each barrel was emptied of its contents it would be filled again with whale oil and sent to the lower hold for the rest of the voyage, and this would be the cargo the *Venus* brought home.

Lafe shaved and dressed carefully for his cousins' visit. The ship was quiet that night as he had let every sailor go ashore with the proviso

449

that they would be on deck fit to work the next day. There would be some sore heads, he knew, but he would have his sailors ashore as much as possible in the next few days, as God only knew when they would see this town again. He had allowed them to draw against yet unearned wages so they could enjoy themselves and store up memories for those lonely nights at sea.

Only the cook crashing away at his pots and pans disturbed the quiet as he prepared the meal for Lafe and his guests, but when the new captain slipped into the galley to order the serving of the dinner he pressed several coins into the man's eager hand and suggested that afterwards he should join the rest of his shipmates ashore.

Lafe met his guests at the gangway personally, brought them down to his cabin and filled their glasses with his best wine. While they ate he outlined his plans to begin loading trade goods and victuals the next day and the water casks the day after. All going well they would put to sea on the tide the third morning after their dinner party. Frederick and Günter did not question his plans, knowing that the sooner the ship put to sea the sooner their investment would begin to pay dividends.

These two had stretched themselves rather thinly at their bank to meet their commitments to Lafe, though they both knew the price he had made them pay was cheap in the long run. They would be facing a judge if Lafe had challenged them over his inheritance and although they would have fought tooth and nail, stalling the decision with delaying tactics and adjournments, they thought the courts would find against them in the end. Their reputations would not impress any judge while this grotesquely-tattooed cousin had somehow won the approval and support of powerful people in the community. This was a far better way to deal with a man who should have stayed dead and left them to spend his inheritance.

Frederick raised his glass high in a toast. 'To the voyage,' he said, and his brother echoed him.

'To this ship and all who sail in her,' Lafe replied.

The ship was silent as a grave now, the only noise the odd groan of the fenders as she shifted in the tide and they were ground hard against the rough planking of the wharf. Lafe's ears picked up the footfalls of the cook as he went down the gangway onto the docks and away to the tavern to join his friends.

'Let's have your papers then, cousins,' Lafe said. 'Business before pleasure, eh?' He read the documents rapidly but he already knew what they contained. They were quittance documents, stating in the dry and convoluted language of lawyers that he agreed to forgo any previous claims he may have against Frederick or Günter Erickson or their heirs. He signed both copies and handed them back to his cousins who examined his signature closely and waved the ink dry before Frederick stowed the documents carefully in his case. Lafe could see the pleasure on their faces, though they tried hard not to show it, and he despised them even more for it. They had a triumphant glow that showed clean through their greasy countenances, he thought. They had skinned the hide off him and had every reason to be pleased, there was no doubt about that.

'Smoke, gentlemen?' he offered, waving his hand in the direction of the ever-present opium pipe. While his two cousins lit up and the sweet cloying smoke filled the cabin, he glanced up at the clock on the bulkhead. He had at least four hours before even the first of the sailors staggered back on board, plenty of time up his sleeve. Slowly and steadily, he told himself, watching the two men as a cat watches a pair of rats, and he waved the pipe away when it was offered.

'I have given that up, for I am going to be a long time at sea,' he told them, though he had to admit to himself that the sweet, cloying smoke tempted him greatly. The cousins registered mild surprise at this information, but that was all. As they smoked Lafe fingered the cosh in his pocket, a foot long leather cylinder with a wooden handle and six ounces of lead shot weighted in one end. He made small talk until both men were as relaxed as they were going to be without falling asleep. Both took on that dreamy, glassy-eyed look he had become used to seeing, and their eyes began to focus on particular objects in the cabin as if seeing them for the first time. Lafe rose and stepped smoothly around the table, keeping his movements slow and gentle until he was in the right position.

'I have something of importance that I want you to do for me

451

before I go off on this great journey,' he said, keeping his voice matter of fact as he stepped around behind them as if to pick something up from a side table. He took the cosh from his pocket, measured the distance with his eye and swung it into the back of Frederick's skull. Without even a groan he crashed forward and hit the tabletop, sending the dinner plates flying. Before Günter's opium-addled brain had time to warn its owner the cosh landed on his head and he too ended up face first in the remains of his dinner. Lafe stepped to the door of his cabin and listened for a minute before turning the key on the inside. The ship was as quiet as a cemetery at midnight.

He took four pieces of cord from his pocket and bound the wrists and ankles of both men securely, sparing no thought at all for their comfort. Then he lifted the heavy table top from where it rested on the barrels, lowering it gently to the deck and leaning it against the bulkhead. From the corner of his cabin he picked up a block and tackle that was to be used to haul the heavy strips of blubber up to the decks to be swung into the coppers. He fastened its hook to an eye bolt in the ceiling that hung directly above the yawning mouth of one of the barrels, took the hook that normally fastened into the blubber and secured it through the thongs that bound Frederick's ankles. Then with a couple of heaves he hauled the unconscious man up feet first to the ceiling until his head hung just above the rim of the great wooden barrel. Slowly he lowered him down head first until only his lower legs protruded from the hole it the top.

'You are not a bad fit are you, cousin? Not bad at all,' he chuckled quietly as he hauled him back into view. The barrel had recently held seventy imperial gallons of rum and Lafe knew that the fumes from the inside would overpower a man very quickly.

'But we don't want you to peg out too soon, do we? I have work for you yet this night,' he told Frederick as he lowered him onto the cabin floor. The fumes from the rum-soaked timbers had caused Frederick to make woofing and snuffling noises.

'You sound just like an old bear waking up after the winter,' Lafe told him callously. 'Never mind, there is worse to come yet.'

He repeated the procedure with the chubbier Günter, and he too slid easily head first into his own barrel and was soon back lying face up on the cabin floor. Lafe washed their faces with cold water and dribbled a little into their nostrils before propping them both up against the bulkhead. While he waited for them to resume consciousness he searched their carryall, took from it the two documents he had just signed and held them to the lamp chimney until they burst into flame. When the fire licked his fingers he dropped them to the cabin floor where they quickly turned to ash.

He took two documents of his own from a drawer, laying them neatly on the table with pen and ink beside them, then casually sipped his wine until Frederick started to groan. He seized his hair, tipped his head back and trickled a little water into his nostrils. This made his victim splutter and shake his head wildly from side to side. After half an hour of such treatment Lafe held their noses and forced them each to swallow a cup of the strong black coffee that had sat on the galley stove since dinner. Before long Frederick was lucid enough to answer to his prodding and Günter was coming along nicely as well.

'I have some papers for you to sign,' Lafe told his elder cousin. 'It is a quittance, you will be familiar with the term. It tells the world that you have no further claim on me, my heirs, my ship or my cargo. Would you like me to read it to you?'

'I won't sign anything,' spluttered Frederick.

'Oh yes you will, it is just a matter of how soon you sign it,' Lafe told him calmly. He bent over Frederick, wrenched his mouth open and pushed a piece of leather into it and then wrapped a gag around his lower face, tying it behind his head. Fredericks jaws worked like a gopher on the leather, but he could not get it out of his mouth. His eyes registered the indignity and shock of what was happening to him. Within seconds Lafe had hauled him up with the block and tackle and once again he vanished head first into the rum cask like a rabbit into its hole. After a minute he was hauled out again and dropped none too gently on the floor. Lafe whipped off the gag and jumped back. A stream of vomit flew out of Frederick's nose and mouth and splattered across the cabin floor, but when he had finished heaving Lafe whipped the piece of leather back into his mouth and calmly tied the gag back on.

'What a waste of good food,' he said quietly, untying his cousin's hands and cleaning them carefully with a piece of rag. He seated the man at the table and placed the pen in his hand.

'Here, practice a little on this piece of paper and then sign away,' he told him in a kindly voice. 'We cannot even think of beginning any other negotiations until you do.'

After several shaky signatures had been scrawled on the page and Lafe had applied more of his own brand of encouragement the signatures became firmer and clearer and Lafe was happy to let the cowed Frederick sign the document. He retied his hands and dumped him back on the floor. After a few minutes of resistance and a spell hanging upside down in the barrel where the rum fumes almost killed him, Günter followed his brother's lead as he had all his life. Lafe let the ink dry and carefully filed the documents away in his drawer. Then he stood over his two cousins as they lay on the floor looking up at him. He could almost feel the tattoos on his face standing out from his skin in the lamplight and he knew he presented a fearsome sight to them. He could smell their terror and it was sweet.

'I have something to say to you both' he told them in an even voice. 'You cannot answer me and I have no wish to hear from you anyway. It is for you to listen and understand what I have to say. You have taken what is mine, and now I have taken what is mine back from you.' He let the silence linger for a long minute before he spoke again.

'Now I would ask you this question. After all the trouble you have put me to, is it fair that we are now but equal?' His voice hardened and the anger in his face was terrible. 'I have no wish to be equal to your sort of person,' he spat. 'There is a word in my country and that word is utu. What a pity I have not the time to explain it to you but it is a long story.' There was not even an ounce of pity in his voice as he grabbed the rope, whisked Frederick off the floor by his feet and dropped him head first into his barrel for the third and final time that night. Then up went Günter and into his, and for a few minutes all that could be heard was the drumming of their heels against the insides of the barrels. It soon became weak and died away.

Lafe took up a wooden pail, unlocked the store and went to where two barrels had been broached earlier that week for the sailors. He filled his pail with thick, sweet black rum and returned to his cabin where slowly and deliberately he poured the rum over the bodies until both heads were completely covered. For a time his cousins twitched and quivered, sending little waves of rum splashing up the sides of the barrel, then they were stilled forever. Lafe took up the pipe and the little ball of opium and dropped them into the rum, followed by Frederick's carryall. It took an hour or more to fill both barrels to the brim then he took up the hammer and belted the wooden lids into the casks, sealing them with hot tar. In the morning he would have the cooper sweat a red-hot hoop onto the top of each cask to seal it properly before the carpenter bolted the table into its permanent position.

'What toothsome morsels you will be by the time we get to New Zealand,' he chuckled. 'All dark and caramelised you will be and tender too after being pickled in my best rum. The question is, who will I invite to dinner?'

At dawn the loading of the ship began and by the evening of the third day the water casks were all filled and hauled on board. The sailors slipped ashore for their last lingering goodbyes with wives and girlfriends, and Lafe left the ship with certain documents in his pocket to say his own goodbyes to the factors and the friends he had made. He returned late to his cabin and stood for a moment with his hands on the big desk.

'Utu!' he whispered, and the blue eyes blazed with a fierce satisfaction behind the tattooed face.

In the early light of dawn the *Venus* spread her topsails and slipped down the river with the tide and out into Chesapeake Bay.